the
'idiot spy'
(the series)
book seven of ten

deific intermediation

c. benjamin lattimore

deific intermediation
Published: November 2021
Printed in the United States of America
ISBN: 978-1-7334945-6-4

a lattidreamer™ publication
© C. Benjamin Lattimore, 2021

to my bride, Marisa.
Your commitment to my passion is off the charts!

ACKNOWLEDGEMENTS

my children, Christopher, Monica, and Courtney--my grandchildren, Isaiah, and Desmond. A heartfelt expression of love to my older sister Mary E., and my younger brother, Darryl A. Yet again, and again, and again, venerate regards to Maurice Cheeks and Reginald Wilkes.

special acknowledgements to Marisa, Dawn Marie, Nikki, and Jill.

lots of love ethereally to, Mary Alice, Walthro M, Barbara Ann, and Walter Eugene. To my friends, Gordon Gant, Joseph Bongiavanni II, Monique Gorham, Rahsaan Stevens, and my newest guardian angel, Mrs. Marjorie C. Cheeks.

CHAPTER ONE

The group's plane landed in New Zealand to take on fuel. Everyone was exhausted. Darryl asked, "So, Uncle, is this your plane or do you guys rent this thing and the crew?"

"No, Nephew, this is our plane, and we have two, or maybe three others that are much smaller."

"Wow, that's amazing. Do you think if I work hard and stay focused, I'll be able to own my own plane?"

"Darryl, your dreams and your actions will determine if those things are important to you. In our case, we spend a lot of time moving around the world and, therefore, for a group this size, it's economical and efficient. We need the flexibility and independence. Eventually, we'll all be too old to get around and these things will become the property of the next generation that follows our path of 'helping people help themselves'."

The Sarge excused himself when he saw Chakes sitting alone. He walked over an asked, "Divorced already?"

"Oh, no, Sarge. All the women are in the gift shop buying trinkets and stuff. What I am concerned about is that history lesson I received the other night. Even if I were inclined to believe it, I still would not believe it. Since I find it fascinating, there isn't much I can say about it. Seemingly, you guys believe there is fact in it, but the important question is--what does that do to our relationship? I mean, it has been stated that my ancestor had your ancestor killed. If I may ask directly, do feel like it could be a problem for us and the team?"

"Oh my God!" Beckmire admonished. I cannot believe what I am hearing coming out of your mouth. I am your brother and you're mine. That was then and now is now. The two shall never meet because we're who we are--brothers who fight, laugh, drink, and will live close by, but not together."

The Sarge hugged him and stated, "My people don't make shit up. When I was told, I questioned the motivation, but the wise guy who slid beside you and gave you the information is much smarter than me and you. It was an information sharing session and nothing more. My people don't instigate chaos, they, as you have learned, are soft and earthly."

"So, there ain't no kind of tension between you and me?"

"Chakes, your ancestor killed mine, and I'll never forget that."

The Sarge looked at him before saying, "I'm just kidding. We're in another space and time, my brother. That information is just that--information. That thing you saw near the water, did it come at you? No, it did not because it's a forgiving spirit and besides, you, Maurice Chakes, had no active involvement in that ancestral ordeal. Are we good?"

Chakes hugged him and said, "I love you man. You, these people and what we do is so important. I never want to cease being a part of this group."

"I have another question for you," Beckmire stated.

"What's that, Sarge?"

"That Luana is one drop-dead gorgeous woman. Her arrival has prompted all the other women to step up their game in terms of how they look and what they wear. We all receive strong and positives vibes from her and her grandmother. This question may be out of line, but I am going to ask it. What on earth are you going to do with her? Are you going to marry her, or what? Dude, you gotta do something. An intelligent and beautiful human being like that will eventually get swept off her feet. And that daughter of hers, Beatrice, is also a heart stopper. Don't fool around with Mr. Macho on this one. If your conscience is right, do the do, and be done with it. If I weren't married, I would have to look at her a couple of times myself."

Wajickee's voice whispered to Beckmire, 'She's part Aborigine, can't you tell'?

"Sarge, I told her, unless there was something about her that was reprehensible, I would marry her today. She responded, 'I would marry you if there was nothing deplorable about you'. I think we're on the right road. I'll tell you this-- I had a dream about a woman having a son, and she had a dream about a man with a strange mark on the back of his leg."

"Did she see your face in the dream?"

"She told me all that she saw was the mark on the back of my leg?"

"Did you see her face in the dream?"

"I didn't. I saw a woman holding a baby boy."

"Now, you know, I'm a guy from a family that believes in a lot of strange things. I asked you those two questions because had you clearly seen her face, or she yours, I would have to tell you the odds of you getting together for a marriage, and not merely a relationship, was slim to none."

Chakes looked at him and said, "Well, since neither of us saw the other's face, what's the deal?"

"It's going to be a grand day in the islands, Man."

An hour later, the group assembled and boarded their aircraft. Ms. Viola said to Chakes, "Man, you sure know how to show a girl an exciting time. I come on this trip, and I'm given a miracle drink which makes me feel like running a marathon. I mean, them people took good care of me. I have you to thank for that."

"Sister, you know if you no have granddaughter, you would be my lady."

"Yeah, Yankee, I know that, but I'm glad I have a granddaughter and great grandbaby and they both love themselves some, Mr. Chakes. Seriously Man, from the bottom of my heart, I thank you for inviting us on this most amazing journey. I have not seen my granddaughter smile and laugh so much. She is happy, and the baby be happy. We all be happy, and it's all because of you--a stranger who took time with an old lady."

"Sister, I be happy as well. I was once jealous of my friends who met ladies from all over the world and fell in love with them. I am so happy I waited until the miracle of the islands showed up so she could steal me from her grandmother. I tell you something else, if that girl of yours will have me, I will have her, and we can learn the good, the bad, and the wicked about each other as we teach each other. I can't imagine living without her and Beatrice. I will have a ready-made family with a grandmother-in-law who I love just as much. Sister, no man lives any better than that. That be heavenly living, Sister. Oh, your color has come back, and I be incredibly happy about that as well."

# # #

Both Rashida, and Marisa, were feeling a little pinkish. Marisa asked Luana if she would conduct school for the children for a portion of the flight. Luana happily agreed. Luana told Maurice what she was doing, and he told her that teaching school created an opportunity for him to get some rest. When Luana went to the back of the plane, Maurice asked, "So, Sister, what are the things your baby doesn't like in a man?"

"Mr. Man, you be having to ask her that question. I no give up any free information about my baby."

"Sister, I didn't think we had a bargaining relationship. I'm just asking for a few hints, so I don't step on spiders and snakes that are not friendly."

"Mr. Man, you be the man and tell your woman what you expect of her. If she no like, she will forcefully tell you so. I didn't raise a chicken."

"Sister, tell me about your daughter, Luana's mother. What happened to her?"

"Mr. Man, I no want to talk about her. As you can see, we don't discuss her."

"Sister, I no press the issue, but it only spikes my curiosity when it becomes a subject that is taboo. I would like to know the fabric she comes from. I found out where my people came from by a spirit in the outback," Chakes reflected.

"We heard the story, but it sounded like a long, long time ago. However, you still be riding shotgun with this group, so who your people were, ain't who you be," Sister stated.

"You have a funny way of stating things. I can't understand why you won't tell me about your daughter," Chakes said.

"My daughter is not for discussion, Man. She be a big heartbreak for me." Ms. Viola started crying and Chakes moved to the seat beside her.

He said, "Come now, Sister, we about to be family. Why you want to go and get upset and keep secrets from me? My world is an open book. There be a protocol before people just get on our plane. I mean a background check, FBI fingerprints, and on and on. You, Sister, and yours, waltzed onto this plane with no questions asked, because everyone knew that a match had been made in heaven and sanctioned. I'm about to ask your granddaughter to have blind faith as I will with her, and marry me immediately at the resort, and before God. As my grandmother-in-law to be, help me understand what my mother-in-law would have been like."

Ms. Viola with a disdainful look said, "Man, I never talk about my daughter. If you think Luana is beautiful then you would kiss the ground, her mother walked on. She was the most beautiful child—and woman, I had ever seen, and she was mine. Man, I will make this short and you will not torment me again. Is that a deal?"

"Sister, you continue to set the terms of our engagement."

"Man, I no get engaged to you. What you talk about?"

"Let me try it differently. Sister, you continue to set the terms of our discussions and actions. Is that better?"

"Man, Luana's mother, was to die for. Men offered her everything and it went to her head. She met a famous movie star who lusted for her. He was a comedian--incredibly famous, one who also had TV shows and many movies. He asked her out and conquered her body. However, he drugged her and had his way with her. When she returned home the next morning, and as his plane lifted off, she had no memory of the evening. She couldn't recall where she had been or who she had been with but knew something had happened to her sexually.

"When it became obviously clear he had deflowered, as well as impregnated her, the pieces began to fall into place. She told me he must have laced the food she ate and insisted she have a sip of champagne with him, which he probably spiked. After that, she told me she didn't remember a thing about the evening. My baby asked me a month or so later, "Why is my stomach getting big when I haven't eaten a thing in a week'. I asked her when she last had a period, and she told me over a month. I asked her had she had sex with anyone, and she screamed at me. 'No'! My poor little girl was impregnated by a man who she didn't know she had sex with. He drugged her, had his way with her, and left her with a baby growing inside of her. She became the slut of the area where we lived. People would say to her, 'You couldn't give that booty to a local, you had to give it to a Yankee who didn't even know your damn name. This how you rep our country, slut?"

Chakes hugged her and said, "People are mean spirited."

"Yes, they are. After months of suffering the torment from the locals, she delivered her child, Luana, and disappeared. She was found hanging by her neck, from a palm tree. She had a note attached to her that said, "Please take care of my child, and if there is a God, please place my vengeance on the man that drugged and raped me'."

Sister began to cry hard and blame herself. Chakes said, "Sister, vengeance is a dead man's game. There be no satisfaction after the fact. If him dead lessens your burden and pain, then I will make it happen, if him be alive. All you need to do is tell me his name and promise me you will never tell Luana. That's all I ask to remove your pain. I must warn you that it's a momentary satisfaction with bigger penalties than you can imagine."

"Man, I no want him dead. I just want him to face justice. How many times he do this thing to young girls and fly away after he gets what he wants? No, no, I don't want him dead; I just want him exposed."

Luana returned to her seat and saw that Chakes was sitting next to her grandmother. She asked, "What are you two scheming about now? I hope it doesn't concern me."

Chakes returned to his seat and said, "Nothing you wouldn't approve of. We were talking about the trip, and her experience, nothing more."

"Speaking about the trip, how did you like it, Grandma?"

"I'm a living testament to the value of the herbs, spices, and pure living the Aborigine people subscribe to. I haven't felt this good in a long time, and nothing hurts me at all. I hope it lasts. The people were friendly and kind. It was never about them; it was always about us, as if we were godly or something. That Mr. Beckmire is one powerful and influential man. They got pictures of Mr. Beckmire's family and the legendary Great Saltie on the cave walls."

Sister looked at Chakes and said, "They told me about your family as well. I mean, as I said, they don't reflect you, but them people were just rotten to the core. I'm glad you grew out of it."

"Sister, frankly, I wasn't sure I believed it, but when that Wajickee fellow appeared next to me without making a sound, I think there be knowledge there I need to heed. I heard the story but was more concerned about the people in the cave and their safety, and that would include you, Luana, and Beatrice. I was distracted because of my selfish desires and wants, convincing you people to trust me blindly and come on this trip. I could have gotten you hurt or killed. That's why I'm not so happy with Mr. Maurice Chakes. If your granddaughter feels for me, what I feel for her, then all would have been okay when I returned from the outback. I placed you people in danger, and for that, I am sorry."

"Speaking about that Wajickee fellow, he said to me, 'I'm going to make you better, Sister'. Did you tell him my name?"

"I did not. That is the first time I communicated with him. The Sarge usually controls the conversations with that guy. You're talking to him one minute, and the next second he's gone, and no one knows where. I don't mess with him or understand him. It's been said that his age can't be calculated. I used to think he was a demon until I saw what I saw last night, a thing I cannot talk about because it was too surreal to be real. Many things can go on in that place we just left. The one redeeming factor I feel from inviting you people is that Sister, you look better, sound better, and move with grace. I be happy, and I say, my account is balanced. Oh, there is one other thing I'm glad about and that is--your granddaughter, kissed me tenderly, and I think she's in love with me."

"Man, I sure be hoping so. When this here bird lands, you two need to go to the farthest part of the resort and tell the stories that are embarrassing to each other. Get that trash out of the way, and you will find yourselves ready to make a commitment for the good of the order and for that baby boy that is yearning for your seed that will brew in that consecrated womb of my granddaughter."

"So, Sister, are you advocating premarital sex?"

"No, man. I don't believe in that belly dancing mess. I'm suggesting sex with the express notion of a marriage to follow within ten days."

"Why ten days, Sister?"

"Why not?"

Luana said, "I hate to disappoint you people planning my life, but I have others who are interested in me, and I haven't made a choice. Believe me, you're both different in meaning and direction. So, before you continue with that mindless conversation, you had better seek counsel from the one who controls this sagacious mind and body. I'm going to sleep, and I do not wish to be disturbed."

"She's in love with you, Man. Tell her you love her."

"Sister, does she like to fish?"

"I don't think she's ever been. Why you be asking that?"

"I want to take her out on a fishing trip and tell her all of the bad things about me. I have a feeling she senses the good things about me. People have made this move before, and it turned into a mistake. I, on the other hand, am convinced that based upon the emotions and dysfunctional behavior of mine when I first saw her, I am for her, and she is for me, the one."

"Man, why you tell me? She be playing sleep right next to you."

"Sister, this way I knock two birds out of the gossip tree with the same sentence."

"You be smarter than you look. By the way, you know I want you to do me a favor when we get back to the islands."

"I know, Sister, I know! I just have to inform our leader about it and get his buy-in and support. If we show a sign of strength down there, all will be well. Just remember, Sister, we don't always shake hands, we sometimes break arms, legs, necks, and heads. We sent an initial message, and I'm sure, they're going to be waiting for us to return. Most likely, how it will go down is that I will escort you guys' home minus Beatrice, and my people will be on the outskirts looking to place a bad hurting on those who think they can mess with us.

Now, Sister, remember, we usually kill people who mess with us. I want you to be mindful of the fact that if this goes south, we will bury the entire group. I just want you to be aware of that piece of information."

"Man, I don't want them hurt, I want them employed or doing something constructive."

"Me and my people humiliated them. I'm sure they're going to want to save face, and, when they do, my people will annihilate them. I'm just letting you know how it works. An innocent act on our part sometimes emboldens our adversaries. Our approach is hard and final, Sister."

"Are you telling me you can't handle this thing differently when you just managed a group of rich white men who were trying to steal part of the country from the Aborigines?"

There was a pause and a reflection by Chakes. He said, "Sister, you continue to challenge me. I will make it happen, but I won't put any of my people in harm's way. I will try to do this thing mildly."

CHAPTER TWO

The plane began to descend into St. Thomas as the sun began to rise in the east. Within the cabin, people were deep asleep. The Sarge stirred and yawned. He looked at his bride and whispered as she stirred, "It will be nice to put our feet on the ground and play in the water."

He stared out of the window for a few seconds and then added, "I'm afraid there will be casualties in this next adventure. We can't be that good that they can't hit us with random gunfire. I'm so afraid for my guys. I really want to send them home and face the final chapter by myself and, hopefully, with you by my side. I would destroy hell if anything happened to any one of those assholes."

Courtney kissed her husband and said, "And they would destroy the universe if anything happened to you."

# # #

As the wheels touched down on the short runway, the sound of the engines turning in reverse could be heard. The plane slowed and made the final turn onto the taxiway that led to the terminal. Sister said, "I be happy to be home, but I no want to be here. I have never felt more alive than when I was on this trip with these people. Everyone is full of energy, and there is no drama. Look at them--they could give a hoot about who said what because they don't do stupid. They know what they have, and don't have to worry about anything ugly. Our people on the island buy fake hair, wear flyaway eyelashes, and get shots in the butt to have bigger asses. Who on earth wants a big butt? Them people on television sporting those small hips and waistlines, are a hamburger away from reality. How many carrots can you eat before you want to taste that thing called, meat?"

As the group began to disembark, they saw Mr. Carter waiting on the other side of Customs. He said to the Sarge, "I've arranged for secure transportation to the bank that has the most secured vault."

The Sarge inquired, "What on earth are you talking about?"

"I'm talking about the diamond you people plucked from the earth in Australia. It's all over the news, someone recorded your sessions, and it went viral."

"Are we going to have an issue getting out of here? Besides, I don't think we have that diamond."

Jong listening in said, "Sarge, remember Wajickee gave it to me to get an estimated value. It's in my bag over there."

"That's right. He did give you that thing. So, Mr. Carter, you're expecting trouble?"

"Mr. Beckmire, I'm always expecting it, but hoping it passes me by. I'm sure some of the locals saw that thing on YouTube, especially since I did, and I don't know how to really use that channel."

"So, what's your plan? Remember we don't split our people up?"

"The local police are going to escort us to the bank, and in each van, we have unlawful tools, should you need to use them in self-defense."

Jong asked, "Sarge, may I have a private word with you?"

When the two men were alone, Jong said, "Now might be a good time to take some of that excess cash and place it in the bank."

"What excess cash?"

"You do know that we have around $15 million on the plane?"

"I forgot about it. Are you concerned it might get lost or something?"

"I'm concerned about traveling in and out of countries with that kind of cash on a privately-owned jet, full of unlikely looking rich people. We don't need that kind of exposure. It could put everyone in danger."

"How do we move the money through Customs?"

"The less you know, the less you can say in court if I'm caught. Let me handle it and this conversation never happened. I think we should have some mad money but not $15 million. I'll get Jilkes and John Lee to count out approximately $1 million and put the other $14 million, or so, in our bank boxes. We also should gradually have Mr. Carter, or perhaps his son--who is more astute in finance--move amounts from the boxes into our various accounts with the money disguised as revenue from the properties. I also think we should diversify and use the bank that tried to rip off Mr. Carter and the others. I think those swindling guys are gone, and we should investigate a relationship with that bank."

"I don't want to mix our partners in any matters that may have future legal repercussions for them. Find another way, but don't involve our partners. What's Mr. Carter's son's name?" the Sarge asked.

"Ah, I think it may be Michael," Jong replied.

The Sarge said, "Let's talk to him later. Do whatever you're going to do with those cases, but don't get caught. It's not like we flew in from Miami. We flew in from Australia with a big ass diamond. Perhaps that's the key and the misdirection. We flaunt the diamond and load the cases onto the food trucks from the resort. Our food, our money, so let's try that one."

Jong bowed and said, "That's why you're our leader. We bring you stupid and you make it smart."

# # #

The people in customs were, as suspected, interested in seeing the diamond and paid little attention to the comings and goings of the rest of the group. Jong and Monica signed all of the necessary forms and never let the stone out of their sight. A customs official said, "I'll have to weigh it. Let me have it, I'll be right back."

Jong said, "You no weigh stone unless you weigh me. Stone no leave my hand. We are the trustees of it. You no take stone away from hand."

Monica looked at the customs agent and said, "That seems highly unusual. As my client stated, the rock does not leave our possession."

# # #

With all of the drama over the stone going on and Ms. Viola spinning a tale of sleeping in the outback and hearing scary sounds, Jilkes asked Michael to watch over the cases. He also told him if he were stopped, disavow any knowledge of what is inside of the cases, and get them involved.

The ride to the bank with a police escort was new for this group. After depositing the stone in 1 of the 8 safety deposit boxes the group rented, they entered their vans and proceeded to the resort.

# # #

At the resort, Jilkes and John Lee saw Michael sitting in the truck and wondered what he was doing. They exited their van and walked over to the truck. John Lee asked, "You be alright? Why you be sitting in the truck like that?"

"Jilkes told me to lock the truck and watch it. I'm watching it from inside."

Jong walked over to the men and asked if there was a problem. He was told that there wasn't a problem and that the cases were in the back.

Jong said to Michael, "I would like to talk to you after dinner. We might have another job for you. The Sarge, or Mr. Beckmire, and I will speak to you. But until then, where can we store these cases securely?"

Michael said, "We have space in the basement that can only be accessed through the meat room. From the rear door to the freezer, there is a secure room that requires an additional key. Only my dad and I have those keys."

Jong said, "Fine, help us take them to that place."

# # #

Meanwhile, Ben Beckmire was in a deep conversation with the other partners in the resort. He asked the men why the construction projects were moving so slowly, especially, considering the fact they should have three crews working around the clock.

Mr. Carter responded, "There is this guy in town who is always trying to organize people into unions. I believe he's doing this so that he can collect dues and not have to work. Anyhow, the only public transportation that comes to this part of the island is on a hit or miss schedule, and he happens to own it."

"We didn't have this problem when we did the resort, did we Mr. Carter?"

"We did not because I organized the transportation and hooked people up the old fashion way."

"Mr. Carter, you're our point man and I want you to work with these guys and get their businesses up and running. I want you to buy buses in the morning and get me solid drivers. We will open a bus route to here and expand the inner island access to our stops. How is that for a solution? If you guys like it, then make it happen while we're still on the island. Why didn't one of you guys say something to us?"

"Mr. Beckmire, we don't want it to seem like every time we see you, there is another request for more money. We appreciate what's been done already and we don't want to seem like we're always in need."

"Listen, guys, we are in need. We have work to be done, and people wanting to work but can't get here. That's a problem and a need. So, we're going to buy buses, hire qualified drivers, have a schedule and uniforms, and offer benefits."

Beckmire heard some people talking, and when he turned around it was Bernstein, Brown, Montomie, and Chakes. He motioned them over and said, "We need to start a bus company. Our partners can't get workers here on a fixed schedule because the only bus in town is owned by a jerk who is trying to unionize the workers here. We are for unions, but this guy is going about it the wrong way. I need you guys to figure this out in the next few hours and give these guys a plan to approve. Is that a problem?"

Bernstein said, "We're on it, Sarge."

The Sarge asked, "Guys, I'm sorry, were you working on something else?"

Chakes said, "We were talking about how to clean up a certain area of young punks."

"You could always offer them the graveyard shift once you get the transportation problem fixed. That's a lot better and builds goodwill rather than beating people up--just a suggestion. That way you have them captured and you can talk to them about the future and their next moves. I mean with three active shifts--it should be at least four to six months of hard labor. By then, perhaps, we could partner with the university and see if they want to work with us on expanding their curriculum into the building trades and other areas that have growth potential on the island."

Chakes said, "Good idea, my brother. We'll try to figure it out and we're on that bus thing."

The Sarge looked at Bernstein and said, "I doubt if we can buy buses on the island. They will probably have to be shipped from the states. Google it and see."

# # #

Chakes received a call from Luana who asked him about his plans for the night. He said, "I owe you guys a stay at the resort. It would be huge to me if all of you would come and stay the night, if you like. I still have to convince Sister to work for us, and this would be my dedicated attempt to sway her. Besides, I want to walk on the beach with you and talk more about our chemistry."

"Mom, that scoundrel is on the phone trying to get us to come out to his place to spend the night and have dinner with him. I'm kind of tired, do you want to go? I'll go if you go."

Ms. Viola said, "I would love to have an early dinner and sit in one of those rooms and watch TV. Tell the Yankee scoundrel to make reservations for three, and if he wants to join us, turn the three into four."

Chakes said in a suppressed voice, "I thought you wanted to see me. If you're tired, then I understand that. We can make it another time."

"Sweetheart, I said that for her benefit knowing she wants to be near the water and in that fabulous place of yours. She heard me say I was tired, and I left it up to her. Don't you think she'll do anything to keep us together?"

"I'm sorry to sound so dejected. I guess I was on a high and your words sent me crashing to the ground."

"Okay, stop it. Dude, I want to be with you tonight, tomorrow, and forever. Just don't hurt me--just love me."

"I am so into you that it frightens me. I don't know much about you, but I feel like I've been waiting my entire life for you, but I have made some bad interim stops along the way. Our dreams and out-of-body-experiences confirm our relationship, and even if they didn't, I would buck the odds because you make me smile and happy. The other thing that is so sweet about this relationship is that Beatrice likes me, respects me, and likes holding my hand when she's in an awkward place. I didn't want to mention this, but your grandmother loves me on several levels as well. So, I'm well-loved, but more importantly, I love everyone three times more. I need to speak to Sister about another matter."

"Hold the phone." A few seconds later, Ms. Viola got on the phone and said, "Is this that Yankee scoundrel?"

"Yes, Sister, it is me. I have a favor to ask of you. I want to send the van for you guys, but I want to send another van for those people I had words with the other night. I want them to come to dinner and see if we can change the climate by showing them and offering them jobs. Otherwise, it may turn into a bad spanking."

There was a long pause on the line and Chakes asked, "Sister, you still there?"

"I'm here. I glad you want to talk to them and not hurt them. I will explain when I see you. Let me go man, so that I can get ready and pack for another adventure with the Yankee scoundrel. See you soon."

# # #

Jilkes, John Lee, Somara, and Yeshida took a walk along the beach when John Lee had an epiphany. He said to Jilkes, "Don't be saying a word. Come and stand where I be standing and tell me, what you be seeing."

Jilkes walked and stood adjacent to John Lee. After looking around, he fell to his knees and said, "At this point, we connect all four properties to one of the greatest beaches on the island and you can see from here, how to connect them.

Damn country bumpkin, what a major discovery. We need to get the Sarge and Mallory here. Do you have your phone with you?"

"I have the phone, but I think everyone needs to be seeing this point of view," John Lee said.

He called the Sarge and said, "Get everyone down here on the beach, and I mean now--it be important." Beckmire sounded his verbal alarm and people came running strategically to where John Lee, Jilkes and their ladies were standing. Courtney arrived first and had her little pistol under her blouse and instinctively scoured the area for the threat. John Lee said, "Doctor Beckmire, ah, you won't be needing that there pistol, and why is everyone else taking up defensive positions? Are we under attack?"

Courtney said, "Damn it, John Lee. You pulled the alarm."

He replied, "Ms. Courtney, turn around and let me know what you be seeing." Courtney turned around, and after close to a minute had expired, she said, "Oh! Oh! Oh my! We accentuate the development of those two properties at the top of the hill. It's a natural landscape, and we should build bigger and better properties rather than little bistros and bars. John Lee, you are amazing."

When the group showed up, Jilkes and John Lee showed them what they had stumbled on. Courtney stared at Yeshida and said, "I don't like your coloring." She then yelled, "Mr. Carter, I need a mule to get me back to the resort, and a van ready to get me to the hospital."

The Sarge said, "Chakes, Gladstone, McArthur, and Whitmore, I need you to do backup."

Chakes replied, "Sarge, I just sent a van to pick up my extended family."

Bernstein yelled, "If you want, Brown and I are on it."

"Execute and keep a small one with you. At the hospital, will be my wife, Jilkes, John Lee, Somara, as well as Yeshida. Let's make this seamless, people, and stay sharp." He looked around and said, "I need Mike, Larry, Zanthius, and everyone else on standby and armed. Why are we short of vehicles?"

Chakes said, "I have two in operation, and one should be here in the next two minutes, with another following it in five to ten minutes."

# # #

The group headed into town with Courtney doing a vital check on Yeshida. She said, "Have you been eating and hydrating?" The responses were minimal.

Jilkes said, "She has always eaten like a bird, and I tell her constantly to drink more water."

Courtney said, "You have to insist on her doing that. She is grossly dehydrated and, therefore, so is your child. That's not good for either of them."

Later at the hospital, after force-feeding and rehydrating Yeshida, the attending physician said, "If you guys want a healthy baby, then you must eat healthy and drink plenty of water. It is a good thing Doctor Beckmire noticed the signs and made haste to the hospital. You must eat and drink smart."

The physician looked directly at Jilkes and said, "And, you the husband, must spend time making sure that she is eating well and drinking plenty of water, and not just tea. Tea has too much tannic acid, and her body and the babies need plain old H2O. I'm going to let you go back to where you're staying, but you must drink twelve ounces of water each hour for the next four hours. Start the regimen in the morning with twelve ounces every two hours."

# # #

Later, when the guests of Chakes showed up, he asked that they be placed in one of the suites facing the beach. They were escorted to their room, and once they hit a button by the bed that opened the drapes, there was the endless view of the ocean and a setting sun. Ms. Viola said, "I've never been in a place this fancy and, just think, it happened because of my rum punch."

Luana said, "Grandma, it was meant to be. I have to tell you a few things that have happened along the way."

"You had sex with him already?"

Luana frowned and then proclaimed, "Ms. Viola, No! He respects me too much, and I him, to rush into that. I want you to know that he had a dream about us, and I mean all of us, and I had dreams about him that were so specific that it focused on a tattoo on the back of a leg. I never saw his face. He has the tattoo. His dreams say that we would have a son and that Beatrice would only know him as her father. That is a sad commentary, but I guess a necessary one. Grandma, I think I'm moving too fast and may be setting myself, and my daughter up for betrayal and disappointment."

"Hush girl. Stop that blasphemous talk. If you can't tell the difference between love and lust, then you might be right. As I see it, Mr. Chakes is respectful, interested, and blinded by your beauty and your body, as well as your brains and your desire for him. He ain't no two-timing son-of-a-bitch like that last thing you married who raised his hands at me. No girl, he be a real man with real emotional desires and appreciation of family and friends. Look at how these people work together. There ain't no drama in this community. They all be about each other and 'helping people help themselves'. I wasn't supposed to tell you this, but the other night when he dropped us off, well the locals said to him, 'Yankee man not safe when mess with island women'. He told them, 'Island man not safe when screw with Yankee man'. He was going to brutalize them but decided to invite them to dinner to see if he could help them instead of beating the shit out of them."

"Why didn't you tell me that?"

"He be telling you tonight as well as ways in which you can engage them and help them move towards a positive existence. Listen, to me, he be like JC-Jr. He's a man to love and cherish. He wants your body, but he loves to discover your mind first. He wants to kiss your lips but would prefer that you held his hand and told him you were happy with him and his people. Him be afraid to move any faster because him be worried that you're going to say, 'I can't leave my grandmother'. That is exactly what your problem be. I be okay, man. You have to live your life, I've lived mine."

"This is not how this is going to be handled, and I don't care what the soothsayer told you. I'm not going anywhere and that's a fact and a promise," Luana affirmatively stated.

"Sweetheart, you don't get it. I want you to leave because I want to know that you're safe, in love, being loved, and happy. I failed with your mother, but I won't fail with you. That son-of-a-bitch that impregnated her after drugging her is the one that I want to haunt from hell and beyond. You will confront your father one day, and you'll laugh at him and say, 'Thank you for the genes and the life, but keep it quiet that you're my father--you're a despicable person with no morals to drug women to achieve sexual satisfaction'."

# # #

Jilkes's phone buzzed as he received a text message and photo from Franco. He immediately sent the message and caption to the crew. It featured a photo of Franco wearing a hardhat, boots, and jeans, with a clipboard in his hand. The second photo was of concrete being poured at the resort site.

# # #

Meanwhile, Chakes and his guests sat down to have a family style dinner. Beatrice asked, "Can I go and play with the other children?"

Chakes said, "Beatrice, I would like you to have dinner with us first, and then if there's time, you can play with the other children. You're going to spend the night, and those children will be up early and ready to swim."

After ordering their food, Mr. Carter appeared at the table and said, "Sorry to interrupt you, but the second van of people has arrived, where would you like me to position them?"

"Place them on the veranda and give them menus. Be sure to mention that the food is free and that I'll be there shortly."

He thanked Mr. Carter and turned to Sister and said, "I have some trouble spots I want to discuss with you. We travel a lot, and we have people trying to kill us. I know this isn't the best scenario any parent would want their child involved with, but we do good work, Sister. We don't go looking for a fight, but when it comes, we're pretty terminal. I want you to know I'm asking Luana and Beatrice to join our traveling circus."

Ms. Viola's head dropped, and she said, "Man, I be happy that you want them to come with you."

"Wait, Sister, let me finish. I say where they go and where I go, you go. Luana will never leave you by yourself. But remember, I gave you a phone, $100, and offered you a ride, and you took the $100 and the phone, so I know you must like me a little."

"You be a real scoundrel, Mr. Chakes. So, you want me to come along and make sure that you're treating my family well?"

"No, Sister. I want you to come along because they love and adore you and I kind of like and almost love you. I just want everyone to know, including Beatrice, that there are bad people out there who will attempt to hurt us. When we leave here, we're heading to Asiram's ranch which is in the middle of nowhere.

"Now, there is one other thing I want to do before we leave this island. I want to ask your granddaughter to marry me and be my partner. In doing so, I will make a life-long commitment to be a stellar husband, an understanding friend, a boyfriend, and father to Beatrice and our yet to be conceived son."

Ms. Viola and Luana began to cry. Chakes reached for their hands and said, "I want you guys in my family, and Luana, I absolutely love and adore you beyond any plastic words that I could manifest. I will be right back. I am working on a project that Ms. Viola has asked me to handle.

Chakes left his guests and walked out on the veranda where he saw the very same people who indirectly threatened him.

He said, "Guys, I've learned that you can't think that there is strength in numbers. A while ago, you guys thought that you could intimidate me based on the fact that it looked like I was alone. We're old guys who fought in Vietnam and we were called the 'killing machine' by the Viet Cong. In other words, I have probably killed more people than you know, plus the number of pubic hairs you have. We usually don't do meetings with people who confront us, but Sister, Ms. Viola, wanted me to try to work with you rather than confront you. I need you guys to stop bullying the older people and try to become proactive and maybe get on the night shift at our construction site. You guys are young and have potential. My people are relentless and only know one outcome from a confrontation—someone dies. I'm not trying to scare you, but you picked on a dude that is a part of a family that will kill everyone on the island to find out who stole his car. Am I making myself clear? Can I redirect your efforts to something positive? Or do we still have a problem?"

One of the guys said, "My name is Richard and Mr. Carter told us to go to church and thank God that we're still alive. He told us about your work in the Nam and we want to figure out how to make it better for all the people. Sometimes, Yankees come into the hood for the wrong purpose, and they leave behind people like us to survive. Our fathers were Yankees that promised our mothers a better life, but apparently got tired of the fruit and left the island, leaving them and us and no support."

"Oh, shit." Chakes walked over to each one and hugged them with watery eyes. He said, "I want you guys to enjoy your meal, have a single beer and be back here in the morning at 0800 hours. A van will be waiting to pick you up at that hour. Is anyone employed?"

None of the guys were employed. Chakes said, "In the morning, let's be civil and try to figure out in what direction you might want to go; job, college, training, or what? Does that sound like something we can do without threatening each other?" They all came together for a group hug. Richard said, "We've never been outside of the projects, this is large."

Chakes said, "If you guys are willing to work hard and study, I can make this thing a part of your life. It just requires that you 'help people help themselves' and never have an expectation for a return favor. You must be about altruism, giving to people, and not looking for anything in return. Okay, listen, enjoy your meal and be at the place where the van will be waiting for you in the morning, to change your lives. I'm glad we didn't have a serious confrontation."

Richard said, "Not as happy as we are that we didn't go up against your group. Thank you, and regardless of the outcome, I think we know what your group is about and that's what we need to be about, not trying to make $15 dollars on a hustle or a swindle. We'll be there in the morning to listen and to begin to work hard."

When Chakes entered the dining room, he saw his group enjoying their meals. He said, "What did you order for me?"

Sister said, "A local fish that is said to have magical powers. My granddaughter said, 'He doesn't need magic, he is magic and good magic at that'."

Chakes looked at Luana and said, "If you said that, then that is who I will be for you and Beatrice. I feel wonderful about where we are and where we're heading. May I kiss you in front of this entire community and your daughter to let them know that we are on the right road?"

Less than thirty seconds later, a single gunshot rang out! Maurice Chakes fell to the floor with blood gushing from everywhere. As the assailant, Richard, attempted to fire another shot, Montomie grabbed the shooter's arm, broke it at the elbow, hoisted the shooter off the ground, and slammed him forcefully to the floor, rendering him unconscious. His companions, after realizing what had gone down, broke out in hysterics and screamed, "What are you doing, what did you do that for?"

Maurice Chakes, lay in a pool of blood, with his positive essence, drifting into nothingness. He was gasping and choking on his own blood. When Courtney arrived on the scene, she yelled, "Get me a damn van! I need to get him to the hospital."

# # #

Much later, at the hospital, the entire group waited for the local doctors and Courtney to come out of surgery with information about his condition. The staff at the hospital was familiar with the group and pulled out cots for the children and pregnant women to rest on. The local priest had heard about the shooting and came to the hospital to offer words of comfort. In another part of the hospital, the police and doctors attended to Richard. Montomie broke his arm in so many places the attending physician said, "I doubt if you'll ever regain full use of this arm young man."

At the police station, the other two associates were interviewed individually. They told the police exactly what happened. They indicated to the officers that they thought they would be given an opportunity to do something other than hustle pennies. They told of how Mr. Chakes, who was shot, had just indicated that he could make college, and jobs available for them, one of the arrested youths stated. All we had to do is catch a van in the morning and be at their resort at 8:00. They independently told how they had a real meal and was looking forward to getting back out there in the morning.

As Mr. Chakes hugged us and said, 'see you in the morning', Richard gave him and us a strange smile. We all started down the steps on the porch and Richard said, 'I forgot to tell him something.' They each told how they stood on the porch and gave each other high-fives. They told their investigators that was when they heard the bang and ran back into the lobby and towards the dining area. Each almost paraphrased their comments and told the detectives that they saw Richard being hoisted off the floor, hearing his bones break, and then being slammed down to the floor.

Elliot, the oldest of the group, told his investigator that he threw his hands in the air and yelled, "What did you do that for? They're trying to help us, and you pull a gun and shoot somebody. I hope they cut your damn head off. You just ruined it for everyone in the hood, you piece of shit."

Elliot began to cry and said, "I told him that I hope his entire family rots, in hell."

David, the other young man, indicated he couldn't believe what he saw and just started crying. He admitted they got into fights and bullied people, but they never knew Richard had a weapon. Both men's stories corroborated the use of a weapon. David said, "We were happy to be finally getting a break from the miserable existence that we have. Elliot and I were so happy, we were about to cry while eating those steaks that they fixed for us.

Elliot said, 'God is good! Now all we must do is make good on the opportunity. I want to take my ass to college. You should come, and we can try to talk Richard into trying it out as well'."

After listening to both individuals, the lead detective said to both men, "What on earth caused him to resort to that kind of violence?"

Elliot revealed, "Mr. Chakes escorted Ms. Luana, her grandmother, and daughter home one night and Richard said, 'Yankee man not safe when mess with island women'."

Mr. Chakes replied, 'Island man not safe when screw with Yankee man'. At that point, doors on another van opened and some large men got out of it, and one was taking our pictures. One literally lifted Richard in the air and told him if he sees his friend, he should run away."

# # #

After bringing Elliot and David together, the detective said, "Richard goes to the resort on the pretense of getting ahead in life, but instead, shoots the man in the back. You guys must realize that you're an accessory to a murder, and if there is something you're holding back, then you had best let me in on it. You are looking at fifteen to twenty years in jail, and you didn't pull the trigger. I'm going to leave you two for a few minutes to discuss your stories. I must admit, they're different in terms of who knew what and when. You seem to indict each other on several levels and that's what my investigators are focusing on. You people shot a person who has invested tons of money in our island, and they do it for the right reasons. They're not here to steal from us, they're here to help us, and you guys kill one of their own. Not sure you know who they are and what they used to do, but I'll give you a little heads up, they've killed more people than you guys know. The most amazing story about them, and it's true, is that they broke into a maximum-security prison in China and rescued one of their own. In a battle that lasted 3.5 minutes, they killed sixty-seven-armed security types."

"Once they finish grieving, you can rest assure they're going to come for you. We may have to secretly ship you off to the mainland and trade your sexuality for your security. Think it over, but when I return, the story had better be a truer version, or you're on your own."

Twenty minutes later, after watching the exchanges on camera and recording the sounds, the lead detective entered the room and said, "I hope you got something for me because you people are going to be charged with conspiracy and accessory to a murder. Why the hell did a little slight like that, evolve into a shooting?"

"We didn't know he had a gun. He never showed us or gave us any indication that he was going to do something stupid. The only thing that he might have hinted at was the comment about respect that he uttered," Elliot stated.

The Detective asked, "What was that?"

Elliot said, "The night after Richard uttered the Yankee stuff, and the Yankee uttered his stuff, and the Yankee's friends appeared, and somewhat manhandled us. Richard said, 'Oh they think they can punk us without a price'? I never inquired what he meant, and neither did David. We just thought it was his way of trying to show that he was a bad *hombre*. We had no damn notion that he would screw us for an eternity. I'm telling you we were so happy to be offered a hand-up and not a hand-out and that we had a promise of options for the future. That's never happened in the hood where the Yankees would come, get our moms, and pay a few pennies. I believe Richard was humiliated by the fact that the Yankee wasn't stupid to come into the hood alone and replied, that's why he uttered that insult at him."

Elliot added, "He has never been that aggressive but has been hanging out with some people on the other side of the island that want to take control of the drug trade. I mean, he would disappear for days and come back sporting new clothes and pockets full of cash. When we asked him about it, him say, 'Got me a new lover across town who likes the way I deliver the goods.' We asked him why he didn't take us with him, and he said, 'You have to do dirty before I can take you into the new place'."

The detective asked, "What's the new place?"

David responded, "That was the end of the conversation and he never mentioned it again."

The detective told them that they would be held over in a cell until the investigation was complete. He told them that murder was a huge crime and that they should seek legal representation. The detective indicated to them that if they were withholding information, the charges would escalate from conspiracy to first-degree murder, and there are a lot of separate charges under that title. He cautioned them about lying to him. As the detective picked up his pad, he asked, "Have either of you guys been in prison before? Not a good place for good looking guys like you. I'm sure you've heard the stories, but you two will definitely become someone's wife on your first day in prison." Both men sunk their heads between their legs and began to cry and tried to rationalize what had occurred and why.

#

At the hospital, doctors feverishly worked to save Chakes's life. The bullet shattered, wreaking havoc on many of his vital organs. He was in good shape and his heart never floundered, which gave the doctors hope that he would survive the surgeries.

# # #

Six hours later, a weary Courtney walked into the lounge and went straight to Ms. Viola, Luana, and a sleeping Beatrice and said, "We've stabilized him as much as possible. Now it's up to him and his God. The bullet splattered in his body creating massive injuries. We were able to stop the bleeding and repair most of the damage, but there was a significant amount of internal trauma. We'll keep a close eye on him and pray for him. I suggest you guys pray for him as well."

Luana asked, "When can I see him?"

"It will be a while before he can have any visitors. We're trying to keep the area as sterile as possible until his natural body functions begin to take control over the various pumps that are working his critical systems. We'll keep you informed and let you know when you can see him."

Courtney walked over to her husband and said, "He's in bad shape. It's as though he was shot multiple times with little bullets that each picked their individual targets. If he lives through the night, he might have a chance. He's lost an enormous amount of blood, and now all we can do is pray for him."

The Sarge asked, "Can we see him?"

"Honey, it's too soon. He needs rest, quiet and prayers. You might want to let your Uncle Wajickee know about this."

The Sarge began to walk away from her and mumbled, "He already knows about this'."

Ms. Viola asked Mr. Carter if he could give her a ride to the church about a mile away from the hospital. He told her if she didn't mind, he would like to go in and pray with her.

A doctor walked out of the emergency area and motioned for Courtney to come back. She went through the doors and witnessed a beehive of activity in Chakes's room. His heart had stopped, and the counter was nearing one full minute. The doctors tried every technique known to their profession, but it was not enough. At 2300 hours, Maurice Chakes flatlined.

Beckmire could see the gloomy faces coming out of the room, fell to his knees and began to cry. Luana screamed at the top of her lungs, grabbed her daughter, and began to feverishly cry. At 2302 hours, Chakes's heart monitor started to beep at an unusually slow pace. Courtney yelled, "I need you guys back in here--he's still alive."

The doctors moved with haste towards the room and saw a slow, but steady progression of Chakes's other vital signs as well as the readings on his heart monitor. The Sarge stood up, and Luana was not going to be stopped by him, or any other human. She was determined to be by Chakes's side, in life or in death. She barged through the doors and said, "I need to be with my husband, and that's the way it's going to be."

A nurse assisted her with a gown, mask, and gloves. She saw the monitors and a very upbeat Courtney and hoped that those were good signs.

At 2326 hours, the heart monitor, flatlined again as well as the monitors for his other vital signs. Luana asked, "Man, you gone get me this far and die on me?" She continued to cry while the doctors attempted to shock Chakes's heart for close to two minutes. At 2331.30 hours, as the doctor was annotating the time of death, the heart monitor started beating aggressively and maintained its beats per second. That would be the final time Chakes's heart would go into cardiac arrest for many years into the future.

CHAPTER THREE

Exactly forty-five days later, Chakes was seated in a wheelchair and was escorted outside of the hospital to an awaiting van. In addition to Courtney, he would have a local doctor attend to him while he was in rehab each day. Beckmire was forced to rescind one of his edicts such as never separating the team. On one of their smaller jets, members of the team had been dispatched to monitor Mallory and Monica as they visited the Catholic Charities. The first thing out of the director's mouth was, "I thought I had lost you people."

Monica said, "Oh, no. We had a friend who was injured in an industrial accident, and we had to provide day-to-day care for him."

"Why do you guys always seem to have security with you?"

Monica started to answer the question when Mallory said, "We have a lot of assets and people sometimes get the wrong ideas, so we have to keep a security detail. Is that in any way an undesirable point for adoption?"

"Absolutely not! Why don't we go back to my office so that I can offer you a few new options that have come to us in the past month or so?"

Monica said, "That's one of our problems, too many options. When you continue to show us new children, we just want to adopt them as well. So, in other words, we want to stay focused and proceed with the two biracial children who are part Aborigine and European--we want the brother and sister. At some point in time, we may visit you again, but our purpose here today is for those two children. My husband and I are emotionally in love with those two."

The conversation continued as the process and paperwork were enormous. Monica and Mallory signed papers associated with the mixed-race brother and sister pair, Elton, and Margo. Monica could barely contain her tears as she read the names of her two children, Elton, and Margo.

Members of the security team looked at John Lee and Whitmore, and said, "Thank you, old wise ones who demanded that we stop at Subway to get sandwiches and from WAWA water and juices. You are all knowing and all wise."

McArthur asked, "How did you know it was going to be so long?"

"You think they just give them babies away without proper paperwork and identification? No, they don't do that. This thing could last another day or two. We might get some time to get back to the island and see our people, but this here thing is long-winded."

Jilkes said, "It's only been three hours. We've sat in the same hole without food and water for days. Why you people be worrying about nonsense?"

Gladstone said, "I'm glad you asked that question, my brother. You do know that me, Mac, Whit, and Montomie met some very upscale ladies at the resort from a sorority out of California? In case you missed the buzz and the fizz, we hooked up with some nice ladies who are smart, independent, and beautiful."

John Lee said, "Them there ladies must be blind too. How they be liking you guys? You guys like those strip clubs where the woman ain't got nothing covering their personal parts and they slide up and down a fire pole. It ain't even no fire."

Jilkes said, "Guys, don't answer that question. We're missing our mission with this craziness. I don't want a Chakes's situation on our plate. I need you to focus and make sure we're good to go or prepared to spit some brass cartridges."

Jong's cousin, the person in charge of transportation said to Jilkes, "Can you speak to my cousin on my behalf about a few things? The first item is to tell him that Darryl is doing fine--school too easy for him. Him too smart and that he studies all night and only sleeps a few hours. Also let my cousin know that he lends me a hand in designing defenses and is conquering our language. The second thing is my number one daughter is crazy about Darryl and he don't even notice her. He speaks to her at dinner, they study together, or he studies, and she gazes at him. He is polite, respectful, a gentleman, and a big help to me in what I do, as well as suggestions about money management. Him been born before to be that smart. Thirdly, my son can move another $100 million for you if you so desire."

Jilkes said, "I only want to deal with one issue right now, and that is, why is Darryl not paying attention to your daughter. Is she too young, or what?"

Jong's cousin pulled out his phone and said, "She is his age or older. She looks okay, I wouldn't marry her, but someone will."

He showed Jilkes the picture and he said, "Oh, my! Perhaps you don't want him messing with your daughter. She is absolutely beautiful."

He smiled and said, "John Lee, come here. Look at this lady, what do you think?"

"Holy pig heaven. She be one beautiful female. Who is this, your girlfriend?"

Jong's cousin said, "She no girlfriend, she daughter and likes Darryl from down under, but he no pay attention to her."

John Lee said, "Well, if I be you, I be glad he ain't looking at my daughter. When he sees her, you're going to be like a pig with one eye--you won't be able to see shit. He be a young man on a mission. Once his elders give him the okay, he be a Romeo and your worst nightmare."

Jong's cousin said, "The thing number four, is that he goes on Spring Break, and she wants him to take her to Daytona Beach. I say, 'No Daytona'. He wants to stay here and help me. Can you take him on the plane with you and my daughter, but keep them from doing what cats do when its dark?"

# # #

An hour later, after an initial visitation by Mallory and Monica, the two descended the steps holding hands. She was smiling, he was smiling, and they stopped on one of the landings and kissed. They kissed until John Lee said, "I would like to be kissing my bride like that. Can you do that once we be on the plane and on our way?"

At the airport, Jilkes said, "I'll ask the Sarge and your cousin about your daughter and his nephew. If he approves of the social occasion, I will send a plane for them. You must make sure your daughter understands that what we say is the rule."

Jong's cousin bowed and said, "You are the most honorable people that I know. It is a pleasure to assist you and you help me. Thank you."

#

The smaller plane landed in St. Thomas and the group went through Customs without a hitch. At baggage claim, Mr. Carter was there faithfully waiting for his partners. Jilkes saw him and made his way over to him and asked, "How is my brother?"

Mr. Carter replied, "He's at 'The Sanctuary', awaiting your return."

Jilkes yelled the rest of the team, "Yo, Chakes is at 'The Sanctuary'. Let's get the hell out of here."

An hour or so later, the returning group arrived at the resort. From afar, they could see a figure sitting in a chair by himself on the beach. The team jumped out of the van, ran down to the beach, and surrounded Chakes. As they hugged and kissed him, they asked a thousand questions. Jilkes said, "Why are you out here by yourself?"

"I asked my family for a moment to reflect on what has happened to me, but more importantly, two of those kids didn't do anything. There was only one person responsible for what happened."

Jilkes looked at him and said, "Brother, we will handle that. You are our primary concern, and we want to welcome you back."

Chakes stood up and said, "Well, hell, I need a damn Coors Light."

#

Chakes played his injury to the hilt. Luana and Sister were his puppets. He pulled their strings and demanded that they stay at the resort until he was able to travel. His biggest conquest was Beatrice. Every morning, she would bring him a glass of orange juice with a note that said, 'I love you and I need you'. She would escort him on the beach and make sure that he didn't need anything. She carried her great grandmother's phone in case there was an emergency. When Chakes was released from the hospital, he privately said to Beatrice, "I love you like I love your mom and your granny. I hope you can find a place in your heart to love me."

Beatrice said, "Silly, I don't have to find a place. The first time you kissed my mom and made her happy, I figured you would be a cool dad for me."

#

Later that evening, Luana and Chakes rode in a mule down the beach for a breath of fresh air and privacy. She said, "I've accepted that what you people do, sometimes backfires, and people get hurt. I also understand that for me and my family there is everything for us to gain, but little for you."

Chakes said, "I'm going to say something to you that may or may not make sense. You know they were about to pronounce me dead at an articulated moment. I was dead I feel, but I was also at peace. My life has been about the destruction of life and the preservation of it for my family. You don't have to believe this, but I want to tell you something that I thought happened to me when that doctor was signaling my time of death. Please, this is very private and is just for your ears.

"The last thing that I recall was a baby boy in the arms of a woman whose face I couldn't discern. The second part of that dream state was that there was a woman who was looking at the strange symbol tattooed on the back of my leg. The third thing I remember was that fellow named Wajickee saying, that I had earned the respect of the spirits and the undying love of a Beckmire. For that acknowledgement, I shall live to see my son born, and to love him and my family for a long time.

"Now, that is what I remember when I heard someone announce, the time of death is. Now, in terms of your statement about me having nothing to gain, I really think you are missing the boat on that one. I gain a world of love, peace, a ready-made family, a grandmother that adores me, and all the support there is in the world. Monetarily, well, that is no big deal. My love for you, your love for me, Beatrice, and Sister's love for me is worth more than any riches I may have."

Luana slithered up to, and under him. She purred, "I don't care anything about none of that. I'm glad that the man I absolutely love is alive and well, and he is holding me in his arms." She kissed his lips fully and tenderly until he started to feel passion, emotion, and desire at the same time. She bit his earlobe gently, turned his face towards hers, and emerged her tongue deep into the essence of his mouth. She uttered, "I need you to make love to me. Love has never been made to me. I need you to love every aspect of my body, abuse my soul with pure lust, and render me unconscious from pleasure. When you were in the hospital, I thought about how selfish we had been with each other by not sharing the ultimate leap of faith and acknowledging our desire for one another. Maurice, I don't even know if I've ever been to that place that my girlfriends talk about. That place where the soul leaves the body and floats around in a euphoric state until it's time to return to reality."

Chakes said, "I will deliver you to that place, but I feel that I'm not capable of sharing it with you at this point. My energy and other issues prevent me from attempting to take the woman I love to a special corner where the only focus is to assure that she is overwhelmed with pleasure beyond her wildest imagination."

Chakes kissed her dearly and began to run his fingers through her hair. He fondled her and felt stimulated. He explored under her blouse and felt her natural softness, all while searching the depths of her mouth with his tongue. He gently rubbed her stomach and parted, ever so slowly, cautiously, but willingly on her part, with a hint of reluctance, her legs. Chakes ventured into a place that had not been touched by a foreign hand in many years. He kissed her with his eyes open. He slowly, and methodically, began to explore areas below her stomach while searching the depths of her mouth. He made contact with her paradise, and her legs gladly opened wider with the expectation of more intense exploration. Chakes kissed her, massaged her erogenous zone, and told her he loved her. On his first time encountering and caressing her valley, he struck an accord that was very gratifying to Luana, and as powerful as an earthquake. Luana was satisfied beyond understanding because she had never journeyed to a place of pure love and pleasure before and had never had love made to her in any sense of the word.

CHAPTER FOUR

With a limp arm from multiple fractures, Richard appeared before a magistrate and pleaded not guilty. The magistrate looked at his calendar and set a date but remanded Richard to jail. When Richard saw David and Elliot, he shouted incomprehensible threats at them accusing them of setting him up and planting the weapon on him because he was on drugs. Richard was led by several guards from the courthouse in leg irons and shackles.

When David and Elliot appeared before the judge, he asked if they had obtained counsel. Both men indicated they were unable to afford counsel. The magistrate indicated that court appointed attorneys would be made available to them. He also ordered that they be held over for trial as well.

#

At the resort, the Sarge saw Asiram playing with the babies at the water's edge. He walked over, sat in the sand, and asked, "How are you making out? I know it's been tough on you and the babies, but I need you to stay with me until we can rid ourselves of the Carbon Factor and my cousin."

Asiram looked at him and said, "Daddy-in-Law, do you honestly think I want to leave this place? Look at that water.

It's calming and it has medicinal powers. It's refreshing as well. We have everything we need. I suggest you come back and ask me that question in a week, or so. I'm not moving a muscle until Chakes is 90% or better. Your sons are trying to figure out the best way to get rid of that damn product but can't seemingly agree on where it should happen. Have you seen Mike? I'd like to know what he's hearing from the underworld."

"You know he's so in love, that boy can't see straight. His only interest and concern is Carla. He has an addiction, and I'm going to have to tell him he needs to let her have her space and time. I think he's smothering her. They need to learn how to make this thing last, and what they're doing ain't the way. Damn, go to the store, or for a walk by yourself to realize you love the other person, and you miss them. That's it--you need to miss them even when they're close by."

"Did you really come over here to tell me that, or is there something else on your mind?" Asiram asked.

"I guess you're too smart for me. I need an unbiased opinion about our group and our security."

"Is there a preamble to that comment, or am I supposed to jump right in just like you threw it out there?" Asiram inquired.

"You're right; I need to give more clarity to it. Do you think we were too lax when we extended the invitation to those young men?"

"Daddy-in-Law, first, we didn't extend the invitation. Chakes extended it and he thought it would resolve a neighborhood issue that was triggered by him escorting Luana and Ms. Viola home. It was hinted that the young boys were a nuisance. No vetting took place; they just waltzed into the dining room and created havoc. Not the other two. They were completely surprised and damned by that guy's actions. We didn't vet Ms. Viola, Luana, and many others. They had a different motivation."

"So did those young men. They were promised employment, an honest income, benefits, and education. That to me certainly are motivating concepts."

"You're right, but once again, no one knew that they were coming other than Chakes, Mr. Carter, and Michael. I suggest we have a logbook that will tell us if a member of our community has invited someone into a zone. I mean that was an execution in front of guys who know and see the world in a different light. You guys were asleep and should have been aroused when three foreign people showed up in your dining room."

"Asiram, we cannot watch everything that people do."

"Well, Ben Beckmire, you had better start, or you're going to witness an attrition of your people at an alarming rate. Could that have happened at the farm? I don't think so, not with Rashida and Juan's anal attitudes towards crossing the property lines. Could it happen in middle America? I don't think so, not with an entire town and its people looking out for us and making sure that no one gets near us without a proper invitation."

"Ben is getting so big. Are you still feeding them breast milk?"

"At night, I like to let them go to sleep with my essence."

"I must admit, I had concerns about you when I first met you. My only concern now is that I have to protect you and keep those beautiful baby boys healthy, happy, and, eventually, horny."

"Ben Beckmire, when I see your wife, I will have to tell her what you said."

"That's okay, she knows how I feel about those two boys. Listen, I can always count on you to give me an unbiased opinion.   In the future, we must vet all strangers.   As uncomfortable as that may sound, our biggest enemy could learn from this experience and wreak havoc on us once again."

"Oh, Daddy-in-Law, the person that was in the hospital with a bullet wound was a Greek priest, who attempted to steal a man's, Gustav Montenagro's, woman.   There was never a Chakes in the hospital. Courtney failed to mention that to you. You'd better have a conversation with that wife of yours. In other words, we're always thinking from the least active of us, to the most dynamic. We are a part of this community, as well as you are, and you'd better start considering our input. You can't have strategic meetings with just your war buddies. You should have meetings with the entire group. We're always on the same plane, and you hand down to us what your current expectations are, much like that new guy who considers himself a president."

"Wow! Why didn't you come to me if you had a problem with the way, I run things?"

"Daddy-in-law, I don't have a problem because you're always right with your gut feelings. This time, you didn't have an opportunity to exercise that intuition because you didn't control the invite list. We, meaning the ladies, could have run interference on that by vetting the invitees."

"Don't mention this to anyone, but I think my Beckmire women are the brightest and most cunning women I know. I love them a lot. Thanks, Baby Girl. Do you want me to help you with the boys?"

"Oh, no. I have an assistant coming, in the form of an ex-lover of yours--Ava. You have to know that she still loves you."

"She has to know that I still love her, but I'm in love with Courtney. My heart, and soul, is hers."

"Daddy, Ava acknowledges all of the things that you do. It's amazing how the women depend on each other and genuinely care for each other but respect the domain and institution of marriage. It is a work of art, and one that I would like to write into the history books."

Ben Beckmire leaned over and kissed Asiram on the cheek and kissed each boy on the head.

When Ava arrived, she said, "I'm five minutes early, I hope that doesn't create an issue."

Ben Beckmire stood up, spoke to Ava, held her hand and kissed her on the cheek as he assisted her to the comforts of the sand where her grandbabies were playing. He turned and walked away but saw a figure at the other end of the beach sitting alone. It was Chakes. He walked towards him, and when he reached him asked, "How's it going?"

Chakes inquired, "Did you know that my heart stopped on several occasions?" The Sarge, fearful of the question, softly said, "I was, my friend, and I cried like a baby."

"Did you, in any way, use magic to restore my heartbeat?"

"Dude, are you serious? Did I use magic? Do I look like a fricken magician who can bring the dead back to life? Have you lost some critical marbles in your head?"

"Calm down, Sarge. I was asking because I want to bow down to you and thank you for all eternity for giving me the opportunity to experience true love with a woman, instead of a group of guys. If you had the ability to bring me back to life through those black magic habits of yours, I would still be bowing down to you. As it is, and since you didn't have a damn thing to do with my heartbeat, sit your big ass down and tell me how much you love me."

"Boy, I thought you were about to trip out on me. Why you do me like that? You know if I could do magic, I would do it."

"Dude, listen. I'm sitting here thanking God, spirits, Sister, Luana, and, especially, Courtney, for my ability to sit here by the water and hear it, touch it, and smell it. I'm sitting here because I have a real family comprised of, mostly men, who will challenge the heavens in my defense. That dude surprised me and hurt the other two. I want to move forward with helping them by asking Luana to legally represent them. I saw them crying before I went blank. They didn't have anything to do with this thing. It was Richard, but who stimulated him and gave him a weapon? Sarge, that's what I want to know."

"And we shall find out. If this is a revenge trip, then I really don't want to be on that train. If you suspect a bigger villain, as well as purpose, then we seek out the answers. I'll be damn! Darryl can get both answers from Richard. He has some stuff with him that Wajickee can't match. This would be a great opportunity for him. Let's get Jong to call his cousin and have my nephew fly down here on his break, next week. He can bring Jong's niece if she wants to come," the Sarge announced.

"Sarge, the son-of-a-bitch shot me in the back. How do you shoot an unarmed man in the back? He has no conscience. He has no soul. I would love to see him passively abused and mentally tormented until he is a ripe old age. I call you to assist you, and you shoot me in the damn back--I want his mind, screw his soul."

CHAPTER FIVE

The arrangements were made. Jong's cousin told Darryl to respect his daughter and do not relinquish to her suggestive techniques, requests, or demands. If he would honor this request, then it would be his honor to completely welcome him into his family. He asked Darryl to not betray his trust. He also asked Darryl if he were sexually active. Darryl frowned at him and stated that the question was invasive and too personal.

In the meantime, Jong sent the smaller of their jets to Washington, DC, to pick up Darryl and Jong's niece, Sue Lyn. At the airport, Darryl turned to Jong's cousin and said, "Your cousin will watch over her and she will not prevail upon me, or anyone else. After I finish school, if she likes, I will ask her to marry me, but I will not disrespect her or you." He bowed and escorted Sue Lyn onto the plane.

The two entered the plane and Sue Lyn asked, "Is this your uncle's plane?"

Darryl said, "I think it is. I hear they have three planes, and this looks like it's the smallest of the fleet."

"Is your uncle a very rich man?"

"He is one of the richest men you will ever meet. His heart is big, and his love for people is even bigger."

The two sat in chairs facing each other and were instructed on the safety features of the plane. Prior to takeoff, Sue Lyn unbuckled her seatbelt, got on her knees, crawled over to Darryl, and kissed him on his lips. It was the first kiss that he had ever received from a female who he thought was beautiful, graceful, affable, sexy, and smart. She giggled and scampered back to her seat as Darryl looked at her in a new light. That little kiss sparked some latent feelings that were hard for Darryl to understand.

Darryl asked, "What was that for?"

Sue Lyn responded, "That was for being such a gentleman and convincing my over-protective father that you would not try to take advantage of me."

"Your mollycoddling father asked me to be on guard against any overt attempt on your part to seduce me. I told him that I would respect you, him, and would ask you to marry me, if you wanted to, after I finish school, if my guardians approved of the union."

"Who are your guardians? Your uncle?"

"He is one of them, but there are many. However, I would like to experience another kiss with you. That was rather dizzying and left me feeling weak."

As the plane slowly taxied to the runway, Sue Lyn, once again, unbuckled her seatbelt and made her way to Darryl. She kissed him on both sides of his lips and then on his mouth. She stabilized herself by placing one hand on his leg. She used her other hand to bring his head to her and that is when she placed her very juicy tongue deep in his mouth. She backed off and made her way to her seat and buckled up. Darryl appeared to be in a coma as the captain said, "We're next for takeoff."

# # #

Once the plane reached cruising altitude, Darryl said, "I guess I've missed out on a lot of things in life. I have never kissed a girl and have never had a girl kiss me like that. My body became weak, and my mind kept looking for the next thing but I'm not sure what it was looking for. Was that kiss supposed to lead me to try to have sex with you? I don't have an experience level with kisses, but that was no ordinary kiss. I still feel vulnerable and weak. Where did you learn to kiss like that?"

"In college, we let the boys we liked kiss us, but they couldn't touch us. We would kiss them until they had their orgasms."

The copilot came out of the cockpit and offered them lunch, he showed them where all the drinks were. When he returned to the cockpit, Sue Lyn said, "Darryl, have you ever had an orgasm?"

"I'm not sure, but on several occasions, I would wake up and down there, you know down here, I would be wet and slimy. Have you ever had sex before?"

"Oh, no. I have had plenty of orgasms by stimulating myself and pretending that I was with a man. I would be afraid to have sex with a man."

"Why would you be afraid?"

"I only want to have sex with the man that I will call my husband." There was a long pause before Sue Lyn said, "I would like to kiss you until you have an orgasm."

"I promised your father that I would not disrespect you or him."

"You will not be disrespecting me by allowing me to kiss you on your lips and make you feel good. I could touch you also, but we will not be having sex. If you allow me to kiss you and touch you, then I will allow you to kiss me and touch me until we both are messy 'down there', as you call it."

Darryl looked at her and said, "Define for me what you think your father's definition of sex is."

Sue Lyn told him, and they both rationalized his definition and interpretation. They agreed that the formal definition of sex was the one that they would refrain from. Sue Lyn stood over Darryl and got on her knees and began to kiss his lips, suck his earlobes, and kiss his neck. Darryl began, in a low volume, to moan and groan. She kissed his lips and used her tongue to seductively suggest matters to his head that would stimulate and complete that thing that was missing in his life— a natural orgasm. She unbuckled Darryl's belt, unzipped his trousers, and methodically began to massage his member. In less than two minutes, Darryl was shooting substances out of his member that hit the ceiling of the plane. Sue Lyn quickly gathered napkins and capped the volcano with one hand and began to return the ceiling to its original condition. Darryl collapsed with fulfillment. His first female assisted orgasm was the result of a desirous woman's soft and determined hands, and a commitment to not disrespect her, or her father in the most technical of definitions. Darryl excused himself and went to the lavatory. Ten minutes later, he returned to his seat to find Sue Lyn pretending to be asleep. He sat in his seat and said, "I want to take you to that place that you just took me. How do I do that, and will you shoot stuff on the ceiling?"

"The first thing I would do, if I were you, would be to kiss me and tell me how much you love me, or describe to me what you felt from my help in your reaching your amazing orgasm. Then, recognize that I desire to experience the same nirvana, and Darryl, females don't shoot like you."

Darryl kissed Sue Lyn but was totally lacking in that skill set. She said, "Darryl, I need you to help me experience what you felt or sit in that chair and go to sleep."

He looked at her and tried to imagine how to accomplish her wish and maintain some notion of respect for her and her father. Darryl asked, "Would it help if I used rubber gloves?"

Sue Lyn said, "Darryl, get some rest. We'll work on your skills later."

He saw the rejection on her face and decided to mimic her technique. He kissed her lips and inserted his tongue in her mouth and became aroused once again. He gently and instinctively began to massage her breasts. He pulled her top from out of her pants and placed his raw hands under her bra. He braced himself against the bulkhead and used his free hand to rub her tiny stomach. She unlatched her pants, and he slowly made his way down to an extremely wet and interesting place. He then placed his fingers on her zone of craziness. With his tongue, ever so deep in her mouth, and his hand feverishly, but gently, massaging her private institution, Sue Lyn began to moan in a controlled manner. When it was her time to blow the whistle, she blew it loud and strong. Darryl was smart enough to smother her sounds by kissing her mouth while trying to get her fingernails out of his back.

Twenty minutes later not a single word had been uttered. Darryl stated, "Technically, we did not have sex. We experienced an emotional conclusion of desire that was shared between two people interested in a final manifestation of a few months of wondering and desiring. We refrained from intercourse, and, therefore, there has been no notion of disrespect of you or your father."

Sue Lyn smiled at him and said, "Perhaps you should use your law degree to become a politician. You are excellent at spinning the facts. Darryl, I love you and thank you for an experience that I can't imagine will ever be achieved again. I literally lost it. I have self-induced, but I have never been touched by a man down there, as you call it."

Two plus hours later, the copilot came out of the cockpit and said, "We're beginning our descent into St. Thomas. I need you guys to fasten your seat belts and prepare for landing."

# # #

As the plane effortlessly glided towards the runway, Sue Lyn said, "I saw you in the shower. I'm not sure if it was an accident, or an unintended consequence of my curiosity. You walked into our home, and I said, 'My father must have lost his mind. Why would he bring a person of color into our home to live? Then I met you and realized you were a mind opening experience because none of us have ever met anyone as smart as you, or as sensitive. It was capped when you saw that poor lady struggling, and you left us in the middle of a conversation to help her with her bags and slipped her money. We all saw it. We also saw how you defused those three little thugs. Now, all they want to do is go to school and become a lawyer like you. And now today, you make me do despicable, but enjoyable things to you, and then I allow you to do the same to me. Ah, you must be a witch, my friend."

Darryl looked at her and said, "I have never felt that way before. Had I known what compromising you would feel like, I probably would not have asked that you accompany me. You see, it is you who I feel possesses the powers of a sorceress. I was innocent until I entered this vessel with you, and then you proceeded to corrupt every known faculty of mine. There is no retreat for me. I am forever going to be in search of that next level, and how do I achieve this knowing that I promised your father that I would not deflower his little girl."

"Darryl, I'm not a little girl. I'm a grown woman who happens to love a, ha,ha,ha, chocolate man from Australia, who happens to be Aborigine, and who is taking me on his uncle's plane for a vacation in St. Thomas. For me, it doesn't seem bad at all, and plus, there was no insertion--just the right amount of touching, kissing, and rubbing. You are the first person that has ever placed his hands on my, you know, down there. I have been the only one in the past to do such a thing, but I guess the altitude discombobulated my brain and allowed your demon spirit to corrupt my inner senses."

"Do you think your father would allow us to marry?"

"Darryl, are you serious? Would you really want to marry me? What happened today is what people do. They don't go and propose after having their first orgasm."

"Sometimes, Sue Lyn, I marvel at your logic. I said to your father, 'I would like to marry your daughter if she will have me, once I finish school'. He didn't answer, but you can confirm that conversation with him."

"You don't know me. You don't know anything about me. Why would you want to marry someone who you know so little about?"

Darryl studied her immediate anxiety and said, "If today I feel as I do, then tomorrow, I will only feel more. I'm from a place where we know those who are just, and those who are lowly. Your uncle is a member of my uncle's family, and vice versa. We on the other hand are by-products of their relationship. Did you hear the story about how my uncle saved your uncle? Remind me at another time to tell you. What's important at this moment is that there are commitments and promises that must be honored. My suggestion and route around it, is to marry you, not because of the passion we share, but because we share passion and not lust. You must confirm the statement I made to your father. Ask him if I asked him if I could marry you."

#

A van picked up the duo and delivered them to the resort, but only after the two had shared in the island's rum punch. Darryl thought it was okay, and Sue Lyn thought it was terrible. When they arrived at 'The Sanctuary', they were met by the entire group and reintroduced to everyone. Ben Beckmire asked, "How was your flight?"

Darryl looked at Sue Lyn, smiled, and said, "Nice airplane, great crew, but terrible rum punch at the airport."

"Well, if you like rum punch, then you will definitely like ours. It's the best on the island." He then looked at Mr. Carter and introduced him to his nephew and waited for Jong to introduce his niece.

Jong said, "This is my niece, Sue Lyn, Mr. Carter."

He then proceeded to hug Sue Lyn and kiss her on the cheek. She said, "Uncle, in as many years as I am old, you have never hugged or kissed me."

Mary Alice announced, "I've been working on him and he's finally leaving that macho mess at the back door. Hi, I'm Mary Alice, the wife to this wonderful and loving man. Nice to meet you. I'll get you settled in your room, and we'll show you around the property."

Ben Beckmire said to Darryl, "In the morning, you will escort Ms. Monica and Ms. Luana to the jail to interview two of the suspects that were with the guy who shot Chakes. Our two lawyers are planning to represent them if they are telling the truth about their knowledge of the situation. In the same facility is the person who did the actual shooting. I need you to try to figure out who was the architect of this crime. It is hard to believe that this guy stumbles upon a new weapon and shoots a man in the back that's trying to help him, without some kind of motivation from somewhere else. What's the motivation?"

Beckmire smiled at him and said, "I saw the look you gave that young lady. Are you intimate with her, and is her father aware of it?"

"Uncle, I have not, and did not, have sexual intercourse with Sue Lyn."

"Okay, Mr. Lawyer. In any way, shape, or form, did you touch Sue Lyn? Did Sue Lyn touch you in any manner? Did you kiss Sue Lyn, and did Sue Lyn kiss you?"

"Uncle, those are pretty precise and interconnecting coordinates. I kissed her, and she kissed me."

"Darryl don't waste my time. What else happened? Be precise and definitive as well."

"We kissed for a long time, and we fondled each other to conclusion. It was spectacular, and it was my first."

"Darryl, there will be no monkey business conducted while in my charge. Is that clear?"

"Most definitely, Uncle."

# # #

At dinner, a subdued Chakes was looking somewhat depressed. Whitmore stopped at his table and asked, "Where is the family?"

"They had a commitment this evening with Beatrice."

"Oh, I see. I guess you're going to have to deal with me, Montomie, Gladstone, and Mac."

"Where are they?"

"Oh, they'll be here in a few minutes or so. What are you going to eat tonight?" Whitmore inquired.

"Not sure, why don't we check and see what the specials are."

Chakes beckoned the waiter and asked if there were any specials? The waiter said, "I'm filling in for someone else. Let me get the menu and I'll let you know."

Ten minutes later, people entered the dining room singing, 'Happy Birthday to You'. It was Chakes's birthday and leading the procession was Ms. Beatrice with a single candle on a cupcake. She was followed by his wife-to-be and his grandmother-in-law to be, Sister.

He said, "I thought you guys had something to do?"

"We did. We had to get dressed, have our hair done, and look good for the man of our lives."

He kissed Luana and said, "I was feeling depressed for a moment until Whitmore came over. He helped stage this event, didn't he?"

Everyone lined up to hug and kiss him. Ms. Beatrice was first and said, "I like you a lot and I know that mom likes you too, and that great-grandmother likes you. We all like you, but I think I like you more than they do." She hugged and kissed Chakes and ran off to play.

Ms. Viola whispered something in his ear. He smiled at her and hugged her dearly.

After all the well-wishing was done, the Sarge walked up to him and said, "I saw your miserable ass feeling sorry for yourself. You know we try to remember each other's day, but sometimes, that ain't possible. You know we love you and would move heaven and earth for you. I must say that woman of yours ranks at the top, along with a few others, in terms of looks and grace in our group. I'll let you figure out who the competition is. I dare not touch that one even though I started it."

Luana, was the last person to hug and kiss her man and wish him happy birthday. Chakes told her that he was a little tired and needed to rest. They left Beatrice in Sister's hands and went to their suite. He said to her, "I want to try to make love to the woman that I love."

"I want to make love to the man I love. However, I want him to be around for a few days after we do. So, if a rise in your nature and your blood pressure don't agree, then we'll have a permanent problem. If you need me to perform pre-marital services that are controlled, then I will. Why don't you get better and then we can make love until you're blue in the face? You've lost so much weight and mass that you need to gain back; we don't want that little head to get you in trouble."

He kissed her seductively and said, "You're right. Why push it when in a few more days, I should have a modicum of strength and stamina back? It is just that it seems like an eternity since I was shot. You know in the Nam, you waited on the bullet with your name on it. Even when the Sarge's cousin tried to assassinate us, your body knew that it was only a matter of moments before the pain would set in. When you're in the midst of trying to help someone, and you're shot in the back, you're more relaxed and the body adjusts to what has occurred. When you anticipate and brace for it, you know it's going to hurt."

"Honey take a nap, and if your little head is still talking trash when you wake up, then I'll take care of my man. Just close your eyes and relax for a while. I know that birthday thing was big and long, but you needed to know your family is with you all the time. Just take a nap, Darling. I'm not going anywhere. If you want me to lie down with you, I will, but I'll have to leave for a little bit to secure Sister and Beatrice."

Chakes closed his eyes and drifted off to sleep. His next waking moment would be at 0800 hours the next morning.

At 0810, he looked at Luana sleeping in a chair and asked, "Why didn't you get in the bed?"

"I didn't want to disturb you. You, my lover, was out like a light and snoring up a storm. I thought that if I got in the bed and stirred, it would have awakened you. I was fine in the chair."

"I'm hungry. Call Sister and see if she and Beatrice want to join us."

"I'm going into town with Monica, Mr. Beckmire's nephew, and a few other people to talk to those two who we aren't so sure about. I want to leave my daughter and my grandmother in your charge. Is that a problem, or do I need to take them with me?"

"Oh, I think I can handle Sister, its Beatrice I'm worried about. She has a boat load of energy and may just tire me out."

"Well, you have all those other members of the group to help, including Marisa and the twins. If you want me to take her with me, then I will."

"No, you go. I got this, and I need to learn how to keep her and protect her. This is a good opportunity, although I'm tired and injured, her world still goes on. I got this."

# # #

At 0850 hours, Monica, Luana, and Darryl arrived at the courthouse escorted by Brown, Bernstein, Larry, and Zanthius. Darryl was included in the group to ascertain any involvement of the two young men with the attempted assassination of Chakes.

At 0900 hours, Elliot and David were escorted into a holding room. Both men were restrained with cuffs. Monica, Luana, and Darryl proceeded to another area where their bags were searched, and they were physically scanned by a metal detector. They were then led to a room where the two men were being held. Luana said, "Hey guys, how you are holding up?"

Elliot said, "This place is scary and dangerous."

She looked at David and asked, "What happened to your face?"

David said, "Just a minor altercation with another inmate."

Luana asked, "Did you report it?"

"Report it to who? That's not how this place works. You snitch, you get shanked."

"Tell me what the altercation was about?"

"I told you it was nothing. Just a minor misunderstanding."

Luana paused for a moment, smiled, and said, "Ok! Let me tell you how this is going to work, or perhaps not work. I ask you a question and you answer it fully. If you don't answer fully, we pack our bags and leave. Which is not a big deal, except you'll just have to defend yourself against a ton of charges that you won't understand. Are the rules clear, gentlemen?"

Both men reluctantly shook their heads. Luana announced, "I take the movement of the heads as an affirmative, meaning that you understand the rules. Now, from this point forward, the shaking of the head will not be accepted, or tolerated. We must communicate in English and clearly at that. Now that we can dispense with the formalities, I'll ask you, David, once again, what was the nature of the altercation with the other inmate?" He bowed his head and started to cry. After a few seconds he yelled, "The guy tried to rape me."

Luana looked at Monica and said, "We should petition for a secure holding cell to protect our clients. If we give notice, and there is no resolution, then we can sue the system for tons of money for our clients if they are molested, harassed or brutalized."

Monica introduced herself and Darryl to the two men. Elliot asked what was Darryl's function? Monica told him that he was an intern who would check past cases to see what direction they should head in.

Darryl looked at each man and said, "In the simplest of terms possible, I'm going to ask you a question, and then I want you to wait fifteen seconds before you consider answering. I will also ask your permission to hold your hands while you conjure up your answer."

"Now, Elliot, did you conspire, have knowledge of, assist in the planning of, or execution of the attempted assassination of Mr. Chakes?"

Elliot waited approximately fifteen seconds and said, "I had no idea that Richard was out to hurt anyone. I knew nothing, and I still don't know why he killed that man?"

Luana was about to say something when Darryl waved his fingers in the air and asked, "Please, Counselor, let me get through my questions."

"David, did you have any information about what was going to happen at the resort?"

David replied, "I didn't know, or hear of anything about trying to kill people. I thought we went there to get opportunities for jobs and education. I didn't know Richard was going to shoot anyone."

Darryl let go of his hands and said, "These guys be as clean as a whistle. They are telling the truth."

Monica said, "Ms. Luana and I will represent you in court. I am between an adoption process and your case. The first thing we must do is to get the judge to isolate you from the general population. Have you two guys looked in the mirror lately? Do you know that you're two good-looking men who look soft? When you enter the world of prisons, the residents look at you in different ways. In your case, you were probably bid on as soon as you entered the general population. Once the winner is announced, you are protected from mass rapes and other demands by inmates. Your initial beating was from the person who came in second place. To avoid any further issues, the person who won, well, you will have to submit and become his property. You guys are not cut out for this life, and unless you like being beaten, raped, and forced to suckle someone's private parts, then I suggest a new path for you two. We will file a motion before leaving to have you both placed in a secure, camera laden cell."

Darryl said, "I'll be right back. I have to find the loo."

# # #

Around 1145 hours, Monica and Luana had filed every conceivable petition to keep their clients out of the general population and made a most chilling threat that everyone on duty, or not on duty, would have to obtain a lawyer because they were going to sue everyone who worked for the system if anything happened to their two clients.

As the group prepared to return to the resort, Whitmore asked, "Where is the young boy?"

Luana said, "The last we saw of him, he was heading to the loo."

Larry said, "I was stationed by the loo. He never showed up there. Zanthius, did you see him go down the stairs?"

"Larry, I was there, and I never saw him either."

Brown said to Bernstein, "Can you imagine how pissed, the Sarge is going to be when we tell him that we lost his fricken nephew? In pairs, everyone searched this place from the top to the bottom."

Zanthius looked out of the window and saw Darryl, sitting on a bench outside of the courthouse. He signaled to the team that the target was in sight, and everyone hustled down to where he was.

Zanthius said, "When you leave our eyesight, we're unable to protect you, and we also expose ourselves. When you travel with us, you always make sure that someone has eyes on you at all times."

"I just went to the loo and then came outside to sit in the sun."

"Darryl, did you hear what I just said? You told people that you were going to the loo, and you never showed up there."

"Zanthius, there are more than one loo in the courthouse. Anyhow, I understand completely, and it won't happen again. Does that include when I'm at the resort as well?"

"Darryl, that includes everywhere. Were you able to get a feel for Richard?" Zanthius inquired.

"I was able to feel his pain, learn about his challenges and, hence, your inability to locate me. There is a group of people on the other side of the island who want to take over the drug and prostitution trade. He shot Mr. Chakes as a part of his indoctrination. Richard terribly screwed up that assignment because he was supposed to shoot someone randomly on the streets, and then disappear into the night. He was not supposed to shoot your friend in the middle of a dining room. He is an extremely unstable person and will probably not make it to his next scheduled trial."

"So, there was no mention, or detection of Walter, your uncle's cousin?" Zanthius asked.

"Insofar as I'm concerned, my other uncle did not appear in any connections that I experienced."

The group mounted up and drove to 'The Sanctuary'. At 1300 hours, Sue Lyn could be seen playing along the shoreline when the group arrived. Darryl said, "If there is no further need of me, I think I'll go and entertain my friend by the water.

# # #

"Hi Sue Lyn. Are you enjoying yourself in the water?"

"This water is salty. I've never been to a beach, but is all of the water salty?"

"No, it depends on where you are. If you are inland and near a body of water, it's probably not very salty. The oceans and seas are, however, salty. I'm going to go and change clothes. Do you have a bathing suit?"

"I do not," she said.

"Okay, come with me. Let's go shopping in the gift shop and see if they have a bathing suit that we can buy."

# # #

All the suits were two pieces. Sue Lyn felt rather bare when she put on the top and then the bottom. She said to Darryl, "Do women really wear these things that show so much flesh?"

"In my country, they don't wear anything except what nature provided them. Here I think people are a bit more conscious of their bodies and prefer to have as much covered as possible."

Later, Sue Lyn walked out of the dressing room and modeled for Darryl. His eyes were glued to her anatomy and snapped mental photos of every part of her. When she turned to show her rear, his eyes almost bugged out of his head. He said, "I've not seen many women's bodies and those that I have seen were relatives and drew no reactions from me. You, on the other hand, have a phenomenal physique that is sculptured in places that I would assume men like to focus on. That suit is so you, but I could be saying that from a lustful point of view."

"Darryl, do you like it and is it too much skin to show to strangers?"

"Sue Lyn, you're not buying that for strangers, you're buying it so that you can comfortably play in the water with me, no one else."

# # #

Later in the dining room, a weary looking Mike ran in and asked Ava, "Have you seen Ben Beckmire?"

"I just saw him walking down the beach with Chakes. They were heading towards the cul-de-sac." He thanked her and ran off. She said to Carlos, "I have a bad feeling about that."

On the beach Mike ran as though a wild animal was chasing him. He saw an image of two men walking and started to yell. He screamed, "Sarge, Sarge, Sarge."

The Sarge turned around and saw that it was Mike galloping at full speed. When Mike reached them, he attempted to talk but the Sarge said, "Catch your breath. Just relax and calm down."

About a full minute later, Mike said, "They're trying to pin the death of both senators on you."

The Sarge smiled and said, "Heck, I kind of expected someone would resort to that kind of bullshit. What took those morons so long? That, my friend, gives them the right to come at us armed to the teeth with tanks, bazookas, and every other kind of death dealing products that man has conceived. Guys, they want us dead, and I mean all of us."

He looked at Chakes and asked, "How much more time do you need?"

He then looked at Mike and said, "Go find my death dealing nephew and his female companion. They are critical to our success; I need to have a private session with them."

As the Sarge turned around to look at Chakes, he was off and running down the beach at a moderate speed, but a speed that would challenge most. The Sarge said, "Damn, I'm whole again. I'm damn whole again."

He threw his fist into air and said, "We gonna get this shit over with, and real soon."

Mike said, "Ah, boss, that was only the first part of the problem. Someone is recruiting a shitload of mercs, and at last count there were 220 applicants."

"Mike, why am I getting this information at this late date? Have your sources dried up?"

Mike lowered his head and revealed, "I screwed up. I became so jealous and suspicious of my wife that I let us all reach 'defcon 3'. I'll not hand you bullshit. I will say that I will take up the most exposed place in any upcoming assaults. I am sorry, but I lost my mind, and all of my responsibilities when on my wedding night my wife and I didn't consummate our marriage."

"Son, your vows were sacred. My wife said Carla was sick as a damn dog. Would you have wanted to consummate your vows by making love to your sick wife and perhaps have watched her die in your arms?"

"Sarge, I'm sick with love because I've never felt this way before. I'm hurting in so many ways, but more importantly, I failed the group by not focusing on the thing that keeps me and this group alive. I'm sorry."

"Son, it will all be okay. We've come too far to fail. They want to draw me out, thinking that I'm the leader. Somehow, my cousin is in the middle of this charade, but we'll find out soon enough. Mike, I need more than ever, for you to work your sources and keep me informed. It's time we made a move to middle America where we can see them coming, going, and thinking about coming. Put your ear to the ground and keep us informed. At the same time, make sure our pilot is in good spirits and is without hassle. If I find that you're a distraction,

Mike, I will have to ground you and replace Carla as our pilot-in-command."

"That information has been noted and stored in my memory banks, Sarge. I will not distract my woman from her responsibilities, that I swear to you."

# # #

At 1500 hours, the Sarge called the group to order. He thanked everyone for coming and introduced his nephew and Sue Lyn, once again. He said, "It has come to my attention that I'm being accused of killing the two US Senators whose deaths were of a suspicious nature. We all know this is a ruse to draw us out and to make me the villain of all that ails our damn government. I surely didn't know that I was of such importance. I want to spend tomorrow here and be off to middle America by the next day. There are several things that complicate that simple wish. I need to have Mallory and Monica at the Catholic Charities. I must make sure that Sue Lyn gets home safely, and then, I must make sure that we all are in battle gear in middle America. My sources have indicated that 225 Mercs have been assembled to conclude our existence. In Virginia, it would be an easy termination process for us with the automated weaponry." Jong raised his hand and asked, "What if we could replicate that process in middle America?"

"That is a spectacular question, my brother," the Sarge indicated.

"I think my niece is as good at video games as anyone that I know, and she is very smart," Jong announced.

"Jong, aren't we supposed to fly them back to DC on Sunday?"

"Yes, we are, but my cousin works for me, and I pay her tuition, room and board and will promise her a nice car. If your nephew comes along, she will tag along like a cat looking for catnip. I think they have a special feeling for each other, but don't know how to express, or communicate it. Why don't we send them ahead to scope out the property and set up some defenses?"

"Damn, great idea. Let's go down to the water and have a discussion with them. In the meantime, the rest of you sit back and enjoy yourselves. We are about to turn the corner on this matter."

The Sarge, Jong, Mallory, and Chakes walked down to the water's edge where Darryl and Sue Lyn were wading. Darryl looked up and saw them and said to Sue Lyn, "I think there is trouble brewing somewhere. Here comes my uncle and your uncle."

Ben Beckmire said, "Darryl, I'm supposed to fly you and Sue Lyn back to Washington tomorrow. I have a problem in another state that I think you two could help both of your uncles, solve. Sue Lyn, your Uncle Jong is going to call his cousin and let him know that we're flying you to middle America to set up our defenses, if you're in agreement to assist us. Darryl, you don't have a choice--its Sue Lyn's decision."

"Mr. Beckmire and esteemed Uncle, I am at your service. I, or rather we, will help you in any way that we can. When you say defenses, do you mean like points of security and/or firing sequences?" Sue Lyn inquired.

Jong said, "That is why I afford you to go to those prestigious institutions. You are the most talented family member that I know, give, or take your father in the development of weapons and remote targeting. I know it was your design with the long guns at our place in Virginia. I need you both to wash that salt off your bodies and prepare to leave this place in the next hour."

The Sarge looked at Jong and said, "I need you to call Clyde and tell him we will need him to pick up our children and take them to the ranch and show them every aspect of our current defenses. Tell him that I want him to respond to their wishes and not judge their youthfulness. Ask him to do that for me."

# # #

After making it crystal clear about what he needed as a defensive position in middle America, the Sarge looked at the two young people and said, "I will allow you to get to know each other, and that may include kissing, feeling, touching, and reaching places of physical satisfaction. I forbid you to consummate the act of sex by engaging in an act that includes penetration, or any aspect of one entering the other. Is that perfectly clear and are the definitions so clear that we won't have to discuss meanings? If you attempt penetration and succeed at it, I will banish you both to a place that is reserved for failed relationships. Now, go take your showers, pack your clothes, and wait for me in the lobby. You will be met by Clyde, a good friend of ours and he will show you everything that you request, or don't, at the ranch in middle America. I sanction touching, and kissing, but not the touching that leads to penetration or the kissing that leads to the kissing or sucking of each other's private parts. I'm treating you as adults. If you fail this basic animalistic test, then you will face a lifetime of unsatisfied sexual experiences."

As they walked away, Jong said, "How did you know they have touched and kissed?"

"Don't you remember when you were their ages? Did you see the way they looked at each other when they first arrived? Your niece, in other words, wants to bang my nephew's' brains out. He needs it, and she needs it, but I'm not sure how to turn a blind eye to this one. You have any suggestions?"

"I have no idea as to how to approach birds that want to flap their wings. They're no different than you and me. I have no idea how to stop flapping wings."

Beckmire yelled, "Darryl, I have a question to ask you." Darryl proceeded to run towards his uncle and when he reached where he and Jong were standing, he said, "Yes, Uncle?"

"Darryl, what would happen to you if you lied to me about anything that I ask you?"

"Uncle, I will not lie to you under any circumstances. You're a Beckmire, and we don't lie to each other."

"Thanks Nephew, I just wanted to hear you say that in public before a witness. Now, go and get ready and be in the lobby in an hour."

Jong called Captain Carla and indicated to her that he needed people transported to middle America in the next two hours and asked if it were a problem. She told him that there were always two pilots ready to fly at all times, and that the pilots who delivered the two young people are legal and ready. Jong thanked her and told her to make sure that the big bird was ready by tomorrow because they might have to get out of town in a hurry. She stated that the plane had been checked, fueled, and food was on board.

The Sarge sought out Mallory and found him lounging at the pool with Monica. He said, "You people prefer a pool to God's wonderful ocean out back?"

Mallory said, "Here I can throw her a rope if the water gets beyond her nose. What's up?"

"I really want to talk to Monica about those kids in jail. We might have to leave here tomorrow or the next day, in a hurry if the heat is turned up on me. I still can't figure out how I could become a person of interest in the deaths of two senators? Anyway, Monica, is there any way we can get those kids out on bail?" Monica was about to say something when the Sarge saw Mr. Carter. He said, "Hey, Chris, can you join us for a moment?"

When Mr. Carter came to their side of the pool, the Sarge said, "I was just asking our lawyer if we could bail those two kids out of jail. Then I thought, if we get them out and they go back to their hood, people may come looking for them. Is there any way you can house them and put them to work on the two properties that are being constructed? Oh, and by the way, do you have a problem assisting us in this matter?"

"Mr. Beckmire, I do not and there is plenty of work to be done here at 'The Sanctuary'. Not a problem at all unless they come out here with a 'tude'."

"I assure you, that will be the last thing on their minds. They haven't been there long, and they've already had a really rough go. Someone tried to rape one of them and the other received a threatening note about snitching. We might have to leave in a hurry, and I don't want to leave those kids in jail. Thanks, Chris, and I'll let you know if we get them out on bail."

He turned to Monica and said, "Wow, I should have asked your opinion before setting that wheel in motion. Do you have any contrary thoughts about what I'm trying to do?"

"No, Man! I looked like that because I am so blessed to be in the company of people who genuinely care about others.

This whole show is about trying to 'help people help themselves', and I love it. I'll call Luana and see if she is available to speak to me about it."

The Sarge looked at Monica and asked, "Is Luana a good attorney?"

Monica looked around as if she were about to share state secrets and said, "She is one of the smartest lawyers I have ever met. She crafted the deal about the coordinates for the outback. She is sharp and disarming. People look at her and say to themselves, 'She can't be but so smart because she's really pretty'."

"I was just wondering. I'm going to go speak with Chakes and see if he wants to take them with us. I'm afraid that this could be a rough road to travel. I heard there are more than 225 mercs being recruited by a phantom in the DC area. We have a better chance of fending for ourselves at the ranch. By the way, I'm sending my nephew and Jong's niece on a plane in an hour to put in play a defensive system, beyond the one that is there."

Mallory asked, "Sarge, why are you sending Jong's niece?"

"The long gun solution in Virginia, well, that was her design."

"You're messing with me, right? That little girl developed that system?"

"Mallory, she is the developer of our entire system in Virginia. Her father, Jong's cousin, is the modifier and installer. That little Miss Muffin, is a tactical genius because of playing video games."

Monica said, "Damn, you just never know who you're messing with. Okay, I'm going to track down Luana and get the bail thing in place. Catch you guys later."

"When are you guys going to secure your children?"

"That is exactly what we were talking about before your big ass came waltzing up."

"Damn, I'm so sorry, or maybe not. I think the heat is really going to be on us this time. I don't know when, but it's inevitable that Walter is trying to close out his business with us. My main purpose is to figure out what you're going to do about your children. Do you want to take them into battle?"

"Gee, Sarge, we were discussing that question, as well, before your big ass waltzed up in our sunshine."

"Damn, Man. I'm trying to cover all these bases and I keep stepping on my own tongue. Hit me back when you guys have decided which direction, you're heading in. I must find Chakes and see where his head is in terms of his new family. Catch you later, and I apologize for interrupting. If you believe that one, then good luck with the rest of the shit I talk," the Sarge indicated.

# # #

Chakes walked up the road to the other properties to check on the progress. He saw one of his partners and asked him if he were happy with the progress thus far. The man told him that it was a miracle it was being done at all, and he thanked him. He told Chakes that the expansion of the two properties would add so much value to the land and the area. He indicated that he and the others had an idea they wanted to present to his group. Chakes asked him if they had bounced it off Mr. Carter, and the man told him they had not. Chakes then went on to tell them that what is happening to their properties is a function of Mr. Christopher Carter. Chakes suggested they get together after he leaves and have some of Ms. Viola's rum punch and try to gather a consensus.

When the Sarge saw Chakes walking down the hill, he didn't recognize him at first. Chakes had developed a slight limp from complications from being shot. The Sarge asked, "Hey man, what's with that limp? Is that something we have to attend to?"

"Not sure, Sarge. I think it gets better and better each day that I exercise."

"Where are you coming from?"

"I walked up the road to check on the progress of the other properties being constructed."

"You walked all the way up there by yourself? Are you heeled?"

"Yeah, I have one of those .308s that the ladies carry."

"Why didn't you take company with you, and where are your people?"

"They're in town and should be here in about an hour."

"Listen, I'm expecting a lot of heat from my cousin. We can't defend ourselves here and in Virginia; there are too many places to guard. I'm pulling up stakes and heading to middle America. My question to you is a simple one. What about your people? You want to take them into the fire?"

"That's exactly why I took that walk. I know the drill, and I've been asking myself that very same question. Do I want to take them into the fire? Absolutely not. I'm thinking they would be a liability and may get someone hurt since they don't know how we work and how the ladies protect our rear. I'm not sure if they could handle it."

The Sarge said, "Well, buddy boy, I believe that's them in that smoker coming around the bend." Chakes turned around and it was Luana, Sister and Beatrice.

Luana pulled up beside him and smiled. Chakes said, "Honey, didn't I ask you to get that muffler fixed when I first met you?"

"And that you did, Sir. I was planning to put it in the shop, but someone keeps calling me and telling me how much he misses us and can't wait until we get here. Do you know anyone who would say such a thing, Mr. Beckmire?"

The Sarge looked at the ladies and said, "Have a wonderful day, and I'll see you guys at dinner. Have fun, Romeo."

Chakes reached into the car and kissed Luana. He then turned to the others and said, "Hi Sister, hey Beatrice. Beatrice, you want to go swimming with me?"

"Oh, yes. Can I mommy? Please?"

Chakes said, "Heck, why don't we all put our feet in the water?"

Sister asked, "Man, have you been sitting in the water?"

"Not really, Sister. I've been meaning to but haven't been in there since you know, my problem came about."

"Man, if you want to get fixed then you should be sitting in that water until your skin starts to shrivel up. That water be as good as any medicine for what ails you. You go and get in the water. We will park this thing and come and join you."

Chakes walked to the water's edge and watched the waves come and go. He wasn't a strong swimmer but was able to do the dog paddle. He walked into the water and ran out in a hurry. Sister said, "What's wrong with you man? You done seen a fish or something?"

"I saw a lot of fish."

"Man, go on get in that water. Can you swim?"

"I can swim a little, but I don't play in deep water."

"Okay, man. Just kneel where you're standing and let the waves rock you slowly back and forth. There be energy in that movement, and the salt water is so good for healing. Just accept it and relax. I no let nothing happen to you. I'll be your lifeguard."

Chakes said, "Sister, how come you doing all that talking on dry land? How come you not in the water?"

"Oh, I was in the billabong in Australia and that was enough for me. I feel so good, and I don't want to feel too good because I might try to start running again."

#

Monica saw the group on the beach and headed for them. She spoke to everyone, and then said to Luana, "Ben Beckmire wants to get those kids out of jail and bring them here to work. My concern is that we might have to leave here tomorrow or the next day and head for Asiram's ranch in the Midwest."

Chakes interrupted Monica and said, "Thanks, Monica, I hadn't talked to them about that yet."

"Oh shoot. My bad. Luana, seek me out when he has finished his sermon. Sorry, buddy, hope it's not a problem."

Chakes said, "Honey, can you come and join me?"

"I don't have a suit on."

"Neither do I. Please come in for a moment. Sister was right, this feels incredible on my body."

Luana walked out to where he was kneeling and assumed the same position. Chakes enjoyed the moment before proclaiming, "The Sarge is being framed for killing two United States senators! Also, there is a group of mercs being assembled in the DC area. We can't defend ourselves at the farm in Virginia but have a good chance of surviving in the

Midwest. This is going to be a large assault and a lot of people may die including, perhaps, some of us. I can't ask you, Beatrice, and Sister to come because it is far too dangerous for you guys."

Luana pondered his statements for a minute before asking "Is it dangerous for those pregnant ladies, Marisa, and the twins. What about for Rashida with her pregnant self and her other child? Why is it that you're trying to make decisions for me and my family? Why couldn't you just ask us what our opinion was, or how we feel about entering a danger zone? Listen, Maurice, we are independent people. We're not afflicted, and there might be a service that we could provide if you invite us, and we select to go. Just ask us and let us decide, rather than telling me about how dangerous it is. It was dangerous in the midst of all your people when you were shot in the back. Let us calculate the danger and figure out what we want to do."

Sister yelled, "Where she goes, we go. Ain't that right, Beatrice?"

"Yes, Granny. That's right."

Chakes looked at them and said, "I can't in good conscience invite you to what could be your last supper. I can't, and I won't. That's the end of that discussion."

Luana said, "I'm so sorry you feel that way, Mussolini. I think we'll head to one of the beaches where the proletariat have a say in what happens to them. It's a despot, free beach. Come on guys, we're heading back to town where the plebs are free to make their own decisions."

Luana stormed out of the water and headed for her car with Beatrice and Sister pulling up the rear. Ms. Viola said, "Honey, this is not how you resolve critical issues. He may have a point! It could be beyond what we're able to deal with."

"Grandma! Let it go. If I'm to leave this earth, and my daughter as well, then I want to be with the man I love and not the dictator that I'm forced to obey."

As they entered the car, Chakes held fast and never turned around to see them depart. Eight to ten minutes later, there was the sound of a horrific accident on the main road. Maurice jumped out of the water and ran full steam up the winding road until he reached the access road. The Sarge, Jilkes, and John Lee also heard it. Jilkes jumped in one of the mules and headed full speed towards the access road picking up people on the way. When he saw Chakes running up the hill, the Sarge said, "Let him get there by his own power. I think I want him to collapse if it's his people. I think he made the wrong decision, and I pray to God that I am wrong. Damn, I pray that I'm wrong."

At the top of the hill and on the access road, it was obvious that two vehicles had fatally collided with each other. The convertible had crossed the lane and impacted a car heading in the opposite direction. The two cars met head on, and no one survived the impact. Five people lost their lives. Luana's car came to a rest in a ditch, approximately ten feet from the collision. She apparently drove her car there to avoid hitting the vehicle that had crossed the median strip, flipped over, and came to rest. The team righted her car and everyone inside was okay. They all had latched their seatbelts.

Chakes opened the door and began to cry. Sister, Beatrice, and Luana, looked a little dazed, but it was obvious they were okay. He fell to his knees and told Luana how sorry he was for not considering their input but would forever learn from that mistake.

He said, "Turn the motor off and get that muffler fixed." They both laughed and embraced. He said, "I would like you guys to take the mule back to the resort. Don't let Beatrice see this mayhem."

Two hours later, the team returned to the resort. Later, they found out the reason why the convertible had jumped across the lane. They were sad at of the unnecessary loss of life because of someone trying to talk on their cell phone and drive. Chakes walked the ladies to their room and asked Luana if he could have a word with her.

Luana jumped his bones immediately, and said, "Mein Fuhrer, how can I serve thee?"

"Come on, Honey. I'm no dictator. I'm just a servant of love who is crazy about you and your family. Do you think my decision was made haphazardly? I would hope not, my lady. We're talking about people trying to kill us over some new bomb, and Ben Beckmire's cousin is leading the charge. The last time we encountered him, he got the drop on us, so he thought, and strapped suicide vests on Larry and Marisa's twins, as well as LaGina. If it weren't for Larry, Okema, Somara, and Yeshida, we would not be having this conversation."

"I have heard that story, and it frightens me. However, you can't tell me what's best for me, or my family. You should have explained the circumstances and asked us to consider all of the things that could go wrong and the possibility of being killed."

Chakes said, "I thought you would understand what I was talking about."

"Mister Man, we almost got fucking killed in a car accident. I'm glad I had the presence of mind to drive into the ditch, or we would have been entangled in that mess, and perhaps be dead like those other people. Stop handing me 'BS'. If you don't think we have a strong enough foundation to weather another storm, then say so. I know the man I'm holding a claim-ticket for. Perhaps he doesn't want to retrieve his bounty from the dry cleaners?"

# # #

All the women in the group assembled and walked to Luana's room. Asiram knocked on the door and Chakes answered it. Asiram said, "Man, go take a walk. We want to see our girlfriend."

They all plowed into the room and began giving Sister, Luana, and Beatrice hugs and kisses. They wanted to commiserate with the ladies following their near tragic accident.

Chakes kissed Luana goodbye and said that he would stop by once all the guests were gone. She whispered in his ear, "Be my man, and not my boss, and we'll live a long life together. Oh, and I saw how you came running up that hill, I hope you saved some of that energy for me."

An hour later, as the women were leaving the room, Luana told Monica that the judge was happy about their requests and indicated that he would release them on their own recognizance in the morning. She said, "I'll speak with Mr. Carter and make sure he has his people pick them up in the morning. Whoever picks them up has to sign a release form and transport them directly to 'The Sanctuary'."

"Good work, young lady. By the way, welcome to an exciting team and way of life. I hope he makes the right decision about your coming with us. Everyone is watching his actions but saying nothing. I think he realizes that life is fragile no matter where you are and how safe you think you are. Look at what happened to him in the midst of his entire family."

"I know. I told him that."

"Oh, and Luana, first chance you get, have him take you into town to buy a real car. That thing you're driving doesn't appear safe."

"Look Girl, I can't afford a new car."

"Honey, open your eyes. Tell him you want a new car, and you want it now. Those guys are extremely rich, and I'm assuming you're his lady, and, if so, he must make sure you ride in a safe vehicle. Just messing with you, but he would enjoy doing that as a gift for helping him recover."

As Monica walked towards the dining room, she saw her husband and Chakes talking. She walked over to them and said, "Baby, we need to talk now. You, Mr. Chakes need to ride into town and buy someone I know a new car for taking care of your ass. Don't think about it--just do it."

The Sarge and Courtney sat down to order a salad when Mike saw them and came over. Courtney said, "Mike if it ain't life or death, then catch him later. We're trying to eat and enjoy ourselves."

"Ah, yes, Ma'am."

"No, you didn't just say, 'yes ma'am' to me?"

"I'm sorry, Mrs. Beckmire."

"Mike, call her Courtney, please. We'll be done in about thirty minutes." Mike started to walk away and said, "Sarge, in thirty minutes you might have the local law all over you. Somehow there is a wanted poster of you floating around in Miami, and someone at the scene today recognized you. I recommend we leave and have Mr. Carter's son put you in the dingy and take you as far up the coast as possible. I've already talked to him and he's on standby. Everyone else should prepare to leave here in the next hour."

The Sarge looked at him for a minute without responding and said, "Find Mallory and tell him I need to see him."

Mike started to walk away again before turning and adding, "I think it might be better if John Lee and Jilkes got in the dingy and we smuggled you in the back of one of the vans. I'm sure they're probably watching us and that would be a simple misdirection on our part. You're not only wanted for murder, but you are also wanted in connection with a bank robbery in DC. Your cousin is pulling out all the stops."

"Thanks, Mike, put the plan in operation. Find Jilkes and John Lee and tell them what has to happen."

Courtney said, "I'm not sure I like this plan of action."

"You have a better idea?"

"No, but I'll be right there if all goes wrong."

"I know you will, darling. I want Whitmore, Gladstone, McArthur, and Mike riding shotgun in the van with me. Honey, have Brown, Bernstein, Montomie, and Jong clear a path. Put the word out--we're out of here in one hour, and the people in the dingy should leave in the next thirty minutes."

# # #

Asiram asked Zanthius, "Do you think we'll ever settle down and live a normal life?"

"Honey, I'm thinking this is the new normal. My dad is working towards that, and this might be the stimulus that gets us closer to concluding at least the deal with the Carbon Factor formula. The business with my uncle is another matter. He's making a final push, and I hear that he's gotten 225 mercs to assist him."

"Zanthius, that's a lot of people with guns."

"I know, but it's also a lot of people in the middle of nowhere who can't communicate and see where they're going. If it's not safe, trust me, we're out of there in a hurry. Pops would not put us at risk."

Chakes got the word while he was seeking understanding from Luana. Mike told him that they were out of there in the next hour. Chakes dropped his head and said to Luana, "I have to leave within the hour. I cannot put you and your family at risk."

Luana's eyes filled with tears, and she said, "Is that your final edict?"

"I'm afraid so. I would simply die if something happened to you guys." She kissed him and said, "I love you so much. Goodbye, my darling."

Chakes said, "That sounded so final."

"It probably is. You don't respect me. I've been down that road of someone trying to protect me while sitting me in a closet to wait on his return. Fool me once, but not twice. I won't be around when, and if, you return."

Chakes said, "I'm looking out for you and your family. What's wrong with you, woman?"

Luana exclaimed, "That's what's wrong with me! You want to dictate, and I want to love. You want to tell me what to eat, and I want to sample everything in front of me. You want to tell me to fix my muffler, but I enjoy the sound as well as the smell. I want a lover, not a protector. I got this far without a wraparound situation and I'm not returning to it. Listen, you must get ready to leave. I'll tell my people you said goodbye. Let it go and let me go. You've made your decision, and I've made mine. We're different and have different expectations. However, I do love you, Maurice Chakes, but not enough to give up my independence."

Chakes looked at his watch and said, "So I guess that's it. You're not going to relent, are you?"

"Maurice, I tried that once and it didn't work too well for me. I am who I am, and I will never tolerate a dictator in my life, and it appears to me you may be just that."

"Because I'm concerned about your safety, you consider me a dictator?"

"I consider you a dictator because you think you know what's best for me and my family. Listen, you have to go, and so do I." She turned to walk away and Chakes said, "I can't believe you would end all that we have developed because I don't want to put you and your family in harm's way. Those women, including Dr. Beckmire, have shot and killed people. Rashida probably has a head count in the hundreds. Will you pull the trigger, if necessary, and will Sister as well?"

"Everyone will say what someone expects to hear to move a moment forward. I'm not promising anything, and, therefore, you need to make your move and join your tribe, buddy."

"I consider you my tribe, as well. Ah, screw it. Let's go. Does everyone have papers?"

"You didn't hear me, did you? I don't want to go now. You've taken all the excitement out of it. Call me, sometime."

Luana started to walk away, turned around, smiled, and screamed, "Does this mean we're engaged? Listen, I almost lost you once. I will protect what is mine and never hesitate."

"Who is the dictator now?"

"All we have is an overnight case for each of us."

"Don't worry, that's all we ever have. There are stores where we're going."

# # #

Approximately one hour later, Jilkes, John Lee, and Michael were on their way up the coast in the tender. Awaiting them at the nearest marina were members of the local police department.

The three men made their way to the marina in a deliberately slow fashion by dropping their fishing lines in the water and then talking loudly. All three men noticed the two police boats that were shadowing them from afar. As the three men approached the marina, the police patrol boats put their sirens and flashing blue lights on. Michael could be seen pouring beers into the water.

The patrol boats told them to head for the marina on their port side. Michael yelled, "That's not where we be heading. We're just out fishing a little."

An officer said, "I need you to follow my instructions and dock your boat at the marina on your port side."

When Michael cut his outboard engine off, he also engaged the choke on it, filling the carburetor with fuel. The immediate response was that the engine would not start. He pulled, pulled, and pulled until he was tired. An officer said, "I'm going to throw you a line and tow you in."

Once in the marina and tied up, an officer from the ground squad asked to see everyone's papers. Jilkes and John Lee showed him their driver's license. The police were familiar with Michael.

John Lee said, "We were being safe out there on the water. What be the problem?"

The officer said, "I'll ask the questions. Why are you people riding around in that tender?"

Jilkes said, "Because we want to. Did we break a law or something? Let me just say this, we are members of the investment team that is financing the four businesses in the cul-de-sac. Our lawyers are somewhere waiting on us, and if you don't have a specific ordinance that we violated to hold us on, then I suggest you let us go. This ain't Alabama, and we ain't no damn sharecroppers. Any additional questions will be asked in front of our lawyers and your judge, as we also prepare a document to sue the living hell out of you for messing with our bonding trip. We come here to this island to bond--spiritually, emotionally, and say prayers to our God to 'help people help themselves'. We don't want any trouble, but if you insist on asking us questions, then so be it."

"Are you threatening a police officer?"

"My words are recorded; you might want to rethink that ploy. We're also broadcasting this entire scene to our lawyers and your judge. What are you looking for?"

The lead officer said, "Have a nice day. Michael, take care brother."

Later, in town, the vans pulled up to the airport and the group was escorted to the customs area. Beckmire got out of the hidden compartment and said to Mr. Carter, "Do I have a problem leaving this place on my own plane?"

"Mr. Beckmire, I've taken the liberty to do something that you do well. I've exercised my authority and everyone who needs to be on board, is on board with my plan. In thirty minutes, the police people will be here and will hold the airplane up until they inspect it. Your captain will escort them, but you will be behind that false bathroom door, and in your own little cocoon. Once the plane is on the runway, have a pleasant trip, my friend. I'll ask the judge to investigate the false claims and find out where this stuff came from."

The Sarge hugged him and said, "You're a true friend who never questions our values, or our missions. Why is that?"

"Your mission is a heavenly one. You help good people and hurt bad people. My kind of group. Safe flight, my friend. See you when I see you."

Captain Carla came on the intercom system and said, "Now, y'all know I like taking off from this airport. I need you to trust the system and tighten those seatbelts. The copilot said something to her, and she loudly asked, "Is everyone present and accounted for?"

Somara and Yeshida started screaming, "No, No, No."

Jong got out of his seat and went to where they were sitting and asked, "Where are the two lovers? Did someone make a plan that I'm not aware of?"

Mike slowly raised his hand and said, "Damn, I'm sorry. I thought someone else had that mission."

Captain Carla called the tower and told them that they were aborting the take-off because they were missing two members of the group.

When Jilkes and John Lee got to the airport and entered customs, the officer said, "I believe your plane is airborne."

John Lee looked at Jilkes and said, "Ain't no way they be leaving us behind. Ain't no damn way."

Jilkes said, "You're right, my friend. That's our plane taxiing back this way."

"Do you guys have anything to claim?" the agent asked.

Jilkes said, "Hell, no. Catch you in a few months."

# # #

As soon as they got on the plane, Jilkes went to Jong and said, "You know you got one coming, don't you?"

"Go to that big guy up front. I did not know about this bad idea of his."

## CHAPTER SIX

Asiram noticed that most of the women on board were all very pregnant, and it was time to start making a different kind of plan. She asked all the women to meet her in the back of the plane so that they could talk. She said, "Ladies, I'm afraid we're going to have to show our men our worth."

She looked at Ms. Viola and asked, "Have you ever fired a weapon before and, if not, if someone was trying to hurt Beatrice would you be able to shoot them?"

Ms. Viola said, "I wouldn't recommend anyone to try that."

Asiram smiled and asked, "Luana, how about you?"

"I've never fired a weapon but would definitely shoot anyone who tries to hurt my child."

"Okay, ladies, no one elected me as the official guide, but I'm going to give you a little history. I was a spy and I have killed a lot of people. I almost killed the man I love. He was on my hit list. Yeshida, Okema, and Somara were once spies and, hell, they still may be. They have ended lives as well. Rashida, our youngest recruit, has terminated more souls than I care to think about. Mary Alice has carried a weapon but has not had to use one. Yvett is a card caring member but has not fired one as well. I depend on each one of you, and you depend on me as well as the others. I want the rookies to meet me at

0900 hours. We're going to go into the field and fire three types of weapons. You're going to fire an automatic rifle, an automatic pistol, and a shotgun.

"When you got on this plane, you subscribed to the notion that this is your community, and it needs your protection. Look at what happened to Chakes before our very eyes. You will fire these weapons, and you will always have one on your person, and be ready to use it safely and effectively. We all saw your man, Luana, take a bullet in the back. Didn't look that bad, but internally it was a disaster. There are safe tunnels underground, and weapon stashes all along the journey there. They are somewhat childproof for the most part. You will fire these weapons, you will absorb the concussion, and you will know that each time you pull that trigger you're intending that someone will die. There are no easy shots like to the leg. You hit the right vein and the target bleeds out in a hurry. In this forum, we shoot to kill. We don't assume that the target is dead because it isn't moving. We make sure it's dead so that it can't rise and shoot you in the back or me in the head. We must protect each other. When we land, you will be fitted with a vest--I suggest that you get used to it because it might save your life. Are there any questions?"

Courtney walked over to Asiram and hugged her. She said, "Damn, I love you and the way you prepared Chakes's people for the ultimate test of loyalty. You done did good, girl."

# # #

As the plane began to descend, Somara yelled, "Oh, hell no. Something is going on in there. Courtney, I need your help. It feels like a fight is in process."

John Lee asked, "Baby, what can I do to help?"

"You go and get drunk and leave me alone. You did this to me and now you want to help? You go away, have a drink, and pass out until next week."

Courtney stumbled to the back of the plane and saw that Somara's water had broken. She picked up the intercom and said, "Captain Carla, unless you put this thing on the ground soon, we're going to have our first airborne baby."

Courtney called out for Jong and said, "Call Clyde and tell him that we have a baby about to be born. Instruct him to call the hospital and have them make ready and waiting on us."

Ms. Viola showed up with cold compresses and began to gently massage Somara's temples who continued to moan, but with less vigor. Somara muttered, "I hate you, John Lee. I love you, John Lee."

Unintentionally, Ms. Viola had showed her worth by doing what she knew how to do to comfort Somara. Somara said, "Your hands are soothing and warm. By rubbing my temples, my body began to relax and let the baby have his or her way."

"Oh, so you don't know the sex of the baby?"

"We just want a healthy baby. I secretly would like a little girl, but I know he wants a boy."

"Well, Honey, if I had two cents in this equation, I would say for sure, you better start picking names for little boys because that's exactly what you're going to have."

Captain Carla turned on the seatbelt sign and told Somara to hang in there for a few more minutes. She told her to look outside of the window and that she would see emergency vehicles coming to the rescue.

John Lee sat next to Beatrice and said, "My name is John Lee, and your name is Ms. Beatrice. I guess we've not been formally introduced. It be nice to meet you."

"You mean, it's nice to meet you," Beatrice replied.

"That be what I be saying," John Lee stated.

"You mean, that's what I was saying."

"That be my wife back there with your great grandmother. She is about to have our baby."

Beatrice looked at him and asked, "Mr. John Lee, how are babies made?"

John Lee said, "I think I'm going to let your daddy, Mr. Chakes, answer that question when he wakes up. Now, don't you forget to ask him, okay?"

Twenty-minutes later, the beautiful flying machine majestically, glided through the air and made a smooth landing. Captain Carla welcomed everyone to Wyoming. Meanwhile, Somara's labor pains were intensifying, and Carla's welcome was barely heard.

The plane pulled into the hangar. Somara and John Lee were unloaded first. Gladstone, McArthur, Montomie, and Mike were assigned guard duty. Clyde was happy to see everyone but was eager to get the group to the hospital. The Sarge asked him how he had been and suggested that the next time the team goes to St. Thomas, they'll send a plane, or get him airline tickets so that you guys can get some sun and have some fun. The Sarge also said, "I see you've changed the color of this school bus as well as the seats. This seems a bit cushy."

"Well, Mr. Beckmire, this is a new bus equipped with all kinds of fancy gadgets and will have a few more when those two young people finish designing things. This bus is a bit heavier because it has armor plated sides, front, and rear. All the windows are bulletproof and there are portholes just in case you want to shoot a deer or something from the bus. Speaking about those two young people, they are well mannered, respectful, and engaging. When they come up with things, they call me over and ask my opinion. They're no trouble and, as a matter of fact, I wish they were mine. I mean they are so considerate and thoughtful. Always asking if they can help me do anything. They've been here for two days, and the things they've accomplished are just short of miraculous. I mean they gave me a list of things to buy including computers, switches, cables, and other things. I had to send someone over to another county to pick up some of the stuff and there's a truck load of stuff coming in from Amazon in the morning. You'll see."

# # #

At the hospital, a team of doctors and nurses were waiting for the group to arrive. When all the people got off the bus, the doctor said, "Oh, I know this group. Welcome back."

The Sarge said, "Nice to see you again. I might have a favor to ask of you, but we'll talk later."

The Sarge said to Monica, "I need a contrived name for the mother and child. See what you can do and see what equipment they might need. It works well out here, a little bribery, that is."

Somara was admitted, and as they wheeled her away, she screamed, "Where is Ms. Viola? I need Ms. Viola or I ain't having this baby."

Ms. Viola said, "Lord, I'll be right there."

She looked at Luana and said, "Take care of my baby, and I'll see you later." She went in the hospital and Somara screamed, "Damnit, where is Courtney? I need my own doctor in here, too. Where is Courtney?"

Everybody scrubbed down and the attending doctor said, "Everything looks like a go, but she hasn't dilated enough. Since she is not dilating, I'll have to probably do a C-section."

Ms. Viola said, "No man, you no have to cut her. Let me relax her. Put on some soothing music, and she'll be ready to drop this load in thirty minutes. You no need to cut her. Just let me calm her down."

Thirty-five minutes later, and appearing as though she had an epidural, Somara popped John Lee Jr. out of his safe house and welcomed him into the world. The doctor asked, "Did you give her anything or make her smell anything?"

"No man, no witchcraft here. I just made her calm down and when she be calm, that big baby inside her be calm too. Everybody calm, doctors and nurses calm, but husband is out like a light."

The doctor said, "You should patent that calm routine."

"No, man, you should come to the island, and I'll teach you how to do it. Maybe you and me could become partners or something. I make them calm, and you just say, 'okay, time to deliver'."

# # #

The Sarge said to Clyde, "I need to split my group up. Ms. Asiram has two boys, and we have a slew of other pregnant women and little children. I want to get them to the ranch, settled in, and leave some of my guys here for a pick-up later."

"When I got the call, I knew there were babies in this group. I made a call, and I have a real school bus on its way."

"Clyde, on the new bus, do you happen to have some tools that my people can conceal"

"I thought you'd never ask. I have, by name, the tools they last used when they were here. Each one has a clip in it and two on the side. Also, in the main bus, I have twenty-four machine pistols and three clips each. On the bus that's coming, well, all it has is seats and heat."

"Good man. You're God sent, buddy. I would like to meet with your people in the late morning for breakfast, say around 1000 hours. There are some things that I need to discuss with them. There may be as many as 225 mean sons-of-a-guns coming out here to end our existence. I don't want you guys involved like before because it's too dangerous."

"Mr. Beckmire, with all due respect, if you didn't want us to be involved, then you should have stayed down in Virginia, or in the islands. How many people did you save in this community? How many ranches did you save? How many bad people did you run out of town, including bankers? How many deeds did you buy back and give to the people? Now, like I said, if you don't want our help, then you should go down to Virginia, or that St. Thomas place."

The Sarge said, "You're such a stubborn old fart, but I appreciate what you just said to me and my people. I'm not going to discuss it any further until we have a joint meeting with everyone involved."

"My misses and a few others have thrown together a small something to eat. There be some new people here. We'll set them up in the alternative place and show them how things work. Seriously, Mr. Beckmire, we're simple farmers who were about to have our land stolen from under our noses. You smelled the rat, and you gave him a trail of crumbs that led him out of town. This don't happen every day, sir. People tend to want to stick it to us, like they did those people over in Jackson Hole. They came in with their suitcases full of money, and, basically, drove them out or burned them out. Here you made it clear that your friends are your family, and your family, are your friends. You will not be able to stop us from assisting and setting up perimeters. As a matter of fact, our people had fun with those two young people, listening to them talk about being in love and wanting to marry."

"My God! What are you talking about?"

"I may be talking out of school, or even considered to be snitching, but she does not want him to wait to finish school before they have sex and marry. She said, 'her uncle told her not to touch, feel and in pure terms, penetrate'. She also said, 'that means that I can touch, feel, and find a way around penetration and still be within the guidelines of my uncle, father, and his uncle'."

"How did you guys hear all of that?"

"Sue Lyn left the channel open. He's trying to do everything possible to maintain his commitment, but she has placed the fire before his eyes in the midst of a blizzard. I'll tell you this and then I won't feel like I've betrayed anyone, he told her that he was an Aborigine and that he believed in spirits, reasons, and the Great Saltie. She asked him, 'What is a Great Saltie?'. He told her to ask his uncle about a time and place where magic was possible, and that love was meaningful. He told her to ask him about the Beckmire Clan, and you will understand when a Beckmire gives his or her word, that there is no reason to question them a second time about a deviation on the theme. When I heard that I yelled, 'Darryl, Darryl, who are you talking to?' I fibbed and told him that the signal was garbled. He told me that it's expected to be since we're trying to cover almost 6,000 acres."

# # #

In the delivery room, John Lee required smelling salts to be revived. Jilkes said, "Country Bumpkin, that kid of yours is human. I half-assed expected him to be a pig. He's a good-looking big boy."

John Lee stood up and walked over to the bed where Somara was holding their son and passed out again but was caught by Jilkes. Jilkes said, "Sissy, wake up and meet John Lee Jr."

The doctor said, "Oh, let me help you." He placed another pack of smelling salts right under his nose. John Lee with blurry eyes looked at Somara and said, 'Are you going into labor now?' The entire room broke out into laughter that lasted for a good two minutes.

John Lee said, "My wife is going to have a baby soon. What's so funny?"

Courtney said to the doctor, "That was incredible. How long will you keep her and the baby?"

"I'll let you know when I come back to the hospital in the morning. I assume you guys will be staying. That wing of the hospital was paid for by you, and it has a special lock and alarm system. You will be safe. The kitchen is fully stocked, and if you need me, just press the red button."

Courtney said, "Ah, Doctor, in case you hadn't noticed, there are lots of red buttons."

"Doctor Beckmire, I did notice all the red buttons, and they all ring at my house. My wife is pregnant as well, and I sure could use Ms. Viola's help if you guys are around, that was amazing. That lady dilated at a record pace and just dropped that baby. I've never seen anything like that, have you?"

"I was startled by what I saw, and then thirty-five minutes later, bam! There's magic in the air."

At the hospital, Mallory zeroed in on Mike, and it appeared that he was crying. He walked over to him and asked, "Dude, what's going on?"

Mike said, "They tracked transmissions from one of the mercs to Switzerland. Someone shot him in the head. He was a good friend of mine who served his country well."

"I'm sorry about that. Should we be overly concerned here at the ranch?"

"Mallory, naw, I don't think so, unless they've found a way to track a signal from Switzerland to Wyoming? You'd have to be the caller or use the ID of the person receiving the call. I placed firewalls all around my phones, and I throw them away like cigarette butts."

When the main group turned off the main highway onto the access road to the ranch, Clyde said to Asiram, "You will notice that we fixed all of those body shattering potholes."

He slammed on the brakes and yelled, "Oh my God! I forgot to call ahead and tell Darryl and Sue Lyn that we were coming back tonight."

Asiram said, "Clyde, we're still quite a distance from the ranch. What's the problem?"

"Ms. Asiram, those two have concocted some space age defenses, and I do mean space age. You heard about that Aegis Weapons System that shot down that Iranian commercial flight a while back? Well, those two have improved upon that technology and have created a series of weapons on their own that can do the same kind of thing. They've invented these drone-like machines that can empty their clips, crash, and explode."

Clyde called Darryl and told him that they were on the access road and for him to cease experimenting. When the group pulled up to the front of the house, Darryl and Sue Lyn walked out and showed Clyde a video they took of the bus turning on to the access road. Asiram asked, "How did you film us that far away?"

Sue Lyn responded, "We flew two drones and placed two cameras on that lone light pole out there on the highway, each with 180 degrees of viewing. We also placed cameras in various places throughout the ranch, all which are activated by motion. Our only problem is that they are solar powered. We're trying to devise an alternative power source, but we can't seem to agree on certain scientific principles. He talks about the earth and sun, and I talk about guns, steel, and formulas. Everything else, we tend to agree on."

Asiram said, "Well, nice to see you again as well, and thanks for that update. Tell me, is there anything in the ranch that we should avoid?"

Darryl said, "Not really. All of our stuff is currently in one room that Clyde told us to use."

"Now, Darryl, we have children here and they're very curious human beings. I want you two to really think about this next question. Is there any way they can unleash some of your, ah, magic? Can they push a button and boom? We don't need any unintended consequences from your ingenuity. Am I making myself clear, guys?"

Sue Lyn said, "Perfectly clear. There are failsafe items installed in my projects, but Darryl's are a little more down to earth and are subject to ancient principles. In other words, his stuff is more tribal, and mine is more 21st century. His projects are outlying and final. Mine are close and terminal. There is a safety quadrant that has been established for the potential help that your neighbors are planning to give. We thought about a lot, but we didn't think about children, although we talked liberally about having a child."

"Sue Lyn, I'm sure you guys will work that out once your parents have given you the okay. I just want you to make sure that we don't have an explosion when we turn on the water, or when one of us turns to Channel 12. Guys don't kill us in the process of trying to keep us safe. No need to respond to that. Just remember it whenever you construct or develop another death dealing apparatus," Asiram stated.

# # #

Marisa said, "It really looks larger than before." She knew that Luana and Beatrice were without Chakes and Ms. Viola.

Marisa said, "So, Luana, I'm going to put you guys next to us if the configuration is the same, and we'll have adjoining rooms, with common side doors. Until your grandmother and Chakes get back, I'll leave it open so that you guys feel comfortable. I know how this works and I know how isolation can make you feel. If you guys want to have a pajama party and movie night, then let me know."

Luana said, "Thanks for recognizing that we're going to be up all night long looking out the window. Marisa, I can't tell you how important that is to me and Beatrice. I was wondering about this place, and now that I see faint lights far away, I'm not convinced that I like this wide-open space idea. I want to take a shower with my baby and wash our hair. I'll let you know if we can hang."

Marisa said, "Look in the closet, and you'll find things that you might need. Remember, we're going to go shopping as soon as Somara is released from the hospital. We have to have a baby shower and a party, right?"

#

Back in town, John Lee was finally learning how not to faint at the sight of his newborn child and wife. He looked at Somara with tears in his eyes and said, "That there boy be big and handsome like me. You be the love of my life, and although I'm no smooth-talking scoundrel, I am the man that be that there baby's daddy. Now, I know you wanted a girl and I be wanting a boy, but I'm the one that got his wish. If you don't be hating me, I'm willing to try this here event again and give you that little lady you so desire."

"My honorable master and lover, you have given me something that I never believed I would ever receive from a man. I love you, and hate you, and I do want to have a little princess. You have John Lee Jr., and I think he's going to keep you busy."

John Lee, look at him and Somara stated, "He's almost nine pounds and is as handsome as you are. Do you really love me?"

"I'm the kind of man that when I be feeling something for someone, it be for that someone and no one else. I love you, but you be having to tell me how to love you. I'm from, well, you been to our place, that be the kind of living I be doing, and you be the kind of woman I be loving. I be making this promise to you--if you stay with me, I will learn to be the best at everything that makes you happy. I just didn't have much experience with that thing called love."

"You are the strangest person that I have ever met. I saw you, and fell in love with you, and I haven't looked back yet. I'm so sorry I swore at you earlier. I just had to blame someone for the pain I was experiencing. Honey, by the way, we need to develop a legal will soon. I have a lot of money and property all over the world. I guess all spies try to diversify, but now that we have a child, we need to make sure our assets are protected, and our child or children, have full access and control over what we've earned."

John Lee asked, "Somara, how much money we be talking about?"

She smiled, looked at him shyly, and said, "Probably, $60 to $70 million. I wanted to tell you from the beginning, but I never really felt there was a need to discuss money. You and your people seem to have plenty of it, and I guess, I didn't want to cause any issues by having money of my own. I was kind of waiting for someone to need something and then I would volunteer. It never happened and, therefore, I kind of forgot the fact that I had a lot of money just sitting."

John Lee said, "Well, that be a lot of money, but I never knew you had money and so it ain't about money. I'm happy about that. Baby, I'm into you, and the only thing I think our marriage is suffering from is a lack of frequent lovemaking. If you love me and I love you, why can't we make love more than one night per week?"

"My dearest husband and lover, have you ever looked at yourself in the mirror? Your animation is satisfying, painful, and aggressive. Unknowingly, you've sent me to the hospital, twice already. Your passion is so desirable, but I can't take the results of your fervor, your nature, your aggression under pleasure, and most of all, your sayings. When you use the metaphor, 'hold on, I'm coming', that is exactly what it means. I'd better hold on, or you're going to bang me into ill-health. You're a big man down there, and you've stretched me beyond what a normal woman would want or could expect each night. Each time we make love, it takes me three days to recover. You need to pay more attention to me and realize that I'm not a machine, my darling. I want you to have me every single night, but my body is having difficulty accommodating your wishes. Please don't think me less of a woman, but your pleasure is insurmountable and catastrophic to my health and well-being. When you love me, it's often filled with pain!"

"Why didn't you tell me this before? I don't want to hurt my woman. I love my woman. You should've told me that when you scream, you scream from pain, and not pleasure. How was I to know this thing?"

"John Lee, calm down. Your pleasure is worth any pain I can endure because I love you so very much. You are my light, my protector, and now my baby's daddy. How marvelous is that?"

"Somara, I don't want to be hurting you when we make love. We gotta talk about that and figure out where there be limits. I thought you were happy with our lovemaking. I'm so sorry for causing you pain. We gotta talk about that soon."

CHAPTER SEVEN

During a senate hearing, a junior senator from Alabama said, "It's beginning to appear like it's open season on sitting United States senators. Two highly accomplished senators, who seemingly had ties to a person by the name of Walter Lassiter, who was a civil servant and, apparently, had an open account, or access to our federal treasury, have suspiciously had an untimely departure from this world. In addition, they both have been involved, in varying degrees, with this phantom new weapon called the Carbon Factor. I, for one, don't like to disparage the reputations and integrity of people who have served this great country of ours and who have given their lives for whatever reason.

"I just want to state that there are connections that deserve investigating, regarding our two departed members of this body. Just recently, I received a video of our two departed members involved in a willingly, and most disturbingly, physical activity as well as engaging in despicable, lascivious, and pornographic activities. I will share these documents with this chamber, if requested. It is clear to me and my people that the activities were orchestrated by Walter E. Lassiter, a civil servant. I'm no moralist, but the physical activities that our two departed senators participated in were beyond anything you can imagine. Our female senator was savagely whipped by our male senator and this Walter, the civil servant, can be seen in the background. In one clip, it appears that from a reflection, gold bullions could be seen in the background.

"Gentlemen and ladies, I do not stand before you in contempt of human nature because I'm neither a Republican nor a priest. I stand before you because the events that I described were sent to my office with a note that said, 'The Russians will discount the very idea of the Carbon Factor, but do not be dissuaded by their continued failure because it is their attempt to misdirect you. The Carbon Factor is factual and the people who have access to it is led by a gentleman by the name of Ben Beckmire.' Mr. Beckmire has also been accused of killing both of our senators but was never near the locations where our people met their demise.

"It appears that Mr. Beckmire is a patriot and received the Carbon Factor formula from his son. Mr. Beckmire and his group were once known as the 'Killing Machine' during the Vietnam conflict. They have certainly earned that title in this country as well. Some of our operatives, by the name of Scottie and Allen, hired sophisticated mercs to conclude their lives. These people are resilient. They survived in Vietnam with millions of dollars in bounties placed on their heads. They also avoided death due to a bad drug deal in the Boston area, several assassinations attempts on Beckmire, and countless encounters around the world.

"Mr. Chairman, I know that my time has expired, but I think it's necessary for me to explain to you what it means if those people have the formula to the Carbon Factor." The chairman allotted the senator five additional minutes.

"Members of this committee, every attempt to conclude the lives of those in their compound has ended in massive casualties. One of our double agents, who is on the run and is knowledgeable of the impact of the Carbon Factor, has stated that the 'idiot spy' has the total configuration of the bombing materials. Mr. Zanthius De Lombardo, the son of Ava De Lombardo and Ben Beckmire, has inaccurately been dubbed the 'idiot spy'. He earned that title when he was sent on a one-way mission to Switzerland and survived the trip, killed an agent, swallowed a capsule, and fell in love with the very woman who was assigned to provide a secondary hit on him.

"I know this sounds like a fantastic fable, but this time good people without any need, or desire for payment, have stumbled onto a new destructive device and formula that is developed from a fuel source that the entire world, except our president, is trying to no longer use--coal. Mr. Chairman, I would like to invite Mr. Beckmire and his group into this chamber with the express notion that the hearings will be closed, and that they will have complete immunity from prosecution. It is highly doubtful that Mr. Beckmire, or his people killed the senators. They are patriots, but it is extremely possible they have the answer to the Carbon Factor."

The debate continued until late in the evening and was concluded when the chairman of the committee said, "I think your comment about Republicans and priest was quite apropos. I'm a Republican, as you know, but I also know what's going on with that product. People are trying to sell influence and buy things that can harm all of humanity. I also think Mr. Beckmire has been offered a ton of money for the product, as well, but appears to be a moral man. I think his people wonder about the ultimate impact of such a dangerous weapon in the hands of those who are only interested in making innocent people suffer. I also don't believe his group has much faith in our group after two of our very own were implicated in schemes to resell the product to foreign governments as well as authorized the hiring of mercenaries to kill people. One senator was filmed trying to make a three-way deal with a foreign government. My esteemed colleagues, why on earth are we dealing with coal when the rest of the world is creating batteries, solar, wind, and other technologies to forge their systems ahead while we inflict people with diseases to mine outdated resources to support our industries? I think we should acknowledge our colleague's request and provide the group with a letter of inquiry that simply does not record the sessions and allows them to discuss, or take the 'fifth', on issues relating to the departed senators."

CHAPTER EIGHT

Darryl and Sue Lyn added the long-gun capability to the ranch. Two ports of eight-long guns and six stations of machine pistols with 150 capacity drums had been installed for a total of sixteen long guns and twelve machine pistols, that needed testing. Over the open terrain, Darryl's back to nature potions were precariously placed with a potion that keeps animals far away from its scent. Each spike had been tainted with a paralyzing chemical that Darryl developed from several household items and a special concoction of his.

When Darryl saw his uncle, he said, "We have made some extreme modifications to the ranch, but I need to show Rashida and Juan how things work and what areas are to be avoided for at least three days unless it rains."

Beckmire said, "I don't understand. Why must certain areas be avoided for three days? Did you put poison down on her land without asking Asiram?"

"Uncle, I would never use poison as you know it. I concocted a series of agents that will render people harmless for hours if contact is made with it. I would never use poison."

"I'll fetch Rashida and Juan in a minute. Darryl, did you sexually penetrate Sue Lyn while you were under my charge?"

"Uncle, you know I will not lie to you. But I must ask you and I beg your forgiveness for asking you to define penetration and where?"

"Son don't play charades with me. Did you have sex with Sue Lyn?"

Darryl paused for a moment and appeared to be having a soliloquy with himself. He said, "Uncle, I did not have traditional sex with Sue Lyn. I never penetrated her vagina and never tried. However, we did manage to pleasure each other."

"Darryl, I didn't ask you about variations on the theme, I asked you if you had old fashion penis in vagina sex with Sue Lyn, and you answered me. Learn to listen to the question and volunteer as little information as possible. Do you understand?"

"Uncle, I was being straight-a-head with you."

"Son, I didn't ask you about pleasuring each other. I asked my question with a clear intent. You happened to provide me with more details than I was looking for. Study the premise and think about what I just said. When Jong's cousin gets around to asking you the question, and he might perhaps have someone evaluate her, the facts remain the same. You did not have traditional sex with her."

# # #

Jong said to his niece prior to saying goodbye to her, "Sometimes adults don't know what they want from their children. My cousin is a good father to you, and the Sarge is a good uncle to Darryl. When we have time to do some accounting, it would appear to me that you and Darryl will earn a sizeable amount of money. It might be time for you two to think about opening accounts for your future. You are both smart people; it's not necessary to start a relationship by becoming pregnant. I know he has told you all about his people, and I'll be the first to admit, there is a lot of truth in what they do and what they say. I make these words to remind you of your oath to your father and Darryl's to his uncle. I know you want to experience sex. Sex, as I believe you already know, can be manifested in different ways. I urge you to be true to your commitments, but do not engage in penetration. The winds that blow, are not in your favor."

Against what he would normally do or say, Jong said a lot. He hugged his niece and said, "We are all counting on you two because you are our future. I love you, my niece."

# # #

Rashida and Juan were thrilled at the added defenses and realized the structure could automatically suppress large numbers of attackers. Clyde realized early on, especially after finding the group and children in wire-ties and hearing about the suicide vests, that there needed to be a 'cross the red line, and we shoot you in the back' strategy. Clyde looked at the ranch from photos and had an excavation crew from Tijuana come up, camp out, and dig tunnels that led away from the ranch in every direction.

The digging teams were screened magnetized and disoriented when they left their assignments. Roughly three hundred and fifteen yards away from the ranch he and his kin opened the earth and made additional exits from the ranch available. It is from those very places that Darryl's earth-based formula and Sue Lyn's mechanized shooting galleries were born. The ranch was fortified and secured against most villains, but Walter was prepared to use extreme force to conclude his nemeses, including rocket-launched grenades.

# # #

Sue Lyn and Darryl were escorted to the airport by Beckmire and Jong. They were prepared to head back to DC when one of their security team, smelled a rat.

Montomie, Gladstone, McArthur, and Mike were the escorts for the group. They arrived at the airport and noticed the odd couple. Sitting in a window that faced the runway, Gladstone said, "At 900 there are two people who are matched like an elephant and a seagull. That is not natural and there isn't enough money to sanction that kind of blasphemy." Slowly and methodically, each man took a mental picture and decided that Gladstone had picked the apple from the tree. Prior to the Sarge, Jong, Darryl, and Sue Lyn walking into the airport, Mike stumbled into the airport lounge as if he were drunk and yelled, "Has anyone seen Luana?"

The barkeep asked, "Who the hell is Luana?"

"That be my wife, mate. She's trying to run off with her lover and I'm going to stop her." He knew that the barkeep would call the police and they would see the bulge in the man's jacket.

Mike yelled, "She's trying to escape on one of those fancy planes, I know she's here." The barkeep tried to calm him down until the police came in.

Three minutes later, the police showed up and began to talk to Mike who was erratic and mumbling at this time. Clyde saw what was happening but did not see the bulge in the man's jacket. Darryl walked over to the police and said, "Officer this is a ruse. The man in the window with that wonderful looking lady, are both carrying weapons. Look at the bulge in their jackets."

The two officers sat Mike down and walked over to the table. One of the officers asked, "Sir, is that a weapon you're carrying in an airport, and if so, who are you and how did you get that by security?"

The man replied, "We're here on official business, and we are licensed to carry firearms for the protection of our client."

"Who is your client, and where is he or she?"

"Officer, we're on a mission and can't divulge that information."

"Sir, please stand and keep your hands where I can see them. Miss, your right hand is not in sight. I need you to slowly move your hand from under the table and place it on top of the table. Please, no sudden movements or my partner will fire on you. Sir, I need you to stand and place your hands on the table. I will not ask you a third time."

The guy stood up and moved as though he was going to place his hand on the table, but with his right hand moving towards the table, he used a convincing slap to the throat of the one officer, disabling him immediately. As the second officer tried to unholster his weapon, the woman caught him in the groin and added an additional chop to the throat. Both officers were incapacitated. The man reached for his weapon. Darryl anticipated the chaos and breached the area with a flying kick to the man's head and a punch to the woman's throat. They both hit the ground and were out like a light. Ben Beckmire said, "Darryl, that was some move, but my guys had them dead to center at every moment."

"I saved them so that you could interrogate them and find out when and how their main force is going to get here."

"Son, I want you to stick to design and leave the violence thing to me and my friends. You could have been hurt in that process."

"Uncle, that man and the woman were going to execute those police persons in front of you. Please realize our ancestor has endowed me with certain abilities. I will only act for the good of humanity, and that is exactly what I did."

"Son, how do you know that is what you're doing? Who decides what is in the best interest of humanity?"

Beckmire paused for a moment and then adamantly stated, "Certainly not you. I mean you're in your early twenties and humanity has a long record of existence before you were even a pimple on someone's anatomy. How do you decide when to invoke the knowledge that is entrusted in you?"

"Uncle, I've been on many strange journeys, and I have witnessed a multitude of things that would make a normal person think that they had suddenly entered a place where the inmates manage the asylum. Uncle, I have seen the conclusion of this event with you, and the Carbon Factor formula. I've also seen my nefarious Uncle Walter, as well as the immoral, the putrid, and the obnoxious of what you and your people will do him. I am unlicensed to speak fully on this, but I can say this is a complex journey that will never end for you and your people. You will make some catastrophic mistakes, recover from them miraculously, and will extend justice to those on the wrong side of the road. Uncle, I think your immediate decision should be about what you're going to do with those two. They won't be unconscious much longer and I assure you, the police are going to want to interrogate them first."

CHAPTER NINE

Clyde transported the couple to the ranch in double wire-ties, along with Montomie, Gladstone, and McArthur. The two were driven to the barn and tied to the horse stalls, facing each other. Montomie said, "Whose turn is it to interrogate? Is it Jilkes or John Lee?"

McArthur replied, "I think it's John Lee's turn. I don't want watch duty if it's his turn."

Gladstone asked, "Why not?"

McArthur said, "Dude, don't you remember what he did to that woman named Scottie? I still have nightmares about that shit. I mean, how do you take a knife and gut a woman from her vagina to her brain, and then take a bite out of her beating heart?"

Montomie said, "John Lee is over the top, but Jilkes is just as bad. John Lee tortures you first, but Jilkes will ask you a few questions, and if he is bored with your answers, he just slits your throat. Either way, they are both some bad *hombres* when it comes to torture."

The female prisoner began to stir and Montomie turned to her and said, "Now, Miss Lady, don't go looking so macho because I assure you when they finish with you, you'll wish you were dead. Oh, and out here, we just drive you out into the field and the wolves, bears, mountain lions, rats, birds, and bugs will do the rest. So, Miss Lady, you keep that smirk going as long as you can."

Approximately thirty-five minutes later, the Sarge arrived at the barn with Jilkes, John Lee, and Mike. The Sarge said, "Hi, I'm Ben Beckmire. My guys and family call me Sarge. That's some sophisticated location devices you guys had on you. Your belt and shoe heel, sir, and her earrings. Who do you people work for?"

There was no answer, and the Sarge said, "I figured you wouldn't answer any of my questions. Nice to have met you. I'll leave you with my specialists and perhaps they can get you to answer some questions."

The Sarge turned to Mike and asked, "Do you happen to have a coin in your pocket?"

Mike reached into his pocket and found a quarter and handed it to the Sarge. The Sarge showed each captive that the coin was indeed two sided. He then said, "Miss, you're going to be heads and, Sir, you're going to be tails."

He flipped the coin high into the air and when it landed, he looked at the lady and said, "Looks like you won the toss Miss."

She looked at him and said, "Stop playing this Boy Scouts game. You will learn nothing from us."

The Sarge said, "I take those words to mean that you want to go first since you relinquished your right to be the victor of the coin flip. Okay, it's settled. John Lee, you're up first, and your patient is this lovely lady that was too stupid to have her friend go first. Catch you guys, or perhaps not, later."

The Sarge turned to walk out of the room and the lady asked, "Why don't you do your own work?"

"Young lady, I make a mess of things. These two are the professionals when it comes to gutting people. Sir, you'll have a front row seat to see how it's done."

Jilkes walked over to the closet and turned on the audio system and played Igor Stravinsky's *Firebird Suite*. He then placed duct-tape over his captives' mouths.

John Lee put on an apron and surgical gloves. He walked in front of the woman and said, "I be hoping your silence is worth the pain you be receiving." He unsheathed his knife, and the woman began to mumble.

Jilkes walked over and aggressively pulled the tape from across her mouth and said, "This only happens once. Make the best use of this opportunity to live, untouched. You have something to say?"

"Since I won the flip of the coin, I want him to go first."

"Really, lady. You want to see your mate get butchered first?" Jilkes asked.

"I don't know him. We are here on assignment. Screw him."

Jilkes said, "That information is of no use to us. You're still first to go."

"What can you guarantee me if I cooperate?"

"We can get you to the airport and on a plane. Where you go is up to you."

"What about payment? I've only received 25% of my money. Will you pay me the rest if I tell you what I know?"

"I'm sorry, but we're not going to pay you a nickel! He can cut what we wants to know out of you. You're stalling for time. That's exactly what you're doing. Mike, call the Sarge and tell him to put the ranch on alert. I think they're already here and that's why she's stalling."

The woman smiled and said, "You're absolutely right. My people are all around this place."

John Lee said, "They won't be here in time to save your ass." He slammed his knife into her right foot and left it dangling in the air with the blood gushing from the wound and into a pail under her foot. She screamed, and Jilkes replaced the tape across her mouth. He walked over to the man and asked, "Do you want to tell us what's going on?"

"Kiss my ass, you worthless nigga."

John Lee walked towards the man and said, "Nobody calls my brother a name like that."

He proceeded to cut away the man's pants and sliced away his underwear. He said, "You apologize to my brother or watch your little pecker hit the floor."

John Lee began to cut close to the man's pecker. He screamed, "I'll tell you what I know, but she's in charge of this operation."

John Lee said, "I don't give a pig's ass about who be in charge. You apologize or, I'm going to cut that little pecker of yours off at the base."

"Damn, man. I apologize. Ain't no thing. They call each other that. Why you so concerned about a word? They sing it in their music, greet each other, swear by it, and call each other all kinds of variations on that notion, and say it freely in front of white people. Listen, I apologized. She's in charge, and all I want to do is go home."

"How many people are here from your group, and who is your employer?"

"Man, I was assigned to accompany her. I was paid a percentage, but I don't know much of anything other than we're the scouting team."

"Did you or she report back to anyone what you scouted?" Jilkes asked.

"She was about to make positive identification when those two police officers came over to us. There was no way she could've sent a message from under the table to her handler. Check her phone, but it has one of those locators as well as a GPS app."

Jilkes asked, "How many of you were assigned to this detail?"

"Just that woman and me."

John Lee, Mike, and Jilkes huddled to decide the fate of the two captured individuals. Mike said, "That woman is going to bleed out unless you do something about that wound."

"It ain't all that bad. She be looking down at it, and it be looking scary. I know how to cut a foot if I want to take it off. Hold on, I'll duct tape it, and she'll last another two hours before she dies. Mike, call Clyde and tell him that someone needs a ride to the hospital in a hurry. And besides, them police people be looking for her ass anyways," John Lee announced.

Jilkes said, "I don't like our exposure on this one. I say we conclude them both and let the animals have a meal. We let them go, and they become added numbers to the people who are trying to kill us. Let's just finish this story and wait for the next book."

"Hey, people, I want to live. I gave you all that I know. You know, I do remember her saying something about a person named Walter who was her handler. There are two other people, at a hotel fifty miles away, who rotate our surveillance and act as if they are in charge."

Jilkes said, "You stated less than five minutes ago that it was just you and her on this detail. Now, you're talking about a rotating detail. I don't trust you, my friend, or anything that you say."

"Okay, I be done stopped her bleeding, but she needs to be getting to the hospital, or we need to kill her and him and be done with it. What's it going to be?"

The man dropped his head and said, "I need to make a deal. I don't want to die in this damn barn. I want to speak to the people that make the decisions."

John Lee asked, "Who you think you be talking to all this time, the kitchen help? You want to live, mister, then you be having to give us something more than pigshit."

"Are you into pigs? Anyway, if I give you a timetable, will you let me go?"

Jilkes said, "Yeah, we'll let you go, you dumbass-cracker. If I let you go right now, where the hell would you go? This ranch is 6,000 acres, or something like that, and you won't be able to tell your ass from your nose because the animals are going to hunt your dumb butt. Now, if you want to make a deal, then you say, 'I want to be let free at the airport'. At least that way, you have some options, and you can take your shit-talking girlfriend with you."

"Listen, she's not my girlfriend and people are beginning to arrive in Laramie and other parts of the state that have airports. A tractor trailer is arriving tomorrow from the West Coast with weapons, and I do mean weapons. That truck is carrying rocket launchers and a bunch of high-tech weapons that were stolen from a military base in San Diego. The mercs will be heavily armed once that truck gets into town. It's taking a surreptitious route with three chase cars, and two drivers in the truck. It only stops for fuel and driver rotation."

Jilkes asked, "What route are they taking?"

"I don't know for sure, but if I had to guess, I would say Interstate 25. In some of the conversations, I kept hearing the number twenty-five thrown around. I honestly don't know, but I would stake a lot on that interstate."

Jilkes said, "You know if we let you go, the leader of your group is going to hunt you down. He's a ruthless man and will spare no expense to see anyone who betrays him, hunted down and their head delivered in a basket."

"Get me to the airport, and you can do what you want with that woman. As a matter of fact, she's one of his women. I mean, you know, like his lover."

"How do you contact your people? Also, how is he planning to pay for such a large undertaking?"

"I failed to mention this because I'm not sure of the validity of the claim, but I hear the truck that's bringing the weapons is also carrying the cash. Everyone involved received a ticket, a stipend, and a pledge of a bonus at a successful conclusion."

"What was the stipend amount?" John Lee asked.

"Once you land in this state, your group coordinator gives you $5,000 for expenses. The contracts are for $50,000 per man for a couple of days of activities. I also heard her confirm the fact that there would probably be a sixty-five percent reduction in their force. I walked away when I heard that. She assured him the number would not be higher than twenty-five percent. Now, I didn't know what all that meant, but I deduced that they were talking about casualties. There was also a constant reference to old guys and Vietnam. I never made the connection until I saw you guys in the airport. Listen, I want out of this thing. It was advertised as an easy assignment with low risk. I've planned jobs before and have a successful track record. What disturbed me was when I heard her flippantly talk about the 'Killing Machine'.

"I do a good job because I study my opponents before I attempt to implement a plan. I googled 'Killing Machine' and it came back with some rock music connotations. I called a friend of mine and asked him had he ever heard of the 'killing machine' and he came back with the same information. He had been in the Nam and between sips of rum, he said, 'There was a group in the Nam called the 'killing machine'. I asked him about the group, and he told me some Herculean stories he had heard. I asked if any of you guys were still alive, and he told me that he didn't think so. By the way, in the airport I reached for my weapon and the next thing I remembered was picking my ass off the floor. What happened? Which one of you knocked me out?"

John Lee said, "It was our leader's nephew. He did the work. We were just about to put rounds in your heads, but he decided there was value in keeping you alive. You be a family man?"

"I am a family man, and may I speak frankly? Sir, I called you the 'N' word because I'm supposed to be a big black-man-hating white man. That's how I got the job, even though I hear the boss is a black man. I'm on every board in my city. I'm on the OIC Board of Directors in Minnesota, the NAACP, several Hispanic Associations, I attend a black church and my wife is a preacher—a black preacher at that. I had to keep up pretenses. I need this job, and I need the money. My family is at risk. My job was to plan the incursion and the extraction of someone called, the 'idiot spy', who is being held against his will. He is also vital to the security of this country and is a member of the new Commander-in-Chief's family."

Jilkes asked, "Where, on earth, did you get that information?"

"Listen, she may be the boss woman, but she is quick on opening her legs. Three drinks and a little weed later, I was told how important she was. She told me a lot of things that didn't make sense to me. I began to get cold feet on this deal when I was told about the truck and rocket launchers. I also became suspicious when she told me there would be close to three hundred people involved in this activity and then I began to hear stuff like sixty-five percent attrition, minimum payout, and other things.

"If you're a relative of that person who calls himself the President, why would you need to hire mercs? We don't have health insurance, and my daughter, by my very crazy ass ex-wife, needs several medical procedures. I'm here for the money to make that surgery a reality for my child. I'm now scared because if what my friend told me is true, we need to start with a bombing raid, then rocket launchers, tanks, and offshore rounds from battleships. He told me it was documented that you people have killed thousands of individuals. Is that true?"

"We're supposed to be interrogating you, and yet, somehow, you've flipped the switch on us, and you're interviewing us. Collectively, that's a low number. Anything else you want to tell us about the group?" Jilkes inquired.

"I can't tell you a thing. I can recommend that you could end this siege by intercepting that truck before it gets here. You'll save a helluva lot of lives. People sign up for jobs like this for many reasons, but mainly, they need the money for an important activity. The people that are coming here are under the impression that they're a part of some noble cause. Intercept that truck and you'll save a lot of good lives, as well as bad ones, and perhaps some of your own. Also, in two hours, she must make a call. If she doesn't, then the routes are changed, and a new player is placed in charge. I've given you all I got. I can't stress enough how important it is to intercept that truck, you'll save a lot of lives."

Jilkes walked over to him, looked into his eyes and said, "Your problem is you don't even know how to say the name you called me. I knew you didn't know what you were saying."

Jilkes cut the wire-ties and said, "I'll have someone escort you to the airport. I hope we won't have to face you in this battle if it comes to that. We need your boss lady for obvious reasons. She will not be making the journey with you."

"Sir, I'm going to rob a bank or something, but I'm not going to commit suicide."

Jilkes reached in his pocket and pulled out a debit card that had some cash associated with it. He said, "I'm going to give you this card, my card. If I see you again, I will execute you. Take this card and do the right thing. It's my personal debit card and it has about $75k left on it. Get on a plane, disappear, and have your family get out of dodge as well. Your boss is not opposed to concluding the lives of women and children."

The man looked at Jilkes and said, "What game are you trying to play here? You give me a simple card and then I get arrested trying to use it?"

"No, it's my conscience payment for not killing you. We have a lot of souls roaming around in hell that are waiting on us. I'm sparing your life, that should count for something when it's my turn to enter hell. And insofar as that card is concerned, that too is a payment on my account. You won't be arrested, trust me."

The man looked at Jilkes and his eyes began to water. For almost a minute not a word was spoken until he said, "I'm not sure, but I think I know the name on the truck. There was constant talk about Vegas First. That could be a bank, but I'm betting it's the name on the truck. Thanks for showing me mercy and for helping me with my cash issue. I can assure you that you'll never see me again in this kind of forum."

# # #

After making arrangements with the scout and after gathering information from him, John Lee turned his attention to the lady. He said, "Little lady, it's time for you to wake up."

After waking her, John Lee said, "You need to be making a call right about now. This is how we can do this. I can put your ass in one of my mules and take you way out there in the field and drop you off. Now, let me tell ya, there be bears, wolves, and other kinds of animals out there. If you make the call, we'll get you to the hospital, and from there, your fate be your own. Your boss man don't be liking failure and he'll probably kill you at first sight. You were supposed to track us, not engage us. What's it going to be? Now, let me just say one more thing, if you try to give a secret message, I'm going to cut that good foot like the other one and the animals will smell the blood on you, and finish your ass off before sunset."

The female member, after considering her options--and none of them were escape oriented--told John Lee and Jilkes exactly what her message had to say and at what time. She made the call, gave the message, and hung up the phone. John Lee thanked her and said, "I'll give you $50,000 for the name of the truck that be carrying all of them there guns for those people."

"Make it $75,000 and we have a deal."

"I'll make it $65,000 and get you on a private plane out of this area." John Lee stated.

"Done. Where's the money?"

"Do you want cash or a bona fide debit card?"

"How can I trust a man who severed my foot with a sword?"

"I didn't sever it. I just gave you a pass out cut. How can I trust a woman who came out here to kill us?"

"I can't carry that much cash. How about $20k in bills and the rest on the card?"

"Done." John Lee said.

The lady said, "The name on the truck is Vegas First and is due to cross the state line in two days."

#

A couple of hours later, John Lee and Jilkes met with the Sarge and Mallory and gave them the intel they had received. Mallory said, "Good job, guys. That was a comprehensive report, and it seems to me a lot of lives would be spared if we could intercept that truck."

The Sarge said, "That would be a major accomplishment. Look, we lower our risk of injury, or death while saving a lot of people who are in this thing to make some money. I mean, if you sell your soul for money to kill others you don't know, then I'm all for killing you, regardless of whether you have a gun or not."

Jilkes said, "Sarge, that's a little hard. If you think about it, we haven't killed a lot of people in a while. I kind of like not shooting other human beings."

"Me too. I mean we done killed a lot of people, and so far, all we got are some scratches and cuts. I want to reduce our risk. I think if we can get a fix on that truck, we hijack it, drive it onto some empty field, and blow it sky high!" John Lee exclaimed.

"Guys, you might have read me wrong. I don't want to kill anyone other than that diseased cousin of mine. If we can save a life, then let's do that. We started that in DC and it felt good to let people cut and run. I wonder if Clyde could get some of his people to drive down the highway and, sort of, camp out and act as spotters? "

John Lee asked, "When are you going to have a full meeting again?"

"I was planning on talking to the group tonight at dinner, why?"

"I just want to thank everyone for being so kind to my woman and John Lee Jr., that's all," John Lee stated.

#

Mallory and Jilkes were assigned the task of speaking with Clyde about the surveillance on the highway. Clyde recommended that they set spotters at the last three truck stops before entering Wyoming on Interstate 25. He called his wife who sent out a group message on their newly established website. Within twenty minutes, twenty-two people had volunteered and could be on the way within the next two hours.

Within the next twenty minutes, Clyde's wife had sent a message indicating that the names had been placed in a hat and that the following names had been drawn randomly.

# # #

As a part of the Beckmire group's influence on the area, their foundation provided each person with a cellphone that did not have a payment plan. Asiram thought it was necessary because, at times, people who worked in the fields needed ways to be in contact with their families. It was a great humanitarian idea, and everyone loved the fact that they could just call and talk to family and friends.

# # #

Clyde's people packed their bags and their field glasses. Some would travel a total of 450 miles, the next group would travel 250 miles, and the final group 100 miles from the ranch. The purpose of this approach was to figure out where the truck was and develop interdiction points that were not near communities.

Later in the afternoon, the Sarge called for a meeting of everyone on the ranch, including Clyde. He said, "I know you're tired and weary, and so am I, but I need you people to stay strong and connected for just a little while longer. We have two issues that confront us and keeps us from living like normal human beings. The Carbon Factor is one, and the other is the most reprehensible person on earth, my cousin Walter, who has hired as many as 225 mercs to conduct, what I'm assuming, he thinks is a final assault on our group. For those of you who don't know my illustrious cousin, he strapped suicide vests on our children. I know we live like vagabonds and that Target has become our best friend. However, I'm living for the day when I can go in a store and have a pair of pants made that fit. This has been an arduous journey for all of us, and for some of you, it's been a God sent.

"We just celebrated the birth of John Lee Jr., and we're looking forward to births by Rashida, Okema, Yeshida, Mary Alice, Yvette, and the additions to the Mallory family, as well. We are becoming a baby farm, and I absolutely love it. Now, for those of you who are new to this area, we carry, and we carry always. I'm going to ask my daughter-in-law to conduct a practice shooting session in the morning for all newcomers. If there are no questions, then John Lee Sr. would like to say a few things."

John Lee stood up and said, "I just want to thank you guys and ladies for the support you be showing me and my wife. That's mighty kind of you and a special shout out to our very own Dr. Courtney and Ms. Viola who calmed my lady down so that she could drop Jr. out.

"I also want to say that the architect has prints, dimensions, color schemes, and landscaping designs for those of you who purchased land on Jilkes and my properties. We're glad to have you as neighbors, and we look forward to taking a trip down there to make sure that everything you want is covered and that building can begin. The infrastructure is pretty much in place with sewer lines, water lines, underground electric, and the gas lines. That's all I want to say, except thank you again for showing me and my wife how great this group really is. Thank you."

## CHAPTER TEN

A day later, a truck with the obvious notation on it, "Vegas First" was spotted pulling into the truck stop at the 450-mile mark. Clyde received the call and relayed the information to the Sarge. The Sarge huddled with John Lee, Jilkes, Zanthius, and Larry and told them he didn't like the idea of separating their forces and taking on a truck full of weapons. Zanthius said, "Pops, give me Juan, Larry, Mike, Jilkes, and John Lee, and I think we can make it happen."

"Son, that plan won't work because I need Juan here on the mechanized weapons. How can you guys do what is needed against two in the truck, and as many as nine more in escort vehicles?"

"If we can isolate them in an area with bad cell service, then we might have a chance. Who is going to suspect us in a blue supercharged school bus? I think it's the perfect cover, and besides, the damn thing is loaded with weapons, has bullet proof glass, and is armored-plated. I figure we catch them at the 100-mile mark, or before, and then we systematically begin to eliminate the threat," Zanthius stated.

"The other problem that I have is that I'm skeptical of the source of the information. It just seemed too contrived to me. I mean she had a dangling foot, and we made him an offer and, they both reported the same information. I just don't want to start putting the lives of our people at risk from information that can't be substantiated," the Sarge remarked.

John Lee said, "I know exactly what you be saying but I kind of think that they be on the level. I did think that she gave up the interstate number rather quickly."

Jilkes said, "If two people had Clyde driving the bus, they could do a lot of damage."

"We can't put Clyde in the middle of this stuff. But Mike and my two boys probably could pull this thing off without a hitch. I'm so fearful of separating our main forces. Besides my cousin is one conniving SOB, and you all know that about the man. He has telegraphed his moves to us before, and we got away with hitting him hard. Why wouldn't he try a different strategy? Wouldn't you? Okay, here's what I think we should do. I know somewhere, someone is watching us from afar. We need to let them see us load up in force on the yellow school bus, but have Larry, Mike, and Zanthius sneak on the blue bus. Does anyone know exactly what Clyde has on that thing in terms of munitions? I know it's armor plated, but is there anything else on it?"

Larry suggested, "Let's ask Rashida. If anyone knows, I bet you it'll be her."

Ten minutes later, Larry came back and said, "I'm worried about my sister. She is so enamored with the idea of weapon systems and guns in general. She told me that Sue Lyn and Darryl installed machine guns in the front and rear of the new bus."

"Where the hell did those two kids get machine guns? We need to find Clyde and ask him about the actual armaments of the ranch and the bus. I say that because Darryl and Sue Lyn fortified both and no one seems to know to what degree."

# # #

When the group caught up with Clyde, he told them that Darryl and Sue Lyn ordered a lot of the materials on-line. Technically, he also added, the armament is not machine guns, but .40 caliber weapons with huge munition drums that hold 150 rounds each.

The Sarge asked, "How many of those guns are installed on the bus?"

Clyde responded, "Two in the front and two in the back for a total of 600 rounds."

"My nephew and Sue Lyn placed those things in the bus?"

"Naw, they just drew the plans and specs. Me and Ned Brown constructed the housing units for easy withdrawal. They were extremely helpful, they showed us a 3-D drawing on those fancy laptops of where to mount those guns as well as to cut out vents on the bus to allow for the air to cool them. They did say that heavy firing should not be done while the vehicle is sitting still."

"I don't have a good feeling about any of this. What if the 'Vegas First' is a decoy? There are too many things we don't control on this one and too much information from suspicious sources that I wouldn't bet anyone's life on. Are you guys with me on this one?" The Sarge asked.

"Sarge, I am weary of the sources and the information as well. We gave them debit cards with tracking devices. Thanks to your nephew, we can signal those cards to kill the holders," Jilkes said.

"How the hell can you do that?"

"Your nephew encoded those cards with spider toxin that we can control from here. At any point when they try to access cash from the card, we can trigger a stop sign from any computer or iPhone that will require them to input their access code three times. After the second time, according to your nephew, the signal triggers a response that opens virtually an unnoticeable chemical from the outback that is lethal on contact with the skin. It can't be transferred and no one else can use it. Unless his shit is all hype, then we're good to conclude those who have given us the information," Jilkes announced.

"Guys, the future of our cause is going to be spectacular. When your kids grow up and meet my nephew and Sue Lyn— wow, our work is going to make us roll over in our graves and thank God we were associated. This group is going to be like the cells that grew in 'Henrietta Lacks'."

John Lee looked at Jilkes, and then at the Sarge, and asked, "Who be Henrietta Lacks?"

The Sarge said, "If I buy you a book, will you promise me you'll read it? That's all I want to know. Will you read it?"

John Lee looked at Jilkes, then at the Sarge, and hesitantly said, "If you buy the book, me and my best friend will read it together."

"Is there anything you two don't do together?" The Sarge asked.

"Oh, there be lots of things we don't do together, but most time we try to stay in touch and do things that won't interfere or take away from our time as brothers."

"John Lee, have you ever listened to the things, words, and sayings that come out of your mouth?" The Sarge asked.

"Sarge, I don't have no idea about what you're trying to insinuate. Listen, he is my brother, and so are the rest of you. I just happen to love him much more than I love you guys, but I'll still take a bullet for everybody in this here unit, and that's a lot of bullets."

Zanthius said, "Asiram is going to insist on coming with me and there is no way I can let that happen."

"Son, I knew she had her right foot up your ass. Now, listen, she's a strong woman and takes no bullshit. As you said, she is going to insist that she accompany you on this journey. I suggest you talk to both of your mothers and explain that you and Asiram are a strategic part of an issue that may save a lot of lives."

"Dad, Marisa and I have mended some of our issues, and she's going to insist that she comes along."

Mike lowered his head, and said, "I think Carla is pregnant, and she too has said that she wants to do battle with her man. As I see it, that provides us with three extra shooters, and we've added another two with Luana and Ms. Viola. It's almost a balancing act, but I assure you, your pilot will be mighty pissed if she doesn't get a chance to do more than fly us."

The Sarge looked at everyone and asked Mallory to walk with him for a minute. The two men discussed issues and their security and knew that the bus would be armed, and it would look like a full-scale assault if everyone fired at the same time. The Sarge turned around and said, "You people need to make ready your trip. Who's going to drive the bus?"

Mike raised his hand and said, "Carla used to be a tractor trailer driver." The group broke into laughter.

Mallory pulled the Sarge aside and said, "You know, we've not followed up on our commitment to him. We still owe him money. Let's tell him that we're going to have Jong place $5 million into an account with his name and Carla's."

The Sarge looked at Mallory and said, "Make it happen, I will tell him about it."

# # #

As the sun began to set, two school buses, one blue and the other one yellow, left the confines of Asiram's ranch. On the yellow bus, there were a significant number of heads sitting in the darkened windows that were not real people, it turned left and headed in the direction of town. On the blue bus headed away from town, it was loaded with people who could, perhaps turn the tide in their favor.

The Sarge gave Zanthius the task of informing Mike that the team was planning to enrich his and Carla's finances by $5 million. When Zanthius gave the couple the news, Mike said, "God is good, and so is my new clan and wife." He and Carla embraced and exchanged kisses.

# # #

On the road to Mile Marker 100 and a rest stop, Zanthius yelled, "People, can everyone make their way to the front of the bus? I want to make sure we have clear assignments and understand what we may be facing. For those of you who may not be aware of the purpose of this mission. I'll be very frank in my analysis. If the intel is good, what we're about to embark on could save our people at the ranch from a lot of unnecessary stress. It has been reported that a truck with the insignia 'Vegas First' is carrying a ton of illicit weapons that are intended to be used against the ranch. If the info is sound, and the truck is carrying the weapons the assault team needs, then a successful interdiction on our part would save a lot of lives on both sides. So, this mission is critical on many different fronts. As such, I trust Carla's driving skills to navigate this vehicle. In the front and rear of the bus, there are two .40 caliber weapons with munition drums that will fire 150 rounds each. Larry, I'd like to ask you to man that weapon."

Larry looked at Zanthius and said, "Brother, I think Mike is a better shot than I am. What's your take on that Mike?"

"You're probably correct. I was considered a marksman."

"Okay, in that case, I will ask you Mike to man the weapons in the front along with Carla. Asiram can man the rear weapons. Remember, sustained fire will deplete the drums quickly, so fire with the idea that each shot must count. Larry, that leaves you, me, and Marisa to cover the sides. I would like to catch this thing away from an inhabited area so that we don't have any collateral damage. We can destroy it from afar. If possible, I would like to take one of the drivers of the truck alive and let him open the back. Just in case it's booby-trapped. If it turns into a close fight, Larry you take the right side, and I'll take the left, and Mike you and the ladies cover us from the safety of the bus. Do not leave the bus under any circumstances. Mike, take care of our women."

# # #

The Sarge called Larry and asked him about their progress. He was told that they were about half-way to the rest station. He told Larry he wanted him to take charge of this event. Larry told the Sarge that Zanthius had developed a plausible plan, and he was comfortable with his directions. The Sarge said, "I respect what you said, but you know what is needed in close up work. You take the lead on any activities outside of the bus. Is that clear, Son?"

"Loud and clear, Pops."

Back at the ranch, Mallory, Juan, and Rashida discussed the firing sequences as well as the escape strategies. Small groups were assigned to cover and escape by the additional tunnels that had been dug.   Rather than destroy the ranch again, concussion grenades were placed strategically around the downstairs for maximum effect. Each tunnel was checked for supplies, water, and portable toilets. In each tunnel, there were ten machine pistols, ten .9-millimeter pistols, with ammo, plus three, 6-shot, shotguns.   The planning was impeccable, and the only thing left to chance was the execution by each member of the group. Ms. Viola had failed miserably at firing pistols but seemed comfortable with firing the shotgun. She and Monica were given the responsibility for the protection of the children. The women were taught to fire strategically. While one fired her weapon, the other one would reload her weapon.

The groups' extended community was on alert and stationed around the ranch, on the roads, in the woods, and in tree houses. The entire town was on alert and the new sheriff, and his deputies had been made aware of the situation and were stationed with medical personnel on Clyde's property. The sheriff was Clyde's cousin and was told about the issue and warned not to do stupid.

The ranch was wired and listening devices were turned on and tuned in. Something that turned out to be a problem for advancing forces in the past. Clyde and his people decided to camp out early, and to openly enjoy fires at their campsites. The weather was mild, but the fires were necessary because the bears and wolves were coming into, that thing called, mating season. Most smart people would have enjoyed the safety of their homes at this time of the year, but this community was going to protect the people that saved their ranches, their dignity, and their town, no matter the cost.

Chakes said to Luana in front of Sister, "I done got you people in a lot of trouble, haven't I?"

Luana, with her head held high, walked over to her man and said, "I've not had this much love, fun, excitement, and danger in my face--ever. I'm loving every minute of it, and I realize the importance of all this. I also realize there is this man, who I happen to be fiercely in love with, admire, and adore his very scent that is a part of this event. I will conclude another's life for him if need be. Dude, we came on this trip with our eyes wide open. If you hadn't tried to pick my grandmother up by offering her a $100 and a cellphone, we wouldn't be here. By the way, have you gotten over your fancy for my grandmother yet?"

"I will never get over my thing for Sister. It be permanent, Man. It be permanent. I just need to tell you guys one thing. It is us against the world. When you run out of bullets, start throwing your guns at them, and when you have nothing to throw, ask God to forgive all your sins and go with him to the great beyond. I will do my best to protect you, but I need you guys to protect me as well. Just pull that damn trigger and pump that shotgun and scream at them. They will hurt us all, if they're successful, including Beatrice. Don't try to be heroes; stay in the position you're assigned, and make sure you listen for the password. We wouldn't want you to shoot one of our own, now would we. I won't be near this part of the ranch, but I will have my ears on and listening to your issues or needs. I will come to you if you're in trouble. I love you, Sister. I love you, Luana, and I'm the luckiest man on earth. Look at you, you're as pretty as the setting sun, and the rising moon, and that makes me special because you selected me out of a field of hundreds."

Luana looked at him and said, "Sorry, my love, you might want to change that number to thousands." They all laughed, and he kissed his bride-to-be and grandmother-in-law-to-be.

# # #

On the road in the blue school bus, Carla said, "We should be coming up on that rest stop in the next fifteen to twenty minutes. By the way, did anyone test the weapons on this thing?"

Larry looked at Zanthius, and he looked at Mike. Larry said, "Shit, I'll call Clyde. He should know."

Larry immediately reached Clyde and asked him the question. Clyde laughed and said, "You people drive 150 miles and then want to know if the guns work? That be just a wee bit late in the game, don't you think?"

Larry said, "Thank God for our pilot who is always in the checking mode. She asked if the guns work."

"Do you think I would let you leave here with that thing without checking out all systems? Hell, yeah, they work."

"Thanks, Clyde. I owe you a beer."

"Larry, I owe you, my life. Thanks, young fellow."

# # #

At the rest stop, Carla asked, "What's the latest intel on the truck? Larry, can you call Clyde and see if it left the other place?"

Larry said, "I'll call him back. Is there a particular reason why you want to know the answer?"

"I'm looking at this map, and there are two rest stops before here. If we drive another forty-five miles, we'll be at a desolate looking town that would be perfect for an ambush and minimize collateral damage. Take a look around, this place is bustling. I'd rather take my chances with fewer locals having the chance of being shot without reason," Carla stated.

Zanthius and Larry looked at the map and agreed. Zanthius said, "If this is a ruse, then that means we're that much farther away from the ranch in providing them assistance. That's why I propose that we drive twenty-two miles from here and hit it hard by this little farm town. I totally agree with you, Carla. If this is just a decoy, then they have drawn six guns from the ranch and left it with less coverage."

"If the intel is correct, this thing isn't supposed to go down until tomorrow. I don't like where my head is on this one. I also believe if this is a ruse and we attacked it, that would allow our adversaries to know the ranch is undermanned. Frankly, I think we should fuel up and move this thing north on I-25 and cut the distance and our response time. Brother, I think we should ride this bus up I-25 until we've cut the distance in half, and, besides, there are no cell towers on that stretch of the road," Larry said.

Asiram's politically correct statement was simple, "Honey, I like your plan because if it is not a farce, then we have the advantage. On the other hand, if Larry is correct, we're that far from our boys. I already think I'm too far from the boys and I'm getting anxious."

Zanthius viewed the surprisingly soft and weak look on Asiram's face and said, "Larry, we're connected. Let's gas this thing up and play closer to our home field. Will you inform dad?"

"I'm on it."

Mike said, "Honey, you get some rest, I'll drive this thing."

Larry called the Sarge and told him what the common thinking was. He indicated that the notion of driving too far was to their adversaries' advantage, and by halving the distance, it gave them the ability to retreat and provide coverage at the ranch in less time. He told the Sarge it was a matter of distance and reaction time--pure physics. The Sarge told him he thought this matter was a decoy, but he wasn't ready to trust the fate of the group on a hunch. After the two hung up, Larry began to stare out of the window. Marisa asked, "Honey, what are you looking at?"

"Damn, baby, you just answered my question." He pulled out his cell phone and attempted to contact Rashida, but to no avail. He tried again, and she answered. He said, "So, Sis, I have a question for you."

"Shoot!" Rashida responded.

"Didn't we install listening devices and motion detectors on the ranch?"

"Larry, you know we did. I mean, I didn't do it, but Sue Lyn and Darryl certainly placed cameras in strange places to detect movement and heat signatures. Why do you ask?"

"I'll let you know once I figure out my own problem. Thanks, Sis."

Larry said, "I think we should take this puppy to the outskirts of town. I mean we should be no more than twenty-five miles from the ranch which would take us, at a high speed of travel, no more than fifteen, or so minutes to reach the ranch. Also, if that truck is in sight, we shoot the fricken tires out first and then focus on those chase cars. I should call Clyde and see if his people have any intel on the chase cars, so we'll know what to look out for. I'll give him a call."

#

Clyde was like John Lee, no quick, or short answers to anything that was asked. He told Larry his people told him they saw two SUVs following the truck, but they didn't see any chase cars. Larry asked Clyde, "Could those trucks be considered chase cars?"

Clyde in a most magnanimous fashion stated, "A chase car is a car out here and not one of those SUVs. When you invade a country, you'd better know the language."

Larry said, "You're correct. Can you contact your people and get a handle on those SUVs? There's also supposed to be another vehicle for a total of three chase vehicles."

## CHAPTER ELEVEN

Mike and his group were twenty-eight miles from the ranch when Zanthius said, "I think this is too far away. I want to narrow the distance to fifteen miles."

Larry who was looking out of the window, said in response, "I'd prefer ten miles, and if anything happens, I know I can run that in record time. What about you, Brother? Can you make that kind of distance?"

"If I did ten miles, I would collapse once I arrived. Mike, can you run ten miles?"

"I haven't had a need to do that in a long while. Without pressure, I'm good for twenty miles if I know the terrain."

Zanthius said, "Let's make it eight miles and be done with it."

Mike said, "Guys, that car has been bird dogging us for the past twenty-two miles." Carla ran to the back and said, "That looks like the same car that turned onto the highway when we left that rest stop."

She moved to the front of the bus and told Mike to put on the flashers and to pull off the road. She hit the smoke button and created a plume of black diesel smoke. Everyone knew that stretch of the road had no cell service and, therefore, felt comfortable if it were the bad guys, they wouldn't have time to radio for help if they engaged them.

Mike pulled the vehicle over, and Carla got out and opened the hood to the bus. The suspicious car pulled slowly next to the bus as if it were going to stop and got a good look at Carla.

Normally, people from the area would stop their vehicles and lend a helping hand, especially if a woman was driving a school bus. Zanthius said, "Now, who would pass a school bus that just blew a lot of black smoke and continue on their way? It certainly wouldn't be people from here."

Larry connected his phone to the antennae on the bus and called Clyde. He described the vehicle and asked him to have his people disable it at the twelve-mile mark which was one of their out-posts. He strongly suggested that they do not engage the occupants but slow them down with a flat tire. He hung up and then called the Sarge and reported what had just happened. He told the Sarge they were coming up on the fifteen-mile marker and would set up camp at the eight-mile marker. He explained their thinking on distance and time. The real matter floating around in Larry's head was much more disturbing than what he would acknowledge. The memory was the one of when he reached the ranch late, it imploded, and his people were nowhere to be found.

Five minutes later, a small explosion could be heard. The vehicle became increasingly difficult to steer. The driver pulled the vehicle to the side of the road, got out of the car, and looked at the tires and saw the front left tire was completely flat. His partner got out of the car and had a huge automatic rifle strapped around his neck. A third man exited the back door on the right and another person exited on the left. They too had large caliber weapons strung around their necks.

The people at the outpost called Clyde and told him that the people in the chase car were strapped with large automatic weapons. Clyde was also told that one of the men was trying to make a call, but apparently didn't have a signal. He told him each man tried to make a call and only one was able to get through. It lasted for less than a minute.

The men opened the trunk of the car and unloaded large duffle bags. The spare tire was a doughnut with a twenty-five mile an hour maximum speed with a fifteen-mile distance recommendation. The lug nuts had been tightened hydraulically, and it appeared that none of the men, individually, were able to loosen the nuts. Clyde's people who were watching from afar, laughed for seven minutes watching these guys trying to undo a wheel lock. One of the guys placed the wrench in a position that would allow him to jump on it, which he did, and the nut finally turned.

# # #

The loud blast from a tractor trailer's horn could be heard as the vehicle passed the blue school bus. Larry said, "Brother, to your point, no one would just blow their horn at a school bus in this place. Did you see the name on the trailer?"

Zanthius replied, "I did not."

Asiram announced, "Vegas First!"

Larry pulled out his cellphone and called the Sarge and reported, "Vegas First just crossed the fifteen-mile mark, and is heading your way with two chase vehicles, one in the front and one in the back. Clyde's people disabled the scout car and if this thing continues past them on the road, then we will engage it. If it stops, we'll just pass it and blow our horn.

We'll wait at the bend in the road at Mile Marker seven and that is when we'll set it ablaze."

The Sarge said, "We have friendlies out there. I need your people to scout your field of fire, and make sure you're firing down and not across or make sure there is a backstop for your rounds. If that vehicle doesn't stop to assist his associates, I need you people to disable it. Tell Mike I need him to throw that little package I gave him onto the roof of the trailer, from the escape vent in the roof of the school bus. And, Larry, no matter what, get the hell away from that thing as fast as possible. Tell the driver to floor that thing and to drop the shield down in the back. I think there is a nitro system on that bus. Good luck Son. Bring everyone back to me the way they left."

As the group pulled onto the highway, a car passed them and a kid in the back seat had a toy gun that lights up. No one paid attention to it, but Carla flippantly said, "I hope those bad guys don't mistake it for a real weapon."

As the bus broke the seventy miles per hour limit, about five minutes later, flashes could be seen from up ahead. The guys from the disabled vehicle, as well as those from the two chase cars, opened fire on the occupants, killing them instantly and without regard. Carla screamed, "Oh my God! They fired on that car that just passed us!"

Larry yelled, "Stop the bus." Mike hit the brakes hard, and the vehicle came to an immediate halt. It was obvious the vehicle occupants saw the toy gun and fired mercilessly on it. He called Clyde and said, "No time to explain, have your people at the outpost begin to fire on those sons-a-bitches. No time for explanation! Call them now!" Larry told Mike to switch places with Carla and man the guns.

Clyde placed the call, and his friends began to systematically force the bad guys to the other side of the vehicle. Larry told Carla, "Drive this thing forward." He said to Mike, "Let's send these people back to hell."

Mike began to fire in an automatic mode and Larry told him to relax and focus. The mercs, one by one, were summarily executed. Carla in the meantime had engaged the overdrive on the bus and was at one time, exceeding 95 miles per hour and pulled behind the truck in a moment's notice.

Mike said, Larry, "I need you to take over this position because I have a package to deliver." He went back to the vent, opened it, and pulled the fuse on the ordinance.

Carla yelled, "In 5-4-3-2-1-now." Mike threw the package onto the truck. Carla engaged the overdrive and the bus pulled quickly in front of the truck. Two minutes later, there was an explosion that was earth shattering. Multiple denotations shook the area, and the night sky was as bright as if it were daylight. Small munitions were spent into the night with some of them hitting the bus. Carla turned the bus around and slowly made her way to the remnants of the truck. Zanthius said, "That explosion shook my very fiber. I'm having a ringing sensation in my ears. Anyone else?"

Everyone was having hearing issues because the explosion was extremely vibrant and destructive. The façade of one of the chase vehicles remained in-tact but the rest were burnt beyond recognition. The group converged on the scene and realized there was enough bad stuff in the truck to destroy the entire town. The crater that resulted from the blast was at least twenty feet in depth and thirty feet wide.

In one of the SUVs, that was smoldering, in the front seat, there was a burnt figure that was slowly being asphyxiated by the aftermath of the blast. "Help me," he whispered. Larry cautiously walked over to the vehicle and saw that the man had lost one arm, and the other one was bleeding profusely as a result of the blast.

Larry looked at him and said, "There's not much I can do for you. How can I make you a little more comfortable?"

The man softly exclaimed, "Shoot me! Please shoot me. If you do, I will unlock the trunk safely."

"What's in the trunk?"

"Payment for the mercs."

"You unlock the trunk and I'll ease your pain. How can I trust you? You came here to kill my family." The guy looked at his tattered arm and hit a button near the steering wheel and the trunk opened.

He begged Larry, "In my pocket is info and a picture of my wife and family. Be gracious and send them some money. That's all I ask. Do I have your word?"

Larry replied, "I'll do that and make sure that they will never need anything as long as they are alive. I will take care of them."

The man responded, "Open the bags with the short zipper. The long zipper is wired. Honor your word and finish me." Larry pulled his .308 out and fired a single shot into the man's head. He then called Zanthius over to the vehicle, and the two men removed five oversized duffle bags containing an uncertain content. Larry walked to the driver's side of the vehicle and removed the man's wallet and placed it his pocket. He turned to Mike, "We can't take this back to the ranch without doing due diligence. This shit is wired. This guy told me to use the short zipper because the long zipper is wired. He lost one of his arms and wants me to take care of his family, and, therefore, told me to not use the long zipper. We either

leave this mess here and blow it up, or we take a chance on a
dead man's story. What's your take on this?"

"Larry, I have no take. We can't take it back without
checking it, and we can't check it here. In ten minutes, the
whole town is going to descend on this place. Let's throw
them on the bus and head towards the ranch. We can make a
detour and gently empty the contents of those duffle bags."

Larry walked over to Zanthius and said, "My brother, if
this goes wrong, I need you to take care of my twins, my wife
and Mike's family as well. Do we have an accord?"

"We have an accord and I swear by it," Zanthius
announced.

Larry walked over to his wife and kissed her and said,
"You know you're the only woman in my life. Trust in me,
and I'll get through this mess. I believe what the man said,
even though I don't know him. Let's not make a big deal of
this. I'm confident I'll be okay."

Mike whispered something to Carla, and she smiled. He
whispered something else, and she kissed his lips. She
whispered something in his ear, and he kissed her lips and said,
"I assure you I'll be back for that."

The two men walked the bags up the road and slowly and
methodically, removed the contents. Larry inspected his first
bag and felt something that was not paper. He removed his
hands and walked that bag thirty feet up the road. Entering his
second bag, the same kind of item was felt immediately. Larry
removed the contents from the bag and walked it another thirty
feet up the road. He turned to Mike and said, "Dude, you
haven't found any devices?"

"Larry, I have a ton of money piled up before me, I don't
see or feel anything out of order." Larry walked over to him
and said, "I'm going to take the bags and walk them up the

road. I need you to pile up the money and make sure that you didn't miss anything."

When Larry returned, he saw Mike looking as if he had seen a ghost. He started to say something to Mike but recognized that he was holding a wired cube of C-4 in his hands. Larry walked over to him and attempted to remove the product from his hands, but Mike wouldn't let it go. Larry said, "Mike, I need you to give me this package, or you and I will die right here and right now. Please, let it go."

Mike began to sweat. Carla could tell that something was wrong from afar. In a controlled voice, she yelled, "Mike, Honey, why don't you give that thing to Larry and come over here to me? Can you do that for me, Baby?"

Mike began to calm down and said, "Damn, Larry, I just froze."

"I know, my brother, now give it to me so I can walk it up the road." Mike released his hold on the C-4, and Larry gently walked it up the road. Carla and Marisa advanced to where Mike was and began to carefully gather the bundles of cash.

Zanthius yelled, "People, we need to make haste. This event is going to draw eyes soon, so wrap up what you're doing." He then yelled to the back of the bus and said, "Darling, is everything copesetic back there?"

"Got my eyes on the road and it seems still for the moment," Asiram answered. "We really need to get out of here."

Zanthius walked to the steps of the bus and said, "Larry, we need to leave now. Either bundle it or burn it. Your choice, but we must leave now."

"Zanthius, have Asiram fire about ten rounds from her weapon, that should scare the curious types away until daylight. Give me five minutes, and I'll have this all wrapped up."

He looked at Carla and said, "You and Mike take these three bags back to the bus. I'm fairly comfortable that they are clean. I'm not sure about this one, and, therefore, I'm not going to go digging around in it at night."

He told Marisa to remain where she was and walked the full bag to the place where he had placed the C-4. He returned, hugged her and said, "Now, that was some scary shit. As soon as we are clear of the area, I'll let Asiram fire rounds at that spot and you won't believe what that little mound of clay-like substance can do."

As the bus passed the place where the unattended bag and C-4 were placed, Larry said, "Asiram, now might be a good time to shoot that bag."

She yelled, "Fire in the hole!" Once again, the night sky was lit up as the bus sped away from the scene. Approximately ten miles from the ranch, Larry called the Sarge and told him what had happened. The Sarge told Larry that Clyde had been informed that a large contingency of men and women had assembled 50 miles to the north and tractor trailers were providing that crew with everything from portable bathrooms to food trucks, to hammocks. His source also said the group looked heavily armed with military grade weapons. Larry told the Sarge that from the size and width of the crater, the Vegas First must have been hauling only explosives. The Sarge asked him what was his '20', and Larry told him that his ETA was ten to fifteen minutes. The Sarge told him to call once they entered the property so that he could have Rashida and Juan shut down the weapons systems.

Larry asked Carla to drive the bus near the barn so that they could scan the bags and make sure there were no tracking devices in them. He then called Rashida and asked her to meet him at the barn to scan some packages. She told him that she didn't have to meet him because all he had to do was place the packages in a line in the first stall, step outside, and flick the red switch.

The system identified two small tracking devices that were useless because the barn was lined with reinforced steel. Any devices that were on the bus, or anywhere on the ranch, that weren't sanctioned were systematically scanned and the signal disrupted. Larry asked Rashida about C-4, and she told him that she loved him and was glad that he survived the blast. She also recommended that he leave the explosives until Jong could examine them.

Asiram exited the bus and said to Zanthius, "The ranch is never this quiet at this hour. Get your dad and tell him I need to see him in the front of the ranch."

Minutes later, the Sarge showed up and asked, "What's unnerving you, Daughter-in-Law?"

"Can't you hear it, or sense it? The quiet is uncommon to this area at this time. Something has spooked the natural inhabitants."

He said, "It is extremely quiet out. It is as though the earth told the animals to stay away because of the impending danger."

He smiled to himself and said, "Earth is what my kin folk know a lot about. You know what I think? I think that Darryl placed some of his stuff in the fields that is offensive to animals and that man can't detect until it's too late. He and Sue Lyn had an argument about what was the most effective, the earth or mechanized weapons."

Asiram asked, "Did you allow him to poison my land?"

"Of course not. I allowed him to use household chemicals and roots from home that keeps the animals away but will sting a human to death. No poison, my love, just substances that are dangerous to humans but make animals think twice about devouring them."

Asiram looked at the ranch and her eyes began to fill with tears. She looked at her daddy-in-law and began to cry. The Sarge hugged her tightly. Between whimpers, she asked, "Will this thing ever end, and if it does, what happens to these wonderful true relationships? I want the killing to stop, and I also want this group to never disband. I know I can't have it both ways, but I love everyone in this group, and I don't use that word love, lightly. The people who were supposed to love me and protect me, dehumanized me. I know the difference."

As he held her tight, the Sarge said, "You know so far, 90% of our group is moving on the land that Jilkes and John Lee own. The other 10%, haven't been endowed yet, but will be shortly. We also have a wonderful place to go in Spain where your mother-in-law is from. We have our farm in Virginia, this ranch in Wyoming, the entire outback in Australia, and, of course, our wonderful resort and surrounding venues in St. Thomas. We have three jets with the best damn pilots that we could find. As I do the math, we're stuck together for life. Besides, we have a lot of causes to bring to the main stage--from bullying, sexual abuse, trafficking in humans, LBGQT, our homeless Vets, college loans for the poor, adoption policies, cleaning out that human shithole called the Congress, the Senate, and a host of other initiatives. I don't think we'll solve them all, but Sue Lyn, Larry, Darryl, you, and Zanthius will carry on our work once we old folks decide to call it a day.

"Sweetheart, I stumbled onto, or perhaps I should say, was 'blessed' to be befriended by a group of guys who are the most honorable, reliable, trustworthy, and loyal people that I've ever known. Then, of course, I found out I had another son that was the zenith of enjoyment, who married a contentious spy, another spy forced him to kiss her and swallow a capsule, that started the quest for the Carbon Factor. Are you serious? Where on earth are these people going to go? We're all sucked into this new drug called family, and we've prospered from it beyond a normal person's imagination. Listen we're family, and the way I see it, you ain't going to have my grandbabies more than a mile from me at any time. You can take that to the bank."

Asiram smiled, sniffled, and said, "You're such a smooth talker, but I still haven't heard anything about my home in Northeast Philly. Yeah, con man, deal with that one. I love you Daddy-in-Law, aka the best con man since that dude in New York became the most powerful man in the world."

## CHAPTER TWELVE

Brown and Bernstein were next door neighbors in the addition. At 0100 hours, Brown called Juan. He asked him if the weapons systems were armed. He groggily stated that they were. Juan acknowledged the fourteen new structures on the property. He told Brown that he was not going to telegraph their firing solutions until the other side provided more intel in terms of numbers. Juan indicated that the Sarge and Mallory were sleeping outside of their command center, and that he would wake them up immediately.

# # #

A sleepy Sarge asked, "What's going on?"

Juan said, "It looks like fourteen new structures have been developed on the property in the last few hours. I have all of them targeted and can decimate all areas immediately, if that is your command."

The Sarge asked, "What are they doing? Are they staging areas, or is there some kind of weapon in each of those structures?"

Rashida asked, "Dad, what's happening?"

"Honey, we have fourteen new structures in the fields and I'm not sure if they're the new weapons systems or what."

"Why don't you zoom in on them and see."

Juan replied, "I didn't know you could zoom in on a target?"

"Honey, you're the boss, but I obviously pay more attention to details than you. It's okay--you're still the best husband ever." Rashida waddled into the command center, hit a couple of buttons, and zoomed in on the new additions. Everyone in the command center was horrified as the images became clear from the zooming effect. Each of the areas was equipped with Rocket Propelled Grenade launchers. The Sarge asked, "Rashida, can you fire on each of those positions now?"

"Dad, yes."

"Then do it."

Rashida hit the laser light switch first and then the fire button on the automatic long guns. The laser light distorted any tracking where the firing was coming from, and the guns pummeled the fourteen positions without a hint of mercy. Mallory instinctively hit the alarm and the ranch was automatically thrown into a defensive posture. People methodically, moved about with weapons loaded towards their designated positions.

Chakes kissed Luana and told her how much he loved her. He also told her that he would officially like to make love to her as soon as they have consummated their marriage vows. She indicated to him, that he had given her pleasure and that he had shared in it as well. The only quest that she wanted him to take on was to conclude the adversaries who were there to kill them all. Chakes then looked at Sister and said, "I be so happy I met you. And you, little one, will soon think of me in another way."

"You're my daddy. I don't know anyone else."

Chakes fell to his knees. He beckoned Beatrice over and said, "I will always be there for you. I'm honored to be given that title by you, and I promise to live up to it in every way. You've just made me the proudest human being on the planet. I love you, your mom, and Sister. I think your great grandmother be having a special kind of drink that hypnotizes people into worlds they don't know much about."

#

In the command center, moments later, the Sarge said, "Those things are Weapons of Mass Destruction. Did you see the way it hit those 14 reference points simultaneously? Sue Lyn and my nephew are too dangerous together. Those positions were hit with machine pistol fire and automatic rifle fire at the same time. No one could have survived that barrage."

Mallory asked, "How did they get that close to our position without being noticed?"

Rashida looked at Juan and said, "Sweetheart, I'll tend to your wounds once they've finished with you. Catch you later."

Juan said, "I didn't pay attention to Sue Lyn and Darryl the way I should have, and I endangered the group. I had them targeted, but I didn't know the right command to misdirect the firing with the laser lights."

"Are you sure you're on board now?" Mallory asked.

"I got this. My wife showed me where I went wrong, and I now have corrected that condition. We didn't have time to simulate firing and it was as new to her as it was to me, but I think she's a bit more anal than I am."

The Sarge said, "That was only their first wave. According to the information I have, there were to be as many as 225 mercs in this group." As he watched the monitors, he said, "I wish we could see as far as the horizon."

Juan said, "We could fire flares over that area or even launch one of the drones. I think Sue Lyn and Darryl may have installed solar powered lights as far away as 1.5 miles that will burn bright for 5 minutes before dimming. I'm sure once we did that, their people would surely disable it."

Juan was about to ask permission to do something when the Sarge held his finger up. He answered his phone. It was Clyde who said, "Mr. Sarge, we done count at least 160 people splitting into four groups. They're going to attempt to engage you from the four points, on the compass, if I had to guess. Now, if they try to do that, they'll receive fire from the rear and from your guys. They won't be in a crossfire, but they'll be catching rounds from the front and back. Unless these boys have another plan that I can't figure out, then I think this group is as dumb as can be."

"Clyde, I prefer that you and your people stay safe and let us handle this matter."

"Mr. Sarge, Ben, Ben Beckmire, how many times do I have to tell you that this ain't going to go down without us? I know you're not a stupid man, but you keep saying the same old shit. Listen, you people saved the farms, set up a fund, ran the carpetbaggers out of town, got rid of the crooked lawmen, and restored our dignity and belief in one another. Now, that's what I call a lot of divine intervention. You're wasting your time and your energy with your protests. On the perimeters of the ranch, I bet you the whole damn town is out there with their hunting weapons. They have all been given firing coordinates. I don't know how to say this, but those people who entered the ranch a couple of hundred yards from where we are, just walked into a killing zone. Hell, I bet you there's over 300 rifles hiding in the dark, ready to shoot anything that moves. You can't just waltz into our town and try to kill our benefactor, and our saviors. We ain't all that smart, but never will anyone take from us what we have worked hard for. No, sir. You might as well just hang up this phone and watch the monitors. I don't see any reason for you and your people to go outside until this thing is over."

The Sarge paused and said, "God be with us all. I hope your people know not to enter that field for the next few days. My nephew put some mighty powerful stuff out there that will fade in the next day or so, and then the animals will have a feast on humans, unfortunately."

"Sarge, when you informed me that you were coming to town, I held a town meeting. My people wanted to find out when and where those bad guys were coming to town to meet them and lay siege to their camp. We wanted to clean this mess up before you got near here, but then there was the notion of that truck with Vegas First on it. I'm telling you this town will make it known that if you come here for bullshit, you'll die in horseshit."

"Clyde, keep your people safe and remind all of them, aim small, hit large, and keep their rounds targeted. No airborne shots, too many people out and about. Thanks, buddy, and God be with us all."

# # #

In one of the tunnels, Beatrice said to LaGina, "I'm scared. Are you scared too?"

LaGina said, "I'm always scared, but grandpa won't let anything happen to us."

"Do I know your grandpa?" Beatrice asked.

"Everybody knows my grandpa, Ben Beckmire. Okay, in the morning, I'm going to introduce you to my grandpa. Maybe he might let you call him that too."

# # #

At 0300 hours, Juan woke up Rashida and said, "I need you to get your dad in here now. Something's going down, and I don't know what it is."

Rashida screamed, "Dad, I need you in the command center now."

On his way to the command center, he yelled, "Jilkes, John Lee, Mallory, and Jong, I need you now." As he approached the center, his phone rang. Once again it was Clyde. He said, "Clyde, I need you to hold on for a minute." He walked into the command center and saw two people waving what looked like capitulation flags.

The Sarge placed his phone to his mouth and said, "Clyde, I need your people to stand down, until I can figure out what's going on? You can reach them, right?"

Clyde said, "Of course, I can reach them. I called you to tell you that I think those people are surrendering."

"Clyde, stay on the phone until I have confirmation about what's going on. Can I trust your people not to fire if we go onto the field?"

"Sarge, my people be listening to you as you speak. They all hear your instructions. We will wait your orders."

Rashida entered the command center and said, "Dad, if I weren't crazy, I would think they are surrendering. Let me cut the audio system on. Juan, hit the switch."

"Honey, do you mean this green one?"

"Yes, darling. I'm glad you're back on board."

Juan hit the switch, and Rashida asked, "You're waving two white flags which is not normal when one surrenders. What is the purpose of the two waving white flags? Speak normally, and we will hear you. What is your name and who is your employer?"

"My name is Jelani Campbell, and I'm the squad leader for this quadrant and overall leader of the advancing forces."

"Mr. Campbell, what terms do you seek?"

"At this point in time, we were supposed to be paid prior to any assault on your compound. Payment has not been forthcoming. Therefore, we want to throw down our arms and evacuate your ranch without further repercussions."

"Mr. Campbell, can you please tell me why we should allow you to egress from our ranch when you are here with the intent to eliminate us? Are you absolutely crazy, or are you smoking too much of that Colorado free pot?"

"Neither Ma'am. We didn't get paid, and benchmarks are what we work under."

"Mr. Campbell, are you thinking before you state your feelings? You're here to kill us and get paid for doing it. And now, you want us to place our defenses on stand-by and let you walk back to your bus and go home to your families? That seems like a bit of a quandary to me, especially when you walked into a killing zone. There are 300 guns waiting for you to retreat. There are all kinds of automated firing schemes that await you as you advance. We don't have to respect your wishes. As a matter of fact, we're considering using this time to teach your employer a huge lesson."

"Wait, you're right on all accounts. Let me and my men leave, and you'll never hear from us again."

"I've heard that before. Mr. Campbell, Mr. Jelani Campbell, your name sounds so familiar to me. I'm not going to make this a social event, but I'm going to ask you a couple of questions? Is your mother's name Monica? And is your father's name Bruce?"

There was silence on the intercom and Jelani, said, "How do you know the names of my parents?"

"They're my friends. You, my friend, should thank your lucky stars. I was prepared to hit a button that would decimate your forces. This world is too small. If any of your people are found with a toothpick in their pockets, they will be summarily executed. I must warn you, if any of your people leave the marked, drone-lit path that I will send in a minute, they will die a horrific death," Rashida announced.

"Several of my people are lying in the field shaking and sick."

"We are aware of that. I'm going to send a drone to your area in a few minutes. It will light and mark a path that you must follow. You should inform the rest of your group that they should remain in place until you and I connect to them. Any aggressive movements will be met with a firing sequence that will be without mercy. Your sick people will perhaps recover, but if a weapon is recognized by our automated system, it will fire in an automated exact fashion," Rashida indicated.

"Understood. We just want out of this arena that has forfeited payment. I will check my people personally, and make sure there are no weapons whatsoever," Mr. Campbell stated.

"I must tell you, once I reengage the automatic system, any semblance of a weapon will be dealt with in a horrific manner. Mr. Campbell, how did you choose this line of work?"

"Ma'am, the money is quick and easy, and this is what I learned when I was in the desert--how to kill efficiently. I have one other request. Can you keep this event between us and not involve my parents in it? They would be heartbroken."

"Wow, Mr. Campbell. You come to kill us, you then surrender, and now you want me to keep your work regime a secret? Is there any other way we can accommodate you and your people? Perhaps you might like a triple latte-moorea-crazy? Is there anything else, Mr. Campbell?"

"Ma'am, no, Ma'am."

"Before anything happens, you must contact your forces and tell them to drop all weapons, big and small."

"Ma'am, that's another problem that we have. I've been sending runners to relay orders. Our communications system does not work out here."

"I'm going to free up the airwaves and it is up to you to make sure they understand what you have agreed to. Your people need to unchamber rounds from their weapons. Leave the clips next to the weapons and remove the bolts as well. Remember, Mr. Campbell, once I engage our automatic system, anyone with as much as pocketknife with be summarily executed by a machine. I know you people sometimes have your favorite weapons and knives, however, if our system detects it, it will fire on the target. Do you understand, Mr. Campbell?"

"Ma'am, yes Ma'am. I will make it clear."

"Your people who are shaking and sick in the fields, you should not try to help them until the drone provides you secure a safe passage. The fields are loaded with toxins and other neurological impacting native concoctions. Everyone needs to remain where they are until we can direct your retreat. Is that understood, Mr. Campbell?"

"Ma'am, yes Ma'am."

The Sarge, Mallory, John Lee, and Jilkes listened to Rashida save the lives of a lot of people. John Lee said, "Rashida, girl, you should be a diplomat or at least a lawyer. You sure as heck saved a lot of lives tonight, perhaps on both sides of the fence. That was remarkable, professional, and you never raised your voice. Now, if that were my African American friend over here doing that, hell, he'd still be screaming words that nobody understands, but his black ass."

"John Lee, you do know that I'm an African American, don't you?"

"Yeah, but you ain't as African American as he is. He is really African American and my best friend in the whole world."

The Sarge said, "Baby girl, you know I tried to teach you everything that I know. I think you can now start teaching me what you know. I'm so proud of you and you're the best daughter a person could wish for. God was good to me and your mom when he opened our hearts and minds and allowed us to become a family. I'm so proud of you. I wish your mom were here to witness how you handled that situation."

"Dad, perhaps when we're out of the stress mode, you can let her listen to the audio and video of what I just did. Everything we do is taped for training purposes."

"Wow, my baby girl. Could you do me a favor?"

"Anything for you, Dad."

"Make sure, Romeo is up to snuff with this, or I'll have to ship his ass out of here."

"Oh, don't worry. He's scheduled for training at 0700 hours tomorrow. However, I still think there should be at least four people who can operate this system. As a matter of fact, I think six would be ideal, but four would suffice. Dad, I'm sorry, I must attend to this situation. Looks like someone is unable to follow rules or didn't get the email. I'll send him a message." Rashida hit the touch screen and was prepared to hit the engage button. The person kept walking so Rashida targeted the individual but hesitated. She concluded that he was drugged, had no visible weapon, and was walking erratically. The Sarge said, "Wow, you have life and death in your hands. Do I have to worry about your mental health?"

"Dad, I like being alive, and I hate it when people strap my daughter in a suicide vest. You come on this ranch, or anywhere that I am, and you're uninvited, then you had better have a big bomb, or I'm going to blow a hole in your ass."

Mallory said, "Chip off the old block. The apple didn't fall too far from the tree."

Jilkes said, "Rashida, I think we should hold them in place until daylight, which is only a matter of forty minutes, or so. We can guide them out of here through the audio system without exposing ourselves. Do you agree?"

"I like that idea because, once again, we're out of harm's way, and they don't get a chance to eyeball us--good idea. Dad, can you buy into that, or do you want to proceed with the night evacuation?"

"Jilkes is right on the money. We control the field during the night and daylight. At this hour, there still may be some nuts out there looking for their last hurrah. Honey let's have them stay in place until daylight and we'll deal with them then.

Tell Mr. Campbell that it is in the best interest of everyone that they remain in place and that it is detrimental to wander, especially since Darryl created some concoction that incapacitates the neurological system. Tell him it would be safe for all if they remain in place until we can guide them out of the field."

Rashida announced their decision and told them to remain in place.

At 0630 hours, Rashida's voice was the obnoxious sound heard by people near and far. She said, "Good morning to my friends and relatives and to our uninvited guests. Those of you who were not invited to this event will probably not recognize a single aspect of the ranch. We can see you, but you can't see us. FYI, you were kept in place because there are some herbs in the fields that will render you unconscious. Once conscious, you will have the shakes, a fever, and you will be discombobulated. In other words, you will have a case of diarrhea that supersedes any you have ever known. So, this is how this retreat is going to happen. There are four groups of you. I want each quadrant to find a stick and place a white cloth on it immediately. In case you didn't get the email, our system looks for weapons. Unlike the x-ray systems at the airports, it targets the Glock and other synthetically made weapons. If you think you're smarter than our system, then I invite you to try to smuggle your favorite weapon off the premises. In case you're not as smart as our system, you will be cut to pieces by our automatic firing system. Now, we know some of you are going to try us, like the two guys in the southern quadrant. You have 5-4-3-2-1, sorry!

"Those people were given a warning along with the rest of you. We consider that a dumb kill because we're trying to allow you to return to your loved ones, but our resolve has been tested. In the northern quadrant, ditch that knife now."

The Sarge grabbed the mike and said, "Good morning. There will be no further warnings. Any individual concealing a weapon thirty-second from now, will be executed where he or she stands. No more warnings, just executions."

Rashida knew that rain was in the forecast and that the product that Darryl developed would wash away without leaving any environmental damage. She looked at her husband and said, "Baby, this happened without a lot of people being killed. I'm so happy to God we didn't have to shoot all those people. Aren't you?"

"Rashida, what makes me happy is that I married a strong and delicate woman who both values and protects life, where possible. I'm not judging or saying with any sense of correctness, but I don't know if this would have ended this way with someone else operating the system. You portrayed an extreme disinclination to fire on those people when others would have just hit the fire button. I'm so proud of you, honey. You're a great mother, wife, lover, and I'm so happy that big ass father of yours didn't break my neck when he found out we were having sex."

"Juan, he knew, and he was making sure you knew he knew. My dad is like no other. When he feels negative, then he plays that card. He knew he was pushing you to your limits as a man, demanded that you respected who he was to me, the group, and most of all, his leadership. You were wise not to try to rebuff his aggression because my father is unnaturally strong. He, unknowingly, lifted you off the ground and held you suspended in the air. When he loves you, he loves you, when you're his enemy, then all gloves are taken off. Other than that, he is a wonderful parent and one that a husband or boyfriend should not anger."

By 0900 hours, 164 individuals had been scanned and were escorted to the road by drones that had audio and video capabilities. At the base of the highway and approximately two miles from the ranch, one of the mercs said, "I sure would like to blow that thing out of the sky. As a matter of fact, how can that thing be operating this far from where we surrendered?"

Rashida broadcasted, "You're welcome to knock it out of the sky, I hope that fulfills your dying wish. Out here, there is a weapon on you always, even when the drone collapses. You would make this easy if you continued to walk and not think about trying to do stupid."

Rashida, who continued to direct the mercs and exercise control of the exit strategy, looked at Juan and said, "Something is about to happen and it ain't good."

Her water broke. Juan screamed, "Sarge, Dad, Mr. Beckmire, I need you in here now."

The Sarge entered the room, told Mallory to find Courtney, and to call Clyde. Beckmire directed, "We need an extraction with the hospital as the designation. Rashida is about to have her baby."

When Courtney showed up, she said, "Find Ms. Viola. Tell her we have another baby ready to come out."

The Sarge said, "Who is handling the exit of the mercs?"

Juan said, "She was."

"Really, Juan? She's about to have a baby, and you're about to become a father, but I need you on those drones until those people are far away from this ranch. Can you do that for me, Son? Can you secure us by doing this?"

"Sarge, I got this. Those people are on the highway, but I need someone to handle this for us. I got to be with my wife."

Jilkes said, "Give me and John Lee a five-minute lesson and be on your way. First, is there a constant scan of the property even though people are leaving from another aspect of the ranch? Secondly, what are the clear indicators that someone is moving in the field? And third, how do we target and fire on suspicious movement in a warning and/or a conclusive mode?"

Juan said, "Damn, Jilkes. Those are the three main questions."

Juan then proceeded to show Jilkes and John Lee how to scan the ranch, find movement, and terminate it. John Lee said, "It's a piece of cake. I told y'all that my African American friend was the smartest person in this outfit, ah, other than the Sarge, ah, and Mallory, ah and I guess me. He ain't so smart after all, is he?"

"John Lee, you keep an eye on movement and I'll handle the rest. You're one crazy redneck."

"Yeah, but you love me. Right?"

"Yeah dude. We're brothers from another mother."

John Lee became uncharacteristically quiet and Jilkes knew what was going to happen next. John Lee began to sniffle and then he broke into a full-fledged crying frenzy.

Jilkes asked, "What's wrong with your country ass?"

"I'm happy, I showed restraint when I kicked your ass in boot camp. I'm really happy I have a John Lee Jr., a wonderful crazy wife, and a best friend that means more to me than life. I'm just feeling a little love for you and the tears are my proof."

"John Lee, I love you too man and you're my best friend in the world as well. I have just a single question for you. Do you know my name?" Jilkes inquired.

John Lee looked at him and said, "I just told people how smart you be and now you be asking me if I know your name? Are you smoking that happy grass, or something?"

"John Lee, do you know that you refer to me as your African American friend more than you use my name? You rarely call me Jilkes unless we're killing people. Why is that?"

"Jilkes, you be too sensitive. You know I know your name, and you know mine. You call me old country. Is this here name calling thing going to be an issue in our relationship? If so, I'll address you as Mr. Reginald W. Jilkes. It don't matter to me, I'll call you Julius Caesar, if you like. I just don't want no stupid involved in our relationship."

Jilkes knew this wasn't going to end well, so he said, "Hey, I thought I saw movement less than 100 yards from the ranch."

John Lee said, "Pigshit, my African American brother. Ain't nobody that stupid except you and me to be moving around with all these push button guns. It's like a shooting gallery at a carnival. You don't want to talk about it, but I want to finish this song. How about if I call you Jilkes without putting in surtitles or adjectives to it like Jilkes, my African American Friend, or something like that?"

"How about I put my foot up your ass each time you don't call me Jilkes?"

"That seems like it might be a whole bunch of ass kicking. Naw, I just want to call you my friend Jilkes. No pig shit, or horse shit--just Jilkes. You know I do want to ask you a question before we move on from this. Did you think I was being offended by calling you that?" John Lee inquired.

"No, John Lee, you weren't being offended, you were being offensive."

"Why you change what I say and make it what you say? Why you always do that. I'll say happy and you'll say some nutty shit like good fortune. Now, what the hell does good fortune have to do with being happy? I know, you're going to say that they be related. They ain't related and you need to charge those teachers who taught your ass."

"John Lee, can we end this conversation? I'm worried about my lady."

"Why, is she planning on leaving your black ass or something?"

"Hey, stupido, she's pregnant."

"Oh, yeah. I forgot about that. Why don't you have Ms. Viola peek at her. She seems to be some kind of special."

"Now, that's the first sensible thing you've said." Jilkes looked out at the monitors and said, "Hey, that's Bernstein running towards here, isn't it? Call the Sarge, something's up."

Bernstein ran into the house and asked, "Where is Courtney? Things are happening to Yvette and she's unable to speak."

Courtney heard this and asked Mallory, "Did you find Ms. Viola, I need her."

Ms. Viola, in the interim, was assisting Rashida. She said, "Mr. Sarge, unless you want to have your grandbaby here on the ranch, I suggest someone get us to the hospital."

She saw her grandbaby and said, "Luana, come help Rashida while I try to help Dr. Courtney and Ms. Yvette." She then made her way to the adjoining property and walked in on Courtney struggling with Yvette. Yvette's delivery was going to be complicated and would happen right there at the ranch. Ms. Viola saw Monica and said, "I need pots of hot water and the strongest bottle of whiskey that you can pick up on your way back here. Are there any women here who aren't pregnant? Tell Ava to make her way here."

Rashida was being helped onto the bus with the military grade armament. She screamed, "Where's my mom? I need my mom."

In another place, Ms. Viola said, "This here baby is bigger than she be wanting, and he be wanting to come out now, and your daughter be wanting to get to the hospital. I'm no doctor, but I say, we bring your daughter in here and you can deliver both babies. If you make a choice, someone will be sad."

Courtney looked at her and asked, "How and why do you say that?"

This one here is ready now, the other one still has some time. If you leave one for the other, or send one to the hospital, there are going to be some very hurt feelings. Since Yvette's delivery appears to be more complicated than Rashida's, Courtney you and I can assist with Yvette. Monica and Luana, will help deliver Rashida's son."

"This one has to come out now and the other one has time. You leave one for the other or take this one to the hospital, somebodies will be sad for a while. This one is critical. Have them bring Rashida here and lets you and I calm this one so that you can deliver her boy."

"How do you know it's a boy?"

"I bet you $50 bucks it be a boy."

"You're on sister."

Two hours and twenty-two minutes later, two women, side by side, delivered two healthy male babies. Courtney rejoiced in her accomplishment but was smart enough to call the town doctor.

# # #

Meanwhile, Beckmire said, "I'm going to send out and separate our forces. I'm sending Brown, Bernstein, Chakes, Mallory and Juan. I need Jilkes and John Lee on the guns and everyone else on alert. I know we don't control these issues, but an advancing force could decimate us easily."

Courtney said, "Babe, your daughter just had a baby, another grandson for you. Go kiss her and tell her how much you love her. We know that if there is a problem, Ben Beckmire and his people will handle it."

# # #

When the group arrived at the hospital, the doctor stated to Ms. Viola, "You had no drugs, how did you calm them down?"

"I made them both do a shot of Jack."

The doctor asked, "What is a shot of Jack?"

"Doctor, you need to get out more often. A shot of Jack Daniels. Do you drink?"

## CHAPTER THIRTEEN

Two additional babies were born to the group, and everyone was excited. Dr. Beckmire thought the assault created a lot of stress for those members of the group who were pregnant. At 1800 hours, the Sarge received a call from Jilkes who inquired about the availability of Dr. Beckmire. He mumbled something and Jilkes said, "I need to speak to Courtney." A groggy Courtney picked up the phone and was startled by the banging on her door. The Sarge grabbed a weapon and said, "Who has the audacity to bang on my door at this hour?"

"Sarge, it's Brown and I need Courtney. Okema is experiencing serious pain and I don't know what to do."

"I'll get her up, and we'll be right there."

"Hurry, Sarge, I'm scared."

Seven minutes later, the Sarge and Courtney quickly moved towards the guest house and saw on the registry that Brown and Okema were in room 227. They knocked on the door but there was no answer, only the sound of someone in agony could be heard from room 229. Courtney said, "Honey, find Ms. Viola because I'm afraid I'm going to need help with this one also."

Courtney followed the sounds, opened the door, and someone clicked on the lights. In unison, the group yelled, "Happy Birthday, Courtney."

She looked at her husband and said, "I'm going to kill you." She looked around the room and saw all the smiling faces, including Rashida, Yeshida and Yvette. She turned to Ben Beckmire and yelled, "Dead Man Walking!"

CHAPTER FOURTEEN

The group enjoyed peace and quiet for little over a month. They remained at the ranch since it provided them with adequate cover and extra eyes and ears from their neighbors. During this time, Okema and Brown, Jong, and Mary Alice, and Jilkes and Somara, all tended to their new baby boys. The group was interested in going south to check on the progress of their homes.

# # #

At dinner, one evening, John Lee said, "I know a lot of you people be thinking that I know exactly what be going on with your homes, but I be here with you. I know you think because Jilkes and I are the cornerstones of this event that we be trying to hustle and flow you people. I have, or Jilkes and me have, ordered a video of the, what you call that process, ah, oh yeah, the production function. I want you to know that Jilkes and I have started tutoring each other in our native languages. We decided to do this so that we could communicate much more effectively. So, saying all that to say, here be the houses in alphabetical order. I will say, all the infrastructure is in place and the houses are in different stages of completion. Can someone hit them there lights?"

The architect and builder spoke personally to each owner and told them how important it was for him to meet each owner's expectations and, in general, supersede their aspirations. The pictures depicted the architectural renderings, and photos of those sites that were in the building phase. Brown said, "Guys, those shots are great. Sarge, when can we make a trip there?"

"I'll leave it up to the women who just had babies. Are they able to travel, and did those guys modify the seats in the back of the plane?"

Jong said, "The plane was modified two weeks ago. I told you about it, Sarge."

Courtney said, "I would like to hire a couple of nurses to support me in all of the trauma and drama you people cause. They could also take over the teaching role with a systematic curriculum. We need to enroll the older children in computer-assisted-instruction and set up clear times for learning and reading. This village is growing by leaps and bounds. So, how many of you ladies think that this is a good use of our resources?" Every female and male hand was raised high.

"Okay, I guess from the show of hands that's an affirmative desire. Can anyone recommend someone?" Asiram's hand shot up into the air and said, "Why don't you ask the doctor who helped deliver a lot of these babies? He may want to help since we're always doing something for the hospital."

"Good idea, my daughter." The place became silent, and Courtney asked, "What the heck just happened?"

Asiram gave one child to Ava, and her other son to Zanthius, and walked over to Courtney and announced, "You called me your daughter."

"You are my daughter unless I've missed something?"

"No, Courtney, you called me YOUR daughter. You've never addressed me in that manner."

"Asiram, you're embarrassing me."

Asiram grabbed her and said, "You and Ava are so important to me and Zanthius. You guys are important to everyone here. Your footprint is all over the children and I just want to say, I appreciate you, I adore your strength, your resolve, and most of all, and I say this for everyone here, I/we love you immensely."

Ben Beckmire strolled slowly to the center of the room and rescued his wife with a strong hug and a few tears of his own. There was no need for words because the entire dining room was filled with tears of joy and love.

After everything calmed down, Chakes walked to the center of the crowded room and said, "That was an emotional moment for all of us. Asiram, that one moment defined who we are and who we are to each other. Most of you have heard things about the Sarge and the Corporal and ten misfits who are represented here today. Our faith and belief in each other, as well as our resolve to be the best, was what got us through the jungles in the Nam. I will not burden you with the sordid details of that adventure, but I will tell you one thing, Sergeant Beckmire and Corporal Mallory were, and are, our greatest inspirations, after God. I just want to publicly thank them both, from the guys, for getting us through one war and entering us into another." The room broke out into laughter.

Chakes said, "I kind of strayed away from my main reason for coming up here and that is to publicly ask Luana to be my wife, Sister to be my in-law and Beatrice, who by the way, has confirmed in public that I'm her dad, to become my family." He walked over to Luana and got on his knees and asked, "I will be a wonderful husband, friend, and a father to your daughter. Will you marry me?"

"Silly boy, I loved you the first time I met you, after you tried to pick up my grandmother by giving her $100 and a cell phone to contact you. I said, 'this guy is either a nut or a special kind of zany'."

"Which one am I?"

"Which one of what?" Luana asked.

"A special kind of crazy or a zany?"

"My darling, Maurice Chakes, you are both and in balance. She kissed him and asked, "Can we have a wedding with sand under our feet and the water facing us?"

"Absolutely!" He said.

Mallory walked into the center of the room and said, "I have watched my amazing wife move from a peace advocate to carrying a weapon on her hip. Now, that's some crazy stuff. Anyway, I want to make this family aware, that we've decided to adopt a brother and a sister who are a year apart. We're going to make the trip back east in a day or, so to confirm, accept, and begin this new phase of our life. We're going to need everyone's assistance because we don't know anything about raising children other than what we've learned from being around LaGina and the twins." The place cheered them on with screams of joy.

Okema walked to the middle of the floor, and Brown lowered his head. She said, "I have become disfigured because of my husband, Richard Brown, aka, Dick- Head. For nine months, I hated him. Along with Somara, Yeshida, and Mary Alice, we conspired to make them fat and ugly. As you can see, they let us eat the ice cream while they ate a banana. We ordered desserts with extra whipped cream, and they ordered sparkling water. I just want to say, I am one amazingly happy woman who was caught off guard by that brigand and swept comfortably off her feet. This message is from me, Somara, Yeshida, and Mary Alice."

From his seat, the Sarge, said, "You people are simply amazing. Let me say that my wife is remarkable, and everyone in this village is astounding. We are bigger and better because everyone here carries their own baggage. We are protective because everyone here will shoot first and ask your intentions later. We are family because we share a common value and that is to 'help people help themselves'. My wife thinks we need nurses and I fully agree with her. As an example, Mr. Jilkes and Mr. Brown, on her birthday, after she had already delivered two complicated pregnancies, orchestrated an appreciation moment. I also agree we need a consistent educational program for all the kids. We need to find our roots and end this adventure that has kept us together and on the move. I say to my friend Mallory, when you go back east, we go back east. When you receive in your heart the responsibility of parenting, we will be right there for you and Monica. Speaking of Monica, if you want to see something funny, look at how she and Courtney carry their weapons— Gunslingers—a doctor and a lawyer.

"Also, listen, there are only a few dictators left in the world. I'm here because the rest of the guys don't want to step up and take command. If there is something, or somewhere, we should go until we figure out our conclusive scenarios, then speak up. I'm no Donald; I'm no Jung-un, I'm no Jinping, and I'm no Putin. I'm Ben Beckmire, a friend of the people and Courtney's husband. Perhaps we need to develop a travel committee? I mean, Luana wants to marry my friend in St. Thomas, Mallory and Monica must pick up their new children, and those of us who are being swindled by Jilkes and John Lee should certainly go and have a look at what we've purchased.

"People, I need two days to make sure that we can rid ourselves of one of the demons that has marked us ever since my son kissed a woman and became known as the 'idiot spy'. I think in two days, I can get the audience we need to destroy the Carbon Factor in public. Two days, people, then we'll only have a single demon left to destroy—my cousin."

Clyde entered the house and said, "I found five huge bags on my bus. Who do they belong too?"

Mike looked at Larry, who looked at Zanthius, who asked, "You guys just left that money on the bus all this time?"

"Hey, brother, you were a part of that situation as well. Anyway, Clyde, I'll help you bring them in. Listen guys, things began to happen in a hurry. Babies were being born and I frankly didn't think about it. Just so that everyone is on the same page, the reason those mercs surrendered was because we captured their payments, but we forgot to tell the group about it. Don't think we were trying to run a scam like John Lee and Jilkes, because we weren't. We forgot about it. We've had, what four or five babies and security has been somewhat lax. No notion of deception was intended, and I apologize," Larry said.

John Lee asked, "How much are we talking about?"

Zanthius said, "We didn't stop to count it. However, we did go through each sack and attempted to detect explosives and tracking devices in the time we had before being exposed. I also recommend we take those bags to the barn and scan them properly before we celebrate their capture."

The Sarge said, "That reminds me, Jong, have we made any headway with all of that cash?"

"Sarge, we began to travel again, and I did not move beyond the two times that were sanctioned. We still have close to $100 million in the basement. I think we can open another account at the local bank here, plus we could place a large amount of it in safety deposit boxes. We have a trust relationship with Clyde and the people here. They could withdraw from the boxes and enter sums into designated accounts."

"Clyde, is that something we can leave in your hands to work out?"

"Yes sir, Mr. Beckmire. I'll make a call to my first cousin and have him call my three other cousins in neighboring cities and we'll make it secure."

Ms. Viola and Luana were listening to the dialogue and were astonished by the numbers that were being thrown around. Ms. Viola raised her hand as Luana tried to pull it down. She said, "Mr. Beckmire, we're simple people, and my grandbaby is in love with that scoundrel, Mr. Chakes. Now, I'm hearing some incredible numbers being thrown around, and I must ask a security question. Is this money stolen, and are people going to try to come and claim it?"

"Ms. Viola, I'm going to give you the skinny right now, and the fat of it, later. Those people who surrendered to us were supposed to get paid with that money once they killed us. We ran an operation on a truck carrying explosives and big guns that were designated to be used against us. By capturing their weapons and their money, we put a dent in their operation. See, these people demand a portion of their payment, and once the job is completed, the balance on the spot. They didn't receive their money on time and, therefore, they surrendered to us. Is that enough for now? I'll have

Chakes huddle with you guys and tell you exactly why we're together again and how my own family tried to kill us."

"Mr. Sergeant Sir, I'm okay with what you just said, I just need to hear you tell me that the law ain't going to be coming for me on some conspiracy charges or something."

"I hope that doesn't happen, but I think we have enough of their money to find you a wonderful lawyer," the Sarge acknowledged.

"I'll wait until that scoundrel of a man comes and tells an old lady what he done got her grandbaby, great grandbaby and her into."

Everyone laughed and Chakes whispered to her, "Sister, I be the best scoundrel your babies can find. I have a solid family and we have values and rules. You will see, this is one marvelous group of people. You know, we may need a little more religion, but after a while, I'll let you impose your need for a sanctuary."

"You be one smooth talking, cell phone giving, and $100 bill offering, scoundrel, man, but I like you."

"If I had known you had a beautiful granddaughter, like Luana, Sister, I may have given you $200. I'm just kidding around. You and your granddaughter mean the world to me. If you guys need to know what we been doing and how many have been trying to do us, then I will take you on that journey."

The Sarge said, "I must remind you guys, we be no choir boys. We don't steal, but if you bring it to pay those who you've hired to kill us, we take advantage of the largesse and put it to good use. Mike is working on a project to serve our vets who are homeless and jobless. I think we should put Juan and Rashida in the armament business that will hire a boat load of people and find value-oriented projects for the ladies. Asiram, for example, wants to stop so many children from winding up in orphanages. She and Monica have already set a tentative date to get research and practical people in place.

"There are so many good things these funds can provide seed money for. We can get local businessmen, governments, and the public to contribute as well. We have work to finish in the outback which is going to be a significant resource for the people there and for us. We have business interests in Spain, in the Islands, here in Wyoming, in Virginia, in DC, and Maryland. We have money in banks all over the world and in our private accounts, as well as massive insurance policies on each member of the team. We'll soon have to take one out on you guys. We're trying to build a dynasty of do-gooders who will 'help people help themselves', like Darryl, Sue Lyn, Mike, Carla, Rashida, Juan, and so on. Have you noticed that no girls have been born into this group of recent? Don't answer that because it's obvious. The next birthing campaign that will happen with this group will be all girls, and guess who their eventual leaders will be? Well, let me clue you people in, it will be our own Beatrice and LaGina. I saw this and other things while in the outback. Mark my word!"

The Sarge banged on the side of his glass and after regaining everyone's attention he said, "We need to organize, and I think this is a great time to do it. Do you people realize you follow me around the globe like robots? You're in Australia one week, the next in the islands, the next in DC, MD, VA. Then you're off to LA, Wyoming, and wherever else I feel we need to be. I know we've talked about this before, but it is time to make it happen. In terms of security issues, my travel destinations come first. After that, you people need to develop committees and establish a travel group. We need a finance group to assist Jong. We, for sure, need a health group to assist Courtney. We need a security group once we're in place in whatever city we might find ourselves. We need people to take the burden of planning and executing off the shoulders of Jong and Mallory. For the next two days, I'm calling some old war buddies to get me audiences with people who, seemingly, are not crooks. I want to conclude the myths of the Carbon Factor and move on towards reconciling the venom I have for my cousin."

Ava stood up and said, "Courtney, I mean no disrespect, but he has got to get his shit together. Ben Beckmire, you run an efficient institution and everyone in here will agree with that. I mean you don't order the food or bandages, but you move us and secure us from place to place. We don't want no damn body else in that position. If there is anyone here who wants to replace Ben Beckmire at the helm of this ship, then stand the hell up."

No one stood up, and the room became silent as Ava began to waltz into her next scenario. She said, "Of course everyone has talents, but no one can put this show on the road like you can. It's precise, methodical, and directional. We know when, how, and where at all times. We never wake up with the notion we're lost and running from the wrong monster. I, for one, acknowledge your request for committees, but I do not want to see anyone other than you, Ben Beckmire, at the helm of this ship."

Courtney stood up and said, "I'm sure that all of you people know who that woman is. Sometimes in introductions, we just focus on the name. The lady you just heard from is Ava De Lombardo. She is the biological mother of Zanthius Beckmire De Lombardo, who is the son of Ben Beckmire. Listen, don't humor me, the world is a fantastic place, it connects people from all kinds of places, and puts them into a little basket. Yes, she once loved Ben Beckmire, but Courtney

Beckmire is his wife and friend. I don't discount anyone's capabilities, but I do know that Ben Beckmire would walk through hell, tell the devil to piss off, and then tell us we were about to get our butts kicked--I stand with Ava. We need consistency in our leadership. Ben Beckmire gets us to and from each axis of the earth, and on time."

Ben Beckmire looked at Courtney and said, "Honey, I want to do this so that we can spend more time together. Our time is always interrupted by emergencies or assaults. I need more time with the woman I love."

Asiram said, "Ah, that's so sweet. I guess we have been a bit selfish in terms of using your time. I recommend Zanthius, but he has no tactical experience. Now Larry, on the other hand, knows how you think and is a good tactician, but lacks environmental experience. How about in calmer places and times, you use Larry and Zanthius to act in your stead? That way, a lot of the burden would be taken off your team and placed on the younger members of the group. If you think about it, your people are involved in every act to support and protect us. You have some young wives and some older husbands. In a place like St. Thomas or Valencia, you guys could take a lesser role and let these guys mature into their roles. At some point in time, we will begin that transition process for when some of us won't be around anymore. We need transitional leadership, and I recommend that you begin turning things over to your two sons, with particular members of your team, to provide mentorship."

A normally quiet Okema said, "I am in favor of what Asiram has portrayed. I am also in favor of the women in this group taking a more active leadership and administrative role. As an example, Somara and Yeshida are strong in economics and business. They could assist Mr. Jong with the problem of transitioning the currency we have into more tangible securities and investments. We never said anything before because we come from a culture where the women are smart but must act dumb. Those are my recommendations."

An even quieter Yeshida rose, bowed, and asked, "May I speak?"

Asiram said, "Yeshida, in America, you don't have to ask anyone if you can speak. You're a part of this group just like I am, Courtney, Yvette and so on."

Yeshida thanked Asiram and said, "I just want to say that Okema neglected to mention that she has a degree in international banking as well as a law degree. If Mr. Jong would be receptive to meeting with us, I think we can settle the issue of cash on hand and make the money work for us rather than sitting in a vault in a basement doing nothing and earning nothing. My only problem is, I would not trust an all-Asian group to handle my money. Just saying! I think this is the correct slang." The group broke into thunderous laughter.

Larry said to Yeshida, "It seems to me you're talking about more than one function. We need an international banker to handle the transactions and accounts that have been haphazardly set up. We need smart people to launder our cash. So, I think if Okema and Marisa would work together on the banking issues, we won't have an all-Asian gang in our midst. In addition, we need some people to handle our investments and develop a strategy as well. We have a lot of money here and there. And people, when I say 'we', I mean everyone in this room is vested in our business model, albeit undefined. Sarge, is that correct?"

"You're absolutely correct, Son, and let me say, this is exactly the kind of dialogue I was hoping for when I was speaking about assistance to diversify our leadership and develop committees. Continue on, Larry."

Larry said, "Zanthius, do you have any input?"

Zanthius said, "As a matter of fact, I do, my brother. Listen, here is the preamble. Pops, you, and your gang do things a little differently than I might do. I'm not saying that's bad, but you guys are the final cut from that cookie cutter. You people are brilliant, cunning, aware of things I would never consider, and you keep us alive. I say all of that to say, I would like John Lee and Jilkes to work with Juan, Rashida, and Mike. Now, Rashida, has that electronic stuff down. She needs the benefit of the environmental aspect of what she does, and that will make her, Juan, and Mike superb. I don't know if you guys know this or not, but Ms. Carla wasn't always the best damn pilot that we've known. No, my friends, she was once in the Marine Corps. She was a hand-to-hand combat instructor. Anyway, she could assist us in developing those skills as well as using that instruction to find ways to reach our center, our core, and our essence. I kind of got carried away, and just so that everyone knows what's going on, we've done due diligence on everyone in this group except the original members. All new members, except those who come from the 'spy world' will undergo background checks. The leadership agreed to this some time ago when they uncovered information about one of our groups."

Larry asked, "Brother, why the separation of those from the 'spy world'?"

Zanthius said, "Larry, that world is full of deceit, misdirection, lies, conniving, cajoling, and a whole bunch of other shit. In other words, if we found a file on Asiram, would you believe it knowing she was a huge spy?"

"Understood and thanks for the education," Larry said.

Asiram said, "Zanthius, we need to talk. I'm your wife and the mother of your two babies. You did a background check on me? I hope you have a stall in the barn to sleep in. Speaking of space, it is time we had a real conversation about this ranch. I love this place and the people in this community. I also know we're away from the lights that so many of you are accustomed to. What is driving this communication is the fact that in the guest house, the space is not adequate for our growing family. Now, I need to honestly know, is this ranch in our future?"

Rashida stood up and said, "Asiram, are you serious? Dad, did I miss the email? Larry, you said, 'you would never deceive me'. Why is this a question?"

"We're trying to come to the end of our traveling road show, and I'm just trying to figure out if it makes sense to expand the guest house or leave it as it is." Asiram stated.

"Ah, Dah! I'll have to admit, I prefer the outback, but I, personally, love this place. When we're not being hunted, it provides the best sanctuary for urban children to witness both sides of living. LaGina prefers the ranch over St. Thomas. Now, how sick is that? I hope we expand the guest house, or you can do what John Lee and Jilkes did, swindle us out of money on a land buying scheme."

The Sarge stood up and said, "You see why it's hard for me and my wife to have a good night? You people have raised some awesome issues."

John Lee stood up and said, "She's a doctor, you shouldn't have any problem getting any of the Cialis or Viagra stuff that'll make you sleep late." The place broke into stitches.

Jilkes pulled John Lee close and explained what the Sarge was referring to. He said, "Oh, sorry, Sarge, and Mrs. Sarge.

I was thinking you be having a different kind of sleeping issue. My bad!"

Larry said, "Pops, when you do this, it's never this rambunctious."

"Son, when I do this, people are in the fields preparing to shoot at us."

Larry smiled at him and said, "Please don't let me overreach my abilities."

"I have your back, son." Larry looked at Zanthius who caught his drift and took the lead.

Zanthius said, "My brother has led us to another dimension of management and administration. We all should think about where he has taken us and decide on the needs of the group. The greatest thing about this group is that I have never heard the words 'I or me'. My dad, our leader, and his gritty friends will always run this outfit. What we must do is not burn them out with responsibilities that we can assume and execute to their standards. I would like to end this conversation for now and allow each of you and your loved ones to have an in-depth discussion to figure out what other issues we need to consider."

Yvette said, "I don't have any technical training, but I'm willing to learn and help in any way that I'm needed."

Bernstein stood up, kissed his wife, and said, "I'm so proud of you for stepping up like that. You're my amazing lover, wife, mother of our child, and girlfriend."

The Sarge said, "I'd like to see my guys for a minute with the new leadership team."

# # #

John Lee started the conversation by saying, "So, Sarge, are you telling me that I have to listen to the new-age bullshit from Larry and Zanthius? You know they couldn't carry our weapons back in the Nam."

Jilkes said, "I like the plan. I have a new baby boy, and I want to spend all my days with him."

John Lee said, "I'm just busting their new asses. You know I don't give a shit because the Sarge knows what he be doing."

Mallory said, "Come to order." Everyone froze and ended their petty concerns.

The Sarge said, "I didn't sanction a damn thing other than the fact that I need to spend more time with my wife. They came up with some great ideas and with solutions. This is what I want to know--do you people have a serious concern about putting our trust in other people? Our survival has been a function of our protecting each other's back. I mean, individually you guys are set for life, financially, right? No man in this room should have less than $90 million in their coffers. John Lee and Jilkes each should have at least $180 after swindling their brothers on a land deal."

John Lee was about to respond when Jilkes said, "John Lee, shut the hell up. Sarge, he and I are on board with this divestiture. As a matter of fact, we support it wholeheartedly. It makes all the sense in the world. Brown and Bernstein, where's your head on this one?"

Bernstein looked at Brown who said, "I speak for the both of us and we agree with it and like the notion." He then looked at Chakes and Montomie and asked, "Where are you guys on this one?"

Montomie said, "Well, Chakes is in love, and, therefore, would sign off on anything. We are not giving up anything; we're just assigning responsibilities to new people. I don't have a problem with that and I'm sure Chakes won't have an issue either."

The Sarge looked at Gladstone and McArthur and asked, "What are your thoughts?"

Gladstone said, "I don't have any issues. What about you McArthur?"

"I'm like you. It's all good."

"Mr. Amazing and Whitmore, you have any reaction to where we might want to go with this thing?"

Whitmore said, "I'm happy with the way things are, but I also realize, Sarge, you're in on every decision and at any hour of the day. Not fair to you and Courtney, so I am in accord with this relationship on a trial basis."

Jong asked, "Why am I always last?"

Mallory said, "Stay on point, please."

"I don't have a problem. I like the idea of more brains involved. Leads to better decision making. I support it on a trial basis as well. However, we're only selectively assigning certain responsibilities to those people, right?"

The Sarge said, "Absolutely! We're not crazy or senile-- yet.

## CHAPTER FIFTEEN

The group made their way into DC where Mallory and Monica met and signed the papers for two adorable children, who were natural brother and sister, thus making them members of their immediate family and the group's extended family. The boy's name was Elton, and he appeared to be a jolly kind of child; his sister, Margo, was much more reserved and calculating. They spent two days on the farm in Virginia under the protective eyes of LaGina and her new running mate, Beatrice. The girls explained to Elton and Margo that they lived in several places and traveled all the time. Beatrice asked Margo, "Do you like flying?"

Margo said, "Only birds and airplanes can fly."

Beatrice asked, "Have you ever been on an airplane?"

Margo looked to the sky and said, "Only rich people fly in planes."

Beatrice then asked, "Do you like me?"

Margo said, "I don't know you, so how can I like you?"

Beatrice said, "Okay, catch you guys later."

She proceeded to walk away when LaGina said, "That's not fair. She was only trying to be nice to you because you're new. I think you need to apologize to her."

Margo asked, "Do you want to fight?"

LaGina said, "We're supposed to be a family. We don't fight each other. Goodbye!"

After watching the dynamics of the discussion from afar, the Sarge walked over to the brother and sister, and introduced himself. He said, "LaGina is one of his grandbabies. Was she nice to you guys?"

Margo said, "She asked too many questions."

The Sarge looked at the child and saw that there was trauma in her eyes. He said, "Do you mind telling me what she said to you?"

Margo said to the Sarge, "We're not supposed to talk to strangers. Come on, Elton, let's go and look at the horses."

As the children walked away, the Sarge thought that the entire group was going to have to break down the barriers that were built around these two kids. When he saw Mallory, he could tell that he too had a conversation with little Ms. Margo. The Sarge asked, "So, Mallory, how are you getting along with the little girl?"

"Sarge, she's an absolute spit-fire. She doesn't trust me and is extremely protective of her brother. We can't figure out what happened from the time we first met them until they came here."

The Sarge inquired, "How are they responding to Monica?"

"With suspicion and reservation. I mean little Margo watches everything we do. It should be interesting when we try to put them to bed tonight, something's not right."

The Sarge watched the children for a moment and out of the blue he said, "Why don't you let Larry have a go at them? He has an amazing sense of figuring out things with people. Let him just take them for a ride in the mule, or something, and see how they react?"

# # #

An hour later, Larry saw the two children in conversation with Monica and he said, "Hi Monica, so these are our new family members? He turned to the children and said, "Guys, my name is Larry, and the twins are mine. What are your names?"

The little boy said, "My name is Elton."

Margo rushed in to admonish him. She said to Larry, "We're not supposed to talk to strangers."

"Well, I don't know your name, so I'll just talk to Elton. Elton, will you tell your sister that everyone here is a family member and not strangers. Also, Elton, have you ever had a ride in a mechanize mule?"

"What's a mechanized mule?"

"I'll be right back." Larry walked to the barn and backed one of the mules out and drove it to the front of the house. He said, "Hey, Elton, let me give you a ride in the mechanized mule." The little boy jumped up and ran towards the mule. He stopped on a dime when his sister screamed, "He's a stranger. You don't know him."

Larry looked at Elton and calmly stated, "Here, we are family, but you have to be with us a while to understand that. No one here will ever hurt you. Everyone here will love and protect you."

Elton announced, "My sister acts like a mother."

# # #

Later that afternoon at lunch, Larry and Marisa paid attention to how Margo and Elton ate. They wrapped their arms around their plates to prevent anyone from attempting to take food from them. Larry walked over to Elton and said, "Your cookies look really good. May I have one?"

Elton, literally, growled at Larry. Larry responded, "Did you know that you can have anything in this place that you see? Look around and see if there's anything you like or want?"

Elton looked at him and said, "I want to have food in my room at night."

Larry looked at him and asked, "Is that all you want, silly boy, food? You don't want your own private Xbox or a drone to play with in the yard?"

Larry looked at Margo and said, "I need you to trust your new parents, me, and the rest of our family. If you don't, you're going to live in fear for the balance of your life. I need you to trust me. How about the three of us go and sit in the middle of those beautiful horses."

As the trio approached the fence, Larry said, "If you don't trust me or yourself, then the horses will sense it and try to hurt us. Margo, I need you to trust me, a stranger, and I need you to do the same thing, Elton. These are not the horses you ride. These horses are wild. I have a pocket full of treats so we should be alright."

Everyone watched the interaction as the group made their way into the corral. Two horses approached violently but backed off and walked away. Larry said, "Elton, I need you to place two treats by that little white rock and, Margo, I need you to place, ah, three treats by that little red flower. This is all about trust, so I need you to pay attention, or someone might get hurt. I'm going to place four treats behind me, and we're going to meet in the center."

Larry moved about randomly and erratically, thus keeping the horses at bay. He said, "Margo, I need you to trust me and tell me what happened to you at the orphanage? Do not try to protect anyone at that place. The horses will sense you are not telling the truth and may hurt you. He looked intently at the frighten girl before asking, "What happens to children at that place?"

"I can't tell you because they will send people out to take us back to that place and put us in the basement with the rats," Margo replied.

Larry said, "No one can come here for you. Monica, Mallory, and the rest of us will not let that happen."

"You don't even know us," Margo interjected.

"Margo, my family members adopted you as brother and sister. No one can, or will, come near this place to take you back."

She looked at Larry and said, "That's what all adults are supposed to say to children."

Larry said, "I promise you on my life that I will never let anyone come here to take you away. Your new mother and father will not let that happen as well. I need you to trust me and the horses. They're coming up behind me and they're soon going to come up behind you, so you must tell the truth."

Suddenly, Elton screamed, "They beat us and wouldn't feed us for days."

Larry was engulfed in pain as well as the entire group. Rashida recorded the conversations and broadcasted it throughout the farm. There was not a dry eye amongst the group.

Mallory and Monica walked out with Asiram to where the three were sitting and held their children. Monica said, "We will not let this happen to another child in the world. We have to make this known and we must go after people who harm children."

Little Ms. Margo cried for over an hour. The Sarge said, "In the morning, we're going to expose that place after we extract, from that bitch, who the perpetrators, or her benefactors are and why they didn't feed the children and beat them."

Monica grabbed the hands of the still crying Margo and her shaking brother and led them to Courtney. As she introduced the children to Courtney, she said, "This is Doctor Beckmire. She is going to examine you and give you something to help you sleep. Children, I promise that my husband and I, will earn the title of mother and father from you through our actions. We will never hurt you. Dr. Beckmire will have to touch you, but she will look into your ears, mouth, and throat to make sure you don't need any other doctors. Your new mother and father will stay with you the entire time. We're also going to take a little blood from you to have it analyzed to make sure you don't need any treatments for issues related to your blood. I need you to trust me and every adult in this group. We are the good guys. Can you guys swim?"

Margo said, "Only in the bathtub."

Margo said, "I'm confused. I was not nice to LaGina, or Beatrice, or anybody else. We were trying to protect each other. I don't like adults--they never tell the truth."

"Monica replied, "They're children like you and they're protected like you will be. If you were mean to them, they will soon forget it. Evil only lasts with the old, the young have the ability to forget and so shall they. I just need one amazing thing from you two and that is for you to trust me and my husband. If you do, we will be the best mother and father combination you could wish for. We prayed over you, and we studied you, we initially only wanted a single child. We saw you Margo, and decided it was you we wanted. We then found out you had a brother and knew we wanted both of you. We hope we, and our family, can earn your trust. We can't change what happened in the past, but we'll try to limit the pain other children might experience. Just give us a chance and we'll give you a chance. Is that fair enough?"

Margo hugged Monica and said, "I'm afraid, because it always turns into the same thing."

Looking into the child's eyes, Monica replied, "I want you to try to trust me and believe that no one will ever hurt you again. I promise you that. I also promise you that your friends back at the orphanage will never have to experience that sort of thing again and those who did those things will be punished. Your new father will make sure they never hurt another child. Isn't that right, honey?"

Hiding his anger, he said, "I will take care of it tomorrow. Put these guys to sleep because tomorrow or the next day, we're going south to see what's happening to our new home."

At 0700 hours, Jilkes, John Lee, Mallory, Larry, Mike, and Whitmore left the compound. At 0755 hours, they arrived at the orphanage. At 0800 hours, Jilkes jimmied the front door open, and the group entered the building. As they ascended the steps, they heard the sound of showers running. John Lee followed the sound and found a man who appeared to be in his late 50s, in a compromising position, looking at a monitor. That is where he would be discovered by law enforcement!

Jilkes and Mallory found the live-in administrator's room, found her in bed with one of her workers, and an old man. He told the woman to leave the room, he placed two rounds into the administrator, as Mallory placed two rounds into her benefactor.

Larry found the central monitoring/recording system and disabled it. He extracted the storage disk that captured incoming traffic. He did a search of the content and found the place had a serious side business. He placed the information into a continuous loop, and it showed repeatedly.

At 1000 hours, the State Police were called to the scene. At 1100 hours, the press ascended on the place and found a well-played out scenario and a documentary detailing random encounters.

As they headed back to the farm, Whitmore said, "I wish we could have taken those children with us."

Larry responded, "That's called child abduction and comes with a serious charge and your picture on a national watch list. We did the right thing by leaving them. The State Police are probably there. It would be difficult to explain a few battered and dead bodies. Let them sort that shit out. And besides, I assure you they're going to come and interview us just because we were the last ones to adopt from there. They'll be at the ranch in the next 48 hours or so."

#

Larry was completely wrong. At 1700 hours, two unmarked cars entered the road to the farm. Rashida hit the alarm, and everyone knew what their roles were. Zanthius and Asiram waited in front of the farm for the uninvited guests. As the first car came to an abrupt stop, spewing rocks everywhere, two men dressed in suits exited the car. Zanthius said, "Sir, you need to learn to drive or at least respect our property." Three officers dressed in uniforms exited the second vehicle and approached them. The driver of the first car looked away and spat.

Ben Beckmire saw that and stormed out of the house. He said, "I don't know what you want, but you need to get off this property before this thing goes south."

"I'll be damned! a voice exclaimed. "Sergeant Ben Beckmire? Is that you?"

The Sarge looked at him and proclaimed, "I know you! You flew Huey's in the Nam. I'll be damned, Son, you look good."

"How are those other crazy guys that used to be in your unit? You ever hear from them?"

"Every single day. They're all here on this ranch, and as a matter of fact, we're flying out of here to Alabama later."

Mallory came out of the door with a Coors's Light in his hand and pronounced, "Damn, Wilbur Jenkins. Boys, this is the guy who used to fly us into those one-way missions and then would have to pick our asses up. What's going on and why are you here? Did we do something wrong?"

"Well, I don't remember your name, but I need to speak with Mr. Mallory and Mrs. Mallory."

Mallory approached, "I am Mr. Mallory, and Mrs. Mallory will be here shortly. What is this about?"

"We got a call earlier today that there was trouble at an orphanage, the same one where you adopted two children," a detective indicated.

Wilbur walked past the detective and said, "You need to leave that one alone. These guys have killed more damn people than you know and the one you're messing with will turn you into a sissy. Swallow that pride, and let it go, or you're on your own."

After an hour-plus interview with Monica and Mallory, Wilbur asked, "If we need to seek further clarification, is this a good place to reach you?"

"It is, but you should call first. We've had some trouble with out-of-town people trying to hunt on our land and we have a lot of kids here. Take my cell phone number. May I speak with you alone for a minute?"

The two men walked into the field and Mallory said, "As I stated, we're going south at some point in time. We have a large foundation, and my wife is interested in taking over that place. Can you find me a person who is not on the take so that we can figure out how to improve that place, put it under our management, and select our people to operate it? As a matter of fact, how much longer do you plan on being a peace officer?"

"I filed my papers two weeks ago, and I'm out of this business at the end of the month."

"We don't know that many vets, but would running a place like that and hiring people who are not freaks, interest you?"

"I've never run a business before."

"Do you have children?"

"I have five and I don't know how I'm going to put them all through school."

Mallory smiled and stated, "Get me a resume. In the meantime, I'll talk to the Sarge and fill him in about what we spoke about. We're also putting together a program to help our homeless vets. I have seen your work, and if you can fly one of those fricken helicopters with rockets and bullets blazing and hitting everywhere, then you can help us alleviate some of the problems our vets are having, or if you prefer, run this orphanage. We're going to expand it if we can acquire the rights to it. You do all that homework for us, and, at the end of the month, we'll settle. If you work for us, you won't have to worry about affording college tuitions. Call me if you have any additional questions about that situation. I know the state is going to have to close it down based upon what my little girl and her brother told me. I guess someone got to them before we had a chance to."

As the officers and detectives entered their cars, the cocky arrogant detective spat in the grass again. The Sarge announced, "The next time you do that on this property, you'll need to make an appointment with a periodontist."

#

An hour or so later, back at their barracks, the detective said, "I should have busted him up."

Jenkins laughed and loudly announced, "Without guns and sticks, all five of us couldn't have handled him. He ran out of bullets, entered the enemies camp, and killed eight men with his bare hands. That group probably has a body count in excess of a couple thousand. The Cong placed a $5-million-dollar bounty on each of their heads. Not the kind of people you want to fight. In other words, he would have whupped your ass bad. Anyone of them could have taken us, including the Asian guy with the limp. It was good to see them, but they bring back bad nightmares."

#

Back at the ranch, Ms. Viola saw Monica and said, "I'll be more than happy to help you with the children. I love children, and they usually love me, I'm just saying. I'll be glad to help, and I think I can calm them and help them adjust, your choice."

"Ms. Viola, why did you say it like that? As if they're a problem or something?"

"Mrs. Mallory, I only say what I know. You can look at those kids and tell that they have been traumatized. I know how to calm children through other children. We no plan a date or something, but perhaps when they're on the plane, I can just drop by with you and tell all the children a wonderful calming story. I'm here to help. I'm not offering pity; I'm offering hope and love, and those two children have a lot of it, but its caged inside of them. Let me help you unlock that love. Oh, you might want to tell Dr. Courtney to bring a mild sedative on the plane for them."

Monica took in a deep breath of air and sighed. She then said, "Ms. Viola, may I have a hug? I need a hug from you."

The two women embraced, and Monica whispered, "Are my eyes bigger than my stomach?"

"No, child, this be the best thing for you and that scoundrel of yours. These two will bring you many days of excitement, disappointment, achievement, and love. I see it in their eyes."

As the two women unembraced, Courtney turned the corner and said, "Ah, so you're cheating on me?"

Monica said, "Ms. Viola has offered to help me with the children and try to put them at ease. She also suggested that you bring a mild sedative for the flight. Speaking of the flight, when are we leaving?"

Courtney stated, "Carla is right over there. Let's ask her."

As the two women approached her, Courtney said, "Why so glum?"

"I came on my damn period the other day."

"Oh, my! You're trying to get pregnant?"

"I could say something smart, but I won't," Carla announced.

"Carla, I told you to use those birth control pills to prevent you from becoming pregnant for at least six months. I told you this because of your damaged tissue. Let me break it down to you. You are injured beyond recognition, and you need to heal before you try to conceive. Listen, I've only been a damn doctor for x-number of years. You're our pilot and, as you said to me, the manual says, that those straight up in the air take-offs are recommended. I asked you about that stunt and you answered me. You asked me about what was going on down below and I answered you. If you don't follow my instructions, then you will never have that take-off that you're looking for. Find a time and come to me so that I can examine you. Or wait until we get to Alabama, and I'll accompany you to the hospital where they have all the right equipment. If you don't follow my prognosis, you will pay forever. I know my business, like you know yours. You're the best damn pilot we have ever known, and I can assure you that I'm the best damn doctor you had better learn to trust, or your ultimate dream will be just that. Ask my girlfriend here. You see how she had to accomplish her love of children. Anyways, are we leaving tomorrow or what?"

"Doc, I don't make the schedule. They tell me, and I make sure the planes are ready, and off we go. We discussed that in the meeting, and this is a prime example of what I mean. Also, I have two other planes floating around, and that's not good for the plane or the pilots. We have two people with families, and we should consider their needs and time as well. Mr. Beckmire invited Clyde and the others down to the resort, but no one said when. We have the planes and, therefore, it shouldn't be a problem."

Carla turned away and said, "You're absolutely correct. I need to follow the protocols we set forth and then hope to achieve my goal. Also, I want to thank you and the entire group for the donation to our family."

Courtney said, "Mike is a true warrior and you're a great pilot. We take care of our own and I/we, consider you and Mike a part of our family."

## CHAPTER SIXTEEN

Courtney said to Monica, speaking about Ms. Viola, "She must be one of those good witches. She has created an incredible calm in the children. Your two new ones were apprehensive to fly because they didn't understand how you could have an airplane. She told them a story, and the next thing you know, they're all asleep, including Ms. Viola. You're going to have to tell your children about your plane and all the other things you have at your disposal. Let's take all of the children shopping once we land in Alabama."

"That's a smart idea, Courtney. A little bribery never hurt, right?"

As the plane approached the airport in the middle of Alabama, Zanthius said, "Honey, I'm so happy I was able to buy this one. You have houses all over the place."

"Yeah, that's exactly what they are. They're houses, except there on the farm and in the Midwest. Those are homes because we're surrounded by our people and our family."

Zanthius asked, "Are you okay?"

"I'm not sure. Ever since those police came to the farm, I've felt uneasy. The quiet one in the suit, alarmed me. I don't know from where, but he looked so familiar to me, and when he saw me, he looked away. Honey, ask your father and Mallory to come up here for a second."

#

Mallory walked up first and asked, "What's going on?"

Zanthius said, "Asiram thinks she recognized the driver of the vehicle but can't seem to place him."

The Sarge showed up and said, "What's up? We're on approach."

"Daddy-in-Law, I think the detective who said nothing and drove the vehicle, I think I've met him before. He looked away from me and never returned his eyes to mine. I think, we're being played. If I'm not mistaken, that's one of the sons-a-bitches that tried to shoot Zanthius and Helga in St. Moritz. He worked for your cousin, and they know exactly where we're heading. I don't like this, and I think we need to change course."

The Sarge yelled, "John Lee, I need you up here."

When he arrived, he asked, "What's up Sarge?"

"I need you to call your people on the ground and see if they've seen a lot of foreigners mulling around?"

"I'll call our hotline, and if they don't answer, that means some pig shit is being stirred up."

The Sarge said, "Why is everything with you about pigs? Don't answer that question."

As the phone continued to ring, John Lee said, "I have to try the other number and that will tell me if there be trouble awaiting us." He dialed another number, and it too wasn't answered. He said, "I think we should park this thing somewhere else because that second number was a paid number, and unless that person be dead, it should've been answered."

The Sarge, knocked on the cockpit door and when it was opened, he said, "Dead reckon to St. Thomas--there is a problem in Alabama."

Carla called the tower and told them they had an emergency on board and that they were going to land at another airport. She then asked for clearance and monitoring to the specific coordinates that she gave them. In the next few minutes, the plane began to slowly climb to 25,000 feet and entered a flight path to the Islands.

John Lee received a text message that read, "All ain't safe in paradise." He immediately showed it to the Sarge who walked up to Asiram and said, "Baby Girl, you just saved us from some trouble. John Lee got a message indicating that paradise was not safe. That person you recognized at the farm is obviously the same person you thought worked for my cousin."

Carla came out of the cockpit and said, "We have a problem. We have papers for everyone on this plane except for Elton and Margo Mallory. I need people to make the necessary calls, or they're going to hold those kids up in Customs and that is not what they need. All trust will be forgotten."

Mallory said, "Call Mr. Carter and tell him our situation and see if he can assist."

John Lee said, "Call that jewelry man and see if he can help."

Ms. Viola said, "That be the wrong strategy. Let me explain to them guys, or girls about what's going on. They will not create a problem for you. Deception will get us into more trouble."

# # #

Two hours later, Carla's picture and voice were amplified on every screen in the cabin. She said, "People, this is some new software that was installed on our other planes by a Mr. Darryl and Ms. Sue Lyn. As you can see and feel, we have begun our descent into St. Thomas, and Mr. Carter and his crew are on their way. I need you people to buckle up those seat belts and pull them tight around your tummies. We have a cross wind that will make it slightly bumpy, but we'll be okay."

# # #

Once on the ground, the plane taxied to the hangar, and everyone got in line to go through customs. Ms. Viola went first and told the agent, her friend, that Elton and Margo Mallory were adopted just two days ago and all they have are their adoption papers. She then asked, "Is that going to be a problem?"

He looked at her and asked, "Where are Elton and Margo Mallory?" Monica looked at the children, grabbed their hands, and led them to the front of the que. The agent said, "Hi Elton. Hi Margo. Is this lovely lady your new mother?"

Margo said, "My mother told me to never talk to strangers." The entire group broke into laughter. The customs agent didn't think it was funny but recognized the group. He said, "Elton, I need you to tell me who you are with and are you with them because you want to be with them?"

"I'm with her, and him, back there."

"Him, who, back where?"

"I'm Corporal Mallory's boy."

"Wow, that's great, Son. And Ms. Margo, I guess you're Mrs. Mallory's new little girl?"

Margo hesitated and said, "Adults always try to confuse children. I'm holding her hand and she loves me. I'm with her."

The agent said, "So, Ms. Viola, am I going to have to find a new job or what?"

"No, man, you just have to find the right forms, sign them, and let us be on our merry way."

"You know I have to follow the rules, but I'm doing this because I wouldn't want my supply of rum punch to be halted. Folks, give me a minute, and I'll get some additional agents out to help you along."

Ms. Viola walked over to Margo and said, "Good job, young lady. Give me five. You acted your part well, and Elton, you did a great job to. Give me five, little-brother."

Monica said, "Ms. Viola, you planned this?"

Ms. Viola stridently stated, "I did not. I told them a story that resembled what just happened before they went to sleep, and I guess they remembered it."

"You, Ms. Lady, are as cunning as a fox. Thanks!"

The people piled into the vans for the ride to the resort. Beatrice said to Margo, "Do you know how to swim?"

"No."

"Have you ever been in a pool?"

"I wouldn't go in a pool if I can't swim."

"Have you ever seen the ocean?"

"I think so. Is that the same ocean that *Sinbad* traveled on?"

Beatrice said, "I'm not sure. I don't remember that one. Did you see *Pirates of the Caribbean*?"

"That's an adult movie. We could never watch anything like that."

As the group entered the access road from the airport, Margo said, "It's really hot here and where is here?"

Beatrice said, "This is my home, St. Thomas, US Virgin Islands."

Meanwhile, Mallory and Elton were talking about going fishing. Elton said, he had seen it once or twice on TV, but wanted to try to catch a fish himself. Michael, Mr. Carter's son, said, "I have the bait, the poles, the boat, and most important, life vests. Let me know when you want to go, and I'll go with you guys if you don't mind. I love fishing. By the way, Elton, my name is Michael."

As the vans turned around the bend and into the sanctuary, Margo's eyes became as big as watermelons. She said, "Oh, my goodness! Look at all that water. It's blue water. Is it warm or is it cold like at the orphanage?"

Monica said, "I'll let you determine that for yourself as soon as we pull up to the resort."

"Are we going to be staying here or do we have to move somewhere else?"

"Honey, you can stay here as long as you like. Mommy and Daddy are part owners of this property along with the other members of our family. Mr. Carter is our main partner and Michael is his son."

"Can I play in the water?"

"Well, since you haven't learned how to swim, you can only play near the shore with a vest securely on. Although that water looks nice and friendly, it can be dangerous. I'll have the life-guard at the pool give you and Elton water safety instructions and I'll schedule swimming lessons for you in the morning."

"Will you be with us at all times?"

"Mr. Mallory or I will be with you guys. Listen, we're a family and we travel a lot and sometimes bad people try to take things from us, but we're always together. All the people you've met and will meet, will be people who are our friends, or business partners and can be trusted. We all must become accustomed to each other. We're your guardians, family, and anything you may want that is realistic, we will attempt to obtain it for you. Did you guys go to school each day?"

Elton said, "Not every day, but most days. They made us do a lot of work when people were not there to visit."

"How did they discipline you if you did something they didn't like?"

Margo's head dropped, and she whispered, "Beat us with a belt."

Monica said, "I promise you Mr. Mallory nor I will never hit you. We will ask that you obey our wishes, but we will never strike you."

Margo said, "That's what all adults say until you cross them."

"Margo, do you realize that Mr. Mallory and I are going to be with you until it's time for you to go off to college? During all of that time, you will understand that what I say is true. We don't believe in corporal punishment. None of the parents here believe in striking children. Our best weapon for unruly children is to talk to them and show them love, patience, and understanding."

"If that's true, why is he called Corporal Mallory? Is it because he's the one who does the beatings?" Margo asked.

"Oh, for heaven's sakes, no child. That was his rank in the Army."

Margo said, "Are you sure and do you promise?"

"My dear Margo, there are a lot of things you will have to learn about us, but I can promise you, being beat by us will not be one of them. We chose you and your brother to offer you our love and our home. We want you to develop into wonderful human beings and help people whenever you can. You won't have to pay us back for anything. All we want is for you guys to be a part of our family and to love us like we're going to love you. There is nothing you can do that will make us want to give you or your brother back to that orphanage. This is about us seeing two children who we know we can love, and they can love us in return."

Little Ms. Margo was kicking out tears by the buckets. She hugged Monica tightly and said, "We won't be bad, I promise you."

"And I promise, we'll love you and Elton with all our hearts. All we want is your love in return, and the four of us, plus the rest of this wonderful family will have a great life together--just trust us. Now, let's go and play in that water."

Elton and Mallory made their way to the water's edge and Elton asked, "Is it safe?"

"It's safe where we are, but the farther you go out into it, the deeper it becomes and that's when it's dangerous. I will take you into it, but I need you to hang on to me, okay?"

They ventured into the sky-blue water until it was around Mallory's waist. He asked, "It feels good, doesn't it?"

Elton said, "I like it, and when can you teach me to swim?"

"How about we schedule you and your sister for lessons in the morning?" As the two headed back to the shore, Elton saw a jet ski go powering by and excitingly asked, "What is that thing?"

Mallory said, "It's a jet ski. Perhaps tomorrow we'll take you for a ride on one."

# # #

At lunch time, the twins, LaGina, and Beatrice sat at their table and waited for Elton and Margo. Beatrice said, "They're pretty slow."

LaGina said, "I think they're still a little afraid of all these people. Maybe we should order and let them eat alone until they feel better about us. I don't know about you guys, but I'm hungry."

Mallory, Monica, Elton, and Margo sat at a table, and Margo and Elton were officially welcomed by Mr. Carter. He said, "My house is your house, so enjoy it."

Margo asked, "What did he mean by that?"

Mallory said, "He was extending you an invitation to enjoy his house like it was your house."

"I thought this was our house and their house and everybody's house."

"Margo, it's a saying like have a nice day, enjoy the sunshine, don't stay in the sun too long, eat your vegetables, or sleep tight and don't let the bed bugs bite."

"Why would anyone let the beg bugs bite unless they were put in the dungeon for being bad?" Margo asked.

"Margo, we don't have any dungeons here and we don't have bed bugs, but it's a saying that people say to each other. It's a friendly thing."

Elton asked, "Will we be able to eat with the other children?"

"Anytime you want to, Son."

"Can I go over now and talk to them?"

"Of course, you can. Do you want to go over with him, Margo?"

"I think I want to stay here close to you guys. I'm still scared."

Monica looked at Mallory and he said, "Margo, please tell me what you're afraid of?"

"I'm afraid of all these strangers."

"Honey, none of these people will hurt you. These people are here to protect you and Elton. They are a part of our family and over time, you will understand their roles, our relationships, and our commitments to each other. We are a family like you and Elton are. We're all family here and we don't hurt each other. We may not always agree with each other, but we don't hurt each other. If I, were you, I would go around, introduce myself to each person, get to know them, and that way, you won't be afraid of them? Do you like little babies? There are six new babies that have been added to our family."

"Are those China people in our family as well?"

Monica smiled and said, "Margo, China is a country. The three ladies are Asian, meaning they are from that part of the world where China is. All three of them recently had baby boys."

"Do you think they could show me how to do kung fu?"

"Ah, if they don't know it, you see that gentleman over there holding a baby, he certainly will be happy to show you how to do kung fu. He is one of your father's best friends, as well as all of those guys, sitting around looking at and holding their new babies."

"Okay, I'm going to go from table to table and meet everyone including the children."

Monica hesitated, but then said, "Margo, you do realize that you're a child, right?"

"Of course, I do. I'm just more advanced than the rest of them."

Monica looked at Mallory and whispered, "I think we have to seek help for her, and I'm afraid to ask her what happened to her and why she feels more advanced than the other children." Mallory hugged her and watched the tears stream down her face. Courtney saw the interactions and went over to Monica and Mallory and said, "Don't worry, it will get better."

Monica looked at her and said, "I'm not sure about that. Margo thinks she is more advanced than the other children, and I'm afraid to ask her what she had to do to earn that title."

Courtney looked at her crying and said, "Shit, I have an idea. Ms. Viola is a special person, let me talk to her. It's okay with you guys, I'll let her ask the question in her own inimitable manner.

"Monica, we'll work this thing out. There are enough of us here to address her issues and, if need be, we fly in the professionals. Let's make sure we know what she means when she uses the word advanced. I'm going over to have a little chat with my good witch friend and see what she has to say about it."

# # #

Courtney saw Ms. Viola and asked, "How are you doing? Where is your daughter? I haven't seen them since we landed."

"Doctor, I be doing okay for an old woman. My daughter is out there with that scoundrel talking with Mr. Carter about their impending wedding."

"Ms. Viola, why do you call Chakes a scoundrel?"

"Him a good scoundrel, and I like him a lot for my babies. Him be a good scoundrel."

"I have a problem, or rather Monica and Mallory have a concern with those two little ones we added to the farm about why they were beaten."

"Doctor, I would suggest that no one approaches the child with questions and let her fit in first. One day, I'll do my good witch work on her."

Courtney said, "You know I meant that in the most positive way."

"She be a child who has come from trauma and evil adults. I suggest to the new parents to watch her, make notes of her actions, and reactions. Let her adjust and then we look inside to see if any damage has been done. Tell Ms. Monica to look carefully at her little body, but don't draw attention to any aspect of it, but hold the question for a future date. In a week or two, after she's adjusted a little more through school, play, meetings, dinner, and shopping, you'll tell all the kids that it is time for their physical examination. Then you can slyly cart them off to the hospital and have them checked from head to toe. Right now, I'm hoping she just needs a lot of love, and everything will kick back into reality for her. Think about it-- she came from that wretched place to the farm, to her own plane, to her own resort, to where she can have anything she wants. That there be trauma right there. I'm still in trauma and I'm an old woman who came from the projects, met some good people, went to Australia, to a ranch in the mid-west, then a farm in the south, and now here at their resort. Hell, I'm as traumatized as can be."

"Ms. Viola, you be so crazy—like a fox. I want to be serious for a minute. You made it easy for me, when all those women started dropping babies one after another. I really appreciated your help. I know you have a small thing going with the resort, but I may want to sneak you away from Mr. Carter.

"Let me be frank, your granddaughter is going to marry a wealthy man who loves her dearly and she'll never have to want for anything. You need your own little stash, so I want you as my assistant. I'll open an account for you the next time we go to town which will be tomorrow because no one has any clothes. How does that sound to you?"

"Doctor, I do what I do for free because all you people do is good things for people. I would be obliged if you could carve out something other than rum punch making for me."

"Great, you'll start tomorrow. We have a lot of first-time mothers in this group, and they don't know much about being mothers. I want you to conduct a class with me about the things that should worry them and the things that are a function of developing. Can you do that with me?"

"Doctor, I'm ready to assist and thank you for considering me. Oh, and Courtney, I'm no witch, I just feel things about people and I'm usually correct. The first time I met the scoundrel, I said to myself, 'Him going to marry my baby'."

"He's a wonderful man and heck of a catch. I'll tell Monica what we're planning and suggest to her the other thing that we talked about."

# # #

Mallory's phone rang and it was Jenkins. He told Mallory that the state had closed the place down and removed all the children. He indicated that most likely, the place would be condemned and demolished. Mallory said, "Can I call you back on this number? I need to check with my people and see if this is something our foundation wants to get involved with. Give me thirty minutes, or you call me back. This is important to us."

Mallory called the Sarge, Asiram, Courtney, Monica, Brown, and Bernstein and said, "The state has removed the children from that place and it's going to be boarded. I want to make a statement and have the place razed, and a new place built with that cop running shotgun for us. All I need is four votes on this one."

Asiram inquired, "So, what we're going to do is make the place better and meaningful, not just better looking, right?"

The Sarge asked, "Mallory, you want to answer that question."

"Monica and I want to make a statement and set the standard for operating facilities for children. That is our mission."

Asiram said, "I'm in with you, and I want to be a part of the planning and review of what we do next. If we can get grants from states to operate, we can build them in a hurry and run them with our people that we train. I love this idea, and I'll put my own money in it as well."

"Daughter-in-Law, we just want your approval to move forward. Are the rest of you with us?"

Twenty-nine minutes later, Mallory called Jenkins and said, "Me and my people want you to develop the concept for that site. I know you don't know shit about orphanages, but you know what you don't like about them, especially, after seeing what they did at that one. I want you to consider this mission. I want you to submit your papers effective tomorrow unless the end of the month brings you a substantial benefit in terms of income."

"Mallory, it doesn't do a thing, but you're asking me to do a lot on faith here."

Mallory paused for a moment and then asked, "Jenkins, do you know the driver of the detective car?"

"I do not know the man. He was introduced as Detective Wilson from the Governor's Office."

"Why would the governor be involved in that kind of a situation? Anyway, my friends think he is working for a real crook. Keep your eye on him."

"Mallory, he disappeared into the night. No nothing on him, no forwarding email address, or phone number, I mean nothing on that dude."

"Okay, back to my initial request. We're going to employ you to accomplish the following: I need you to engage lawyers to petition the state to turn the property over to our foundation, so that we can destroy it and build a model for the nation in orphanages. I want you to find an architect, or we'll give you ours and have him develop plans for the site. I want you to employ three shifts of local talent to work around the clock to open a state-of-the-art home for children. We will place you in contact with a member of our foundation who will provide you with bank information and operating funds. Call me in the morning if you want to be a part of 'helping people help themselves'. Oh, I'm sure they will pay you at least $200k to start. Think about it."

Asiram said, "Mallory, you and my daddy-in-law just blindly trust people. You just met him and look what you're doing."

"Asiram, any man that flies into bullets to get people out is deserving of an opportunity to rip us off, but I don't think that's what he's about. We'll see if he can convince the state to let us convert that place into a sanctuary, from the devil's den."

Minutes later, the Sarge looked out on the beach and saw Margo, Elton, LaGina, the twins, and Beatrice imitating Jong. He said, "Well, I'll be damned. Jong is getting involved with the children. Now, that makes me happy. He's teaching them some form of martial arts, now that's great. I think being a father has turned him into a different kind of person--that's great. I need a picture of that. Now, that's another venue for the children and for us old ass adults. That stuff would keep us limber and ready for Freddy if need be."

Asiram said, "We should discuss that at dinner. That's a wonderful sight to see, Jong of all people, helping the young."

Monica ventured to where Jong was holding lessons and asked, "Hey, Jong, can I join in, or is it just for the kids?" He motioned her to join the group.

Mary Alice watched as her husband showed another path to the children who would one day appreciate the knowledge of restraint, control, and attack. Okema asked Mary Alice, "Do you think you're getting too much sun?"

"Naw, I'm here to watch the man I love, and the baby is covered and sound asleep. How's your baby doing?"

"Oh, my God! I don't know what to do and I'm lost just like the other ladies," Okema announced.

Mary Alice looked at Okema and said, "Guess what, I think the Doc and Ms. Viola realize that we're novices and they're going to conduct classes starting tomorrow. Don't spread that rumor, I just heard it, but it hasn't been confirmed."

Okema said, "Yeshida, Yvette, Somara, and probably you, all need some training in this thing called motherhood. Do you know my husband tried to attack the zone last night? I told him he had better drink more and pass out and then come home."

Mary Alice said, "My little *conejo* out there with those children, tries to do it every night. I want to run away. Maybe, we can have the doctor put that in her training package and tell them we just had babies. The box needs a break!"

At dinner, Mr. Carter said, "I wasn't expecting you guys, but as usual, I'm glad you're here. When you turned the corner to the resort, I'm sure you all saw the progress that has been made on the expansion properties. We meet weekly and discuss issues relating to the construction process. We're at the point where we will need your input on the interior decorating. I told them about how the ladies in the group got together, suggested what other women would like when they visited a place, and they agreed. So, we need that wisdom and that special touch the ladies in the group have in terms of decorating."

Monica stood up and said, "I think we would love to assist in decorating something because we haven't decorated our own places yet."

Asiram said, "Now, that's what I'm talking about. We do all this good and live out of paper bags. I have more houses than money, and I can't stay at any of them because people are still hunting us. I vote we take this thing to them and conclude it ASAP." There was a rousing response by the women. It was obvious that those who could do the night-time thing were not going to be doing it any time soon.

## CHAPTER SEVENTEEN

As a result of the women going on strike, and the men having to assume more of the day care work than normal, it was decided over dinner that in two weeks, the Carbon Factor would be turned over to the Governor of Ohio. The governor was one of the former Democratic finalists for president, along with female senator from Massachusetts, and a sitting senator who was also a war hero from Arizona. All the details had been worked out with the people from the sewers who Mike considered reliable, resourceful, and would protect their backs because of the things the group was doing and planning to do for veterans.

Somehow, there was public chatter about the matter on the airwaves and in dark back offices. The Russian spies, who had been spread around the country to listen for any intel on the Carbon Factor formula, had implanted a listening device in one of the four persons articulated as one of those who would be given the formula for the Carbon Factor. Although the Russian contingency was small it had the resources to recruit the kind of people who could do a job and not have any patriotic attitudes.

From the sewers, where many of the people who provided Mike with credible intelligence work, an "SOS" came in requesting a meeting immediately. Kremlin types were in the hood trying to recruit people for a mission with a significantly higher payday than any of the others had offered. The only exemptions were no drugs or alcohol abuse.

Mike showed the information to the Sarge who said, "I thought we carefully picked those people because they could be trusted. Seems like someone has made a deal with the devil. Are all our people on the take? Are there any politicians who are honest?"

Mike said, "Perhaps we stand a better chance of destroying that stuff in front of eyes at the Vatican."

He continued, "Let me know if you want me to take the meeting, or try to figure out another way of communicating with my friend?"

The Sarge stared at Mike, dropped his head, and asked, "What the hell did you just say?"

"I said, let me know if you want me to take the meeting with my friend."

"No, not that. What did you say before that?"

"I said, we might do better destroying that stuff in front of eyes at the Vatican. Oh shit, that's a home run! Oh my, that was off the cuff. Zanthius and Larry's notion of misdirection would work beautifully in this case. The people in DC would be expecting us. We show up in Italy before the Holy Father and burn it right in front of him."

"Brilliant, but the Vatican has a lot of loose lips as well. How on earth could we pull this off? We need to meet with the group and discuss this thing. Tonight, we have a wedding to attend. Keep that under your hat until we talk again. I don't want any noise on this issue until I bring it up formally."

## CHAPTER EIGHTEEN

Elton and Margo were adjusting to the group and to their new parents. Each night before bedtime, Mallory would read them a story, but never finish it because Mr. Sleepy would catch the children. The kids, often fell asleep as soon as they were tucked in. The previous night, before he started reading a story, Margo inadvertently asked, "Can I call Monica, Mom?"

Mallory smiled and said, "Why don't I call her in here and you can ask her yourself." He walked into the suite and said, "Monica, Margo has a question she wants to ask you."

Monica walked in and said, "It's kind of cold in here, isn't it? Anyway, what's your question, my little princess?"

"Can I call you 'Mom'?" Monica started to cry and walked out of the room without saying a word. She thought Mallory had put Margo up to it and that it was not of her own volition. Margo started to cry as well and said, "She doesn't love me. Nobody loves me."

Hearing that, Monica walked back into the room, hugged her, and said, "I have been waiting all my life to share my love with children, and I was just shocked when you asked me that question. I am your mother, maybe not natural, but I am the person who is going to look after you and love you no matter what. This is new to us as well. We're a little older than most people who adopt, but I wanted to love a little girl and when I walked into that place, I saw you, and I fell in love with you. You asked me if you can call me 'Mom' and I say, that is what I expect you to call me from this point forward, my princess."

"Are you sure you love me?"

"Oh, yes! I'm quite sure overtime, you will learn to understand what it means to love someone unconditionally, or without limits."

Mallory feeling a little left out said, "I guess we'll read a bedtime story tomorrow. You guys get some sleep."

Margo said, "So, Mallory, does that mean we can call you "Dad'?"

He kissed her on the forehead and said, "I would be honored if you and your brother called me 'Dad'."

The following morning at 0900 hours, Monica woke up and saw that Mallory wasn't in the bed. She staggered out of the bedroom and saw breakfast on the table. Mallory and the kids had ordered room service, a thing they had never done before. Margo, said, "It's time to eat, Sleepy Head. I hope you like what we ordered."

Monica was not a big bacon, sausage, or ham eater, but said, "Oh my, these are all the things that I like."

During breakfast, the family talked about what a family is and does, and Mallory told them they were going to go shopping in town in an hour.

Margo stated, "We don't have any money to shop."

Monica reached over, took her hand, and said, "If you stay humble and respectful, the world will be yours. There are somethings that parents are supposed to do for their children and one of those things is to take them shopping for clothes and perhaps a few toys if they want them. Also remember, Beatrice's mom is getting married this evening and we should buy them a gift. Oh, honey, can you arrange for, ah, some eyes on us?"

Margo asked, "Why do we need eyes on us?"

"That's a great question and one that your dad will explain to you in the coming days. Enjoy your breakfast and Margo, you're first in the shower and then you Elton."

"Hey, you guys didn't eat a lot. Was the food not good?" Mallory inquired.

"We've never seen this much food and, I guess, we're afraid to eat it." Elton said.

"I'm going to have Dr. Courtney examine you guys soon along with the rest of the children. Don't worry, I'll be there every moment, and, by the way, she is my best friend in the whole world. I've known her for years. We'll do this to make sure you're alright and that we don't need to treat you for any issues. Is that okay?"

Margo said, "It's okay by me as long as you're with me."

"You know, Margo, your dad may have to be with you sometimes. Is that going to be okay with you?"

"We have been here longer than any place else. I'm happy; Elton is happy; and we hope you're happy with us. We don't want to go back there."

In a strident tone, Monica said, "Margo and Elton, you're not ever going back to that place again. You're going to be here with us, and I don't want you to think about that place ever again. This is your home, or wherever we finally settle down."

"May I ask a question?" Margo inquired.

"Why, of course," Monica responded.

"When we go shopping, can we wish for things even if we can't have them?"

"Oh, my God! Child, if you can wish it, perhaps your dad can make it come true, if it's reasonable. Now, you must define what is reasonable and you and Elton abide by your definition. Do you understand what I mean?"

Margo said, "I think so. I shouldn't wish for a spaceship, but it would be okay to wish for a home for Christmas, with a fireplace."

"Oh, baby, I promise you, for Christmas you'll have a fireplace, and the biggest tree we can cut down and haul back to our house. I promise you that."

Mallory looked at Elton and said, "You seem to be low maintenance. Do you have any wishes and wants?"

"I just want you to take me fishing tomorrow with Michael. Oh, I also want to learn how to swim. Christmas is okay, I guess. I would like to have a tree with presents under it. Can I work or do something to earn an allowance?"

"How about me and you talk with Michael tomorrow and see if we can find a job for you that will pay you for your work?"

"Now Dad, I like that idea. I want to earn money so I can buy people things or help some of the children in the home we left. I miss them, and I want them to get away from those mean people."

"Son, how about you and I work on a plan to knock that place down and build a better one in its place and find people who will not hurt children, to operate it? Can I count on you to work with me on that?"

"Dad, I will do whatever you want me to do. That place is where the devil lives."

"I want to help also. I had a lot of friends there and I miss them," Margo stated.

Monica said, "We have thirty minutes to shower and get dressed. Margo, you and me in my shower, Elton, you, and your dad in your shower. Let's go people."

Monica pretended to dismiss the fact that Margo was in the shower with her. Margo rinsed the soap off her body and Monica noticed whelps across her buttocks. Monica got out of the shower first, looked in the mirror and said, "Honey, put lotion on your body when you get out of the shower."

Margo yelled, "Don't leave me in here. How do I cut off the water?" Monica reached in and pushed the lever down and the water stopped. Monica handed Margo a towel and she smiled.

Monica asked, are you ready to go and have some fun?"

Margo responded, "I'm not sure if I have really had a lot of fun before."

Monica sighed and then exclaimed, "Well, today is your lucky day! Let's get dressed and go shopping. It's time to have some fun and buy some crazy outfits and look real pretty for tonight. What's your favorite color?"

"Black is my favorite color because that's all I've ever known."

"Would you do me a favor and try some other colors today, just to see if you like them?"

#

In town, the children had a field day picking out things and deciding whether they wanted them or needed them. When Monica, Mallory, Margo, and Elton walked into the shop, the owner who was prompted, asked, "Oh my, aren't you hot in all that black? Honey, down here we dress as if we're going to be in a parade every day. I would like to show you some outfits that I usually save for all the queens on the island, but I sense your parents think you're a queen as well, so I'm going to show you my best outfits."

She grabbed Margo's hand and said, "Come with me." A confused Margo said, "Mom, come with me." Thus, was the beginning of a special relationship between an adult female and a child who was looking for love and protection. Mallory saw it and acknowledged it by saying, "Your daughter is not going to let you out of her sight. Listen, Elton and I are going to head over to that shop for guys and see if they have anything that will make him look as handsome as me."

The two guys left the store and Mallory looked to his right and left and saw his escorts. Whitmore and McArthur were to the left and Montomie and Gladstone were to his right. The vehicles were driven by Michael and Jong.

Before the group drove to town, Ben Beckmire had summoned Michael for a conference and explained who they were and their mission. Five minutes later, Beckmire grilled him and asked about his proclivities towards drugs. He asked if he were loyal and protective of his dad now that he had the most desirable place on the entire island and whether he would swear allegiance to him and his people?

Michael said, "My dad and I are getting closer, he's showing me more and more things relative to the business. He even took me up the road with him and told me how the four partners, once enemies because of envy, were about to own the place to come, to be, and to stay. He told me about you guys and kept saying to me that he was waiting for some slick activity to happen where you people would try to buy him out and that he also went to the university and talked to legal aid people. They told him the way the contract was written; he didn't even have to repay you guys. Is that correct and, if so, why would you structure a deal that leaves you in the hole?"

"I thought I called you to find out if we could trust you and here you are doing your daddy's bidding. Listen, one day we'll have you come to our properties on the mainland and talk to our neighbors. The carpetbaggers were trying to take over several farms and had literally lured farmers into deals that were designed to fail. They were about to foreclose on nine or twelve ranches. I mean beautiful places with 4,000 to 18,000 acres of land each. We got involved in the game and gave those baggers a deal they couldn't refuse. That cheating ass bank in town had your daddy and the rest of those guys set up for foreclosure and we smelled a rat. We don't like rats. We went in and paid off their loans, gutted their places, rebuilt them, modernized them, and when they're all finished, they're going to be six-star resorts. That bar at the top of the hill will have sixty or more rooms instead of that sleazy screw joint for the locals.

"All these guys will be trained and you, my friend, will play a major role in putting this cul-de-sac on the map. Now, back to your main question, 'we help people help themselves'. We couldn't stand by and watch those developers manipulate those people's loans and call them in during the same week, that's crooked. Listen, if your dad or any of the others try to screw us, it will be their loss because we'll shut down this part of the island. If they do good by the people and hire local and not import those blonde haired, big buxom women, then we're happy. They know our percentage and it's low. We rebuilt these places, and they don't have to pay us a dime."

The Sarge paused and said, "I am running out of time, and I want to fast forward this conversation. Now, can I trust you to protect my family, even if it means putting a bullet in a man's head?"

Michael looked at the Sarge and said, "You already know how I roll. Why you be asking me that question?"

"Because I need to know if I can send my people with you. I want to make sure they come back without a scratch. You know the penalty for having a firearm on the island. We'll take care of that, but you have to act responsibly."

"Mr. Beckmire, why are you trying to help me?"

"You disposed of a person who once tried to kill me. To me, that spoke volumes about your character. We don't do mean, or evil things to people, but a lot of them would like to see us dead, and I mean the children as well."

"Mr. Beckmire, can I speak freely?"

"Let it out."

"I want to know one thing--will you, your people, or those who come behind you, ever try to take this place away from my dad?"

"Oh, goodness no, Son! He's our friend, as well as those others. As soon as we get a big monkey off our backs, we're going to concentrate on that area where Ms. Viola lives and clean it up. This resort and the other properties will make you rich, us rich, your dad rich, your mom and sisters rich, those other guys, and their families, rich as well. If someone attempts to screw us, then the whole scene gets shut down. You are going to be that glue that keeps that from happening."

"Mr. Beckmire, is my father aware of this conversation?"

"He is, and he told me that you would have a lot of questions."

"Mr. Beckmire, I will be what you want me to be on this island for your group and the people of St. Thomas. I will deal honestly with everyone and not try to make a dime off a dollar."

Beckmire stood up and shook his hand. Michael said, "Damn, that's some grip."

# # #

Later, in town, Michael saw Elton and Mallory come out of the shop with four bags each. He walked around to the back and opened the trunk and placed the bags in it. Mallory asked, "Why are you carrying."

"I had a talk with Mr. Beckmire, and he gave me this item."

"I'm glad, because we've been watching you and giving you dirty jobs to do to see if you had the right stuff. He talked to you and asked you to make us safe and it looks like you're in. Thanks, Michael. Have the ladies come out of that store yet?"

"Mr. Mallory, you know women don't have a need to rush for anything."

Mallory asked Elton if he wanted to go into the electronics store to see if he saw anything that he liked.

He asked Mallory, "What do they sell there?"

Mallory looked to the heavens and said, "Let's go and see."

When the two entered the store, Elton's eyes became as big as saucers. He said, "Is this where they sell computers?"

Mallory asked, "Did you have use of a computer in that orphanage?"

"I don't really know what a computer is. All they told us was that it was the rich man's way of buying things online and staying away from poor people like us. She told us that we would never own such a thing."

Mallory saw a notebook that he was familiar with and told the clerk that he needed two of them and two internet hot spots with international capabilities. He then told the clerk he needed the latest version of MS and some electronic games that teach and don't addict. It was at that point a bell went off in his head and he said to Elton, "Do you know how to read?"

"I don't think I know what you mean. I know the pictures from Bugs Bunny and the Road Runner and what they mean. What do you mean by read?"

"I mean, Elton, if I gave you a book, would you be able to read any of it?"

As Elton looked at drones, he said, "They said books are full of lies and change after you've read them." Mallory's head dropped, and he realized they should know how to read simple eye impacts like McDonalds, Coke, hotdog, milk, and water. He stopped analyzing and began to enjoy the excitement that Elton was enjoying by witnessing things that had been blocked out of his development. He said to himself, 'screw it, we're going to have some fun and worry about reading tomorrow'.

He purchased two drones, walkie talkies, two iPods, cameras, and everything that Elton couldn't want before. He felt Elton was solid and that he would be there to be a positive influence on him. Mallory was happy he made the decision on his own, that he did not enter this new adventure blindfolded, and immersed in Monica's obsession.

When they came out of the store, Michael asked, "Is there anything left inside?"

Elton said, "Yeah, there is a lot left in that store."

Mallory asked, "Did they come out of that place yet?"

"They have not. I became concerned and whispered to the others that I was going in to make sure they were still in there. I walked in and they were having their toes and fingernails painted in the clothing store. That little girl was amazed at how her toes looked. She asked your wife if it was okay for a child to have painted toes. Your wife asked her, 'Who's the mother here? If I let you, do it, then it's okay'. What struck me as telling was when your wife said, 'I'm your mom and I'm going to introduce you to the world tonight. You're going to be the bell of the ball'."

As the women were prepared to exit the store, Michael leisurely turned his head to the left and saw the flash of either binoculars or a scope. He dove into the door, pushing Monica and Margo back in, shattered the glass, cut his hand, and yelled, "Get down, I saw a sniper."

Montomie and Gladstone responded first after watching the heroics of Michael. Whitmore said, "We're heading to the top, keep your eyes on that building to the southeast. I see a scope flash as well."

Mallory said, "Elton, do not move from this spot until I return. Do you understand?"

"Yes Dad."

Mallory breached the building where the flash had come from, with Whitmore and Gladstone following up. He sent Whitmore to the left and Gladstone to the right and gave them the thumbs up. Whitmore threw a bottle of Coke against the side of the building and Mallory bolted on to the roof with his .308. He searched the area and discovered the cause of the concern. A small piece of metal that had broken away from its host and fell in a place that would allow it to reflect an ominous light. It was a mirage, a simple by-product of a storm that had left a piece of aluminum laying in a position to cause concern to those on the ground.

When Mallory returned to the store, he saw Monica wrapping towels around Michael's hand. She said, "Honey, we need to get him to the hospital. He's bleeding a lot."

The team was glad that the hospital was less than a mile away. When they entered the emergency ward, the doctor said, "Michael, what did you do to yourself?"

# # #

An hour plus later, the team was on their way back to the resort. When they arrived, Mr. Carter was standing in his normal, royal position, and saw that his son had a huge bandage on his hand. He walked over and asked, "What happened? Michael told his father about his first day, at trying to be a spy. The two men laughed. His father, uncharacteristically, hugged him, and told him that he needed him whole so that he could run the family enterprise. Michael looked at him and asked, "Do you think once the group leaves, we could seriously sit down and talk about your vision for the operation and management of the resort?"

"Absolutely, Son. As a matter of fact, I would like our partners to be a part of that discussion, so that we can get their ideas about what they expect as well. It's hard to tie them down, they usually tell me that I know more than they do so make the decisions."

"They're a new breed of humans. They don't take, they don't act bossy, they ask instead of demand, and always end with a thank you so much. I've not encountered one of them who is not kind. That Mr. Beckmire asked me a lot of questions about loyalty and family. He wants me to be the glue that ties the cul-de-sac together. I'm going to have to go and meet the others, Dad, without you, to make sure, that everything is cool and that they understand I'm representing Mr. Beckmire. Is that okay with you?"

"Son, Mr. Beckmire expects more than that from you. He wants you to oversee the construction of the two properties because there seems to be too many issues for such a small project. You might want to speak with him again tonight after the wedding to make sure you understand exactly what he expects from you.

"You're probably going to take over the accounting and payments from me because I can't handle it, it's too stressful to try to account for someone else's funds. You know what I mean? Son, this is a great opportunity for you. I only ask that you do a good job and represent us well. God knows, they're a lifesaver, our friends, and we don't hurt our friends. Tell the truth, did you dive through a glass door to save Mrs. Mallory and her daughter?"

"I saw the flash as I told you, and I thought it was from the scope of a rifle. I didn't think about it, they were coming out of the store and my reaction was to knock them back in and cover them from harm."

"Boy, you're going to get a lot of credit for that. Damn, you sacrificed yourself for one of them. That's colossal, Son. That's enormous. He's going to take care of you. Wait and see."

"Dad, I wasn't looking to be no hero. I was not going to let them get hurt when I was supposed to be watching them."

# # #

Meanwhile, Mallory and Elton tore open the packaging on the drones and were disappointed that the batteries had to be charged for a full 24 hours. Mallory began to read the instructions to Elton when he noticed that Elton had put his drone together and had started the charging process for the battery. He said, "How did you know how to put that together?"

"Look at the pictures Dad. It shows you how it should look."

Mallory looked at the photos and said, "Son, it says the drone should be put together following these steps to make sure it flies properly."

Elton looked at the pictures and said, "That's how mine is put together. Do you want me to put yours together?"

# # #

Jilkes and John Lee sat under a palm tree holding their newborn babies. Jilkes's phone began to buzz, and it was Franco texting him from Spain. Franco attached pictures of the construction project. Jilkes said to John Lee, "Look at what happens when you don't kill people on the first date."

John Lee looked at the pictures and said, "You should broadcast them pictures to the rest of the group."

# # #

At 1600 hours the resort seemed to be asleep. Everyone was taking a siesta except for Chakes, Luana, Beatrice, and

Ms. Viola. They were preparing themselves for a life altering experience called marriage.

Montomie asked Chakes, "Have you really stayed away from that beautiful woman?"

"I kid you not. However, tonight, I'm going to shake the very foundation of 'The Sanctuary'. I can't believe that woman loves me. She's the most beautiful human being I've ever seen, and she wants to marry me. Wow, I'm still in shock."

"Yeah, I know what you mean because I'm in shock that she's marrying you instead of me. I'm better looking than you are, I'm sure as hell smarter than you and I certainly have a better conditioned and sculptured body than you. I can't figure that out. Why is she marrying you instead of me? I should ask her that question before you get married."

"You're so stupid, but one of my close friends. This has been some ride that we've been on. It started with that damn Brown and Bernstein trying to help the poor guys they fought with. Now look at us--we're set for life beyond our wildest dreams, and it keeps getting better, at least for me, because I'm about to get married, but you continue to chase strippers."

"Why, you hating on me? You used to chase those pole dancers, as well."

"Yeah, yeah. I remember, but those days are over and done with. Perhaps you and the other single men should shop around for a real woman without an agenda that includes looking for someone to take care of them."

"Oh, stop being a hypocrite. You got lucky, and I'm still going to ask her why you and not me? You need to read over those vows I wrote and make sure they reflect your feelings. You can't just use my words. You must make them your words. I only gave you a road map! You have to turn my directions into a wonderful place in your mind that you want to share with Luana for the rest of your life. You can't use my words. Transform them, Brother, or I will say them myself to your ex-bride to be."

"Thanks, my friend, but that won't be necessary. I know what I'm going to say. I just needed a guide to what people say when they get married."

"Oh, I see. So, you ask a person who is not married, to write you a script, right? Damn, that's dumb, and different."

# # #

In another location, Michael met with the owners of the other three properties and told them that Mr. Beckmire had asked him to be the glue that held this group together and to manage and correct the issues with the construction process and the bus issue. He asked if anyone had any questions or concerns and if they felt uncomfortable with his new assignment? Everyone agreed that if Mr. Beckmire could fund it, then he could make recommendations about how to make sure it gets done. They welcomed Michael into the fold and Michael said, "I have to ask you guys to do me and them a favor this evening. I need you and your people at the top of the road, and on both sides of the beach to screen for intruders. This is an event that will require, at least, you guys to carry weapons. Is that a problem?"

Mr. Miller said, "Son, I like what they're doing here, and I know they got our backs. Me and my people will cover the east and west sides of the beach to the rocks. The rest of you guys can manage the road, I hope."

#

At 1745 hours, everyone was in place and dressed to the nines. The one thing about the .308s, is that they're small enough to hide under a shirt that is not tucked into the trouser.

Montomie walked Chakes to the beach and the two men stood there waiting on his bribe-to-be. Chakes was decked out in white linen pants, a white linen shirt, and soft white sandals. Montomie was appointed with a matching outfit. What became a sub-highlight of the festivities was when Monica and Miss Margo showed up dressed exactly alike from head to toe with matching nail polish on both fingers and toes, and identical sunglasses. More startling to the group was the dazzling duo of Mallory and Elton. They had matching linen suits, sandals, sunglasses, and thin summer mesh shirts. They were as clean as a Chitlin should be. Elton looked at his sister and said, "You look good, Sis. You too, Mom."

At exactly 1800 hours, festive music began to play, and a light was focused on the base of the tent where a beautiful little figure dressed in a soft pink linen dress with matching bows holding her hair in place. Beatrice walked slowly, spreading rose petals with a smile on her face that would melt an iceberg. Ten paces or so behind her was her mother and great-grandmother. Ms. Viola wore a soft pink, full-length dress with accents on both sides. Luana wore a white and pink fitted dress, that flowed with a train to it. She looked beautiful, radiant and in love with a man who her grandmother lovingly called, a scoundrel.

When the group reached the groom, Luana was overcome with emotions and had to be attended to momentarily by Courtney. She was almost at the point of hyperventilating.

When she finally reached her husband to be, he said, "You are the most loving and beautiful person I have ever known."

He then looked at Ms. Viola and said, "Sister, I no recognize you in that outfit. You look absolutely lovely."

He turned away from her and fell to his knees, looked at Beatrice and said, "I need your permission to marry your mother and to become your father. I beg of you to give me that opportunity."

Beatrice looked at him, cautiously gazed around, and then whispered in his ear so that no one could hear her. She said, "I already told you I love you, and that you are the only person I know as a daddy." He kissed her forehead and hugged her tightly.

Chakes then rose to his feet and said to the audience, "Beatrice has given me permission to marry her mother and to become her father, a responsibility that I say before God and you, I will execute to the fullest."

The two were married in the eyes of God and before a wonderful group of friends who witnessed and sanctioned their union.

CHAPTER NINETEEN

The stage had been created for the handling of the Carbon Factor formula. Four prominent, allegedly honest American politicians had been selected, and apprised of the Carbon Factor formula, and its alleged horrific impact on mankind by a full-bird Colonel who was homeless, connected, and living in the sewers.

The four politicians were also apprised of the Russian's efforts to create bombs that could be packaged in milk cartons. The Governor said, "How can anyone capture the by-products of carbon, add some unknown substances to it, put it in a milk carton, and say it has destructive powers equal to that of a nuclear bomb? How can this lunacy continue in this day and age?"

The retired colonel replied, "Much like the last election was stolen, and the riots at the Capitol were peaceful visitations. I'm not sure of any of it and unlike you, Governor, I'm not an expert, but I did hear that a helluva lot of people died trying to get their hands on the formula my friends are trying to give up. Now, would you rather have people who are maniacal get their hands on this thing, be it a joke or otherwise? And since I'm not a scientist and don't know squat about formulas, I still wouldn't summarily dismiss the notion as impossible."

The senator from Arizona asked, "When do these people want to make this happen?"

"I'm told as soon as possible because it has been alleged that Russian operatives were recruiting mercs in our country to obtain the information at any costs. My associates are concerned for their safety."

"Colonel, I know who your associates are, and I doubt if they're afraid of anything. They may be tired of killing people, but I doubt if fear plays a part in that equation," the senator from Arizona acknowledged.

"Senator, are you sure we're talking about the same people?"

"Colonel, I know their story, I know their names, and I know what they did to people out in Virginia, where a recently departed senator lived. Oh, yes, I know exactly who you're talking about, and I support them a hundred percent. Hell, those boys almost ended the Vietnam war by themselves."

The ex-presidential contender asked, "How did I get mixed up in this? I'm not an elected official."

"Sir, they said, if you no go, they no go. I believe they are staunch supporters of yours and their foundation contributed to your campaign."

"Colonel, I have to ask you a question. A year or so ago, you went missing because your wife had, well, was indiscreet. How are you attached to these people? I hear you're living in the sewers. Is that correct?" the Governor inquired.

"Yes, sir, that is correct, and you should come and visit. So many of your veterans who are homeless, jobless, penniless, and hopeless, live here. It's people like that group who keep us with food, medical resources, legal aid, and things such as this to do."

"I would be honored if you would find time to escort me to where you and others who have served our country, live. I find it so hard to believe. Will you do that for me. To me that is more important than that damn Carbon Factor. Can we leave here now, and you take me there?" The senator from Massachusetts inquired.

The governor chimed in and said, "I want to go as well."

The Arizona senator stated that he was in. Ten minutes later a car was ordered, and they made the first of several stops into the sewers.

In the car, the colonel told the driver to take them to North Capitol and K Streets and make a right heading east on K Street. Once at 1st and K, the colonel told him to pull over and wait for them. They got out of the car and the Governor asked, "Will we need security down here?"

"Naw, you're in good hands. Here are the only rules you'll have to follow. Never shake a person's hand, only fist bump them. Never accept a drink and never offer a drink. Never wander off, stay within my eyesight, and don't be skittish."

#

Exactly one hour and thirty minutes later, the people departed a sewer under a bridge that was used to bring the mail to high profile businesspeople in Washington, DC. The senator from Arizona looked at the group and said, "Now, that's a national crime and disgrace. Those kids fought for us, their friends died in the line of duty to protect our freedoms, they come back here, and this is their welcoming committee? I have just received new marching orders along with the hundreds of others, but this one, my friends, is going to get my overtime attention.

"I swear to each soul in that hole, I will be back and not to look, but to find ways and means to help them. This is a public/private/non-partisan/call to arms, and I need each of you to help me move this mountain. I need everyone to work closely with me on this one, even if you're not in government. Your voice is a respectable one and with the governor and my colleague from Massachusetts we will get those boys out of that squalor. We need a plan before we take cameras into that appalling world when we show them how we treat our veterans. We need a plan of action and Colonel; you're going to be our focal point," the senator from Arizona stated.

In the car on the ride back to the hill, no more words were spoken, but each of the occupants dedicated their souls to helping solve this problem. Once they arrived back on the hill, the senator from Massachusetts said, "That was damn enlightening, most assuredly."

CHAPTER TWENTY

After a full night of celebrating the marriage of Chakes and Luana, those who had partners helped Chakes shake the very foundation of the resort. Lovemaking was in the air and on the minds of everyone at the resort. Those who didn't have legitimate mates, met some freelancers at the top of the hill and enjoyed themselves on the beach. Montomie was the only one who was robbed. One of their partners sent an urgent message to the women who worked near 'The Sanctuary' that items were missing and must be returned before morning.

As the bachelors stumbled blindly back to the resort, McArthur said, "I think I'm in love."

Montomie said, "Dude, those ladies do that for a living and not for love. Let's go to church, or to the library for love. I think it's about time we bit the dust like the rest. I'm tired of my only options to openly have a date in the community is with one of you nuts."

McArthur said, "You know we did have good words with those ladies in Valencia. I mean the one I was with was a schoolteacher and didn't seem to give a hoot about money. All she talked about were the players in Barcelona and Valencia, and how they destroy your name if you didn't add your name to their plaque."

"Yeah, I was struck by the one I was with as well, for some odd reason, I didn't get much from her. Didn't know what she did for a living, just thought she was cute and sexy in a deliberately honorable way," Montomie commented.

"This life of leisure and non-commitment is becoming meaningless. I sometimes want to wake up and hear the sound of children, my own, but I feel that I'm 'too old' for that shit," McArthur concluded.

Montomie said, "Mallory and Monica just adopted two children. Jilkes, John Lee, Brown, Bernstein, and that fricken, Jong, just made babies. What is this too old shit you're talking? You like to have sex, don't you? Unless there is something mechanically wrong with us, then why are we too old?"

"After that first disaster, I kind of resigned myself to being solo. But with Chakes finding Luana, and what a find she is, I'm starting to reconsider the single life. That woman is not only beautiful, sexy, bronze, kind, and smart, she's a woman of passion and love. She always touches him on his arm, hugs him, and gives him small sneaky kisses, and smiles that are genuine. He hit the damn Powerball with her. You ever look at her closely? Next time you see her, look at her eyes and her face. She never wears makeup, but her skin is almost perfect," McArthur said.

Montomie said, "Why are you looking at that woman's face so closely?"

"Because I'm in love with her as well. I know that you're in love with her too. I will never violate my brother's trust, and I will never speak about this again."

Montomie looked at him and said, "That's some sick shit. I respect the fact that you acknowledged it to me. I didn't say anything to the contrary which makes me feel a little awkward.

I could say a lot of things about our friend's wife, but I won't. I will say that I'm in accord with you about our feelings. I even told him if he blew this ceremony, I would repeat it to her for myself. He thought I was joking, and I was, but in my heart, I realized I love his wife in an honorable way. It has nothing to do with sex. She is an amazing friend to him, and I'm jealous and envious of my brother, but I won't do stupid. Now that we've gotten that shit off our minds, it's a conversation that will never come up again because we're both drunk and don't remember shit. No Sir Lancelot!"

"Agreed, my brother. However, we need to find separation to find our own Luana. We're always so engrossed in the family--we neglect our own desires. I want to start my search in Spain and not necessarily with women who are there for a purpose. You know what I mean?" McArthur asked.

"Yeah, I do. Now, you must admit, John Lee, Brown, and Jilkes hit home runs as well. Those three Asian ladies are spectacular. Oh, and by the way, Mr. Bernstein knocked the ball out of the park with Yvette as did Jong with Mary Alice. Now, you are talking about a stroke of luck. Jong cooked that clock from the moment he saw her. Word has it, she calls him the *conejo* because he always wants to open the box up and play in it," Montomie indicated.

#

At 0930 hours, Mike struggled to find his cell phone. He answered it and recognized the voice on the other end. He asked, "Colonel, what makes a full-bird fly so early in the morning?"

"Son, it's already time for lunch according to my clock. I need you to wake up your guys so that we can have a conference call. We're getting a lot of traction on several fronts. Do you know I had a governor, two senators, and another VIP down in the sewer yesterday?"

"Stop hallucinating. Ain't no way in hell those people are going down into that place where the stench is stronger than the misery."

"Mike, they were down with the guys for over an hour and a half, and they left with a sense of urgency to provide help to our veterans. Anyway, that's just the preamble to the conference call. They are hesitant to believe the stories behind the Carbon Factor. They think it's a myth. I don't know how to convince them of it one way or the other. If I'm not mistaken, you want to publicly destroy the disks that have the formula on it. Is that correct?"

"Not only is that correct, but we want to destroy it on national TV with live cameras watching so that we can get our lives back. Those are the group's objectives. We want out and away from that whole scene."

"Mike, is this some publicity stunt, or are the Russians ready to make a frontal attack to secure this thing?"

"Colonel, I'll have the leadership team on the phone in an hour. I can only say that we've not attempted to decipher the formula, but it must have some merit because there are in-excess of six hundred souls roaming around in Hades because of it. I'll hit you back in an hour. Don't get your hopes up too high with those politicians--they tend to cry a little, move on to another cause, and then nothing gets done. I think you have a better chance of showing the world what happens with these guys than you do with the politicians. They never want to show what's wrong. They need positive press, not depressing issues that people can equate them to."

# # #

Mallory, Elton, and Michael were preparing to head out in the tender to do a little fishing. Mike saw Mallory and called out to him. When the two men met on the beach, Mike said, "The colonel needs to discuss the Carbon Factor issues with the leadership team. I've arranged to reconnect with him in an hour."

Mallory looked at the excitement on Elton's face and whispered, "Mike, I can't start disappointing a fragile little guy, so soon. I'm not going to be a part of that discussion because I'm taking my son fishing."

Mike looked at him and said, "You know what, Mallory, I'll rearrange the call until later when you return from your leisurely fishing trip with your son. Have a great time."

When Mallory returned to the boat, Elton asked, "Are we still going fishing, or do we have to wait until another time?"

"Son, we're going fishing, and we're going now." Elton smiled and high-fived Michael.

Mallory asked, "How's the hand?"

"It's good and bandaged, and this is a rubberized glove. I'll need you to stabilize the boat while I pull on the crank cord."

Mallory asked, "What does something like this cost?"

Michael said, "I'm not sure. This is a hand-me-down tender with a motor that I purchased from a shady character."

"Where do they sell these things, or bigger and safer boats?" I don't want to go too far from shore with Elton. Can we catch anything close to shore from the boat?"

"Mr. Mallory, if the fish be hungry then they come for this bait that my mom makes. It never fails us."

Michael took the dingy about sixty feet from the shore and the depth was approximately thirty feet. He baited Elton's hook and cast it twenty feet away. He also latched Elton's life vest to the side of the dingy so that nothing could pull him into the water. He explained all of that to Mallory who was feeling uncomfortable with the whole scene. Elton was comfortable and patient. Michael grabbed a hold of his line and jerked it a couple of times. Mike asked Elton if he felt that movement and was told that he did. Michael then said, "That's exactly how it's going to feel when a fish grabs a hold of your hook. Are you ready?" Elton gave him another high-five and the wait began.

While they were sitting in the hot sun, Mallory said, "I want to buy one of these, but a little bigger and much sturdier. Will you take me to a place where that can happen?"

Michael said, "It would be my pleasure." He watched as Elton's pole jerked once, then twice and then there was a full bite on the hook. Elton began to reel the fish in, but it was obvious that he was no match for whatever had bitten the bait. Mallory started to get up and Michael said, "Mr. Mallory, I need you to stay exactly where you are to keep balance in the boat."

Michael then reached over to Elton and said, "My young friend, you have caught yourself a big fish and it's going to take all of us to bring it into the boat. I need you to do exactly what I tell you to do--understood?"

Twenty minutes later, Elton was completing his final turn on his reel. Michael with the glove on to protect his cut, helped keep the stress off the line and reduce the amount of work Elton had to do. Mallory saw what he was doing and appreciated the special attention that was being given to his son.

#

When they arrived back at shore, Michael said, "Elton, I want to take a picture of you and your fish. I'll take one of you alone and then one with you and your dad." Mallory took a picture of Michael and Elton and felt happy about the trip. Elton said, "Dad, I really want to do that again. That was fun."

Mallory rubbed his head and said, "Yeah, we'll do it again, but in a bigger tender."

Michael asked Elton if he would like to have his fish for dinner? Elton said, "Only if my mom, dad, sister, and you can have some."

As they entered the resort, people saw the fish and asked who caught it. The two adults pointed to the little boy, who was happy to be loved.

Mallory saw Mike and asked about the meeting and was told that it was going to take place sometime after lunch. He looked at his watch and asked Michael, "Can you take me to the place where they sell those tenders. I just need to get a few friends for backup."

Mallory called Montomie and McArthur, and asked them if they would escort him to a place that sells tenders? Of course, they didn't know what a tender was and inquired about it.

#

The five of them, including Elton, piled into the van. Michael drove them to a marina at Red Hook Bay to look at tenders that were for sale. Before going into the office, they walked the docks and admired the majestic fishing boats, with their rigs, poles, and their amenities, which included heads and gallies.

When they walked through the door, there was a noticeable lack of attention from those selling the crafts. Mallory asked the lady at the desk if there was a salesperson available. As she looked around, individuals seemingly tried to act as if they were on their phones and or otherwise, busy. Both Mallory and Michael noticed the atmosphere as well as did Michael.

Michael said, "Perhaps we should have bypassed this place and gone over to where the bigger boats are. I apologize, Mr. Mallory."

Mallory said, "That's okay, I know when people judge a book by its color and presentation. Screw them; they must be making a shitload of money since they don't need ours. Let's go to that place over there."

In less than an hour, in the adjacent boat yard, the group boarded a thirty-foot fishing boat with twin-in-board engines and were out on a demonstration ride.

When they returned, Mallory said, "This seems a bit crowded. Perhaps we need a fifty-foot boat that will allow us to go out and stay overnight if we want to."

The young African American salesman said, "Perhaps you want to start small and work your way up?"

Mallory said, "I want to start big and work my way down."

He pointed to Michael and said, "Talk to him and figure out a training package, and everything else. I want a boat that my son, family, and friends can spend the night on if we want to."

The salesman said, "I would like to compete for your business, but I need to try to find the precise product that you might like. Listen, I usually sell small things. I sell parts, small motors, and sometimes a small dingy. You're talking about a yacht. I would like to broker such a deal, but I can tell you that at the fifty-foot range, you're looking at a number that is close to $1.6 million."

"Listen, what's your name?" Mallory asked the young salesman.

"My name is Ben Martin."

"Really? Listen, get me several configurations in terms of the cabins and try to convince me to spend my money on one of them. Bring me at least five variations on the theme and let me choose. In the meantime, we're going to take that thirty-footer to fish close to shore. How much is that thing, by the way?"

Boom! Like a small explosion, a member of the group became the owner of a thirty-foot fishing boat with his eyes towards a fifty-footer. Ben Martin's boss came over and said, "Ben, I'll take this from here." He introduced himself to Mallory and indicated that Ben wasn't really a salesperson and that he only sells parts and small engines.

Mallory looked at a dejected Ben and then at his boss and said, "That's a damn shame because if he doesn't sell us this boat, and the one he's researching for us, then we'll import our boats from the States."

Mallory said to Elton, "Son, you have to always help the little guy. Come on people, we're out of here."

Ben's boss said, "Wait a minute now. Let's all take a deep breath and start all over again."

Mallory said, "We're done, if he's not the guy filling out the paperwork, taking, and getting the full commission for this boat."

His boss looked at him and said, "You know what you're doing, carry-on."

As the man walked away, Mallory asked Ben, "Did he just try to cut in on your commission?"

Ben smiled and said, "I have to work here." Ben started pulling out papers to start the financing process. Michael indicated to Ben that he thought the boat would be paid for in full and wanted it delivered for fishing in the morning. Michael walked over to Mallory and said, "Pardon the interruption, are you financing the boat or paying for it?"

Mallory fished out his credit card and told Michael to use it and to sign for him. He stated, "We're going to leave you here. Do you think you and Ben can get that thing out to the beach before dark?"

Michael walked over to Ben and said, "If I give you instructions, can you deliver the boat with me to their resort?"

Ben replied, "Absolutely. I presume you're going to be the operator and I'll come out tomorrow morning and go over things again with you."

Michael said, "We have some heavy life vests. I'm going to need new ones. The boat had all state-of-the-art electronics, including radar. Is there anything else we might need on it?"

Ben said, "The boat is designed for deep water fishing and has an electronic distress signal, ship-to-shore radio, radar, fish finder, chart plotter and comes with a satellite radio/phone as well. Michael, I need you to tell the buyer he should demand ten to fifteen percent off sticker price, especially since he's paying cash."

Michael walked over to Mallory, who was fitting Elton with a vest, and told him what Ben had said. Mallory walked over to Ben who had the figures in front of him and picked up the paperwork. He said, "When I buy a car, I expect a discount. When I buy a boat, I expect a discount as well. Why are you guys making it hard for us to do business?"

Ben excused himself and went into his employer's cubicle and said, "The guy wants a discount, and he wants between ten and fifteen percent off sticker price."

"Offer him eleven and a half and see if he bites. That sucker doesn't know nothing about boats."

Ben went back and pretended to discuss the figures and on a scratch piece of paper wrote, "He called you a sucker'.

Mallory said, "Listen, fifteen percent or we walk and that's in the next three minutes." Ben excused himself again and walked back to his employer's cubicle and told him that the sucker wanted fifteen percent, or he was walking. The guy mumbled something under his breath and told him to conclude the sale.

After running Mallory's card through American Express, Ben was surprised that all they wanted was a signature from Mallory. Ben also wasn't familiar with the *Black Card*, either.

On his way out of the door, Mallory said, "Michael, you good? You and Ben are going to deliver it, today, right? You'll get me the specs on that other thing, right?"

Mallory and Elton walked out of the store with Montomie and McArthur trailing. McArthur saw a dingy with a motor and said, "I like that thing. Hey young fellow, give me fifteen percent off and you got yourself another sale."

Ben pulled the tag off the dingy and walked into his employer's cubicle and said, "The other sucker wants to buy that dingy, but with a fifteen percent discount as well. Do you want to sell it?" His employer told him to close the deal.

McArthur gave him his credit card and asked him if he could deliver it as well? Ben told him he would tow it back to the resort as soon as he filled the tanks on the first boat and equipped the dingy with vests and everything else such as running lights because the anchor light was removable

Elton asked, "Dad, did you really buy that boat? Why didn't you bring it with you?"

"Son, they have to check things out on it first. They'll deliver it later today or tomorrow so that we can go fishing again. I like fishing; how about you?"

"It's fun, but sometimes I just want to ride on the boat. Can we do that?"

"Whatever you want to do, Elton. Whatever you would like, my son."

# # #

When the group turned into the cul-de-sac, they were happy with the fact that people were putting the final pieces together on the two properties. At their resort, Mr. Carter stood in the shade and watched as his guests enjoyed themselves basking in the sun and on his beach. He walked towards the beach and made sure that the guests did not need anything. As he approached a couple wading in the water, the guy said, "Mr. Carter, your place is fabulous. Why don't you build docks here and have fishing trips and maybe even a high-end fishing tournament?" Mr. Carter looked at him and smiled.

# # #

In the meantime, the leadership was preparing to speak with the colonel about the Carbon Factor formula. The Sarge asked, "Where is Mallory?"

Mike replied, "I informed him of the call this morning, but he was going fishing with Elton and Michael. I called the colonel and told him the call wouldn't happen until after lunch."

When Mike got the colonel on the phone, he said, "Colonel, I have the decision-making people in the room with me. I briefed them on our conversation this morning and as I said to you earlier, they want to get this monkey off their backs."

The Colonel replied, "Hey guys, I met with two senators, one governor and one ex-Secretary of State. They seem to think that the Carbon Factor formula is a hoax, just in case it's' not, they don't want the formula finding its way to some third world, America hating country. I told them that you guys were solid and were not offering it to the highest bidder. My question is simple--how can a product in a milk carton make a nuclear bomb detonation, miniscule?"

The Sarge said, "Colonel, we are field soldiers and there is not a scientist amongst us. My wife is probably the only person who has taken a course in science, and she hasn't seen the formula in any format. I say that to say, my son, who I didn't know existed, kissed a spy, swallowed a capsule, and created enough problems for us to last a lifetime. We don't know shit, about its capabilities, but we do know that a lot of people have gone to Hades trying to secure the product. We don't know anything about its capabilities. We only know that people are trying to kill us to obtain the formula. We want this monkey off our backs as Mike stated earlier."

"Okay, Sergeant, humor me. How can something the size of a half-gallon milk carton be so destructive?"

"Colonel, I guess I have to repeat myself? We don't know shit about this mess. All we want to do is publicly turn it over to the authorities or destroy it in public. Our gut feelings are that we want to destroy it in public. All of us agree that we don't think the world needs another weapon to destroy itself. We've not seen it at work, witnessed an explosion, or anything."

"Sergeant, I will try to get an audience and the press in the next week or so to witness your actions. I know our government is going to want to test the efficacy of the product to see if it can be another weapon in its arsenal. You guys are between a rock and a hard place. I'm not sure if this is the best venue for you guys. Let me attempt to schedule the meeting and let's gauge the interest by when it's scheduled. I have a suspicion if it's attended to immediately, then I wouldn't trust those involved. If it takes a month or so, then I think that they don't give a shit."

The Sarge said, "Colonel, let me change the subject a minute. Have you heard of any recruitment activities going on for people to bear arms and do light security work?"

"It's funny you asked that question. I have a meeting with a person tonight who wants to recruit a small security force to breach an institution and secure a product. When I inquired about the product, I was told that it was scientific in nature and personal. His client's computer had been hacked and someone gained access to key elements of a new drug that is designed to minimize heart attacks in victims with high blood pressure and high cholesterol and is worth approximately $100 billion in its raw form. My only problem is that he sounded like Nikita Khrushchev."

The Sarge asked, "Do you have a report date and execution date?"

"Funny you should ask that, as well. The report date is next Thursday, and the execution date is one week from that, and I've been offered a $100k to lead the recruitment process. Don't worry, I'm on one of the phones that Mike left us to use.

No one can track, or hack this call, this is Mike's phone, not mine. My source of contact, seemingly, is interested in capturing someone called the 'idiot spy'."

The Sarge didn't appear interested in that information and waltzed over it. He said, "Why on earth would anyone want an 'idiot?"

The colonel said, "From what I'm also told, he has the executable formula scanned on him that makes the myth a reality."

"What the hell does that mean?"

"Sarge, a female who also contacted me and who had an accent, told me the 'idiot spy's' body has a scan point. I asked her who she was, and she flatly stated she discovered him. She told me her child was his and that his current wife was mothering both of their children. I asked her why she was telling me all of this and she said, 'because I'm broke, and I need money'."

The Sarge proclaimed, "I'll be damned. Seems like some things never end, and others keep finding a way to defy the odds. Colonel, did she seem to be working with Nikita?"

"Sergeant, I'm not sure who is working with whom. I did ask her how and why she reached out to me and how she knew my name? She told me on the internet there are details of odd jobs that a group of homeless vets are willing to do for compensation."

"Colonel, can I call you in thirty minutes? I'm missing a significant part of our team and I just want him here when we make the final decision. Is that possible?" The colonel told him he had all day and that he would call back on a different phone.

The Sarge asked Jilkes if he would secure Zanthius for him as well as his wife? The Sarge tried to figure out what was Helga's role in the grand scheme of things. He knew she couldn't be trusted and wondered if this was a ploy to somehow try to retrieve her child.

When Zanthius and Asiram showed up, Asiram said, "Oh mighty master, what is your wish today?"

The Sarge said, "You're a funny girl. I just heard from the colonel who heard from your nemesis, Helga."

Asiram's funny face turned to stone, and she said, "I'm going to have to kill that bitch. She can't have our baby under any circumstances."

Zanthius hugged her and asked, "Dad, what did she want?"

"Well, for starters, she told the colonel she's broke. Now, does that mean she can't pay her rent or can't buy a new airplane? I don't know with her, but you people are familiar with her. I don't think we should keep being her bank. Every time she runs out of money, she calls us with some nonsense. Also, she told the colonel that Son, somewhere on your body there is scanned information that brings the myth of the Carbon Factor to life. Have you noticed any strange points or rashes on your body?"

"Dad, be serious. I haven't noticed anything and besides, how on earth could she, or anyone for that matter, scan information onto my body without me knowing it?"

"Son, I hate to mention this, but you do recall that time in the hospital when we deciphered writings on your intestines? You do remember that almost miraculous occasion that left doctors, scientists, and normal human beings, metagrobolized by what they were seeing. You do remember swallowing a capsule. You do remember that day, don't you?"

"Dad, I hardly remember anything from that day other than what you guys told me."

"Zanthius, that's good, Son. Truly, I mean it's good that you can block shit out, what, sixty years of education by various people and you knock them back in kindergarten. I saw it, you saw it, your wife saw it, and everybody else who was there saw it. So, why do you think it's impossible that you have a barcode on your body somewhere? You kissed a woman and swallowed a capsule, and people from all over the world wanted to find you and cut it out of you. I say all of that to say I don't discount anything anymore, and especially, from the foes who apparently still want your body."

Asiram said, "I agree with you, Daddy. We can't keep paying her. More important, why does she show up when new people are being recruited? Is she in cahoots? I don't trust her, and I think the only person who can deal with her, is me.

"Okay, we're not going to settle this at this moment, but I want your opinion on something before I take it to the group. Jilkes, you and your girlfriend, get in here."

The Sarge continued, "I've been thinking about that misdirection thing you and Larry talked about, Son. I'm not going to give you the fat of this idea. I'm only going to give you the skinny of it. First, I want to set a date to destroy the product on camera and in public with the two senators, governor, and ex-Secretary of State. I also want to let the world know that we'll be flying in from Australia to the west coast and then on to Washington, DC. Now, here is my misdirection. I have a friend who I met years ago who loves Rome so much that he moved there and became sort of an unofficial ambassador to the Vatican, or more precisely, to the Holy Father. His wisdom and intelligence have endured three Pontiffs. When the Holy Father has questions about defining intentions, or meanings from world leaders, he calls on my friend, Captain Ben. Yes, I see your confused looks and, yes, there is another one. Ben Hackney used to work for the Chief of Naval Operations. I befriended him during a bar fight years ago, in Rome. Ben Hackney was a senior spy on policy, whatever that means. Here comes the misdirection, on our way back here, or wherever we stop--we stop in Rome and Ben connects us to the Holy Father and we destroy the means for man to kill man before the eyes of the Holy Father, the world and not have to expect an ambush when we get to DC. What do you think?"

Zanthius shook his head in disagreement and said, "Man, I have your genes. You are one cunning son-of-a-priest. Dad, that's incredible. Can you trust that Ben fellow?"

"First of all, Mike gave me the idea. Oh, and Son, I can trust him with my life. You see that fight was a setup and the people who initiated the fight knew he was the mouthpiece to the Pope without protection or sanctions. Fortuitously, he was the reason I was in London when I met your mother. He asked me to help him get rid of some scum that was crawling up a wall to hurt him. I was on leave, I stopped in Rome, got the pictures of the aggressors, and paid them a visit and no, I didn't kill them. I don't like killing people, I just happen to be good at it. I broke them up and told them if anything happened to my friend and brother, I would be back with a force and would kill everyone who was related to them."

Asiram asked, "How bad did you hurt them?"

"Honey, not that bad. I broke arms and legs, ankles and jaws, that's all."

Zanthius asked, "Dad, that's all?"

"I could have broken their backs. Anyway, that was a long time ago. Oh, I then left there and went to London where I met your momma. Whew, what a romance that was, Son. Anyway, I'm getting off target."

Jilkes said, "You know, Sarge, I've always told the guys to leave you alone when we have a problem, and you'll work it out. I'm one hundred percent attached to your plan and so is my country ass friend. Ain't that right?"

Asiram asked, "Do you two ever say anything nice about each other?"

John Lee said, "You didn't think that was nice? I be thinking like my minority friend, I like that plan. What we do is trick them and do it somewhere else. I be liking that a lot. You know that time when we didn't kill all those fellas that came to kill us? Well, I be like trying to give people a chance to live. If they come at us, I got to put them down, but I would rather not have another soul in that there place called hell, waiting on me."

The Sarge looked at Asiram and said, "Two things--you know we're going to have to kill his baby momma and the second is, what are your thoughts about my plan?"

"I like your plan as long as we're going back from Spain, and not Australia. On the other point, leave her to me."

The Sarge said, "I need you guys to really consider what I'm presenting and look for holes in the plan. Tonight, oh shoot, whose boats are those driving up on our beach?"

The group walked out of the room and towards the beach and saw Michael. The Sarge asked, "Michael, did you buy a boat?"

"No sir, but Mr. Mallory and Mr. McArthur did. That's McArthur's dingy floating behind Mallory's boat."

"Wow, that's nice. Where is Mallory?"

"I'm not sure, but he left an hour or so before I did, and we came by water. Oh, Mr. Beckmire, this is Ben, he's, our salesperson."

Asiram exclaimed, "Oh, my God! Another Ben in the same day? Bens are overtaking the world."

Michael said, "He should be arriving, ah, soon. Here comes the van, I guess he and the guys are in it."

The Sarge meandered over to where the van stopped and waited for Mallory and his other men to exit the vehicle. Instead, an older gentleman got out the van and said, "I was paid $200 to drive this van back to Mr. Carter's place and to give him this note from the guy who gave me the money."

The Sarge expected that his cousin had landed on the island. He opened the envelope and read the note aloud— "You have four hours to bring $100,000 to this address, or we will kill your friends."

The Sarge's face contorted, and his smile turned into a frown. With controlled anger, he said, "Damn, I thought my cousin had invaded the island, I need my daughter. Jilkes, can you make that happen?"

Ten or so minutes later, Jilkes showed up with Rashida and her protector, Juan. The Sarge said, "Honey, some novices have abducted some of our people for ransom. I'm hoping that at least one of them is wearing those items you gave them in middle America and that you can track them. Is that possible?"

Rashida asked, "Who's missing Dad?"

"Mallory, Elton, McArthur, and Montomie."

Rashida opened her laptop and said, "No problem, Dad. They got my friends and I'm going to tell you exactly where they are in less than five minutes."

After her computer booted up and she engaged her private internet carrier, she said, "Dad, it looks like they're in a place where they've been before. Oh, shit, Dad, that's where Ms. Viola lives. They're in that building."

He grabbed her and said, "All of my children are smarter than I am, and I thank God for that."

He looked at Michael and said, "I need you to put your people on full alert. I want the cul-de-sac locked down until I find out how my people got suckered by locals."

Michael said, "Mr. Beckmire, I know a backway into that area. If you go trouncing there in force, it may lead to a problem."

The Sarge looked at him and his father and said, "Put that plan in play."

The Sarge said, "In the meantime, I'm going to put my ladies in charge, and I wouldn't recommend a soul going near them. Mr. Carter, can you and the others lay the first line of defense for my family?"

"Mr. Beckmire, unless they come with tanks and submarines, they don't stand a chance. There are some things my son has encouraged us to do which is amazingly simple. We push a button and things get shut down. If we push that same button twice, the cul-de-sac gets shut down—no one in and no one out."

Beckmire said, "Damn, I'm glad you're on our side."

Beckmire looked at Zanthius and said, "I need you to put the women on level five alert, and that means shoot first and ask questions later. I need you, my son, to take control of this area and make sure that our people are safe. I need your brother to do some dirty work. Find him and tell him that Larry the Wanderer is being called to action."

Monica walked into the dining room with Margo and asked Beckmire, "Have you seen Mallory and my son?"

Beckmire beckoned her over to his side and said to her, "Do not show alarm and scare little Ms. Margo. Your husband is being held captive by locals who want money. We're on it, but I need you and the rest of the ladies to move to level five where you shoot first and ask questions later. Now, Monica, you know that I will not let anyone hurt my man. I'm leading this expedition and I will not take any prisoners. Trust me, you touch mine, I destroy all that you are."

Monica looked at Margo and said, "Your brother and father have been sidetracked, but will be home soon."

Approximately, fifty-five minutes later, John Lee, Jilkes, Bernstein, Brown, Jong, and the Sarge were on their way to town and were almost in position for Larry the Wanderer. Fifteen minutes later, a homeless, dirty, and ugly person appeared near Ms. Viola's building. He focused on the trash cans, but the food he ate that seemingly came from the cans was actually placed there by him--the art of misdirection. One of the gang members on lookout duty called on a VHF frequency and said that a bum was eating shit out of the trash cans. Jong zeroed in on that conversation and said to Jilkes, "They're amateurs. Are we doing a full assault?"

Jilkes looked at him and asked, "If it were you, would you want me to ask them to dinner or breakfast?"

"I understand but, a simple yes or no would have sufficed. You don't have to make me look stupid."

"My brother, I'm not passing judgement, I'm just saying I don't go in easy when your life is under the knife. I go in with a killing mindset, the switch is hard to turn off, if you know what I mean."

Larry staggered to the doorway and two guys pushed him down. Larry attempted to get up when one of the guys said, "You piece of shit, go eat garbage somewhere else." Larry pulled out his .308 with a silencer on it and placed a bullet into the man's head doing the pushing and another into his partner's. He then signaled Jilkes, and the group proceeded into the building. He picked up one of the VHFs and hooked it to his pants. As Jilkes and the group entered the building, John Lee said, "Damn, Larry, they be only kids." Larry looked at him, but never responded.

As they began to scale the steps, John Lee said, "I be out of place. We must protect our family. We shoot first and ask questions later. I be sorry, Larry."

On the fourth floor of the building, the VHF began to squeal as if it were too close to another unit that was dialed to the same channel. Larry began yelling, "Charlene, I be sorry man. I don't love that girl, I love you, please baby, open the door so that I can talk to you. Please baby, I don't love her, I love you." He got the reaction he wanted. A tall slender young man walked out of a door with one hand behind his back as if he were concealing a weapon. Larry yelled, "What the fuck you be looking at man?"

"Shut up you drunk, before I smoke your ass!" Coming from the other direction, Jilkes was on the move. He hit the guy so hard, he shattered his jaw. Larry entered the apartment and saw a guy reaching for his gun. Larry said, "Please don't do that."

#

Later, Larry looked at Elton and said, "You've had a busy day, haven't you?" He said to Mallory, "Is there anyone else on the prowl?"

"Those two are the only ones I've seen throughout this ordeal. How were they able to get the drop on Montomie and McArthur?"

Mallory said, "It's a long story and one that I would prefer to discuss at the resort. My little man is hungry."

As they left the site, Brown and Bernstein had loaded the two bodies into the van under cover of night. The group left the hood with two young bodies in the back that would never see the light of day again. The Sarge said, "Those guys were packing and, Son, we don't hesitate when we call Larry the Wanderer into action. Good job, Son. Always shoot first and seek answers later. Mallory, what on earth happened?"

"We were loading up the van with all of the stuff that Elton picked out for he and his sister and suddenly this innocent looking kid walked over to Elton and told him how lucky he was and placed a big ass gun to his head. His compadres placed guns on Montomie, and McArthur and we figured we would wait to see what they wanted before we assaulted them. We all were afraid for Elton because the kid who had the weapon on him had strange wandering eyes. Clearly a person who seemingly liked to hurt others. He was scary and disarming at the same time. The last thing we expected was that someone would try to take us on, but it goes to show you, we can't relax at any time during our trips."

In the rear of the van, a quiet Larry sat looking out of the window. John Lee was near him and said, "I've made that same decision you made tonight, a thousand times. I distracted your actions by bringing in pigshit about them fellas' age. If someone ever catch me, or my minority friend asleep, and we need to be rescued, please come in the same way, and shoot everybody except us. That was some professional shit back there, and I be proud to work with you on any job, if you would be selecting me."

Larry studied John Lee's face to extract a hint of insincerity but couldn't discern any signs. He laughed and said, "John Lee, if you ever want to speak Spanish, I'll teach you."

"Now, why would I want to be speaking Spanish. You people don't understand my English, I don't want to confuse you guys with another language. It wouldn't be fair."

As the group rounded a bend in the road, the Sarge pulled out his phone and called Mr. Carter. He told him they were a couple of miles away and to have his people stand down. He then called Zanthius and told him they were entering 'The Sanctuary' and for his group to stand down as well.

When the van pulled in front of the resort, Margo stood patiently and finally saw her brother. She said, "I thought they were trying to do to us what they did to Katy and Sarah. I guess not, and I'm glad you're back."

Monica heard the conversation and placed her hands on their shoulders and said, "Stop this kind of conversation. You are not going to be separated. My husband and I adopted you both, and you both will live with us until God makes the call. I need you to stop thinking that something is going to happen to you and him and that you guys will not be together. I need your trust and your love. We are new at this, and it just might be to your advantage to push the envelope, if you know what I mean, until we understand the art of parenting. We love you both and you're what they call a package deal. We can't have one without the other. Do you understand?"

Elton said, "I do, and those guys tried to kidnap me today, but dad's friends came to our rescue."

Ms. Margo said, "Elton, stop making stories up. You'll start to believe them."

The Sarge in a one-on-one with Mallory asked, "Okay, I know you didn't want to throw the guys under the bus, but what really happened."

"Sarge, a child-like warrior placed a large caliber weapon to my son's head. No alternative information is available. That's what happened, and I cautioned the guys to stand down and stay down," Mallory stated.

"What's the learning curve on this one? Do we send more men? Do we stake out a place prior to going to it? I don't know, but you have to decide how we do this from now on," the Sarge stated.

Michael slowly moved to where Mallory and the Sarge were sitting, and once they acknowledged him, he made his way to their table. He said, "Sorry to bother you, but I do have two bodies that need to be deep sixed. Can you designate someone to help me?"

Mallory said, "Sarge, John Lee prematurely said something to Larry about the stiffs, but later apologized. I think Larry may be a little down and might need a man-size-hug from his father."

Mallory, then turned to Michael, and said, "Take John Lee and Jilkes. Take them on that old boat, not the new one."

The Sarge said, "Yeah, what's up with that boat thing? When did you get into boating?"

"My son likes to fish. When we were out on Michael's dinghy, but I didn't feel safe in it, so, I purchased a bigger boat, and I have the salesperson looking for another one in the fifty foot plus range. I was thinking, perhaps we should build docks. We have four other places, and a large dock would bring in private yachts and larger boats. We could keep the sanctity of 'The Sanctuary' and move the docks to the beginning of the cul-de-sac or the end. Anyway, Michael, talk to your people and see what they think about the idea. I'm taking this project on personally."

Michael stood there, and Mallory was wondering why he was still in their presence. He asked, "Is there another matter?"

"Mr. Mallory, I'm not accustomed to telling your people to come and assist me in disposing of dead fish. They might want to hear that from a higher authority."

The Sarge laughed and said, "Michael, see if you can fetch them and tell them that I'm looking for them. One will not be that far from the other."

The Sarge then said, "If we had to interview for people like him, we would never find a guy like that. Wait a minute, the Sarge exclaimed!" The Sarge got up and bellowed into the night air, "Michael, I need to see you."

A minute or so passed, and Michael cautiously and startled because of the booming voice of the Sarge. He stood in front of him and said, "You called me. How can I help?"

"I want you to know we run a tight ship and that you're a welcome addition to it."

Mr. Carter hurriedly walked into the room expecting to hear some disturbing news. The Sarge, after recognizing him said, "Come on in. You and your son are great assets to our group. I'm sure the entire island has asked about us, but it's apparent you guys keep us out of the press. Michael, we've asked you to do some dastardly things that we hope won't rise to the surface, at some point in time."

"Mr. Beckmire, there are places in the water that only people who live here know about. There also be fish in the water that will strip a body to its core in a day or so and then feed upon its bones. You helped my dad when he, stubbornly, refused to admit that the bankers were going to shaft him. He wouldn't listen to me because his generation needs to be all knowing, but that doesn't stop me from loving the man. He's a proud man and it hurt him to have you guys help him. But now he realizes you are good people without a bottom line, and he adores the group and what it has done for his ex-wife, and children. You really don't know me, but my father does. He knows I'm a loyalist and when challenged, I can't remember shit! I'm employed. You've asked me to coordinate the toxic relationships between the owners in the cul-de-sac and I've gained their confidence, even being the son of Mr. Chris Carter. I owe you, and I can only pay you with loyalty, a thing my dad told me is greater than money."

The Sarge held his hand out and shook Michael's hand until it hurt him. He said, "Your family is my family, and my family is your family, and I swear that to you in blood." He pulled a blade from the back of his pants and slit his hand. He gave the blade to Michael who passed it to his dad who, without hesitation, slit his hand. Michael then slit his hand and the three men joined their hands together and swore an allegiance. The Sarge said, "Until death do us part."

# # #

Later as the Sarge was about to have a drink, he saw Larry walking on the beach. He called out to Larry, who stopped and appeared to be mentally engaged in conversation with himself. The Sarge said, "Looks like you're having an argument with your best friend. What's the deal?"

"Dad, I shot two kids today and perhaps I was a little quick on the draw. Maybe I could have disarmed them, but I don't think I had to shoot them."

"Son, that's a fine line you're walking. Remember the kid that shot Chakes in the back and the other two that were with him, and that was after he brought them here to help them? I wasn't there with you and, therefore, I can't assist you in trying to figure out if you did the right thing. What I can say is this--I've never known you to be anxious while we were in the field. I only remember you calculating the odds of surviving and I'm sure that's what you did today.

"Son, listen, we're not Boy Scouts. There are people who want us dead. Those two young men were a part of a scheme to extort money from us by kidnapping our people. I'm damn glad you seized the moment to save our people and, yes, I'm sad you had to end the lives of two young men. However, both were carrying weapons and one placed a loaded weapon to the head of Mallory's newly adopted son."

The Sarge paused, placed a hand on his chin, and said, "Let me see! What would I have done? Well, Son, let me tell you what I would have done. I would have assessed the situation and acted expeditiously, realizing the magnitude of the threat. I say all that to say, good job! I assume if you have a weapon on you, you're going to use it at some point in defense or offense. You didn't know those guys; all you knew was that they were armed. You can't rationalize what happened. You didn't go there and, purposefully, target those two men. Let it go, Son. You did what's right and your family will be forever grateful to you."

"Dad, but their families will never see their child or brother again."

"Son, their profession was not an honorable one. They tried to kidnap our people and steal our money--they were crooks. Sooner or later, if not you, someone would be pulling the trigger on them because they were not honorable human beings. Let it go, Larry."

The two men headed towards the resort and Larry said, "I think we need docks here so that yachts and other watercrafts can come and enjoy the ambiance of 'The Sanctuary'. Everything is so fancy here. I ordered a hamburger the other day and it came with fresh melon, strawberries, sliced apple, and pieces of coconut. It was served on a roll that was thin, but strong enough to handle the juices. The fries were in a cup, wrapped in paper with a bag of mustard on one side and ketchup on the other. Every time we order food, it comes to us like a work of art by one of the old masters."

"Larry, we should talk to Mr. Carter about that. You do know that Mallory brought a boat and dinghy today, and McArthur purchased a dinghy."

"I saw that boat out there and was wondering who the heck it belonged to. You know if Mr. Carter has rights to the land heading east on the beach, then it might be worth having that discussion. I was considering the stretch of beach on the other side of 'The Sanctuary'. That would be great."

## CHAPTER TWENTY-ONE

As the group prepared to board their plane for Spain, and as the planning for the destruction of the Carbon Factor formula continued to be discussed, the colonel called Mike with news that would be unsettling to all. He told Mike that the Russians had teamed up with the leadership of China, Turkey, Algeria, Venezuela, Cuba, the Philippines, and Syria. They pledged that they would secure the product and wreak havoc on America for all its atrocities across the globe and on their people. He said, "Mike, I'm afraid some of the countries in the world that are ruled by dictators have forged a secret alliance and have committed resources to obtain the formula at any cost. You and your people have been put on the worlds 'hit list' and I advise you guys to go into hiding." Mike asked him to try to keep them informed and that he would be in touch.

Mike walked over to the Sarge and asked, "Can you assemble your brain trust for a moment? I have some very disconcerting news I think we should consider before we head out."

The Sarge looked at him and said, "Damn, Mike, it's that bad, eh?"

"I'm afraid so, sir."

"It must be. You never call me 'sir'."

As the brain trust assembled outside of the plane, Mallory had to convince Elton that he was not going to leave him. He told Elton, "I want you to sit on the top step and don't move unless I turn away from you. We, my son, are going to play a game of trust. I'm going to win because I love my son and I think he's beginning to love me."

Of late, wherever Mallory went, Elton was not far behind. When Monica moved, Margo moved. When they were all together, they, seemingly, moved as one always touching each other's hands as a sign of constant communication.

John Lee, Jilkes, Mallory, Beckmire, Jong, and Mike stood outside of the plane and discussed the information that had been gathered by Mike. Jong said, "If this is that big of a problem, then they know where we're heading. I think we should go away and figure out how to handle this issue."

"I don't like having to make sure I can protect my family. This one doesn't seem like it can be fixed on the fly. We need to gather our resources and make them come to us. I be thinking that the most unfriendly place would be in that there outback," John Lee stated.

Jilkes jumped in and said, "Damn, now you finally make sense. We let everyone know we changed our minds and decided to head to the outback to do some fishing and sunning in a remote village that is only occupied by the indigenous animals. To the rest of the world, that means, wild dogs, spiders, and snakes. They don't have a clue that it means giant size saltwater crocodiles, dingoes that hunt in packs, poisonous spiders and snakes, and a shitload of other things that can kill you if you're not focused. Screw Spain: we can catch it on the way back. From what I've heard, we need an advantage. The outback is the perfect cover and a place that we can effectively manage our business."

John Lee said, "What bothers me a lot of times is that my minority brother hears me thinking and then throws my thoughts out there as if they be his. The plan he just laid out, my plan, I be endorsing. It don't seem to me that if we surrender the product that them there fellas will go home and have sex with their mates. I think their contracts require them to make people dead, and I think the dead people under consideration, be us. In that there outback, hell, there be too many things going against them. My plan is the same one that the minority guy stole, and I be endorsing it," John Lee professed.

The Sarge said, "I want to put an end to this color shit right now. Jilkes, do you want to fight him again?"

The Sarge then looked at John Lee and asked, "Do you want to be embarrassed again by him?"

Jilkes looked at John Lee and, simultaneously, they both looked at the Sarge. John Lee asked, "Why you want to see us fight?"

The Sarge said, "You keep saying that minority shit and he keeps waving you off. I want to know if you two have a problem with each other?"

Jilkes said, "Sarge, all's good. He is who he is, and I accept who he is and that is my brother. I don't fret about his innuendos, I know that if someone comes to me in an aggressive manner, this cracker will kick the shit out of them. All's good, Sarge."

John Lee asked, "Did I say something offensive?"

The Sarge said, "Damn it man, you keep calling him 'minority this' and 'minority that'. Honestly, John Lee, you don't think that's offensive? Suppose every time that he referenced you, he called you a *cracker*? Eventually, wouldn't you get pissed off about that and want to kick his ass?"

"Now, Sarge, he don't be calling me a cracker that often. I call him minority, but he knows that I love him. If he thought my words be offensive, he would say something. I don't know why everyone else puts their pigs in the same pen with mine. I just don't get it."

The Sarge looked at him and shook his head. He asked Jong to have Carla come down from the cockpit because he had a few questions to ask her.

Five minutes later, Carla walked down the steps after having a brief conversation with Elton. She asked, "Mr. Beckmire, you requested me?"

"I did, Captain. I think we need to change our destination from Spain to Australia. Do you have the correct number of pilots in pocket to make that happen, as well as fuel and service?"

"Mr. Beckmire, when we travel abroad, I always bring in a second set of crew members to make sure we're legal and can leave at any time. I know how we must roll and, therefore, I keep my people busy. If Sydney is our destination, then I will have to change our flight plan to include Los Angeles for refueling and then the long trip across the pond to Sydney where we'll refuel again before flying to the Northern Territory."

"Wow, Captain. The Northern Territory, I like that. Anyway, that is our destination and I need you to make the changes."

"Mr. Beckmire, there is one small problem that remains. We don't have clear paperwork for Elton and Margo. Can your people over there help us with the paperwork?"

"Damn! I hadn't thought about that. Well, we have the paperwork from the adoption agency, we have their access stamp into St. Thomas and from there, I think we can make it work. We shall see."

The Sarge walked on the plane after consulting with his brain-trust and said, "People, I need your attention because I need to make a major announcement. Please, may I have your attention?"

After the occupants settled down, the Sarge said, "I am so sorry to disrupt your lives as much as I have had to do, but I am about to make another adjustment. We will not be flying to Spain as previously scheduled. Instead, we will be flying to Australia."

The Sarge continued, "Several countries that are run by dictators have joined forces to obtain the Carbon Factor in an effort to wreak havoc on our beloved country. I'm a patriot and I believe in what our country stands for. If this thing called the Carbon Factor is real, then I surely want to destroy it publicly. Now, I know you've heard this speech before, but what you may not know is that there are reportedly, six nations under dictatorships that have bonded together to retrieve the formula. We will not be able to defend against these people in middle America, Virginia, and/or St. Thomas. There are, apparently, simply too many.

However, that place where my ancestors are from has many opportunities to discombobulate these people. I say all of that to say, I've directed Captain Carla to point this thing to Sydney and then to the Northern Territory. Is there anyone who would like to discuss or negate my directions for the group?"

The occupants of the plane were silent.

Finally, the Sarge said, "I thank you for your trust and we will need the vigilance of every person in this group, including the children. We are honorable and decent people and, therefore, God is on our side. We can delay this trip by two to three hours to allow people to purchase things that they don't need. Oh, it might be smart if everyone invested in boots and socks or perhaps it might be better to do that once we get there."

CHAPTER TWENTY-TWO

Almost a full day later, the weary group's plane landed in Sydney, Australia. Okema, Somara, and Yeshida conducted mandatory yoga classes to keep the blood flowing throughout everyone's veins. Even the Sarge and his crew participated in the much needed, stretching and relaxation exercises. The back of the plane was essentially a nursery. Elton and Margo were much more relaxed and enjoyed the fact that their seats on the plane had their names on the trays in front of them. Yes, the two children began to adapt to their new family members and became less guarded and displayed socialization skills that were indicative of members of a clan.

#

In Sydney, the group left the plane and headed to Customs where, fortunately, familiar faces greeted the group. Once through customs, Yvette was welcomed by fifty or so people who were related to her and to Ben Beckmire. Beckmire was given the honor of presenting Yvette and Bernstein's son to family members who had gathered in the waiting room. Elton and Margo's paperwork was sketchy at best, but the agent knew the group and was not going to let details stand in the way of welcoming the children to Australia.

The second flight crew made their inspections of the plane and were followed up by Carla and her co-captain. Two hours later, the plane was refueled, and the group reboarded it.

After departing Sydney, Carla sat in the jump seat and watched the relief crew handle the plane. Once it leveled off, Larry unbuckled his seatbelt and walked to the front of the plane and sat on the floor next to a sleeping Beckmire and nudged him. He said, "Dad, I have a plan that might lessen the odds against us. Do you know what time it is?"

Beckmire looked at his watch and said, "Really, Larry? You wake me up to ask me what time it is?"

"Dad, I meant to ask, what time of the year is it? And of course, you know, being a descendant of this place, what season it is. It's summer, and it exceeds a hundred degrees daily in the outback. When we get to the village, we inform the people of the impending dangers. We move everyone deeper towards the center of the continent, where if you don't know the land, you will starve or die of thirst. We move our group deeper and deeper into the outback, but we have our friends pick up the enemies discarded weapons and circle around them and bring them to us. Here's the beauty of my plan--I'll bet you $10 they think it's better to travel during the night because of the heat during the day. You and I know that at night, you can't see where you're going and there are things in this place that look for lost and evil travelers. Any thoughts on my plan? Strategically, they would have to have helicopter support to deliver them provisions once we embark towards the center of the country. They are going to be heavily armed, carrying way too much water, and will probably begin to kill each other once they run out of it. If they go near any billabong, the crocs will certainly be hungry. I think in the absence of any other plan, this is one that can be tweaked and set into motion."

Ben Beckmire placed one of his massive hands on Larry's forehead, and said, "Heal."

He patted his head as he thought about what Larry had said. He thought about going deep into the outback but felt hesitant and knew that the natives would share his sentiments. He turned to Larry and said, "Son, my people know there are times when you don't go towards the center. When we get there and if we can convince them, we need their help, and, if they agree to take us deeper into the land, then I think it will work. Wajickee told me I should trust your instincts, even though you're not a Beckmire by blood. He said, 'My love for you and your love for me is as strong as any love he has ever seen.'

"You know Larry, it was a lot easier when we put drug dealers out of business. This thing is so complicated that it appears to me that everyone we encounter is on the take. Wake Mallory and Jong. I need to know exactly what we have on this plane in terms of weapons."

"Dad, in Vietnam, you and your people were called the 'bow people'. Why are you worried about weapons?"

Beckmire looked at Larry and said, "You are so special to me, and I love you so much, Son. I know we have small caliber weapons for everyone on the plane. If we follow your plan, we use those for close work and fashion weapons out of local resources. They'll think nighttime is the best time, but we'll prove to them, that it ain't necessarily so."

Larry started to get up when the Beckmire suggested, "Stop by Yvette and Bernstein's to get her input. She is from here, and I hope she has some recommendations. Just humor me and check with her."

"Done, Dad."

As Larry made his way to where Yvette and Bernstein were sitting, he said, "Hey guys, I need to have a serious discussion with you about our defenses once we're in the outback. We only have small caliber weapons because we're not naturalized citizens and, therefore, we can't own weapons. Yvette, how can we fashion bows and arrows in a place that's so hot and dry?"

"Oh, Larry, there are all kinds of trees and bushes that you can use to create weapons. By the way, if people come here to hunt us, they will also have to deal with the locals. Listen, your father, my uncle, is like a God here. They have days, festivals, feasts, sermons, rituals, stars, and holidays named after his namesake. I can assure you that an ill-wind has blown this way and they're preparing for a reckoning. In the morning, I'll take you city types for a walk through the outback, and we can pick the right trees to fashion arrows from, and those to make bows from. It'll be fun, but first, we must make sure everyone has boots and long pants. That bull stuff about wearing shorts in the outback is as stupid as wearing a fur coat in St. Thomas. Where we're going, you cover the body unless you be Aborigine. There are things that can sting or bite us that will cause a problem. For my sweet and loving husband, a simple mosquito bite could be the beginning of the end. We eat everything that moves and, therefore, develop a resistance to spiders, mosquitoes, some snakes and even the box jelly fish, to an extent. That's a stretch of the folklore, but I wouldn't want to test it."

"Thanks for the update. I'm recommending to the Sarge that we move farther into the interior and create a water issue for the people who we're speculating are going to come here for us."

"Larry, trust me. Our friends have already moved their camps towards the center and have stored their weapons along the way for easy retrieval. Don't ask me how they know. Did your dad call them? Did I send a text message? No, I did not. Larry, and my beloved, this place is magical and that's all I'm going to say. If you haven't witnessed it yet, you will."

"So, Yvette, you, me, and Bernstein are going to go for a walk once we land?"

"No, Larry. You, Marisa, Bernstein, and I are going to go for a walk in the morning. That woman is such a catch, and those twins are so adorable. I hope my husband wants more children because I do."

Bernstein looked at her and kissed her forehead. He said, "I love you so much and whatever you want, I want. I just want you to be happy with life and me."

Yvette looked at him and said, "Something is troubling you, my husband. Are you having those dreams again? If so, I can only tell you that my dreams are more powerful than yours because yours are focused on the Nam. My dreams are about family and love." Larry wanted to ask about the nature of their dreams but realized that it wasn't his business.

# # #

The captain came over the speaker system and said, "We've begun our descent into the Northern Territory. I need everyone to self-check and make sure they're in the correct position for a safe landing, and that means, seatbelts, babies, small children, and older children are all secure and in place. Come on people, I need feedback."

On the final approach, a violent crosswind pushed the plane sideways and caused everyone concern. Without hesitation, as if this were a repeat performance, the captain rode the wind sideways and at the right moment, gunned the port engine and backed off the starboard. That action corrected the direction of the plane and it landed smoothly with a lot of claps, signs of the cross, Hail Marys, and a few other religious gestures.

As the plane taxied to the only covered hangar, Beckmire said, "Wow, what another fabulous landing from our crew. Let's give them another round of applause. On this occasion and in this land, we will never be out of each other's eyesight. I have the strongest feeling this is where it all ends, except for one aspect of it. If we're successful here, we begin the hunt for Walter without any impediments. We're also expected to present the formula in Washington, but you all know what our intentions are on that one. How can a single government be operated by everyone who has their hands in the cookie jar? I'm appalled at our system, and I want to expose each one of those crooked bastards and, pardon me, bitches for that matter."

No one texted or called, but a school bus was waiting at the airport for the group and was prepared with history plus information about how to proceed. When the group disembarked, the driver said, "We have been waiting for you and everything is in order. We have twenty people who will watch the plane and its crew. Once we're at the familiar village, you will find clothing that will fit everyone, including the new additions. It is time to conclude one aspect of this matter, but our family member will be hiding in a conspicuous place once you return to the land of evil."

The Sarge asked, "How do you know so much about our plan and those who will be coming here to conclude our existence?"

"Ben Beckmire, your family is the source of legend and truth. In this land, there is a testament to your heritage and certainty, and anyone foolish enough to confront that reality and legend will face an unforgettable transition to hell. All is well here, and all is protected here. It is also fortunate you have those two smart lawyers with you. People are also trying to find holes in our rightful ownership of the land where that huge stone was found. In the interim, we have purchased barren land from the east, west, south, and north, because of a little-known tenet that was not exercised, and or questioned, and was omitted by their high-priced lawyers. Their omission allowed us to purchase without contest, for a modest fee of $600 dollars in each direction, 2,000 acres to the east, 2,000 to the west, another 2,000 to the south, and 2,000 to the north. While the north and south land's look to provide us with significant revenue from the discovery of oil, the east and west lands promise to provide us with large amounts of diamonds and gold. We've begun to prepare for a full-scale war. As such, Mr. Beckmire, we have unearthed some weapons that were left by a group who thought they could waltz in here and conquer the land. They all died of thirst."

Beckmire asked, "What kind of weapons did you capture?"

"Ben Beckmire, I don't know anything about weapons. I'm your driver."

The Sarge turned around and yelled, "Larry, I need your help up here."

When Larry walked to the front of the bus, the Sarge informed him, "The driver just told me that they unearthed some weapons that we could possibly use. I need you and Bernstein to handle that charge. I know he's unlikely to want to move without Brown, so I'll include him as well."

#

As the bus neared the first village where the group had stayed, they noticed the place looked deserted. Ben Beckmire was told that in anticipation of problems, they moved to the interior until he had finished his affairs. They also set up preliminary borders and defenses were so happy to help in defending one of theirs against bad people. Ben Beckmire asked who oversaw developing their defenses, and he was astonished when Darryl's name came forward, followed by Sue Lyn's next. He pardoned himself and went back to Jong who said, "I know exactly what you're going to say, and there was nothing I could do about their trip. I found out late when we were taking off that they were on their way. They took a commercial flight as soon as Darryl heard the news."

The Sarge asked, "How did Darryl hear the news and from whom?"

"Sarge, these be your people. I don't understand half the things I see and find the other half hard to believe. You tell me, Brother."

The Sarge sat next to Courtney and said, "Darryl and Sue Lyn are here setting up our defenses."

"Really? How did they know about what was going on?"

"My only answer to that question is that, somehow, Wajickee made a call."

"I won't ask how he knew. You haven't explained to me how he could be hundreds of years old. I'm a doctor, I don't believe in spirits and stuff."

#

An hour or so later, the bus pulled near a billabong, and everyone got off. Ben Beckmire asked, "Aren't we a little too close to that billabong?"

The driver said, "This is where I was told to let you off. There's your nephew, mate."

Darryl walked over and said, "Good day, Mate! You took your time getting here."

"Darryl, why aren't you in school?"

"Uncle, it's the weekend and Sue Lyn and I thought you could use our help. We're out of here tomorrow, so, therefore, we need to bring Juan and Rashida up to date on what we've done."

"Darryl, how did you know we were going to have an issue and that we wanted to settle it here where we could control some of the environment?"

"Oh, my God! Uncle, you're Aborigine and we know all. Oh, and by the way, thanks for introducing me to Sue Lyn. We plan on marrying once I finish school."

Beckmire was about to say something when Darryl said, "I know what you're going to ask, and I have not, and I repeat, I have not, according to the parameters set down by those who control everything, violated my pledge. She is as virgin as that new Roo calf over there behind the bushes."

"Darryl, shut up before you out talk yourself. Speak with Rashida and Juan and let me know what and where we have coverage after you and they have agreed upon the deployment. Make sure you have transportation out of here tomorrow in time for your flight. By the way, does Jong's cousin know where his daughter is?"

"Uncle, we are trying to communicate with adults, like adults, and truthfully. She told him where she was heading, and he did not give his approval. She told him that she loved him but was also in love with me and that we had not violated our pledge. He later recanted and asked what we needed in terms of software. I told him I loved his daughter, that I would ask him to acknowledge our relationship, and at least let me show him how I will be able to afford to care for her. I also, honestly told him we desire each other and at each juncture of our union we recall our pledge. I told him that I'm not sure how much longer I could submit to my pledge and that I wanted to run off and marry Sue Lyn as soon as possible. Uncle, I could hear a sigh of approval in his voice, but I have not, or we have not consummated our relationship through the true definition of sex or making love."

"My nephew, you're a cunning little beast with a lot of talent and bullshit. If you violate my guidance and you consummate your relationship, I will banish you from the family. My friend--her uncle, and her father would follow an old tradition and that would pit me against them. That ain't going to happen, so you'd better keep 'Richard' in his cave, and you need to arrange for a ceremony as soon as possible. You risk everything, including her dignity, if you violate the agreement. Wajickee can marry you without certificates and it will be a ceremony approved by the Spirits. Don't touch that flower again until you've bargained with your demons to make sure that this is not an exercise in the satisfaction of carnal feelings, but one that is rooted in the essence of love, respect, and fidelity."

"Uncle, I was told long ago that you are a man of great wisdom and who has a silver tongue. I now know what that means. I will ask Wajickee to join us in marriage on this continent, but I will not use that opportunity to by-pass our obligations to her parents. Uncle, you are wise, and your words are important to my ears."

"Darryl be the man that I know you can be, and the entire world will know your name and that of Sue Lyn. You and the younger members of this group will inherit a shitload of money, assets, land, and other things that can distract people from their true missions. Your mission should always be 'helping people to help themselves', and your money should follow your conviction. This group walks a tight rope. People are always trying to conclude our existence. That's why we're here."

"Uncle, that's why Sue Lyn and I are here, to give you an extra added capability against odds that seem insurmountable. Any fool that comes to this land is truly a jester. This country is unforgiving, and it certainly will wreak havoc on those who are here to hurt a relative, especially one with the name of Beckmire."

"Boy, you're beginning to sound a lot like Wajickee. Do you speak with him much?"

"Uncle, I will not tell a lie. Almost every day, I feel his presence and it comforts me. He frowns on how much time Sue Lyn, and I spend on manufacturing ways to kill people, but he also remembers the lawlessness that almost wiped our people from this earth."

The Sarge looked at him and smiled. As he turned to walk away, he said, "Do not come between me and my brothers. Honor your pledge and marry right, not expeditiously."

Near the billabong, Sue Lyn, Rashida, and Juan were discussing that the only way into their new camp was straight on from the hills. Sue Lyn asked, "You guys keep focusing on the land in front of us instead of the water behind us.

Suppose they decided to pull some special forces mess and use rubber boats?"

Rashida said, "Sue Lyn, I personally haven't seen any crocs and hope I never do, but I've been told some incredible stories about the things that inhabit that particular billabong. Let me say, if we're successfully attacked by water then it is our time to perish in the outback." Sue Lyn looked a little confused, smiled and walked away in search of Darryl.

In a clearing, Ben Beckmire sat in the position most demonstrably illustrated by Rodin and his statute *The Thinker*. Sue Lyn saw him in that renowned position and mused. She decided to be bold, walked over to Beckmire, and said, "Mr. Beckmire, do you know who Rodin was? Have you ever seen a picture of his sculpture titled, *The Thinker*? Anyways, if I get an internet signal, I'll fetch you and show you the infamous statute. Can I get you some water or something?"

"Sue Lyn, may I speak freely with you for a moment?"

"Of course, you can. Do I have to assume the position of *The Thinker* as well? Just kidding."

"I'm not going to treat you like a child. I had a long conversation with Darryl, and he assured me you two had not crossed the bridge that was placed in front of you. Now, I'm an old man who has broken so many promises that I could build a bridge if each one was a brick. In your situation and his, that is not the same. If you and he move to the next level or get to the next base, it could mean ruin for me, Darryl, your uncle, your dad, and our relationships. It's like a conundrum."

"Mr. Beckmire, I've had dreams of culminating a beautiful event with Darryl and then the nightmares that follow from us deceiving everyone who loves us. They frighten me, and I can never explain them to Darryl. I challenge him, and he challenges me and, somehow, we back off each time from what seems appealing, good, and pleasurable. I so desperately want to experience the real event, and so does Darryl, however, we both know it would start our lives together off with a huge lie, a lie that would ruin our relationship over time."

"Sue Lyn, do you trust me?"

"As far as I can see you, Mr. Beckmire. Just kidding. Of course, I do."

"Once you complete helping us with our defenses, I'm going to have someone take you to the airport and I want you to fly home alone. If you fly together then there will be a snowball that won't be able to be stopped. Will you do that for me, your uncle, and your father?"

Sue Lyn assumed the position of *'The Thinker'* and said, "I know this is best and I need to face father and tell him that I'm still his child."

"You're making the best decision for everyone. I will hold Darryl over and let him experience what aggression looks like. Therefore, if you want to see your man, make sure this area is fortified and strategically situated."

"Uncle Beckmire, not even a single mosquito will be able to enter this area once we set it in motion. That I can promise you."

# # #

That night, Diablo was at work trying to seduce Darryl and Sue Lyn. From the bush, members of varying tribes came into camp to offer their services. McArthur and Montomie had their canteens filled with various drinks. Courtney thought that Ben Beckmire was trying to make a move on Ava, and Marisa thought that Larry was being seduced by Mary Alice.

The camp seemingly was in chaos when Beckmire stood up and fired a single shot into the air. He said, "People the devil and his disciples are trying to create problems for us. I need you people to find your niche and remain alcohol free tonight. That is not a request, that's an order."

Ms. Viola saw Chakes acting hyper and aggressive and called out to Beckmire. She said, "Mister, I need your help with him. His demons are trying to control him, and he be letting them win so far."

The Sarge walked over to Chakes and said, "My brother, this is going to hurt in the morning." He cold cocked him.

The Bush people began to chant and display their defiance. When Wajickee entered the scene, everything became normal again.

He asked, "Was I missed?" He walked over to Ben Beckmire and said, "Two plane loads of people will be arriving at the airport early in the morning. I be thinking they will land around sunrise. You have come to the right place to have this interaction. People believe in all kinds of things, but you have always held fast with your beliefs, even when others have thought you to be missing parts of your brain. Your people will be called to task, and your forged weapons from the land will be your biggest protector. My friends have fashioned many arrows, you have some mechanized weapons, and you also have the dingoes, wombats, and crocs. This invading force has picked a time when the country is out of balance because of that thing they say that doesn't exist, global warming. The animals feel it and are confused by it.

"My friends have created a perimeter that the animals will not breach. Any fool who comes up the billabong will be a hearty meal for the festival of crocs that are all in heat. Oh, by the way, the dingoes are also in heat. All the animals in this area are out to get laid, eaten, or destroyed because of this false weather pattern. They are aggressive, and the snakes and spiders are on the move as well."

Beckmire interrupted him, "I should know better than to question your wisdom, but I have a lot of children here."

"Ah, Ben Beckmire, these children will have lots of children to carry on the work that you and your people have signed on to do until death do you, and them, part. Where did you find that little Beatrice? She's a fire storm and will make everyone proud."

# # #

That night, in the middle of the outback, the Beckmire group and locals had a feast of the earth and listened to the sweet and mellow sounds of the didgeridoo.

Courtney said to Ben, "I think we're most at peace when we're here and surprisingly, frolicking in the outdoors with all kinds of weird animals not far away. How do they keep them and the bugs away from us?"

"Honey, we're the good guys. The bugs prefer to eat the bad guys."

At approximately 2100 hours, Beckmire was summoned by one of the locals who told him that he had received word that a large contingency of men would arrive via a freighter that was on its way here. He told Beckmire, the men had different dialects and that some were Asian, and others appeared to sound French. Beckmire thanked him and told him that he needed eyes on those people, and when they started to move, he wanted to be alerted. He asked if there was impending danger tonight, and the bloke told him that most of the men appeared too drunk to fight.

Beckmire found Mallory and asked him to round up the team. He told Mallory that unwanted guests had arrived on the continent.

Fifteen minutes later, the entire team met, including Mike, Larry, and Zanthius. The Sarge began the discussion by telling them that this group was not procured by his cousin but was the result of every bad person who is a dictator that had funds to support this incursion. He indicated they had some artillery, and this fight was about capturing and distributing weapons of the fallen.

John Lee asked, "Perhaps we should go out and meet them?"

Jilkes looked at him and said, "Perhaps you're right. I'm assuming, they don't know exactly where we are, but like in all conflicts, some people are for sale. I think we've made enough noise for everyone to know exactly where we are. I think we should do some sniper work and retreat. I'm talking about being as close as 700 to 1,000 yards kind of work."

The Sarge asked, "Any other ideas? Come on guys, don't let the two lovers out do you."

Brown said, "I would use a different strategy to deplete their numbers. I would start where they are by adding a little something to their food or water source for that matter. By the way, how many people are we talking about, and who's the no-good traitor that's tracking us and giving them information?"

The Sarge said, "Oh, we know who they are, and they will be dealt with appropriately. Where is Juan, Rashida, and Carlos?"

"I neglected to tell them about the meeting. I'll get them," Mallory indicated.

# # #

Fifteen minutes later, when Rashida showed up, she asked, "Dad, how could you forget about me? How could you?"

"I'm sorry, Baby Girl. You know I have so much on my mind that I sometimes forget things. What you got for us?"

"Well, Darryl and Sue Lyn gave us a lot of ideas. We've created some interesting firing scenarios. Those guys will probably have the latest military hardware, it will all probably be automatic. We have 8 cameras—8, .40 pistols, and that equals 120 rounds per weapon, or 1024 rounds that can be controlled by cell phones. These guys will have heavy equipment including vests and, therefore, all shots must be head shots and out of sequence to distort where the firing is coming from. The cameras and weapons are in separate places and, therefore, we have Okema, Somara, Yeshida, Asiram, Juan and me, so far, who have an orientation for weapons that are assigned to us. Juan and I can handle two cameras each.

"Now, Daddy, without your input, we established our position approximately 1.5 miles away from here because each of us can run an efficient two miles in sixteen to seventeen minutes. We will be approximately 400 yards from where the action will take place. Our receivers are good for 600 yards, so they say, but we're going to test the range tomorrow. Darryl said he guaranteed the distance, but you know me, I like to check things for myself. Another surprise is that your family is not going to let these foreigners come to town to hurt you without providing some hick-ups along the way. Approximately forty arrows will fill the air from all directions as soon as they cross the imaginary 'red line'. It's unlikely that they'll split their forces in search of those who fired the arrows. By the way, how many people are we talking about?"

"Baby Girl, I wish I knew. Right now, I'm more interested in what plans you've developed to secure us." He looked around the circle and the guys knew what he was thinking.

"Okay, so, Dad, if they chase the directions of the arrows, they will fall into thickets where there are poisonous snake pits and plenty of Australia's deadliest spiders. Your people know where to run and where not to. These guys are nuts to try this event in a foreign land that they know nothing about."

"Baby Girl, that's where I feel your assumptions go awry. They have natives who are helping them and showing them the way."

"Dad, that's great. They can only get to this area by traveling along that other billabong two or more miles away from here. Your family has assured us that it will be the place where they set up camp, but the things that they will disturb seems to be mighty creepy to me. They're going to see that clear water and want to swim in it, and the guide is not going to know that crocs now inhabit that water. According to your family, that billabong didn't exist a week ago and was just formed two days ago along with all this bush."

John Lee said, "Damn, you be a Beckmire from head to toe. You done gone and planned this whole thing out for us old farts. Damn, Rashida, I want to thank you."

Jilkes jumped up and said, "Best damn plan I've heard all day. All we need is specifics and points of engagement and pull back and places where we can lead them where the animals won't be so friendly. They're going to give us some of that stuff to rub on so that the animals don't find us appetizing, right?"

Rashida said, "Knowing you guys, I know you have a better plan than that one."

Bernstein said, "Rashida, actually, our plan mirrors yours, except we hadn't gotten into the specifics of who is going to do what, when, and where. We had a forward contingency in our plan, but ah, had not assigned specific resources to it. I think we're all in agreement with your plans, so far. My only question is, what is our last line of defense?"

Juan was about to say something when Rashida asked, "Honey, may I finish this one?"

"Our last line of defense is actually our first line of offense. You guys are going to be buried behind them as we implement this plan. Your mission is to be snipers and pick up the hardware of the fallen and to charge at them from behind. You'll be assassinating them with their own weapons. If there is another group and this first group is a ploy, then we're screwed. We'll have bows and arrows, spears, and our small caliber .308s and six clips each. I've suggested that we put the children in several crafted boats and set them adrift in the billabong behind us. Don't ask me where that came from, but I had a dream about this event and Darryl told me to do the same. He indicated that people will be on the other side of the billabong to receive and care for the children, if we're massacred."

The Sarge bellowed, "He, said that? That little shit actually said that to you?"

"Dad, I asked him if all went wrong, what about the children? He told me that according to his sources, these men would butcher them and that the safe thing to do is to place them in the billabong before the trouble starts and have faith in ourselves and the spirits. He said, 'no animal, small or large, will harm them'. I have to say, I didn't like the finality in his tone when he said that."

The Sarge said, "Larry, I asked you Brown and Bernstein to assess our inventory. Is there any good news to be shared?"

Larry said, "Dad, we have six shot guns, and four .357 magnums, with about 100 rounds for the pistols, and six boxes of old twelve-gauge shells. Brown and Bernstein in their spare time have fashioned six bows and about forty arrows. We're talking about a primitive defense, but one that we can win with what my sister has planned out. I know, we don't know their strength and they think it's just the guys fighting. When we were last at the farm in Virginia, I saw the targets from each person's practice. Those women aim small and hit large and they are damn good. My mother, the doctor, had a perfect score at a hundred yards. Not a small accomplishment, if I must say."

Chakes asked, "Did my wife participate in that event?"

Larry bowed his head on purpose, raised it, looked Chakes directly on and said, "Behind Asiram, she had the third-best score. She's an expert marksperson and if I were you, I wouldn't piss her off. Now, your grandmother-in-law had the lowest rating with a pistol, but a steady high rating with a shotgun. Back to Rashida's point, I would put Ms. Viola in the boat with the children and let her be their guide. At least I know she's someone we can trust."

John Lee said, "I just became a daddy. I want to remain a daddy. How is she going to handle all of those children by herself?"

The Sarge said, "She won't be by herself. She'll be with our spirits and my people. Now that we have decided how we're going to die, I want to know, how we keep these sons-a-bitches from getting this close to our families?"

Bernstein said, "Hell, I'm like you, John Lee and everybody else in this group. I will fight these people with rocks if it comes to that. Rashida, what's the last line of defense again?"

McArthur said, "Guys, you know that takes us away from our protocol. If one goes down, we don't leave him. What I'm hearing is if anyone goes down, we leave them and protect the future kings and queens, is that correct?"

Jilkes said, "John Lee if you get hit, then I'm going to leave your ass. I'm not going to feel good about it, but I know you're going to want me to take care of your wife and little John Lee. If I go down, then I want you to do the same damn thing. I want you to leave my black ass, go and protect my woman, and my son. No long goodbyes or wait until my eyes close. When I'm hit, I'm hit. Don't linger or you'll have me to deal with in hell."

Rashida said, "Dad, your people must have been fierce in the Nam. It scares me to think about the kinds of things you've done to survive and to protect each other. It's almost like me and my brother, Larry."

Zanthius looked at the group and said, "I think we need prayer. That's right get your butts in here. We're going to pray for the things we feel are right and have pity on the souls who come here to engage us. Get in here people, your religion don't matter squat to me, or how you pray. Just get your hands in here."

## CHAPTER TWENTY-THREE

The next day, the bush was awash with rumors of an impending attack on the Beckmire clan. The night before, those who had sold their souls to the intruders met with various kinds of death. Two of the conspirators died from snake bites and the third one died from a bite from the Sydney Funnel-Web spider.

Some members of the strike force thought that the possibility of their deaths being coincidental was a little hard to fathom.

Each group planned their offense and defense. The offensive team was unable to recruit other Aborigines to join their cause. From the discussions and points on the map that had been circled as to where the group had stayed, and the likelihood of them being at those exact spots, it appeared that it was an easy in and out operation. The last intel the invading forces received from the departed Abos was that the group was holed up near a billabong that was full of crocs.

Rashida and Juan had checked and re-checked their security systems and were confident that they were viable. Beckmire and Mallory met with the locals and made sure that their throwing of spears and firing of arrows were completely covered by the higher terrain.

At breakfast, Asiram rose with both boys in her arms and said, "Ladies, it's time to get busy. Rashida and Juan would like for us to conduct a dry run of our reactions to being overrun by these people. Now, those of you who were with us in Wyoming, remember the images of our children dressed in suicide vests. Ladies, that ain't ever going to happen, again. If they ever get that close, we offer them sex while we reconstruct a new manner of eliminating them. In any event, Ms. Viola will have our babies in the middle of that water with a bunch of hungry damn crocodiles nearby. I don't know how you control an animal that likes to eat things, but hey, we're in Australia, and apparently, everything goes. I'm trying to make light of this because I'm afraid for my babies, as well as all the babies, and for my family. To each one of you, when this thing starts, pull the trigger. I can promise you that you do not want your last thought to be of someone putting suicide vests on our children."

#

In a rushed training exercise, the women also participated in firing a bow with and arrow. Initially, their results were catastrophic until Juan yelled, "The guy you're shooting at is going to place suicide vests on the children. Is that how effective you plan on being? Come on little girls, this shit is major. Now, aim that thing and pull it with meaning."

Unbeknownst to members of the group, Aborigine tribes from as far away as fifty miles had made their way to the massive billabong and were camping out with their distant family and friends. They, seemingly, had come up with a plan of their own that would be counterfactual to what Beckmire's group was envisioning.

In Australia, there are many plants and mushrooms that produce hallucinogens and dissociative drugs. One of the Aborigine tribes came with a plethora of the product to use to incapacitate the foreigners. Exotic fruits such as lychee, rambutan, black sapote, and others were going to be sold outside at the harbor, only to individuals leaving the ship. Most of the day, the tribes spent their time spiking many of the referenced fruits by injecting them with a special concoction that would save many lives. Those eating the fruit would not feel the impact of the drug for hours and not until they became thirsty. Water was the kick-starter for the drug.

Wajickee showed up and had a conversation with Ben Beckmire. He told him that it was estimated that nearly 500 or more mercs had assembled in the harbor. He also told them that they had mechanized vehicles with weapons ports and that they were a formidable looking group of killers. Ben Beckmire told him that they didn't have enough weapons or ammunition to handle that kind of a force and wanted to know how he could get the women and children out of there safely.

Ben Beckmire was reminded that he came from a regal family and that at the start of trouble, everyone including the children would play a role. He was told not to despair because his nephew and his lady friend had constructed a powerful defense system and that his indigenous family members would be on the fringes to create chaos and to save as many lives as possible. Ben Beckmire inquired about that statement but was not provided with a clear meaning. Wajickee suggested that he should, for once, decide to separate his forces. He was told that earthly hiding places had been excavated for ten people and that strategic firing places had been constructed for ten others.

Ben Beckmire vociferously stated, "I can never separate my men. I can't help them if they're hurt."

Wajickee stared at him and looked towards the heavens. He said, "You, Ben Beckmire, are from a bloodline that is royal in this land. I'm just a seer."

Ben Beckmire fell to his knees and said, "Please forgive me old wise one. It is as though I feel everyone's pain when I'm here and no one feels mine."

"You, my friend, are destined to be your brother's keeper. As your seer, I must suggest, but you must implement, the idea is really from your daughter."

Ben Beckmire knew he had pushed the wrong buttons and said, "I will follow your wisdom and divide my key personnel as you suggest. Please forgive my defiant behavior, my liege."

Wajickee said, "You remind me so much of Andy, Andy Beckmire, your great-great-great grandfather. He, too, took me to task on occasion, but we always found our way to the right road. You're supposed to challenge me and others who provide you with information, for you're responsible for all of these souls, my friend."

Wajickee could see that Ben Beckmire was about to fall into a funk and said, "Ben Beckmire, you're the leader of this group and everyone knows it. Protect your people and especially those wonderful children."

Ben Beckmire saluted Wajickee and walked over to where Mallory was sitting and said, "I need to talk to the group. I have what could be a one-way mission for some people."

Mallory stood up and embraced the Sarge. He said, "As long as my wife and my children are protected, I'll carry the fricken bomb by myself."

Beckmire gave him a man-size hug and said, "I know you would my brother, and I would take care of your wife and your children, if it would come to that as I would expect you to do the same for me."

# # #

Twenty or so minutes later, the entire group showed up including Larry, Mike, and Zanthius. The Sarge said, "Guys, this operation may cause you to become insubordinate. This may be a one-way mission for you, and, therefore, I need you to consider your options."

Zanthius said, "Dad, every mission we undertake, is one-way. How can I, or we help?"

"I need ten of you to go and lay in the ground until those people start making their advance. I want to implement an attrition model, just like my daughter outlined. I need you to collect their weapons and advance forward while inflicting damage to their rear. At a to be determined interval and place, you will no longer advance on their rear because they will be bombarded with spears and arrows. After the barrage of arrows and spears, ten of us will fire strategically from our position. Mallory and nine of you, will eventually be positioned behind the invaders and will be in the most precarious situation because there may be others coming from behind the group's first wave. I'll lead the other group. I'm not sure if we'll survive this action, but I'm praying that our babies will. We don't have a lot of weapons and we'll be doing some real primitive shit out here, but if we execute the plan that I've laid out, there may be a chance in heaven that we will not succumb to a superior force and firepower. I need your support, but I must warn you, you might not survive this storm."

John Lee didn't waste a minute and said, "Hell, every time we fly, or eat, or take a run, there be a chance that somebody is going to drop the hell dead. What on earth you be talking about? For the years we be together after Nam, we've almost equaled the number of people killed in that so-called uncivilized place. At least here, they don't shoot your favorite pig and leave it in your front yard. If I be dying, then it be that time. If I be dying, I want my African American friend to die too, so that we can die together."

Jilkes said, "Why you, country ass, pig loving, redneck. If you die, I will cry at your funeral and perhaps, tell some of our stories. I don't want to die because your crazy ass got killed. I want to live, celebrate and tell stories about a wonderful redneck that I had to beat the shit out of, to bring him into the new century."

"Sarge, forget that shit. He's all in because he can't live with, or without me. Don't be listening to his, ah, charades. He be wanting to die if I die," John Lee announced.

"Listen, no one is dead yet and hopefully, no one will die. I need you guys behind their lines taking advantage of any weakness and assassinating their asses for coming this far to earn blood money. All I need you guys to realize is that they will butcher your children if you're not successful."

All the silliness left with the wind and a different mindset woke up. The Sarge said, "Mallory, you take ten people."

# # #

As the evening began to make its presence, Mallory came back to the Sarge with Brown, Bernstein, John Lee, Jilkes,

Montomie, Carlos, and three of his men. He told the Sarge, that they understood the problems associated with this mission. The Sarge told them that two locals would escort them to their hiding place. He also told them that they were not to cross into the opening that would be marked by a bush fire because Juan, Rashida, and some of the ladies would be operating pistols with their phones. He essentially told Mallory's group that their mission ended at the clearing, and they should watch for stragglers and reinforcements.

The men threw their hands into a circle and had a moment of silence. The Sarge said, "Protect each other, and I'll cover the rest. Be smart, safe and listen to the locals, they know when it will be time to move."

CHAPTER TWENTY-FOUR

Mallory and his group were literally laying in graves that had been neatly excavated by the locals that contained water and energy bars. The sounds of the didgeridoo and drums could be heard in the background. The didgeridoo was to continue playing, but the drums were to cease, which was notification that the group had left the harbor.

The ship that carried a significant number of people was searched from the top to the bottom and no one from customs could find any contraband. The captain of the ship was a genius and a seasoned smuggler. He was paid extra because he assured the various associates of the dictators that he could smuggle the arms into port without the weapons being discovered and that he would guarantee his success.

Prior to arriving at port, and approximately thirty miles out, the captain transmitted that he was having engine problems. He slowed the ship to a crawl while his engineers fixed a nonexistent issue. On deck, there were two large, camouflaged containers equally stationed on the port and starboard sides of the ship. He knew that the depth of the water in the harbor at low tide was fifty-five feet. He also knew his ship drew thirty-two feet of water and that the two airtight packages were ten feet in depth giving him a need of forty-two feet of water. He flooded tanks on his starboard side to offset the balance issue as well as the additional load on the port side of the ship.   Cables were unlatched from a hidden compartment and were attached to the sides of the containers. On both sides of the ship, elevator like contraptions off-load merchandise in small ports. As the water level was increased on the starboard side of the ship, the containers were lowered into the water until there was an equal balance on the port and starboard sides. The captain of this ship was truly a pirate with a vessel that was cunningly laid out to hide illicit cargo. His cost for transferring cargo was usually 60% higher than most companies because he was the most knowledgeable in compensating weights and balances, as well as submerging cargo in air-tight containers beneath the hull of the ship. It was an ingenious operation, nevertheless, illicit.

Once in port and after the customs personnel had left the ship, the retrieval process was conducted through several camouflaged compartments near the water line of the vessel. At this juncture, the balance of the agreement had to be wired`. This was also the time when the clock began to tick for the mercs. Once they were handed their weapons and munitions, they became official and were clocked in as mercs at the agreed upon rate. The only problem that existed for them was their paperwork with customs who knew they were mercs, allegedly on their way to East Africa with an interim date in South Africa for a freedom movement. They were not allowed to disembark onto Australian soil.

At 0230 hours, all was quiet, and the ship appeared to be a party boat with lots of booze and drunken men who were confined onboard. At 0300 hours, two shots were placed through the window in the customs office hitting two agents. The mercs walked towards awaiting buses to take them to the brink of the outback.

# # #

When and you want to communicate in the outback, you need to have your own systems in place and channels that work--a common mistake made by the departed mercs in Virginia and Wyoming. The two Aborigines who were assigned to alert Mallory and his crew, threw rocks on the boxes that the men were hiding in signaling for them to stay still and quiet.

# # #

When Mallory and his group got the sign to exit, he looked at the two locals. They indicated that many men and women had crossed into the area. Mallory asked, "Fifty to one hundred?" There was no answer. Finally, one of the men pushed his spear into the air repeatedly and Mallory said, "Two to three hundred?" The man continued to pump his spear into the air and Mallory said, "Four to five hundred?" The man then inverted his spear and threw it into the ground.

Mallory looked at his guys and said, "I want to die before I see someone butcher my wife and children. I'm going on the east flank with four of you. Jilkes, you take four; we're in this to the end. Are you with me?"

Jilkes looked at the group heading out with Mallory and said, "Damn, we need to have a drink when this is over." Jilkes had John Lee, Brown, Bernstein, and one of Carlos's men with him. They headed west and could hear the invaders, who did not know their every move was being monitored.

# # #

Mallory and his group, fired the first volley, and then the group led by Jilkes joined in. At that point, the invaders were near the open area and the two groups backed off their pursuit, but not their firing for effect.

Whistling sounds were in the air, and arrows and spears met their targets in various places. The mercs turned to fire in the direction of the incoming arrows and spears but did not hear the arrows and spears coming in from the eastern side of what appeared to be a gully. The Sarge and his group began to fire from approximately one hundred yards, or so, and hit their targets, driving them closer and closer to the center of the established killing field and away from the billabong. Retreat was not an option for the group because they were under assault, from all sides. They continued to randomly fire at targets that they could not see and subsequently they were picked off, summarily. Groups of mercs began to charge the area where the spears and arrows came from. When they reached the top of the hills, the area was abandoned on both sides of the gully. Gunfire continued from the groups led by Jilkes and Mallory and created a problem for the mercs advancement because their numbers were being reduced, by a force they couldn't see.

Suddenly, the mercs began to fire continuously in all directions with their automatic weapons. Bullets began to hit trees and mounds and disrupt the nature of the outback. The repeated gunfire woke up every living thing within a hundred miles.

As the mercs moved within three hundred yards of the billabong, Rashida and her ladies began to target individuals. The women with phones did not hesitate to target and destroy mercs. Courtney, although not using a phone for targeting, ended the lives of two men and one woman who tried to breach them from the side she was assigned to protect. It was a bloodbath. The captured weapons and munitions from the fallen mercs were then used to target the remaining mercs. At that point, over three hundred mercs were out of commission. Some forever, and others with wounds ranging from superficial to life concluding. They blindly entered a killing field with superior numbers, when they thought, they were going to enter a snake's den and catch it sleeping.

From the east, west, south, and north, spears, arrows, and bullets laid waste to hundreds of men and women. Some were lucky and received an arrow in the leg or arm, or a spear in the shoulder or foot--injuries that would not end their lives. Their problem was that the animals had been awakened and were hungry.

It is said that a dingo is worse than a shark when there is blood in the air. Literally, hundreds of them descended on the area in search of the source of that strange, but intoxicating substance—blood.

Forty-five minutes later, approximately one hundred and forty men and women surrendered by extending their hands in the dirt with their arms stretched out and their weapons out of their immediate reach. The Sarge knew that a lot of bullets had been fired because the mercs, without clear indication of who was shooting at them, fired indiscriminately into the surrounding areas and may have by chance wounded some of his men.

At base camp, the Sarge took role call and was satisfied that his people were accounted for. He tried to ascertain the severity of the injuries to Montomie, John Lee, and Bernstein, but Courtney and her newly drafted medical team, consisting of Monica, Ava, and Asiram, were too busy trying to help those who had sustained injuries to give a status report.

After inquiring about the injuries to his people, the Sarge was told that John Lee suffered a wound in the side that looked like a gut shot initially, but the bullet went clean through him. He was also told that Bernstein was bleeding profusely from his shoulder and Montomie had a thigh wound that was jettisoning blood.

Courtney told the Sarge that her interventions were momentary and that the men needed to be taken to the hospital. The Sarge was about to say something when the sound of a shotgun being continuously fired, filled the air. He yelled, "Keep your positions and your eyes on the prisoners, and if they sneeze or belch, shoot them. Remember, what I taught you, 'shoot first and we'll discuss it later'. I'll check on the children and Ms. Viola."

# # #

In the meantime, Courtney was in denial and crying because she had once again, gone against the Hippocratic Oath, and shot and killed three people. When the Sarge said, "Honey, I don't know what you did, but I have three people bleeding, and we need to get them to the hospital, but first, I have to check on Ms. Viola."

# # #

Luana, Yvette, Okema, Marisa, Somara, and Yeshida were assigned to watch the prisoners. As Luana walked by a group of outstretched hands, she heard the sound that a weapon makes when a round is being chambered.

Instinctively, she turned, scouted the sound, and fired her weapon three times. She yelled, "If I hear that sound again, we're going to, indiscriminately, terminate your existence. The choice is yours."

The Sarge, Larry, Mike, and Zanthius boarded a skiff and headed out to where a lone red, green, and white light was visibly floating in the billabong. Mike yelled, "Oh, shit, look at that croc heading our way."

The Sarge said, "Breathe in and out, and focus on something else. Don't draw attention to us." As their skiff got closer to where Ms. Viola was, the view of another vessel became apparent. The Sarge's crew pulled their weapons and scoped out the territory. Zanthius moderately yelled, "Ms. Viola, are you and the kids, okay?"

"We be fine, but I think them fellows in those two rubber boats be having a problem. There were three boats, two made of rubber and the one behind me. I didn't know them fellas, so I just started shooting until this thing didn't have any more bullets.'

"Ms. Viola, where are the people from the rubber boats?" the Sarge asked.

"Man, I don't want to think about it. They hit that water and some big things came up immediately, and that's the last I heard from them. Now, those other people, well, I guess I must tell the truth. I shot them cause, they come up on me and the children in the dark. They should know better than to be coming up on a woman and her babies in the dark. Yes, sir, I shot them fellas. I hope I don't have to go to jail for protecting babies in the middle of a war."

"Ms. Viola, are all of the children in the boat with you?" Zanthius asked.

"Now, that sounds like a question that scoundrel of mine would ask. Where you be thinking they be, Man? They all here on the floor sleeping like babies. I gave them a little coconut water, mixed with a little rum, and some roots from that wizard fellow. They all be here and them babies, wow, them babies just be sleeping their little heads off, all of them."

Zanthius said, "Ms. Viola, I'm going to come up beside you and two of us are going to row you back to the beach. Do you promise not to shoot us?"

"Zanthius, stop doing stupid and get these children back on solid ground. And besides, I'm out of bullets."

The Sarge said, "Zanthius, you and Larry get the children back to shore, Mike and I will attend to those guys in the wood boat." The Sarge pulled up beside the boat, gathered the weapons and capsized it, providing food for the inhabitants of the billabong.

On land, Mallory assumed command and carted John Lee, Montomie, and Bernstein to the local hospital with Courtney, Okema, Somara, Carlos, and Ava. Word had been spread that the hospital staff needed to be in attendance that night in case there was an emergency.

As the skiff that had the children gently came to shore, some of the parents took charge of their children, as well as Okema's and Somara's babies, and escorted them to a cave near the billabong. McArthur, Chakes, Brown, Jong, Gladstone, and Whitmore stood watch over the aggressors. A merc asked, "Hey Mate, can we at least sit up like human beings?"

Brown looked at him and said, "My friends are on their way to the hospital because you guys wanted to make some money by killing people."

Brown then announced, "Screw it!" He then shot the guy talking and the men on both sides of him. He then said, "Ask me another dumb ass question and I'll kill the whole fricken row of you."

Whitmore sauntered up to Brown and said, "Take a break and check on your family. You just made it easy for us to watch these thugs. We got this."

An Aborigine who the group was familiar with walked over to Whitmore and told him that his people were going to collect the weapons that were laid out. He wanted those in detention to strip to their essentials while he and his people made sure they did not have weapons hidden. Whitmore said to the captives, "We're going to collect the weapons in front of you. If you make a move for them or a weapon is fired, we will fire upon the entire group. Make no mistake about it, we have killed more people than you know, collectively. In Vietnam, we were called the 'killing machine'."

People buzzed, and one guy said, "We were told you were missionaries-- selling babies to old men for debauchery."

Whitmore walked back to the area where the sound came from and asked, "Who said that?"

In broken English, an Asian merc said, "I, respectfully, said that. This job was about stopping people from selling our stolen children and others to bad people."

Whitmore looked at the guy and said, "Please stand up and follow me." He walked with the guy until they were out of hearing range of the rest. Whitmore, along with Jong in attendance asked, "Who among you is the leader of this assault?"

The Asian guy said, "All orders come from the captain of the vessel. He the man who also make payment upon completion of job."

324 c. benjamin lattimore

"What does completion of job mean?" Jong asked.

"Everyone in area was target. We were told that children live to become adults, so they were targets as well. That's when we knew that this mission was not legitimate. Our job was to terminate all things that talk, small and large but save the leaders of this group for interrogation, and at all costs, spare the life of one called the 'idiot spy'."

Jong asked, "And you joined up to get paid to kill us?"

"My people joined to rescue children taken from our village, and to buy rice, blankets, and medicine for the winter. We no actively kill people unless they're bad people. The captain told us that each man will make $25,000 for this adventure and earn a place in heaven for ending the lives of people who would do wickedness with children."

Whitmore asked, "Who among your Asian brothers is the leader?"

"I'm the leader of my brotherhood."

Whitmore asked, "Why when I mentioned Vietnam did you speak up?"

The guy smiled and said, "I was a young man there, as well as Viet Cong. I had many dreams of earning the millions of dollars bounty for your heads. I was on many operations in search of you people. I had an encounter with you people in a small village in the south where you slaughtered my entire group with arrows from hell. Yes, I was there, and now I'm here, but once again, with bad information."

Whitmore looked at him and said, "I'm going to let you and your people stand and then sit. However, you must first disrobe, and let our friends from here make sure you're not concealing any weapons. When our leader arrives, I'll let the two of you speak and figure out how you can stay alive, perhaps get paid, and get back home. How does that sound to you? I must tell you one thing about us, as you've seen, if one of you attempts to do stupid, a lot of you will die."

"Understood. We don't do stupid, and we don't want to die."

"Yeah, but you came here to earn money by killing us."

"All my people are accounted for. We don't shoot without a target, and we don't use our other weapons, without a real purpose. Purpose directs us--not money. It was alleged you were holding many of my people in bondage. Money is not the motivating factor here. Purpose was our mission, exact information was not forthcoming and, therefore, we are alive and they're dead!"

Jong said, "You have a silver tongue my friend, and if any part of what you just said is not true, I will make sure that you never utter another word again. Is that clear?"

"Clear as the night becomes day, and the day becomes night. You must understand, we were bested by the few, but my people never fired a shot because there is no honor in shooting a shadow. We are warriors and could have bested you at every corner, but the purpose that was provided to us was not obvious when we entered your nest--we are the best. You concluded or injured approximately, four hundred people and yet, my people are alive and well and without a single injury."

The guy looked away for a moment and said, "What are those strange looking dogs at every point of entry."

Jong said, "Come now, I know you people aren't afraid of a few dogs?"

"We've never seen dogs like these that tend to herd their prey. It was strange and most confusing to my people, and plus, this place has been called the seminary for deadly creatures."

"They're called dingoes, but I've renamed them, 'body snatchers'." McArthur studied the man's expressions and said, "Three of yours were shot by one of mine. How can we trust you to do the right thing?"

"So sorry, not my people. My people talk through me, and they never say a word until they hear the talk about the Nam and more stunning to them, the calling of the name, 'killing machine'."

# # #

As the group continued to assess the injuries, things were a bit chaotic, and people were on edge. At base camp, it was discerned that five Aborigines had succumbed to gun fire on the ridge and four others had sustained minor wounds.

The Sarge said to Mallory, "That fricken guy that brought all of those people here on his boat needs to be put out of business. I want to sink that tub. There are a lot of bodies being consumed by the indigenous animals of this continent. I'll have the locals help us remove many of the remaining bodies to the billabong, so our friends in the water can feast on their bodies as their souls descend quickly into hell. However, I want a few people to help me sink that damn ship."

When the Sarge saw Whitmore and his Asian captives, Whit said, "Sarge, the captain of that ship provided them with their marching orders and told everyone that we were having sexual affairs with children, and that many of the abused kids came from his village."

The Sarge looked at the man and studied his face and composure. The Sarge said, "Where are you from? Apparently, you speak enough English so that my people understand you. Is that correct?"

"I understand and speak your language."

The Sarge said, "Who told you we were having sex with children?"

"The captain of the ship, who is also the director of this assault, and the pay master after the completion of the work."

The Sarge said, "Why should I believe you?"

Whitmore said, "Sarge, I need you to hear the full story before you start to pass judgement."

"Okay, Whitmore. Now, sir, why should I believe anything you have to say, especially, because I'm thinking about forcing all of you into that billabong to become croc food. Why should I believe you?"

The guy said, "Once information is obvious, then decisions and thoughts become clear."

The Sarge interrupted him and said, "I don't need to hear that cloud shit, I need to know why I should believe you. You answer me, or I'll blow your damn head off."

At that point, ninety-nine men rose from the ground and stood tall. The person who the Sarge was addressing said, "Then you will need more guns. If you shoot me then you will have to shoot all of them and without knowing the reason. You do not appear to be that shallow.

"Once again, we were told you were dealing in babies for carnal satisfaction. In fulfillment of that notion, many of our children were abducted. Many families were destroyed. To me now, it is clear, people in my village sold their female children into slavery in response to an advertisement and blamed you. From the moment we entered the ship, no one trusted anyone and lots of confusion was about whose children were more important. The captain kept people at each other by serving antagonistic food stuff--pig parts to Arabs and stale meats to the English. It is clear to me this drawing was not a work of art. We had a plan for capturing your place, but no one had time to listen. As a result, all my people are alive and everyone else is dead, wounded, or a prisoner. No one can explain that. It is what it is, and it is what it shall be."

The Sarge looked around and saw that the people in front of him were of Asian descent. He whispered to McArthur to summon Yeshida to see if she understood their dialect. He wanted her to randomly question people and see if the same story prevailed. In the interim, McArthur provided the Sarge with the conversation he had with the guy about Vietnam. The Sarge asked the man for his name. The man responded, "My name is Hutang. What is your name, if, I may ask?"

The Sarge uncharacteristically, threw his hand out to an adversary to shake. The guy looked at his hand and followed through with his hand and felt the strength of the man whose hand he was shaking.

The Sarge said, "I was named Ben Beckmire and this fellow is McArthur. That other guy is Jong. I asked him to summon some of our friends so that they can have an in-depth conversation with you and your people to look for consistency in what you've told us. I need this to figure out how to proceed in trying to decide what I should do with, and to, people who came here to kill us?"

The Sarge in front of everyone said, "Since you're still on my shit list, I'm going to have you and your men help the locals transport those bodies down to the billabong. There I have friends who need nourishment."

Hutang asked, "What if a person is only injured and in need of medical attention?"

The Sarge said, "Medical attention will be provided at the billabong."

"This billabong you speak of, is it where people can seek help?"

The Sarge looked at him and realized he did not know much about Australia, and especially the outback. The Sarge answered, "Hutang, that is where those who came here to hurt my family will find their final resting place."

"This thing you call billabong, how can it do what you just said?"

"Because it is full of saltwater crocs who will savagely tear and strip those bodies of all earthly resemblances."

# # #

At 0500 Yeshida, seemingly, had a good time speaking in her native tongue with the captives. In some cases, they were bowing to each other and demonstrating a sense of détente. At the end of each individual session, she reported to Jong that everyone in the group was on a mission to recapture children taken from their villages who were transported here for indecent activities.

At 0530 hours, a weary Sarge said to Hutang, "Perhaps there is a business relationship we can enter. What time were you people supposed to report back to the ship?"

Hutang stated, "An all-clear signal was to be sent by 1000 hours, and at such time, the captain of the ship, after certifying the work had been done, was going to report the murder of customs agents after our return to the ship. The planning for this event has been suspicious from the beginning. There are forty people on that ship providing redundant services. I think they are mercs assigned to kill those who return to the ship."

The Sarge asked, "Hutang, when you hunted us in the Nam, why weren't you able to find us?"

"You people would do work in Cambodia, and then be flown to Saigon and to various parts of the country. We did not have the use of copters like you did."

The Sarge looked at him and said, "You know, sometimes people feel they were put on this earth to accomplish a simple task, then after that, well, they don't really care about the conclusion. Are you satisfied that the war in Vietnam is over? And a second question is simple, are you still trying to fulfill that task of eliminating the 'killing machine?"

"Sergeant, I lost that desire long ago, but signed up for this when two of my nieces went missing and were reportedly being used by you people for sexual pleasures.'

"Hutang, I assure you on my children's lives, we are wholesome people who cherish children. I will allow you to accompany me to the shore of the billabong and look at our children and grandchildren. We love children, we don't hurt them. We nourish them and attempt to send them on successful paths. We would never kidnap children. We would never place them into slavery of any kind. Now, that is the formation of a relationship that I'm proposing to you. We can automatically shoot you now, or we can work together and feed that captain to the Great Saltie. The choice is yours, but this opportunity has a time limit. In addition, I'm willing to split the spoils of the ship and the fees for all those dead souls, right down the middle. I bet you he figured a way to get the work done and eliminate the workers to keep all the money for himself, then that is the plan he has in place. If he offered you $25 thousand, he's making $50 to $60 thousand on each head that dies. I know people like him and their mathematics. Trust me; I'm no thief and we don't hurt children, we help them and never hurt them."

"Mr. Sarge, I think me, and my men can help with a joint venture and pull off a ruse. There is only one problem, it is alleged he has a detonator on his person at all times."

"If he comes into the outback, he will have no connection, plus we can scramble signals and disrupt service. This place is unforgiving, without mercy and like no other on earth." The two men began to discuss specifics and an approach to the ship and its captain.

At 0900 hours, a seemingly workable plan was in place as an investigation unfolded at the docks. The captain created a sinister scene and filled the pockets of customs agents with cash and bags of drugs. The camera system in place was not working and it seemed a drug deal went bad and ended in the death of two people who were under investigation for previous malfeasance. Their bodies wouldn't be discovered until that Monday because the port was a regional stop that required all ships entering the harbor to anchor until given permission to enter.

The Sarge assigned members from his group to Hutang's team. He used Brown, Mike, Jong, Okema, and Yeshida. Rashida, Larry, Mary Alice, and Yvette were their backups. Rashida and Juan brought along their signal directing unit, and as soon as the Sarge's group got close to the ship, they engaged it. The Sarge and Mallory accompanied their group. Hutang gave the group the layout of the ship. The Sarge began to look at the ship through field glasses and noticed that people were moving freely about on the vessel. As the Sarge looked closer, the people onboard were armed and taking-up defensive positions. He said to Hutang, "This looks like a damn ambush. And you know what else, they have eyes on us from the ground, for the moment."

The Sarge kept scanning the area and saw where the intel to the boat was coming from. He signaled two Aborigines dressed as workers by running his hand across his throat. In less than a minute, two boomerangs went swirling through the air, hitting their targets.

The Sarge exclaimed in a loud voice, "Damn, that had to hurt."

He lowered the glasses and told Hutang, "I just saw two boomerangs hit their eyes on the ground, and it happened in less than a minute, absolutely amazing. As I see it, you've already been reported and the longer we stay here, the more suspicious it's going to look. You told me they know that the captain kept you guys at odds based on race and food. If that's so, showing up with some white and brown guys in your group, is going to be suspicious. How do you want to play this thing?"

Hutang looked at the ship and noticed the double lines from the starboard and port sides tied on double cleats. He asked, "Are your people too old to scale those lines?"

The Sarge asked, "Have you lost your damn mind? Look at us, we're trying to figure out how we're going to scale that gangplank. Now, smartass, I just happen to have a few people in training who can handle that task easily, but we have got to be on that ship when they get to the top to provide reinforcements. The bad thing about that plan is that I never place my people without me being in spitting position."

Hutang said, "We're running out of time, and we've been spotted and reported. He hasn't been off the ship and I'm sure he's going to want to know what happened. The ship is scheduled to leave as soon as the mercs are back on board. I assume he will also want a report about the assassinations of the two agents as well. I'm going to have my men stagger as if hurt. Can your back-up crew handle long shots?"

"Dude, we captured some of your weapons and I have some of the best markspersons in play. Give me two minutes and let them scope out their targets and we'll all have a chance to succeed. Any thoughts?"

"We're at least six to eight hundred yards away. Your people who shoot bows, can they do that work?"

"My people can hit targets moving at eleven hundred yards. Today, you had better hope that they're on target," the Sarge responded.

"This is so confusing because you're not the villains we hunted. I now need you to protect me and my men under a clause of blind faith. Your man Jong said that I was a silver tongue rogue, or something like that, but I wonder what he thinks of the shit you say."

The Sarge smiled and said, "They consider me the hustler, the pimp, the boss, Diablo, the con-man, the finisher, and the Pope in fatigues. I really don't know what they think, but I assure you, it's something along those lines. What they will tell you, however, is that if I sign on to do a job, I deliver, and I bring my people back, dead, or alive. I personally, want to sink that, damn ship. My problem is, how do I safely get you and your people off the continent and to a neutral place? As it looks to me, you and yours killed those people, and that is the story that I will stick to in this country. I wish I had time to give you a history lesson, but my forefathers were pretty big deals here. My name is associated with spirits that are 'kingly' in this part of the world. My ancestors were a part of making this country responsible to my race, the Aborigines. If we all survive this adventure, I promise, one day I will tell you the second greatest story that was told to me by my father, who received it from his father, who received it from his father, who received it from his father. It is truly a remarkable story, but right now, you've got to make a decision."

Hutang told his people in their native tongue that they were going back to the ship and to keep their weapons in a firing mode. He turned to the Sarge, and said, "If they start shooting then I need your people to help out."

# # #

As the Asian group walked slowly back to the ship, the Sarge looked through his glasses at the lines leading from the deck to the dock. What caught his attention was a large rat struggling to ascend the line. He concluded that the crew had greased the lines to keep unwanted humans and non-humans from fetching a free ride. The Sarge looked at the group making their way back to the ship and decided to intervene. He gave his people the signal to takeout the snipers on the ship. The Sarge fired rounds at the feet of Hutang to disperse his men. He told Larry, Zanthius, and Mike to follow him as they raced towards the gangplank.

The group reached the gangplank, Okema and Somara began to rapidly fire their weapons in that area. The Sarge yelled to Hutang, "This is a setup. You need to trust me and help me take the deck."

Hutang yelled to his men, "We must breach the deck."

# # #

Approximately thirty minutes later, the forward and aft decks were secured, and all the hatches were monitored. Larry surveyed the ship and told his dad that they needed to secure the bridge. Larry, Zanthius, and Mike were trailed by Jong and Brown as they made their way to the bridge firing indiscriminately on their way up. Larry looked behind him and thought, "If they throw a grenade, we're all screwed". He backed the team down a stairway and told the Sarge that it was a suicide trap.

Larry explained, "One grenade in that stairwell would kill us all because we would be stepping on each other to get the hell out of that place. Let me go alone from the stairwell. Mike, you and Zanthius scale those ladders leading to the windows and let's secure it that way. All of us bunched together is a recipe for disaster."

The Sarge looked at his boys and said, "Larry, you're in charge of the internal breach and Zanthius, you handle the outside."

Larry walked over to Zanthius and suggested that he wait a few minutes until he was in place. Larry saw what he thought was a huge cushion and said, "I'll be damned, that's a bomb retardant blanket. Dad, they were going to seal us off and annihilate us with damn grenades. Until we reach the captain, we grant no quarters."

From a distance, Okema, and Yeshida had their high-powered weapons focused on any movement on the bridge. There was a small disturbance behind them, but Rashida, Mary Alice, and Yvette handled it efficiently. From the weakest to the strongest, the team had jelled and would never again, watch their children be strapped in suicide vests, they hoped.

Once on the bridge, Larry huddled low in wait of support from Zanthius and Mike. He slowly spoke through his unit and said, "Okema, I am on the bridge and I'm waiting for the gang. From where you guys are, can you see me? Please copy because I don't want you to shoot me."

Okema said, "Larry, I see you huddled in front of the twin wheels. I need you to stay there because there are two shadows moving behind you."

Yeshida said, "I have one. Okema, do you have the other?"

"I do not have a clear shot because he's directly behind that metal seam that holds the windows in place."

Larry said, "I can force him to move, but I need to know that you can cap him when I expose my ass."

Okema said, "Larry, on 3-2-1-now."

Two shots rang out from approximately five hundred yards and tore through the windows and frames and into two human beings. Larry proclaimed, "Great shooting!" He then peeked carefully around the helm and saw the two bodies stretched out. He then said, "Zanthius, I need you and Mike to breach those windows now. I'm awful lonely in this foreign place."

"Don't worry, Bro, we got your back. We'll be there in a jiffy. Okema, do you have eyes on us?"

"Got you, bro!"

Hutang's people swept the port side of the ship and Beckmire and his crew took care of the starboard side. Hutang, was the only one who had a listening and talking device, and when Beckmire gave it to him he told him not to lose it.

The Sarge asked Hutang, "Approximately how many men were left aboard the ship to protect it?"

Hutang responded, "There were thirty-seven; eleven are dead on the deck, four were terminated on the bridge, two were finalized by Aborigines, and that would leave a force of nineteen plus the captain."

The Sarge said, "Hutang, we're going to breach this vessel from the bridge, both port and starboard sides. My men will identify prior to pulling the trigger. Can I count on your men to do the same, just in case we meet somewhere in the middle of this big ship?"

"I can assure you my people will exercise caution. I suggest that we first secure the forward part of the ship where people sleep. As we work our way back to the stern, we should be able to weed out the captain's personal guard."

Larry and the rest of the people were listening to the exchange and acknowledged the plan. Zanthius said, "Okema, if anyone comes up behind us, send them to their next life."

"Zanthius, we will shoot anyone that comes near that vessel."

Okema confirmed, "You guys just secure the inside and we'll take care of your retreat. If I might be so bold, tell your dad to use those stun grenades they got from the people on the forward deck. It provides a concussion and blindness."

"Thanks for the heads up, I'll be sure to tell him," Zanthius replied.

Zanthius asked his father if he heard what Okema had suggested, and he acknowledged that he had. Hutang and his people, as well as the Sarge, removed the stun grenades from the bodies.

As they began their mission, Larry suddenly paused and threw his hand in the air. He stood fast for a full minute and said to Zanthius, "Bro, I hear a ticking sound, and I don't like it."

Zanthius paused, and said, "Larry, I don't hear shit. Mike, do you hear anything?"

Mike held fast and said, "I'm with Larry on this one. Call your dad and that Asian guy and tell them to hold still until we can discern where that sound is coming from." Larry tried to raise the others on their network, but as the Sarge and Hutang's men descended deep into the belly of the ship, the signal decreased incrementally and eventually was non-existent.

Larry looked at Zanthius and said, "Dad is entering a boobie-trap. Mike, I need you to head to those stairs over there on the right and Zanthius, you to the ones on the left. I need you both to simultaneously, pull the pins on those stun grenades, and throw them on the landing. Don't, throw them down the steps. Wait, 20 seconds, and throw a second device. After that device goes off, Dad should realize that something is up and abort their descending into the bowels of this beast. Dad, and hopefully Hutang, will recognize that those explosions came from the bridge area. He'll try to call and then realize the steel hull is disrupting the communications system."

Later, after the detonation of the devices, and as sure as there is a heaven, the Sarge and Hutang's people realized that something was amiss and that they needed to abandon this mission as they tried to navigate a ship that was not theirs.

Once on deck, the Sarge asked Hutang, "Was that you and yours blowing the boat up?"

Hutang threw his hands in the air, and exclaimed, "No! When we heard the explosions, we began to realize we were out of communications range."

Larry, Mike, and Zanthius walked from the bridge with smiles on their faces. Larry said, "Chalk it up to youth. You guys, as you descended deeper into the bowels of this ship were completely cut-off, communications wise. We hoped that you would recognize the distress signal and sound of grenades going off, gunfire, and figure out you were about to be assassinated."

The Sarge looked at the trio and smiled. His pride would not let him tell the guys he was afraid that they had walked into an ambush. Instead, the Sarge said, "I'm so happy you newcomers think that you did something miraculous, and you saved my guys and Hutang's men from devastation. Hutang and I are old adversaries, and we agreed to enter the belly of this beast until we couldn't hear each other, and, at that point, we would retreat and figure out another strategy. However, I want to thank my boys and Mike for saving our lives, even though we were never in danger."

Zanthius said, "Dad, you could at least act like we tried to do the impossible."

"Zanthius, the truth of the matter is that you saved Hutang's people and my guys. I was just posturing. We realized we were in another man's bedroom and the only way out was over his balcony. That is why, my sons and friend, there is really no command of this rag-tag-group. Yes, you saved our asses! It is greatly appreciated."

Zanthius's head dropped and the Sarge asked, "What's with the head dance?" Zanthius balked, but said, "It was not my idea. It was Larry's."

Larry vehemently jumped in and yelled at Zanthius saying, "Who gives a damn? Dad and everyone else are alive. Let's not go there with this horseshit, we're a team. On this one I had a notion, on the next one, you'll have an idea and before this, who was the one who asked all the right questions? Come on now. It was you, so why go there?"

"Larry, there is the human part of me that wants me to be the best that dad has ever seen. It is driven by the fact that you've been with dad forever, it seems like. I'm not sure he is as comfortable around me, as he is with you. Hell, I'm a little jealous and in need of acknowledgement. Sorry, Larry. I just need recognition and purpose in his eyes, but I would never try to purposefully undermine you in any way."

The Sarge said, "What a helluva time to have a family relevance discussion. Can we table this to after we figure out how to flush these rats out of their hole?"

Zanthius said, "The helm has a radio that can broadcast throughout the ship. Also, I saw a switch that controls everything electrical on this ship. If we want to end this thing now, and I mean right now, then we pour gasoline down the stairway and tell them that in ten minutes we're going to ignite the entire ship. We tell them that the only resolution to this situation is that the captain make himself available for negotiations, or we set off detonating charges that will sink this ship."

Larry said, "Seems like you have the script, so execute it, my brother, and let's see what happens?"

Zanthius looked at his father and asked, "Dad, you have any input on this issue?"

The Sarge said, "At this stage of engagement, and as a function of being trapped in stairwells, hearing gunfire, grenades explode, I'm still a little tone deaf. If you think it's a good idea and it will limit the loss of life, then I'm on it and in agreement. I must admit, I'm tired of sending people to the afterlife. I want to help people live, be happy, and not do stupid. Let's stop doing stupid. Our problem is that our commander-in-chief does stupid daily."

Zanthius said, "Dad, there's only one problem, my brother applied the brakes because he and Mike heard what sounded like a clock ticking down. I think we have to first solve that concern."

Larry said, "Once we fill the stairwells with fuel and explosives, that issue will come to a head, and will be resolved in a hurry, I am almost sure of that. Zanthius, let them know that we're prepared to cook their asses in the next five minutes. Tell them to deal with the fact that a double-cross didn't work and that we, the intended targets, are prepared to watch the ship explode and disintegrate in a matter of minutes."

Zanthius engaged the public-address system and said, "Captain, you're in a very precarious position. My people, in a matter of 5 minutes, are going to begin filling the stairwells with fuel. We will also place both normal grenades and stun grenades at a series of emergency exits. We will then attach C-4 to the key structural tenets of the ship. Let me say this very carefully, so you understand who you're dealing with. The people in charge once operated in Vietnam, subsequently, large amounts of money were offered for their heads. That was during the police action. Since then, and in America, they have terminated a significant number of people who were working for blood money.

"Now, once we set the ship on fire, you'll begin to feel your skin boil and ache, you'll want us to be merciful. I ask, would you have been merciful to us, or our children? Or would you have been okay with strapping those little children in suicide vests? In any event, I'm going to set the timer on my watch and as it counts down, we're going to extract our people to a safe area. At the two-minute mark, I'll just push another button and demolish this wonderful ship with all you lovely people on it. Oh, and by the way, I'm not sure about our impromptu deployment of your munitions, but I do know there are more on the starboard side. This is our last transmission and at the appointed time I will push the button.

Your problem is trying to figure out when my counter began. I have to say, I am a little devious."

Forty-five seconds passed, and a voice came on the radio and said, "What exactly is it you want from us?"

Zanthius replied, "Well, to begin with, how about you and your people make your way to the forward deck with your hands up and no weapons in sight. Our long-range shooters will fire on the entire group if one of you attempts to do stupid. Once you prove to us that you can follow simple instructions, we'll move to our second request."

"What guarantees do we have that you won't shoot us?"

"At this point in time--none. If you think that stalling for time is a good tactic, I will say this, my clock is still ticking."

"Give me a moment without the threat of killing us." As the captain spoke, men started appearing on the forward deck with their arms extended above their heads.

Zanthius called on the intercom system and said, "Captain, some of your people have made the decision to concede. This process must happen orderly. Please have your men refrain from independent actions and please coordinate their surrender."

"Listen, I want to come up and have a conversation with you before the rest of my men concede. I'm sure you people are business minded and I have an offer that I think might satisfy you," the captain said.

Zanthius responded, "Captain, this thing cannot be done in pieces. I need you and the rest of your men to appear on deck, and I need this matter to happen now. Please don't delay the inevitable any longer. I think a conversation will be in order once we're sure that all your men are accounted for."

"Okay, we're hoping you people are honorable and hold fast to any agreements and the safety of my men."

In the meantime, Larry huddled with two of the prisoners and questioned them on the ultimate objective. Both men independently stated that their mission was to kill anyone who returned from the bush. Larry questioned the men as to the purpose of that action and was told that the fewer the people to pay, the larger the split. Larry remarked, "Something like no honor among thieves, right?"

Five-minutes later, the captain said over the intercom system, "Alright, we're on our way up."

When the group arrived on the deck, Zanthius asked, "Who is the captain?"

A portly-looking fellow walked forward and said, "I'm the captain."

Zanthius reached for his hand to shake it. In doing so, he decided immediately, that this guy was not the captain. He said to the man, "Captain, you have some rough hands. They remind me of a plumber's hands." Zanthius placed his pistol to the man's head and said, "I'm tired of the bullshit. Point him out, or tell me where he is, or I'm going to execute each man in front of me."

A voice from the rear said, "I'm the captain." As the man approached, he repeated, "I'm the captain."

"Sir, do you surrender your vessel and everything that's on it in exchange for your life and the lives of your men?"

"Sir, I respectfully request an audience with you to discuss any terms."

Zanthius looked at his hand and saw that it had a trigger taped to it. He asked, "Are you prepared to use that finger switch? Are you prepared to die on this vessel? If not, I suggest you hand it over to me and tell me where the ordinances are located. If you are concerned about us capturing your vessel, and you would like to discuss terms,

I'm sure our leader will grant you every consideration. I must warn you--we are aware of the plots to kill the men who returned from the outback as the notion that less is good, and it is beneficial to those who eliminate the excess. Not a very family-oriented plan, but I must admit it seems quite efficient. I must ask you, how many men remained on the boat to tidy up any stragglers?"

The captain responded, "Including myself there were thirty-seven. If that's the case, according to our calculations, there should be twenty-one people, including you, on deck, I only count seventeen. Captain, should I show you our resolve and have our long guns shoot five people. They're watching and listening to us, your call. Also, unless you think that finger trigger gives you bargaining power, I suggest you hand it over to me. Otherwise, we will leave the vessel and let you attempt to diffuse our ordinances, your choice, captain."

The captain removed the trigger, handed it to Zanthius, loudly stated that it was a ruse, and it was hoped it would lead to a bargaining session.

The captain raised his right hand into the air and clinched his fist. Four men came onto the deck with their hands in the air.

The Sarge said, "That activity minimizes your ability to negotiate. I'm Ben Beckmire, you can call me the Sarge. I think you already know Hutang. Okay, I'm going to be brief. Your men were assigned to kill anyone who returned from the outback. For that action, you were going to sweeten the amount of money they signed on to make by thousands of dollars. In addition, you were going to betray them because we found cylinders that were marked oxygen but are actually cyanide. What kind of human being are you? I have a question and please answer it honestly, or I will blow your head off. What were you going to do with all of that money?"

The captain paused for a few seconds and bellowed out, "I was going to change my life and stop dealing with people like them and you!"

The Sarge gave him a moment to realize what he had confessed to and said, "You know your crew is going to kill you? You do realize that don't you? How and when were you going to pay them?"

"This is a unique vessel. It can be operated by as few as five crew members. Every aspect of the ship is computerized. I can, literally, from my stateroom set a course, and watch the systems steer-clear of debris, reduce, or accelerate speed when required. The people who came out of the shadows and surrendered were the individuals who would assist me in operating the vessel in the emergency mode."

The Sarge looked at the man square on and asked, "How much cash are you carrying on this vessel and where is it?"

The captain looked at the Sarge and said, "You're just a bunch of pirates."

The Sarge's weapon accidently, or intentionally, went off near the captain's foot. The Sarge said, "Did I hear you correctly, or was that an invitation to blow your foot off? You tell me."

The captain nervously replied, $35"I think you heard the information correctly. I was politely going to say that we are transporting $25 million dollars. That amount made me think twice about our mission and made it a soul-source relationship in my mind--I wanted it all. I wanted every penny, so that I could get away from people like them and you. I want to retire to a gentleman's life."

"How can you sleep while you're a gentleman, after killing twenty-one people, that's a hard pill to swallow? You think that $35 or even $25 million will ease your burden? Let me tell you one thing, there are thousands of souls waiting for my entry into hell, I'm afraid to die. Here's the deal, I'm going to confiscate all money on board the boat. I'm going to pay $6.1 million dollars to Hutang and his people. I'll give your minimized crew a fee to get them back home including expenses. I'm having my people re-rig the finger switch and they'll give it to Hutang. Also, let me assure you, once my people take pictures of you, well, we will execute a contract on you and everyone that is important to you. If you don't comprehend, let me say it another way. While you're alive, anyone and everyone who is important to you will be assassinated in the most horrific manner. You will be last. We're going to implant you with three miniaturized GPS signaling devices that have explosive capabilities to make you bleed out after detonation. That little gem was developed by my daughter. You can travel to the moon, but once the signal finds you my friend--boom. Secondly, we will place a sizeable contract on you with the money you were going to confiscate by killing all those who returned from the outback. I know you probably heard that we're a bunch of bad people who are generally lucky."

Rashida walked over to her dad and gave him a phone with pictures of the captain's family. The Sarge asked, "Did you place a number on them?"

"Dad, I followed your instructions. Each person has a $500,000 marker on them, including the little girl."

The Sarge looked at the captain and said, "She's probably one amazingly, beautiful, and smart child. In the time we've been trying to figure out who's on first, my daughter found your family and engaged people to bid on their demise. My daughter is brilliant and sinister—oh my! Now, here's the deal. A couple of us are going to walk you to where you keep the cash. Any false movements, or if I don't respond to my daughter, your baby girl will be decapitated. You came here to kill me and mine, therefore, the rules apply to you and yours."

The Sarge showed him pictures of his family and the man panicked and said, "Listen, can we start all over again? Please don't hurt my family."

"You came all the way here to terminate me and my family and you want me to extend your family quarters? I'm going to show you our resolve and let you decide who we kill because you came here to hurt me and mine. You pick one. I know one of your children must be a pain in the ass, so maybe you'll pick that one. I'll give you two minutes to decide and after that, my daughter will send a text and you'll see the body of the person you selected. If you don't select one, then two will summarily be executed. You coordinated by air and water, five hundred mercs, to the outback, to lay waste on me, my family, and friends. Thus, it's only fair to me that at least two of yours should die unless you select one. See that way, you'll always know the one you selected and the one who was executed was chosen by you, a burden that will eventually drive you insane."

"You people are mad. How can you do that to my family? They didn't cause you any harm. Why are you going to hurt them?"

The Sarge cocked his arm back and slapped the captain almost into a coma. He then said, "Why you, sanctimonious son-of-a-bitch, I should have my daughter select your oldest daughter and have her first violated by the contractor and then decapitated. That's what your people were going to do to us. Select someone, or I'll give the signal to have them all slain. After them, we go for your mother and father, you fricken bastard. It's okay to violate and kill my family, but now you've become mad because we want the same act performed on yours."

The Sarge looked at the man and screamed for all to hear, "Which family member is expendable to you? Tell me now, or I'll force you to watch the mayhem that will be reaped upon them in a matter of minutes. You're going to pay as well, but not until you've gotten Hutang and his people safely back to their port. You delivered them here and disavowed any knowledge of their mission. Do you think you have a pass? Let me tell you, *mi Capitan*, you're more responsible than those who did the shooting in the outback."

The captain began to cry and said, "I'll do anything to keep you from hurting my family. Tell me what you want. You want gold? You want drugs? Tell me what you want."

The Sarge looked at him and said, "We only want peace. We don't do drugs. We don't have a need for gold, and we don't need anything that you can provide."

The captain said, "I'll give you an alternative safe with $50 million in it, if you'll allow me to keep what's in my other safe."

The Sarge said, "Your first mistake with us, was to call us pirates. We're not pirates, we're just family. What's in the other safe, captain?"

"Sarge, we're transporting some of the best dope ever fused by man. It's some good shit."

The Sarge said, "Show me where the money and drugs are. You should consider changing your way of life. We don't do drugs and are totally against anyone who transports substances that addict people and eventually causes horrible issues in society. All that shit has to be destroyed, or you and yours will be exterminated, like grubs on a lawn, your choice."

The captain said, "If I go back to home port, there will be a thousand questions about what happened? Those people will kill me if I can't prove that the people, they selected were amateurs."

"You will transport Hutang and his people back to where you collected them. Insofar as the crooks that hired you, tell them to watch the news in three days when we destroy the product in front of the Senate Office Building in Washington, DC. It's going to be a big bonfire."

"Sir, do you realize how much money you can make by turning that formula over to one of the countries that financed this trip?"

"Actually, I do! I am just not that interested in turning on CNN and watching the results of my greed--despair of innocent Americans forfeiting their lives, while not having a clue as to why. Have you been watching the news lately? Have you seen what has happened in London, Toronto, Paris, and even in Iran? Can you imagine what your bankers would do with a product that is small and deadly? Have you no conscience, and how much money do you and your family need to exist? How many billions? To me, you're in the life destruction business and all for a profit. You sell drugs, weapons, transport people to commit heinous crimes, and then you whine when we show you what is about to happen to your own family. Captain, you're next to the lowest piece of shit that I have ever encountered. Save my cousin. You top all bottom dwellers that are on earth. Say no more to me."

The Sarge started to walk away, and Jong said, "Shall I complete the business here and make settlement with Hutang and his people?"

The Sarge turned around and said, "I think you should hurry and do that before I put a bullet in his head."

In front of the captain, the Sarge said, "Tell Rashida that I want active contracts on his family, executable within two hours after confirmation."

"Mr. Sarge, I'm giving you all of my money. I was hoping that it brings me safe passage?"

"It brought you safe passage, but if you show up on our radar, or that of our contractors, a video will be sent to you illustrating the way your family died. I can assure you that we have people who are experts at gutting humans."

Hutang asked, "May I have a word with you, Sarge?" The two men huddled near the bow of the boat and spoke in soft tones. He said, "We are proud people, and we did nothing to earn payment. We cannot accept any money."

The Sarge studied the man to see if he could discern any notion of bullshit but failed to realize it. He said, "You saved me and my men from a disastrous fate as well as an ambush. You're going to need that money to make your village safe. I'm not certain, but I think I know who the architect of this event is, also, he is not a forgiving person. You must keep the pressure on the captain, or he will find a way to annihilate you in your sleep. Place his people in the lower deck and seal it. The money is yours and if you don't take it, they'll use it to hire people to kill you. You, my friend, know too much. You and your men must take this money, or it will remain with that bandit. My people will not take it unless you and yours do the same. They, and I, find you people honorable and worthy competitors.

"You came to kill us because you thought we kidnapped your children and placed them into sexual slavery. You realized we're family-oriented people and that we never hurt children. The captain has information about your children. Go brutal on him. Cut his fingers off or slice an ear off. Extract the information about your children, and if he was a part of their demise, if in fact they have been killed, then cut his legs off at the knees and his arms at the elbow. You're dealing with people who would kill their mother for a few dollars."

## CHAPTER TWENTY-FIVE

At camp, the elders illustrated through dance, the wonderful victory that they participated in to save one of their own. They began crafting the story that would be told over and over throughout time. At the hospital, Montomie, Brown, and John Lee had received the finest care possible in the outback. Along with Courtney's assistance, the young idealistic doctors handled the wounds and bound them as if they were in a New York City hospital triage center. The men would stay in the hospital overnight and late into the next day but would have their family members nearby.

Mike said to the Sarge "You know the whole world will try to intercept us prior to reaching the Senate Office Building. You do know that don't you?"

"One battle at a time, Mike. I have a friend who just might be able to help us out of this saga. If you have a suggestion, I'm all ears."

"Sarge, I suggest we do our destruction of the information somewhere else but let them think we're coming there."

"Damn! Really, Mike? Did you come up with that all by yourself?"

"Sarge, I'm serious. If we head to that town, it might be the last time for all of us."

"Mike, I asked the question about you coming up with the plan because that is exactly the plan, I'm trying to work the kinks out of. I wasn't putting you down, I was just thinking how this entire group is always on the same page."

# # #

Later, when the Sarge saw Jilkes, he asked, "Any word on our injured?"

"The only thing I heard is that everyone is recuperating and will be fine. I think I want to go on the next rotation and let the others get some rest. I know he's worried sick about me, so I'd better go and hold his hand," Jilkes stated.

"His wife is there to do that," the Sarge indicated.

"Yeah, but she doesn't know how to hold his hand like I do without even holding it. It's a mental thing that he and I have that no one will ever understand," Jilkes announced.

"Not true, I think we all have that for the members of this group. Boy, we've been through hell and back and when we got back, another hell was waiting to test our resolve. We've got to end this thing, and soon. I was considering taking a small contingency to Rome to deal with this mess if, in fact, I can reach my friend Ben, and he can make it happen," the Sarge stated.

"Rome is not around the corner, and if things jump off in the wrong manner, then you're isolated without the proper backup. I consider that a flawed plan and you need to keep looking at options. You can't do this without the entire clan. Check with Mallory and see what he says. I doubt if he'll agree with you," Jilkes stated.

#

Three days later, the wounded warriors joined the rest of the group near the billabong. Each man looked good and responded well to movements. John Lee said, "I sure been missing you people. It was like being in jail or something. I want to thank all of you for your support. I want to especially be thanking my wife, and my girlfriend, Jilkes."

Montomie said, "I never knew how tired I was. I slept like a baby, and thanks, guys, for caring. Oh, and Dr. Courtney, you are the best."

When it was Bernstein's time to thank the group, he hugged and kissed Yvette and said, "This woman is God-sent, and I love her dearly. It's been hard for her to make some adjustments, but she is as solid as any other person in this group when it comes time to defend us. I also must acknowledge the care and expert work that the doctors at the hospital did, under the direction of our very own Dr. Courtney Beckmire. All of us in this group will always be in your debt. You do more than fix us, you heal us as well."

A moment of quiet came over the group before John Lee said, "I be needing to add my thanks to Dr. Courtney. You people know I don't like this here public confessions, but thanks, Doc."

The Sarge bellowed out, "Listen up, people. It is time for us to end this damn war that my son started by kissing a spy, swallowing a capsule, almost getting his entire family killed, and thus, leading the way for me and my guys to join in fellowship again. Since that time, we've had weddings, injuries, trying times, found untold wealth just lying around, purchased homes on property owned by our very own crooked real estate salesmen and most of all, we have had divine intervention. Each of us, and I do mean each of us, has had to conclude the existence of another human being in defense of the group. Our newest member, Ms. Viola, put a hurting on a group of people trying to backdoor us by using the billabong. This is not a thing to be proud of, but it is what one does to protect their own, and especially the children. Speaking of children, we almost have enough to start a football team, and they seemingly keep being, ah, created by our members. I'm going to leave that alone before I fall into a box that I can't get out of. Anyway, I want to officially welcome our wounded back home. Our friends here are going to fix a feast for us in honor of the beginning of a new tale that will span an eternity."

"Ah, Sarge, how can a tail expand eternity? I know something about tails, and they don't have no special staying power," John Lee declared.

Jilkes looked at him and said, "He's back! Listen, you Alabama dirt farmer, he's talking about a story, and he used the word tale--'T-A-L-E', to describe it. Your country butt be talking about tail--'T-A-I-L'. You get it?"

"I got it now and that is exactly why I allow him to be my friend. He ain't the dumbest pig in my pen. I just love this here minority member."

The Sarge said, "If you two lovers are through, I would like to express an opinion for input." He looked at Jilkes and John Lee, and Jilkes motioned for him to continue.

"Now, that we've had our spelling lesson for today, I want to talk about our upcoming trip back to the States. Earlier, and in the presence of some of you, I expressed my notion of attempting to misdirect the location of the destruction of the Carbon Factor files. I have a friend in Rome who has been the unofficial ears to Holy Fathers for years. Everyone will be expecting us to honor our commitment to turn the data disks over to the people selected, at the Senate Office Building. I propose we continue with that ruse but divert our plane to Rome and make an emergency stop. If my friend can arrange it, we will then be escorted to the Vatican and in St. Peter's Square, there we will destroy it in front of the Pope and swear before him and God that this is all we know and have of this cursed product designed to destroy humans. Any questions?"

John Lee stood up and said, "That there be a brilliant plan. Did you come up with that by yourself?"

"I had help defining it. However, I want you people to shoot holes in it and tell me why it won't work."

Rashida stood up and said, "Dad, is there any way your friend can get us secure travel arrangements? I mean, after all, it's a text, or phone call away by the FAA."

"Good point, Baby Girl. Can I ask you to keep account of the questions that need to be followed up on?"

"I'm on it, Dad."

"Any other questions?"

Zanthius stood up and said, "Now, Pops, if you want to really hoodwink them, then we should send our plane back to Washington without us. We could hire another plane, or several planes to ferret us to Rome. We time it so that when our plane lands in Maryland, Virginia, or DC, our real mode of transportation would have landed in Rome, and we would be at the Vatican. I think timing is everything and we need to make sure we can execute to the minute. The plan is an excellent one, but we need to make sure everyone is on board."

Ava stood up and said, "There is just the matter of passports. How can a plane take off without a manifest of who is on it?"

"Good question, Mom. That is one that we need to try to figure out. Carla can such a thing be done?"

Carla appeared hesitant to talk. She held Mike's hand and said, "With this group, I've found that if it hasn't been done, then let's try it and see what happens. The law is specific. A pilot could forfeit his or her license for a year or so if they participate in a conspiracy to circumvent the laws of the land. I know, that's broad and it becomes a definitional issue between lawyers and judges. On the other hand, why would a group of people fly knowingly into a hornet's nest realizing the ultimate outcome was to be stung to death? No practical human being would proceed to a place aware that their very existence was being decided by forces unknown to them. My only problem is that we worked hard to obtain these licenses. I would not want to ask any of my people to consider this action. I, on the other hand, am pregnant. It would appear to me that with such good lawyers as Ms. Monica and Ms. Luana, there is the potential for relief. With a person who can explain the nature of the ruse, Zanthius, they might forgive my violation of the law and perhaps forget the entire event. Also, with the politicians involved in this event, it might never be brought up for review. I could also say that I brought the plane back to the area to pick you people up."

Ava stood up and asked, "Carla, can you fly the plane by yourself?"

"Yes, but it is against a mountain of rules and regulations. However, I'm sure that if I ask my crew to volunteer, they will all accept the challenge like your people do when the Sarge asks for nutty."

The Sarge cleared his throat.

Carla added, "No disrespect intended."

"None was registered other than a few coincidental details to work out. It seems like a workable plan. Carla, can you ask your people to consider the risks?   In the meantime, I need

Jong, Mallory, McArthur, and Gladstone to meet with me privately. Guys and dolls, food will be served in twenty minutes along with a native brew. Please remember that what the indigenous consider mild is like doing a shot of straight whiskey to us."

# # #

The Sarge looked at Jong and said, "I need you to find us alternative transportation. The question is from where? I need your people to coordinate with the group and figure out the best place to leave our beautiful plane and perhaps board some less than reliable aircraft. What country is the best that gives us proximity to Rome, and allows our plane to travel and land in DC or Maryland the same time we do our thing in Rome? Think about it and figure it out. Get back to me asap. I'm going to walk along the billabong and hope that I can get a secure line to a friend in Rome."

# # #

Out of range, but not out of sight, the Sarge used a connection through Rashida's system to place a call to Rome. The phone rang 22 times, that allowing the caller and the person being called to establish anonymous numbers and locations. On ring tone number 21, a sleepy Ben Hackney said, "This had better be important to get a call at this hour."

"My brother, Ben, how the hell are you? So nice to know you're still among the living. This is Ben Beckmire, and this is a secure line. My daughter has flipped this call all over the world, and I have four and a half minutes left to ask you for a favor. Not sure, but have you heard of the Carbon Factor?

Don't answer that question. I'm involved with that product because of my son who is called the 'idiot spy'. I need your help. I'm expected to turn it over to a group of people in Washington, DC, but I'm afraid that we'll be arrested or assassinated once we land. I want to keep the notion of DC, but I want to destroy it in St. Peter's Square, and in front of the Pope. The Carbon Factor is, allegedly, a vicious product that is carbon based and is as destructive as a nuclear bomb. It is another way for humans to kill humans.

"We have been tracked and assaulted by mercs from all over the world. Unfortunately, the third world countries are aware of it and its ability to destroy massive numbers of people and, more importantly, it can be contained in a milk carton. Can you get a message to the Pope and ask him to be a part of the process to destroy the formula of another weapon designed by man to destroy man?"

Ben Beckmire looked at his watch and said, "We have two minutes left. What say you?"

"Damn, Ben. I've heard about your issues but dared not reach out to you for obvious reasons. That's a remarkable plan and I will send a text to the Father in a few and see what he says. He's a different kind of a Holy Father and is concerned about the ability of nefarious people to do dastardly things to his flock."

"Thanks, Ben. I will wait to see a text from you about submarines. Thanks, my brother."

Ben Beckmire used the submarine euphemism to certify that it was he and Ben Hackney would use the understatement aircraft carrier. When Hackney was based in the States and Beckmire did some clandestine work for the Navy, he was given clearance to experience a nuclear submarine and an aircraft carrier.

## CHAPTER TWENTY-SIX

Two days later, there had been no communication from Ben Hackney, and the Sarge began to believe that his plan fell on deaf ears. Also, two days later, Montomie, John Lee, and Bernstein were healing remarkably well and fast. Courtney attributed their recovery to all the indigenous roots, potions, black magic, and the waters in the billabong. During the same time period, Luana announced to the group that she was pregnant. Ms. Viola added that a scoundrel and dark spirit had corrupted her child and seduced her with fire.

Wajickee appeared on the scene and asked Ben Beckmire to accompany him on a short stroll. Courtney was near and she asked, "May I come along?"

Wajickee paused as if he had fallen asleep. He sprung upwards and said, "Yes, it is time you know that all medicine is not learned from books. Please, join us."

As the trio walked deeper into the bush, Courtney said, "Perhaps I should have let you two mysterious men bond without my being in the equation."

Wajickee said, "Mrs. Beckmire, rather, Doctor Beckmire, behold the Great Saltie." Courtney turned to her right, saw the magnanimous creature, and immediately fainted.

Wajickee and Ben Beckmire held somewhat of a séance with the Great Saltie. After communing with it, they gently revived Courtney and led her back to the base camp. Courtney said, "Honey, I will never doubt you again. I cannot believe what I think I saw. It looked like it was manufactured. Nothing could possibly be that big and, according to you, the age is unfathomable. I believe in all that life has no explanations for. I believe in you, my husband, and will never doubt you again when you talk about hocus pocus."

An hour later, Rashida saw her dad and said, "Some dude is trying to reach you to talk about submarines and aircraft carriers. Do you want me to connect him? He sounded like someone straight out of an asylum."

"Baby Girl, that would be my friend Ben Hackney. Please connect us."

A minute or so later, Rashida and her internet device connected the Sarge to the one person who had an answer to one of the group's main issues—the resolution of the Carbon Factor formula.

After a few pleasantries and 'BS', Ben Hackney said, "Get on your plane and head this way. When you get two hours away, give me a call on my number. If someone intercepts the call and starts talking shit, you know the two things that connect us. Everywhere you go, or are, my brother, people want that formula. My Father is willing to pay a tremendous spiritual price for it, so get here as soon as possible. Let me know when you leave and when to expect a call from you. Stay safe and submerged, my brother, hope to see you soon."

After the call, the Sarge asked Rashida to schedule a meeting of the group in one hour. He told her to make sure that everyone was in attendance.

One hour and five-minutes later, the group, with their backs against the billabong, sat patiently as the Sarge thought about how to announce his plan. As he prayed for divine intervention, a threatening sound came from the billabong, and everyone turned around in time to get a glimpse of the most menacing amphibian that they would ever see in their lifetime.

Asiram yelled, "We need to move this meeting. Did you guys see what I just saw?" The entire group expeditiously evacuated their positions.

When they reached the base camp, Yvette said, "In this country, there are many things that don't appear normal. If you have pure thoughts about mankind, then your exposure to those things that can hurt you will avoid you like the plague. Spirits are real, and here the world operates in a backwards mode. That which you think you saw and, perhaps did see, is a relative of mine and my uncles. I want to thank my husband, and uncle for rescuing me many moons ago from the evil that affects our land. I know I don't say much, but I want to make sure you realize that this is not Maryland, this is Australia, here there be demons and spirits."

"My family, my niece is right. This place is as weird as can be. Some of you have seen me with my friend Wajickee. Now, that fellow allegedly provided protection over my great, great, great grandfather and he doesn't look a day over sixty-nine. Now, if you believe that, then you are subject to understand the nature of Australia, the place where my people began their quest for justice for all people. I don't want to talk about demons and spirits, I want to talk about that damn Carbon Factor formula.

Everyone is expecting us in Washington, DC in a few days, but I'm afraid that if we head that way, it might be our last trip. Larry and Zanthius spoke to me about something called misdirection, and I want to try this one on you guys. Some of you know what I'm going to say. As I said, we are expected in DC soon. As I also said, I don't feel safe about that trip. I have been in conversation with a friend of mine who has been sort of the sounding board to Popes for over thirty-six years. I want to fly into Rome, while they're expecting us in DC, and destroy the data files in St. Peter's Square in front of the Holy Father, as people seize our plane in expectation that we're on it.

"This must happen when our plane leaves from somewhere and heads back to DC without us on board. We then hire another plane or try to act like we don't know each other on a commercial flight. The goal is to destroy this thing and swear before God and the Holy Father that this is what evil doer's want, and it is for the sake of mankind that we destroy all knowledge of this in front him and God. We can't continue to be under siege for something we don't understand. I swear to you, if I ever see my son kiss anyone other than Asiram, I will personally cap his ass."

The group broke out into laughter. Zanthius and Asiram did not see the humor in the statement. The Sarge then asked Jong, Mary Alice, Rashida, and Yvette to prepare the group for immediate departure.

The Sarge continued with his instructions, "Once we are cleared and have filed a flight plan, we will decide which place is smart for us to stop and solidify our plan. I know there are some obvious reservations about the plan, but I can only improve upon it or abandon it, based upon input from you guys."

# # #

Later during the day, the Sarge, Mallory, Jong, Chakes, Gladstone, and McArthur went back to the ship and were met by Hutang's men. Hutang welcomed them on board and said, "I need you to follow me, the captain is not an honorable man. He deceived you about what he was carrying as well as how much. One of my men became intrigued with the sound that a bouncing ball made on several panels of the ship. There was a hollow sound and then a dead or occupied sound. As he rotated around to the other side of the structure, he noticed the same imperfection. After further investigation and meddling, he uncovered this movable panel. This is what he found when he flashed his light into it."

The Sarge said, "So, he's running guns and drugs. Do you know where they were destined?"

"Mr. Sarge, I do not. It is not the guns that are of concern. Look behind the guns and in the other gun cases." Mallory cracked open a case and found tightly compressed $100 bills stacked in gun boxes. Hutang suggested that he open the three boxes under the stack in the corner. Mallory complied and found that he was unable to lift or move one of the boxes. As he flipped the lid, he found shinny gold bars staring back at him.

The Sarge said, "Hutang, why didn't you just keep this secret and make a deal with him?"

"Mr. Sarge, you can never be sure of the deal that you make with the devil. This box is what I want you to see." He opened another box that said grenades on it and the Sarge almost passed out. It was a box full of uncut diamonds.

The Sarge said, "Hutang, you could buy your own country with this."

"Mr. Sarge, you are an honorable man, and you are aware of such a treasure. We are ancient warriors looking for our last fight. This means nothing to us and will compromise us if we handle it directly. Now, as your partner, we're willing to split it equally with you and trust that you will make sure our part is forwarded in pieces on a precise schedule. We don't have the skills to handle diamonds and gold. You offered us a part of the bounty from that crooked captain, and we now believe we can do good with it, but we need someone to manage and invest it for us."

"Hutang, I have three people who can do what you need. I will ask my friend Jong to assist you immediately, then I will have my nephew and Jong's niece to take this on as a project. My nephew and Jong's niece are perfect for the job because they are loyal and smart. They're both from strong clans. We must act expeditiously because we have a date with a demon in a few days. Jong, you, and McArthur collect all the gold and diamonds. The only safe place for those spoils is in the billabong."

McArthur, hesitated and looked at the Sarge and asked, "Sarge, are you sure?"

"Well, Mac, would you go into that water knowing that there are large saltwater crocs? Oh, I see! You think that you can shoot them all and then go treasure hunting? Mac, if I put that booty in that water, that means every weird animal that you haven't seen will protect it. Spiders, ants, rats, and every other animal here. Remember, my friend, demons, and spirits. This ain't Maryland."

The Sarge looked at Hutang and said, "We are honorable people, and our kin will provide you with a balance take. They will figure out the best institutions in your area for you to deal with and they will keep them honest. Although they're young, this is the project we want them to do, and this is the project that they will do. You came here to kill me, but you realize it was not us who captured your children and, therefore, you made an adjustment. That adjustment saved many lives, maybe some of ours, but mainly yours. We had you targeted, and I hope we never have to do that again. I do hope that if we need a group of mercs to slip in and do a job for us, I can count on you and your people."

Hutang looked at the Sarge and said, "As long as it's reciprocal, then we have a deal. Once we show up with money and ways to improve our infrastructure, the local thieves are going to come out in full force. I think we have the workings of a long-term relationship that is built on integrity and trust. Thank you, Mr. Sarge."

# # #

When the Sarge and his people arrived at basecamp with the illicit fruits from the pirate, he headed directly towards the billabong where he instructed Chakes, Gladstone, and McArthur to load the oversized skiff with the new booty. Once it was loaded to capacity, the Sarge said, "Okay, guys, what're you waiting on?"

Chakes said, "I just got married, I'm not going in that water in this little boat, where I know there is a beast that is from another world."

The Sarge looked at McArthur and Gladstone, and asked, "How about you two?"

McArthur said, "Man, we love you, but this is where it ends. What I saw today was not the normal size of a croc. Sarge is there another way?"

The Sarge said, "Yeah, guys, I was just seeing if you are as loyal to me as I am to you. I'll do this by myself." As he pushed the skiff into the water, Chakes yelled, "What the hell. I'll go with you."

Gladstone said, "You're important to this mission, if anyone has to be eaten then I think it should be McArthur."

The Sarge said, "Gladstone, keep your ass on land. I got this. You people are funny as hell. Listen, none of you can go out there. I'm the only one in this group, save Yvette, Darryl, Zanthius, and Larry who can make this happen. Let me acknowledge the fact that I knew you would come around and put yourselves in danger. You should also know that I would never accept or suggest a task that I wouldn't do myself. I love you guys. I'll be right back."

Prior to the guys pushing the skiff into the water, there was a breach and a strong flap in the water. The Sarge said, "I hope he recognizes me."

#

Much later, as the group prepared to leave the outback, the Sarge and Wajickee were seen taking a stroll towards the billabong. The Sarge said, "Old friend, my people are brittle, battle worn, and weary. Do you see a hiatus in these unfortunate events that leads to death?"

"Ben Beckmire, in the hunt for peace there may occasionally be a war. During that war many great and honorable souls will perish! As usual, and as throughout time, evil will not prevail. Only when you despair is when you will find the most hated moments in your life. Rely on your people and your children. Rashida is blossoming into a wonderful human and tactician. Zanthius is Zanthius, but Larry is your hold card. When you need the impossible done, call Larry and let him assume his other identity."

# # #

That evening, all the gold and diamonds had been transferred to the billabong. Those precious items are safer there than in any bank. Jong had all the necessary information for Hutang and his group. He indicated that he was going to begin a corporation as soon as they were near a banking center and asked Hutang to develop a name for the company.

John Lee, Montomie, and Bernstein were the hold up. They were permitted to fly by the onboard doctor, Dr. Beckmire. The Sarge received a call from his friend in Rome and the plan was about to be placed into action. Ben Hackney gave Ben Beckmire details to follow once they landed their plane in a to be announced location. Ben Hackney told the Sarge that he would have a commercial plane available to fly them to Rome as their plane took off for the states with only the pilots on board.

As Hackney was about to hang-up the phone he said, "You remember my other favorite place, Ben? Don't answer, that's where you'll be landing and boarding another plane at that time. Good luck, and trust very few."

## CHAPTER TWENTY-SEVEN

Milan, Ben Hackney's other favorite place in Italy, was the welcoming place for the weary Beckmire clan. The group was immediately escorted from their plane into a hangar where they boarded a medium sized jet for Rome. Ben Hackney told Beckmire that these costs were going to be billed to him and his clan.

Twenty-eight minutes on the ground, the group was airborne again, but this time in an unfamiliar plane. In the jump-seat was the legendary Ben Hackney. After the plane leveled off, the cockpit door opened, and he scanned the plane for a glimpse of Ben Beckmire. When he saw him, he headed aggressively back towards him, however, being stopped along the way by Jilkes, McArthur, and Mike. He said, "Listen, I'm the reason you're on this flight. I need to hug that big, bad, and ugly Ben Beckmire."

The two men embraced and cried. The Sarge said, "Damn, at least I'm not on a submarine or an aircraft carrier. How the hell are you?"

After talking about everything under the sun, Ben Beckmire said, "I'm sure you know the details of this thing called the Carbon Factor formula. We just want to dump it so that no one can use it against each other. It's ominous, deadly, miniaturized, and easy to conceal, if it's not a hoax. We don't know if it's the real deal, but there has to be a thousand dead people roaming around Hades looking for that answer."

Ben Hackney asked, "Are you married? You got children? What's the deal with you?"

The Sarge introduced him to Courtney and everyone else on the plane ride that would take over an hour. He told Courtney about Ben, how they ran into each other in St. Peter's Square, and how he got him access to places in the Vatican that normal people will never see or believe. He told his wife that Ben was in the friendship line behind his family and his men.

# # #

When the plane landed in Rome, Ben Hackney was met by his longtime lover and roommate. As planned, she led the group into vans and whisked them from the airport without a single moment of intervention from security types. Brown said to Okema, "We just flew international on a plane, and no one has asked us for a passport. It is because perhaps they don't want anyone to know we arrived here?"

"My husband, I have noticed the same thing. It's unfortunate that the aggression is led by men. The ladies have smuggled their little weapons on board. I've sent the signal to the group that there is concern about our host and his people. I think someone is interested in making a lot of money."

"Baby, what are you saying?"

"I'm thinking that Mr. Sarge's friend or his lover, have found a buyer and wants to embrace the Carbon Factor formula and sell it for themselves."

"Okema, the Sarge has a keen eye for people and has talked about Ben Hackney for a long time. What makes you think he's dirty?"

"My husband and commander, I think the Mr. Hackney is a puissant man and great friend. I don't think he is contaminated. I think his woman is tired of him, has perhaps, found a new partner. Look at how nervous she appears. She looks at her watch frequently, that makes me think she's waiting on some act or someone to rescue her, to our demise. We shall see, but I find her nervousness extremely suspicious."

Brown said, "Honey, everyone is not a spy or has an agenda that is counterfactual to our mission here."

"Yes, I acknowledge that. However, something is causing her great concern. Look at the way she is acting. She's looking for someone or something. And yes, she would be a terrible spy. Please inform the Sarge that I have concerns about his friend's partner," Okema stated.

Twenty minutes later when Ben Hackney and the Sarge were talking about old times, the van pulled off to the side of the road. Ben Hackney asked the driver, "Is there a problem?" He received no response. He moved closer to the front of the van and a voice said, "Sit your ass down or I'll turn this shot gun on all of you."

The Sarge looked at Ben and said, "Your people have turned on you."

"These brigands are not my people. My only connection to these people was through my longtime lover." Those words hardly parted his mouth when the door to the van opened. His lady friend appeared and said, "Honey, I love you, but I need a more productive life." She pointed her weapon at Ben

Hackney and pulled the trigger. The impact threw his lifeless body against the back of the van.

The Sarge said, "You know we don't have those disks on us. How could you shoot my friend and your lover?"

She snapped her fingers, and a petite woman, who looked to be about thirty years of age, stepped forward and salaciously began to kiss Ben Hackney's longtime lover. She then said, "This is the only person in my life. I just want to say to you, I have people in the other vans, and an assortment of explosives. Now, this is how this is going to play out. You will call the 'idiot spy' and have him make his way to the forward van."

Zanthius was about to make a move when Larry held him in place. Larry realized they didn't know who the 'idiot spy' was. Larry said, "Please don't hurt my family. I'll do anything you want. There's no need for violence."

When Larry entered the lead van, he asked, "What's this about? If it's about the Carbon Factor formula, then I'm afraid you guys are too early. It will be posted to me tomorrow. You really didn't think we fully trusted Ben, did you? Oh shit, is he, is he, dead?"

Ben Hackneys' lover said, "He is, and so will you be. Give me those damn data disks."

"Listen, we have been double-crossed, tripled-crossed, and deceived by so-called honorable individuals with titles such as senators and congressmen. We have been shot, cut, tortured and our children have been placed in suicide vests. If you think we value those disks more than any member of our group, then you don't know what we've been through, and who we are.

"Listen, three FedEx couriers will show up in St. Peters Square at 0900 hours. Until then, there is nothing that can be done or given to you. If anything is amiss in the morning, they will set their packages down and walk away from them. At precisely 0910 hours, they will be detonated by timers. I'm the only one who has the key, and the rotation knowledge to defuse the packages since, I'm the one who developed the bombs."

She looked at Larry and said, "You're a smart little twit. Suppose I just shot you in the head?"

"You could shoot all of us in the head, including our children, and you will not achieve your objective. If you harm any of us, you will fail to reap the rewards you think the product is going to provide you. The Carbon Factor formula is straight from hell and so far, over a thousand people, have died trying to obtain it. You might want to reconsider getting your hands on it because all we want to do is rid ourselves of it."

"Why are you called the 'idiot spy'?"

"That's a long story, one I would love to share with you if you chose another path. The one you're embarking on, well, is full of deceit and death."

"Me and my people can handle ourselves."

"The over a thousand dead souls I referred to, were all seasoned mercs from around the world. Paid assassins, not inexperienced robbers."

"Shut the hell up! From now on, I ask the questions and you give me short answers. Is that clear?"

"Very clear," Larry confirmed.

"What hotel are you staying in?"

"We're booked at the Holiday Inn in Aurelia."

The woman looked around the van and said, "I need you to stay in the van with me. You, in the red shirt, go back and get in van number three." She was addressing Jilkes who slowly made his way back to the designated van and was happy to be with three pistol packing women, Ava, Courtney, and Asiram. The three women were feverishly trying to calm the boys.

Ava asked Jilkes, "What was going on?"

One of the *bandidos* slapped her and said, "No chatter, unless I ask you a question."

Asiram cocked her head from east to west, Courtney grabbed her leg and said, "Let me hold one of the babies and try to calm him down." Asiram got the message but was not going to forget how easy it was for the guy to slap her mother-in-law. Ava was stunned, but maintained her wits, dropped her head into her lap as if in a submissive manner. In that position, she placed a suppressor device on her weapon.

Each van had two people guarding it and another driving. It was the women who continually broke protocol and smuggled weapons in and out of foreign countries. Okema and Yeshida were in the first van. Rashida, Marisa, and Yvette were in the second van. Monica, Mary Alice, and Somara were in the third van. Ms. Viola, Luana, and Carla were in the fourth van.

One of the men pointed to Luana and said, "You, get out of the van now." When Chakes made a move to intervene, the other guy pointed his weapon at his head and said, "Yankee, I will kill you, and still screw your woman."

The other guy pulled Luana violently out of the van, and that's when the shit hit the fan. Carla surprised the man who pointed his gun at Chakes head and said, "Smile, motherfucker." She blew his head open, and Ms. Viola shot the driver.

When the man who violently pulled Luana out of the van attempted to secure his weapon, Luana said, "You won't assault another woman, you piece of shit." She shot him in his pleasure zone. That was the unofficial signal. From each van, the sound of gunfire could be heard, and it was the women who were protecting their men, children, and families from yet another attempt to obtain the Carbon Factor formula.

Larry looked at Ben Hackney's lover and said, "You're a real piece of shit. You shot your man so that you could gain access to a weapon that kills innocent people."

#

The Sarge hoped that Ben Hackney had a vest on because he never knew who he could trust. The Sarge slapped him and threw water on his face, causing him to jump up.

The Sarge said, "Don't fret. Your woman tried to kill you. We kept her alive so that you could have the pleasure of dealing with her. We must leave here now, our ladies, apparently, killed her people. Ben, we must go. What say you about her?"

Ben Hackney, half dazed and disappointed, looked at his former lover and said, "If she dies here, her death will connect her to me. I have a friend who can assist me in this matter and dispose of her efficiently as well as the others. I feel so violated by her. How could she have listened in on our conversations and amassed a group of rookies to obtain the product? Someone tipped her off. She must have a handler. I'm sure she has report times."

Hackney said, "Veronica, who's your handler, when do you have to report?" She looked at him and said, "Take your best shot."

Ben Hackney looked at Ben Beckmire and asked, "Did she just tell me to take my best shot?"

Ben Beckmire replied, "It sure as hell sounded like that to me."

Ben Hackney said, "I guess I have to follow orders." He sucker-punched Veronica in the stomach, and everything she had eaten in the last week was puked onto the side of the road.

Ben Beckmire exclaimed, "Damn, Ben!"

"Did you not hear her say, 'take your best shot'?" Ben Hackney inquired.

"I guess she won't ever say that shit again," Ben Beckmire stated.

After her violent catharsis, Hackney said, "My next punch will be to your beautiful face. However, I assure you one thing, I won't enjoy it, but I will break bones in your face." Veronica attempted to say something, but it was inaudible.

Beckmire said, "I take that as a stalling technique. I'm going to give you one minute to gather your senses, give me correct information or I'm going to let my friend, here, gut you from your mid-section to your brain and leave your carcass alongside this nasty road."

Hackney moved close to Beckmire and said, "Now, that be some bad shit."

Beckmire said, "I know, we've done it before."

Hackney said, "You're full of shit."

"No, Ben, my boys have done this thing before. One of my guys even took a bite out of the heart before it stopped beating."

"That's some sick shit! And you're the leader?"

"Whatever! You must really feel good about your woman shooting your ass."

"Yeah, I felt something was out of place two nights ago. First, I couldn't understand how that beauty could like a nerd like me.

"Many months ago, our meeting was so random and inconsequential. I literally walked into a grocery store, and when I saw her, I thought how beautiful she was. She never saw me until I approached the checkout counter. At that point, she took a double take when she saw me, and she shyly smiled like a little girl. I never frequented that store, I never walked that way home, but this day, I changed my routine and there she was. Our chance meeting took away all the fears that I had that I was being played because I never ventured into that part of the city. It was purely random, and that is when I made my move.

"I played the old, little spider trick on her. You know, I always kept a fresh dead spider in my little bag. I said to her, 'I don't want to alarm you, but you have a small spider crawling up your back'."

She looked at me and said, 'There is a large snake about to strike you'. I ignored her trivial nature, casually distracted her, turned her around with moderate force, slapped her back, and in the palm of my hand, presented her with the venomous critter. Once she saw it, she said, 'I thought you were trying to come-on to me with that lame nonsense, that happened to be true'. She then said, 'I'm Veronica and I would like to buy your provisions, if you'll let me'. Well, the rest is history. The bad thing is that I must kill a woman who I love, admire, and enjoy the wildest sex with. What a freaking bummer! Don't call me anymore after this, Ben Beckmire. I'll get you into the Vatican, but I must admit to you, she provided me with the best sexual experience a person could be a part of. Ben, I mean she could do things that seemed unnatural, but oh, so stimulating and exciting. She loved bringing foreign ideas to my bed and watching me participate in pagan events. I loved that dog, but I must put it down. It bit its master."

Near the hotel, Ben Hackney announced, "I don't like this idea. There are too many of you and you'll all be spread out. Why don't we let the women and children freshen up, and then we'll camp inside of the Vatican walls? I'll feel a lot better after what just happened. However, I'm expecting a visitor in the next ten minutes to dispose of my sick dog and her puppies. As I said, hate to put her down, but she bit me."

Fifteen minutes later, a medium size truck pulled up and Ben Hackney waved to the driver. The driver and his associate placed the dead bodies into the vehicle. Ben Hackney escorted Veronica to the back of it and listened to her blame others for her actions. Ben Hackney without saying a word, placed a round in her head and told the driver that he would compensate him tomorrow.

Later, after everyone used the hotel to freshen up, the group headed to the Vatican. They would, for a few hours, sleep huddled up and close in the vans. Mallory collected all the weapons from the women and secured them in the van with him.

## CHAPTER TWENTY-EIGHT

At 0800 hours, a gentle tap could be heard on the hood of the first van. It was a smartly dressed young fellow who asked if Mr. Hackney was available?

Ben Hackney left the van and motioned for Ben Beckmire to exit it as well. He instructed Beckmire to wake his people and prepare them to meet the Holy Father. Hackney was told that the Holy Father was aware that women and children slept in vans inside the gates of the Vatican. He was obviously upset by that revelation and invited the group to breakfast.

The Vatican is a well-oiled machine that operates efficiently and on schedule. However, this morning, it would keep photographers, journalists, and camera persons waiting for over an hour. The Pope spent time with the group and enjoyed meeting the children, as well as blessing, the new babies. He unofficially performed an impromptu baptismal on the children and blessed the group. He thanked the group for weathering the storm and not leaning on the side of profit to deploy another manner for man to indiscriminately, destroy man. He also admonished the group because of the lives they had ended but understood the nature of predator and prey.

On the other side of the ocean, a new jet began its descent into the Dulles Airport. It was the Beckmire's group plane that only had the captain and crew on board. It landed at precisely

1600 hours and was immediately descended upon by individuals wearing CIA, FBI, HS, jackets.

That morning, St. Peter's Square would be heavily guarded by the Swiss Guards. At 1000 hours, a cadre of armed guards escorted the Pope into the Square followed by the Beckmire clan. The Pope stated the reason for the press conference, that he admired people who could have earned billions of dollars but were instead turning over the formula for a weapon that man could use against man. He stated that in front of him and God, the entire group swears that what they will unveil is the formula for a weapon called the Carbon Factor. He indicated that many lives had been forfeited in search of this weapon. What the press and the world were witnessing was the conclusion of any known manner of manufacturing another weapon of mass destruction.

Ben Beckmire escorted Jong, Asiram, and Zanthius to the front of the group and they each handed him data disks. With a small pen knife, Ben Beckmire pried the units open. One by one, he laid them on a plate that had been provided by the Pope's staff. He was given a small accelerant and a lighter. In front of the entire world, the Pope said a prayer, asked the group to swear before him and God that the information that was in front of him was the only copies to their knowledge. He asked each individual to swear that their statements are true.

Ben Beckmire then set the plate on fire.

At the end of the session, the reporters began to ask questions, but the group was whisked away by the Swiss Guards into the Vatican. The remnants of the formula were placed in a bag and labeled.

Across the ocean, senators stood perplexed at what they were watching. The current Secretary of State said, "Smart move on their part. If they wanted to sell it, they could have. This way, our government can't corrupt, or threaten them, because they destroyed the essence of it at the Vatican, in front of the Holy Father. I wonder how they pulled that off?"

One of the senators laughed and said, "I bet you 500 bucks I know the jackal behind that ruse."

# # #

At the Holiday Inn in Aurelia, Mallory returned the products that belonged to the ladies. He told each of them he was glad they had no concern for international law and the carrying of weapons.

Jilkes and John Lee convinced the manager that they needed to buy out the entire wing and they would pay each guest $1,000.00 in cash and payment of hotel costs for the balance of their planned stay in Rome. It turned out to be a free holiday for the guests.

In the hallway of the wing, the group was staying in, they had the hotel set up tables against all codes so they could dine together and in safety. It's amazing what cash can do.

Beckmire called the group to order and said, "I want to reintroduce you to a good friend of mine, and a person, if he should call on you, I would expect you to consider his request and oblige him--if it's not too crazy. People, once again, this is Ben Hackney. He is the person responsible for getting us direct access to the Pope and arranging for all those cameras and journalists to be in attendance. Give Ben a hand."

# # #

After a single drink, Ben Hackney said to Ben Beckmire, "I have to go. I need to find me a new crazy lover. I don't like sleeping alone and I don't do sex-for-pay. Catch you later and, Ben Beckmire, don't call me--I'll call you."

Beckmire walked Hackney to the lobby and hugged him. Hackney whispered to him, "There are six agents on duty. Try to keep your people on their floor until tomorrow when I can get you a military plane to get you the hell out of Rome."

"No need for a plane, ours will be here tomorrow evening and we'll be out of your hair. Don't hesitate to ask me for anything. I'm your friend, and, as a matter of fact, you need to come and spend some time in St. Thomas. We have a six-star resort there and you just might meet the right lady there. I'll send a plane for you and whoever, just come and hang out with us. You're my friend, and you know that friendships, true ones, are hard to come by."

# # #

On the other side of the ocean, a new jet was being refueled, stocked with provisions, and a change in crew. Jong called them and told them to bring their plane to Rome with lots of booze on it. Jong also asked Gladstone, McArthur, Whitmore, and Mallory to assume first watch, in pairs. He told them that he, Beckmire, Brown, and Jilkes would handle the final watch.

The quiet of the night was disrupted by loud snoring from the group. At the mid-point, the second shift took over the guard duties. At 0700 hours, a van pulled up to the hotel and three men exited. They flashed their badges and asked for Ben

Beckmire. The hotel clerk told them he would call his room, but Beckmire was on guard duty and was aware of the three men.

As his people surrounded the three men, the lead guy said, "My name is Alenandro, and I am one of the security details of the Vatican. The Holy Father made a choice and selected a potential winner that did not win. He then, in trade of course, agreed to have his adversary and her group meet him for breakfast once again."

Ben Beckmire asked, "Are you basically saying that the Holy Father made a bet with one of my men?"

"Mr. Beckmire, I'm not saying that all. He offered terms without payment on the other side, and he lost. I'm not sure I would call that a bet."

"And who did he make this bet against and what was the activity?"

"The activity was basketball--the non-wager was made against Beatrice."

"Beatrice is a child. He lost a bet to a child?"

"The Holy Father does not wager. He selected a team, the Cleveland Cavaliers, and she selected a team, the Golden State Warriors, and her team won. When he asked her what she would like, well, she said a day of exploring the Vatican."

"Oh, my God! She is such a little charm. So, what's the resolve?"

"Breakfast is at 0900 hours, and a visit into places that mere mortals never see. I'm here to tell you that our bus will be here at 0815 to pick your group up. You don't have any say in this matter, you'll learn a lot about that place called 'down under' which I understand to be an important part of your history."

The Sarge looked at him and said, "We'll be ready at the appointed time. Thank you, Sir."

As the guard started to walk away, he turned back to Ben and said, "Please ask your ladies to leave their weapons in the lockers in their rooms. They won't be needing them."

The Sarge smiled and said, "I didn't know they had weapons. I'll make sure, if they do have weapons, they secure them."

#

The Pope cleared his calendar and waited with a sense of anxiousness on his face. His aides asked him about his day and what he expected to accomplish, and he flatly stated he was hoping to be inspired by a child of great foresight and a group of extraordinary people who couldn't be purchased.

#

At 0845 hours, the bus arrived at the Vatican gate, and everyone was escorted and ushered through metal detectors. On every occasion, Jong set the detectors off, repeatedly. The Pope finally asked, "Are you Catholic and do you swear not to try to cause a problem while you're here?"

Jong said, "I am Catholic and I'm no problem, Holy Father."

The Pope said, "There you have it. Let's go because I've found a child who is smarter than her age and wiser than most adults. I want to spend time with the group and take you to secret places people don't get to see or even believe exist. I want to pray silently at mid-day with believers and ask for protection for all when you enter the final phase of your journey. I know a lot about this group, and I know if there was a model for family and friends, I would replicate this group. The one is the whole, and the whole is the one.

"As Pope, I enter each day with pretty much the same routine. When Ben Hackney told me about your amazing saga, I became so enchanted with it that it was I who wanted to meet you more than you wanted to meet me. I also talked quietly and only for a few minutes with Beatrice and my spirituality was restored. I saw within a child all the Godlike things that man should believe in--family, spirits, choices, survival, love, inclusion, and adaption/adoption. I feel as though I should kiss your ring, rather than you kiss mine. The entire universe is at risk, and it is how you people live, and mind you, I don't condone the way you conclude adversaries, but I do believe in the survival of the fittest, doctrine. I hope to have a glorious day and would like to encounter you on a frequent basis. Although I'm the Holy Father, you, my children, are my source of rejuvenation. My need to explore outside of the traditional church teachings. I want to make a difference, I want to destroy poverty, hunger, ignorance, and disease. If I can make a dent in those four domains, then I believe I can lead the church outside of itself."

At breakfast, the Pope observed Beatrice and her mannerisms. He told Ms. Viola that inspiration does not have a calling card. He told her that her baby was a child of faith, and it is through faith we see the other side of the equation. He said, "Her father has never really been in her life and the person you call scoundrel, is clearly the epitome of a father to Beatrice".

Ms. Viola asked, "How you know so much about my family?"

"Ms. Viola, the status of the Carbon Factor formula is presented to me daily. When the scoundrel realized he loved your grandbaby, my people watched and provided protection over the group where possible without involving the church. I've been following this event and its participants for over two years. I've found strength through my daily briefings. This has been a source of, how can I say it, believable fiction to me. I'm enthralled with the story. My people keep coming up with parts that excite me, such as when the 'idiot spy' kissed a spy, seduced her, swallowed a capsule containing parts of the formula.

"As Pope, I'm having a blast watching the good this group does. By the way, in my view, there are no limits to Beatrice's options and capabilities. That scoundrel will become the father of fathers to her. I will become a long-distance mentor, and I will help her understand the stupid, but that scoundrel will help her manage the complex. Your granddaughter is in good company, and she is with child."

#

After breakfast, the Pope prayed with the group and told them he had a surprise for them. As the group toured the Vatican and visited areas that are off limits to even the highest officials, the Pope said, "This is where I come to gain strength to resist those within the church who are, as Ms. Viola calls them, scoundrels. No connection to you, Mr. Chakes."

An assistant hurriedly approached the Holy Father and told him that a high-ranking Cardinal was waiting to honor a meeting that was scheduled. The Pope told him to tell the Cardinal he was celebrating life and the destruction of a weapon that could kill people and that he would reschedule.

He told the aide to thank him for his patience and understanding.

The Pope told another aide he wanted to go to the real library. The aide started to say something but was met with a scornful look from the Pope.

The Pope said to the group, "I must insist that all recording devices, phones, and cameras be stowed in baskets that will be provided to you. I also must receive an acknowledgement from you that you will never talk about what you see in the library. No one from the outside sees this place. You will be given gloves and you must wear them at all times. Furthermore, please do not touch anything in the library. You will be amazed at the things that are stored there and the historical significance these items play. It is a world of the unbelievable, where only the true of heart will understand and appreciate some of the artifacts. If I have your word, and I'm sure I do, we can proceed to the library and enjoy a rare reflection of the history of the world."

#

One hour and a half later, an uncertain group emerged from the educational catacombs of the Vatican. Discussions were being stoked by members of the group as they thought history said one thing, but the reality provided another. LaGina asked her mom about the stories she had told her. Rashida flatly told her she will never tell her those stories again. Everyone had a surprise, or realization, that what they thought to be true was false.

Beatrice asked, "Mr. Pope, can I see the Sistine Chapel?"

"Oh my. What do you know of the Sistine Chapel?"

"In school, they told us that a man painted it by lying on his back. I don't think that's true."

The Holy Father looked at her and said, "Your looks deceive your age. In the Apostolic Palace, my residence, is where you will find the chapel. Do you know who the alleged painter who laid on his back to paint it was?"

"Everyone knows that. It was Michelangelo."

"You truly are refreshing and insightful. Someday, I would like to visit with you and your family. Would you like that?"

"Mr. Pope, I would like to introduce you to my friends at school. The only problem is that I might have to do a book report. I don't like doing book reports."

"I'm sure I can fix that. Do you and LaGina go to the same school?"

"No, Mr. Pope. We've been home schooled because of the bad people trying to hurt us."

# # #

In the meantime, the Pope escorted the group to the Sistine Chapel and was told by an assistant that it was time to take his medicine. Overhearing the conversation, Beatrice said, "My granny takes medicine. She says a lot of older people take medicines. What is your medicine for?"

Luana interrupted her daughter and stated, "Honey, it is impolite to ask people about their medications. It's a personal matter."

"Sorry, Mom. Mr. Pope, I would like to come here again to see things that I don't understand. If I wrote you a letter, would you answer it and invite me here? I wrote the Tooth-

Ferry, but he never wrote me back. I asked him why was my tooth worth only $1 dollar? He gave Megan $5."

The whole group broke into laughter and the Holy Father said, "Beatrice, I'm going to give you my card that has my personal email address and cell phone number on it. In giving you my card, I hope that you respect my privacy and do not share any information about me with your friends."

"I would never do that. I would only tell LaGina and the twins, but I wouldn't give them your number."

"I appreciate how respectful you are, young lady. When your parents and their associates have completed their business with the forces of evil, I will make it a point to come and visit with you and your family. It has been my esteemed pleasure to meet you."

"Mr. Pope, what does that mean?"

"That means, I hope I've made a new friend today and one who will always educate me in the ways of the young."

# # #

The Pope continued, "In the Sistine Chapel, the Holy Father was presented with Rosaries, and he blessed them individually and gave them to each child. His last gift was to Beatrice.

He said, "I have never met a young lady like you, Beatrice, and I want to make sure that you always remember me. This Rosary, belonged to my mother, a simple woman who loved life and challenged what she did not understand. It is you who created a new challenge in me, and I want to bless this rosary and make it a gift to you. On my word as the Holy Father, I will seek you, and your family out, and pay a casual visit. On your word, you must agree to come and visit me within the next year. God bless you my protégé."

   "Mr. Pope, what does that mean?"

CHAPTER TWENTY-NINE

The group realized they had just shared an ecclesiastical experience that involved the Holy Father, himself. Zanthius said to his father, "Dad, he blessed all of the children, but none of us. What's your take on that?"

"Son, we just witnessed an incredible transformation and interchange with the Holy Father. He could not, or cannot, bless us for we have sinned beyond the basic guidelines that define a sin. My son, we kill people. He is not condoning our actions, but he realizes there are forces on the horizon that want to end our existence. He has transferred spiritual power to little Beatrice because he feels she is special. I'll accept that as a testament that he indirectly blessed us, as well."

As the bus appeared at the security gate, Ben Hackney came from out of the shadows and asked, "How did it go? I mean the tour and all."

"It has been a Godly day. It was just the thing my people needed. We're so far left of religion in our actions that it was humbling to pay respects to the symbol of the Catholic Church. Anyway, let me know when you want to visit us in St. Thomas, middle America, Valencia, or in Virginia. Actually, our houses should be ready in a few months, you can come on down to Alabama and watch nothing pass you by."

"Ben Beckmire, it's been a pleasure to see you and meet your family. You don't owe me a thing. If I had to bargain, I would say we're even. I do recall how you assisted me with a bunch of bullies that I could have killed but didn't have the cleaners that I have today. I'll give you a call soon. Right now, I'm mourning the loss of a wonderful lover. Seems to me you got rid of one problem, and one problem remains, your cousin. I wish you luck, with him. From what I know and have heard about him, he ain't dead until his head is severed. He is the Anti-Christ in more ways than one."

"Ben, I'm going to do more than sever his head. I'm going to gut him like a pig, from his tiny dick to his brain, then I'm going to take a bite out of his beating heart before it ceases to thump. I will spread his ass all over the world so that he can't genetically be assimilated, or his DNA established."

"Where does your cousin get the money to hire people to try and kill you?"

"I, personally, think he has a key to the Treasury Department. He had stash houses on Capitol Hill that we hit, but that act didn't damage his resolve or finances to kill me, and everyone associated with me."

"Yeah, I heard about that stunt in middle America. You know I get my information from the agency. They've been watching him and you for some time with an emphasis on you, until your cousin went rogue and became the chief perpetrator in the deaths of a couple of United States Senators. Oh, by the way, who came up with that misdirection idea? Was it you?"

"Ben, I may be old, but I'm not too old to learn new tricks. My people didn't think it would work because of the manifest issue and passports. I guess I got lucky."

"The word out of DC, is that a low-level sergeant, from the Viet Nam era, beat the entire United States Government's intelligence arm. He made his way to the Vatican, had an interview with the Pope, and destroyed the Carbon Factor formula, live on international television. What a feather in your cap. However, my brother, keep your eyes open, always- -your cousin, I hear, has spent a lot of time in Ethiopia where he had terrorist relationships. I think he's in the recruiting business once again, and his target is big Ben Beckmire and his troupe. Good luck my brother. Give me one of those man-size hugs and let me disappear into the walls of this place."

A little later, Jong approached the Sarge and asked, "Are we good?"

"I hope so, my brother. We have the one problem facing us and that's my nefarious cousin. I'm afraid we're going to need your cousin, my nephew, your niece, and all of our relatives to help us on this one."

Jong said, "Speaking of my niece, she is apparently being influenced by your nephew, and they are inseparable. Your nephew is being influenced by my niece, and she won't leave him be. My cousin wants to break it off, but can't find reasons that are satisfactory, even to himself. He loves Darryl and has decided to allow them to officially date with the goal of marrying. He also continues to forbid them to copulate until such time they consummate the relationship by marriage."

"Jong, are you serious? They're kids, barely wet behind the ears," the Sarge retorted.

"I think that's the best time. No one to talk you away from how you feel. Carefree like me. I'm not old, I'm wise."

"You're nuts. What's the status on the plane? Is it time for a conversation about a new plane? I mean have we outgrown that plane, or a better question is, can we get one that has our blueprint before manufacturing rather than after-market alterations and modifications. Just a question that only you can answer in consultation with Carla."

"Sarge, do you know how much money we have?"

"No, I don't, and I don't need to know that as long as you're alive to take care of the small details. Why do you keep asking me that question? You know damn well that I don't have a clue. Is that your way of humbling me?"

Jong bowed and said, "You're our master and friend. It is because of you that babies are being born and people have met their soul mates. You unite us and lead us. I would never humble you. I just wanted to make you aware of the fact that we have over a billion dollars in investments. To be more precise, we have in excess of $500 million in cash that needs to be washed and is stored in some of the most retarded places. Also, we just placed a significant amount of assets in a billabong, guarded by saltwater crocs—the first such banking relationship with amphibians, in the world. No need in trying to earn interest on the gold and diamonds. Oh, Sarge, that is after each person in the group, including the children, received $3.5 million in their personal accounts."

"That's amazing and fantastic. You are truly Mr. Amazing, a title that will follow you to the great beyond. How about the pilots?"

"I recommended that each one receive $1 million in addition to their salary for the next two years," Jong indicated.

"Wow, by accident we found a lot of money," Beckmire stated.

"By skill, we invested a lot of money and it's paying big dividends to us. Do you realize that in Facebook alone, we made close to $100 million dollars in profit? I won't bother you with the details of Amazon and Google, and that Tesla. I'm afraid we're going to need someone to handle this thing daily," Jong stated.

"Jong, we have Sue Lyn and Darryl. They're smart, we just make them smarter, and let them figure out what to do with that booty in the billabong. Now, that money along with the diamond business, we can rebuild every Aborigine village from Sydney to Perth. Wow, that is some spectacular news. I'll share it once we're all on the plane and heading towards the states. Oh, where are we going?"

"I did not canvas those people. I'm sure they're going to say to St. Thomas," Jong indicated.

"We need to get Asiram back to middle America and to Virginia. We also need to check out what's going on in Alabama. Let's see where the group wants to go and then we'll tell them about the issues on the table that we must address, such as Asiram's places."

"Sarge, suppose she wants to visit for a day or so? Why not send her on one of the other planes if she agrees?"

"That sounds like a good idea, but we're vulnerable when we're not together. I'll ask her in the general forum, see what she and Zanthius think about the idea. I don't like the notion of separation because we have a slimy predator out there looking for a chink in our armor. He will publicly execute one of us if he can successfully capture a team member and place a horrifying image on YouTube or some other social media platform. I would feel so much better if we stayed the course until he is destroyed before we get tired of each other and start wandering around the world blindly and independently."

Jong said, "The likelihood of that happening is small. You should sit around and watch the way people talk to each other. Their plans are the plans of a group. Some of the things are stupid, such as, I had eggs yesterday. Do you want eggs today?"

"What did you have--and on, and on, and on? The bonds here are stronger than any family I have ever seen. They're all connected. Sorry, we are all connected, and they're as strong as we were when we were in *the Maiden from Hell's Kitchen*—with a little divine interference.

the end

also in the 'idiot spy' series

Available at Amazon and BarnesandNoble.com

www.ingramcontent.com/pod-product-compliance
Lightning Source LLC
Chambersburg PA
CBHW051518250626
47156CB00001B/139